ISBN 0-8317-8797-X (Hardcover Edition)
ISBN 0-8317-8798-8 (Paperback Edition)
LOC 80-82169

Copyright (Text) 1980 by Malcolm Edwards & Robert Holdstock
Copyright (Illustrations) 1980 by Young Artists & Artist Partners

All rights reserved under International and Pan American Copyright Convention.
Published in the United States by Mayflower Books Inc, New York City 10022.
Originally published in England by Pierrot Publishing Limited, London.

Designed by Julie Harris & Steve Ridgeway
Assisted by Alison Daines & Jill Gambold
No part of this publication may be reproduced, stored in a retrieval system,
or transmitted, in any form or by any means, without prior written permission
of the publishers. Inquiries should be addressed to Mayflower Books Inc.

Manufactured in Singapore.
First American edition.

TOUR OF THE UNIVERSE

THE JOURNEY OF A LIFETIME: THE RECORDED DIARIES
OF LEIO SCOTT AND CAROLINE LURANSKI

MALCOLM EDWARDS
ROBERT HOLDSTOCK

MAYFLOWER BOOKS · NEW YORK CITY

WEST EUROPE GUARDIAN

BY AURORA!
London Couple Win Tour To Magellanic Federation

IT WAS THE COMPETITION THEY SAID WOULD NEVER BE HELD, and it's been won by a couple who said they hadn't got a hope! Leio Scott and Caroline Luranski, a liaisoned couple from London's Ring 7, won outright the SEVEN WONDER BREAKFAST Competition that attracted so much interest, and so much controversy. Their simple answer to the question, *"What has intergalactic space got to offer you?"* was enough to satisfy the panel of six judges and four Logprimo Molecumatrix computers. Their prize: to join the first package tour to the Aurora-Magellan Federation!

When the competition was first announced, a year ago, it attracted a large amount of criticism, mainly from the Supporters of Freedom for Individual Planets, who are bitterly opposed to the militaristic regime of the A-M Federation. But APOLLO FOODS, creators of SEVEN WONDER BREAKFASTS, have long been fighting for inter-system trade with the Aurorans, and they jumped at the chance to part-sponsor this first non-diplomatic flight out to the Lesser M-Cloud.

The full size of the tour has not yet been disclosed, but will probably be in excess of 300 persons. Most places on the tour have been allocated by Central Solar, to worthy citizens, sportsmen, artists, businessmen, and thirty underprivileged young adults from the outer world colonies. Six competitions have been held to dispose of fifteen places. Leio and Caroline won against an entry toll of more than four million forms.

The full extent of the tour, which has a visit to the Magellanic Cloud as its high point, also includes a visit to several fabled worlds such as VandeZande's World in the Altuxor System, Refuge in the Pliax System, and their choice of one of the Galaxies largest casino worlds. They will be allowed a brief visit to the Tombworld, in the system Draconis B, where the tombs of a billion Galactic Kings are to be found. Normally restricted to a few select tourists per year, Tombworld is the subject of more than twenty thousand research projects. Lucky Leio and Caroline will have a scant fourteen days to explore the galleries and passages and find the legendary Jaraquath Treasure. Lucky Kids!

The whole trip will take six months and Caroline Luranski is already on leave and preparing for the tour at the small, comfortable module she shares with biochemist Leio.

INTE Herald

Aurora-Magella System frontier
First visitor set for next

A REPRESENTATIVE of the Galactic Co-operative Department of Commerce announced today that arrangements have been concluded with the government of the Aurora-Magellan Federation for a resumption of cultural and trade contacts between the two blocs. The first concrete result of this historic agreement is expected to be a package tour of parts of the Federation, tentatively scheduled for September next year.

The breakthrough follows extended negotiations between top-ranking officials of the two sides. These began immediately after the 2573 summit meeting at the Pliax Stargate. Talks were on the verge of collapse last year during the crisis over the starliner *Cassiopeia's* inadvertent violation of Aurora-Magellan frontiers, but sustained diplomatic efforts by both sides averted a breakdown.

In a statement issued by the Aurora-Magellan Legation at Sao Paolo, Federation representatives expressed satisfaction at the outcome of the talks. "The government and people of the Aurora-Magellan Federation of Independent Worlds look forward to welcoming visitors from the Cultural and Economic Co-operative of Democratic Worlds

WORLD Tribune

THE NEW EARTH TIMES

opens its

his century ar

d to a continuing growth of de and cultural contacts ween our two great systems."

A stride back from the brink

by our POLITICAL CORRESPONDENT

THE FIRST STAGE agreement concluded today between the Galactic Co-operative and the Aurora-Magellan Federation may appear trivial at first sight – a reciprocal arrangement to allow a few thousand tourists each year – but its symbolic importance can hardly be exaggerated. It marks the first significant thaw in relations between the two great power blocs since the outbreak of the Aurora-Magellan War of Independence in 2445. Agreements on trade negotiations and full ambassadorial exchanges are expected to follow in a matter of weeks.

Since the termination of fighting in 2453 the galaxy has lived under the constant threat of renewed conflict on a catastrophic scale. Mutual suspicion grew steadily during more than a century without direct diplomatic contact, but since the first tentative steps towards rapp-

rochement were taken in 2569 both sides have shown themselves anxious to reach agreement. Despite a number of setbacks, observers seldom doubted that the talks would ultimately prove successful.

As yet the agreement does not signal any progress towards disarmament. Indeed representatives of the right-wing Human Unity party were today calling for an increase in military expenditure to counteract what they described as "a transparent attempt by the totalitarian dictatorship of Aurora-Magellan to lull our people into a false sense of security while planning a surprise attack." However, these arguments are unlikely to impress representatives of the majority parties, who are hailing today's news as the most significant step towards permanent galactic peace for more than a century.

QUARK-LINES QUIZZED OVER QUESTIONABLE CRAFT

Star-liner time-slip scandal stops sponsorship of Galactic Tour

THE LONG WRANGLE between Quark-Lines, a branch of Intersun Haulage, and Pan-Galactic over the transport rights for the first passenger tour to enter Auroran-Magellan Federation Space has at last ended. PanGal emerge the winners by default, and will now begin preparations for their most auspicious guided tour ever.

Fourteen days ago a Quark-Line passenger liner, the *Solar Voyager*, experienced a time displacement of four thousand years; all three hundred passengers, returning from vacation on Rigel 17, have undergone seven weeks' displacement ageing, and have appointed Central Judiciary to sue the space line. They charge gross dereliction and negligence, claiming that the older Quark-Line craft are not properly serviced, or equipped.

Time Rescue Inc., who each year are responsible for more than four million years of travel to save space-yachts and rickety freighters from the swamps and deserts of different times, claim that the final bill for the rescue of the *Solar Voyager* will be in excess of a million galactic units.

Counsel for Intersun deny negligence. The case has been adjourned pending detailed scientific investigations, which our legal experts estimate could take three years to complete. Meanwhile an attempt by the EurAmerican Society for the Safety of Interspace (EASSI) to have the entire Quark-Line fleet grounded was rejected by the court. Nevertheless, Intersun have lost their right to carry passengers on the much heralded trip to the Lesser Magellanic Cloud.

Our science correspondent writes: why *do* these older ships fails so frequently to maintain maximum hold on time during the Time-Space-Matrix-Distortion travel (TSMD drive) that reduces a light year to an hour's travel? Quark-Lines state categorically that these accidents are mere flukes, citing the handful of incidents that have achieved national press coverage. But the fact remains that one in every three flights by such older vessels slip in time by, perhaps, no more than a few hours – not enough to worry the passengers, perhaps, but a distinctly ominous portent. Researchers at the Aldebaran Institute for SuperCee Studies have now found evidence that it is the triple thick zirontix-steel hulls which are to blame, and point the finger at the high rate of radiation of charmed quarks when the ships begin to cross the Cruntznick Meridian into faster than light speeds. Modern ships, with hulls made out of Titronix Diamond Tuff-Shield, never show any dislodgement, or high sub-particle radiation, when channelling time through their Irridon Plasmaspan High Coil Rotunda thrusts.

Personal diary Lelo. 1st June 2577: If this holiday doesn't make a Quikbook then I — or should I say we — don't deserve to have had our stroke of luck. It was Caroline's idea that we should each keep a diary of the holiday and that'll help a lot. I'm sure that at the end of six months we'll have forgotten half of what we saw and heard. Caroline treated us to these tiny wrist recorders and the only problem now is getting over the embarrassment of speaking to my arm in public. How she afforded these little gadgets I can't imagine. I hope she used her personal account and not our joint account. I daren't call it up and look. This is being recorded at home, a sort of pre-holiday check-in. I also want to get used to the diary. I feel like I'm being very incoherent. At the end of each recording we can slot the crystal recorder into any Homefax print console and get a copy for inspection; or we can just leave the data inside until we get home. So. We go to Earthport (Andes) in two days' time. Caroline is still working, but I got my leave from this morning. Six whole months! I shall have to eat more Seven Wonder Breakfasts. Strangely, I can't remember which of us it was who came up with the winning caption in the competition. Such a stupid caption too. I still can't grasp that we've actually **won**. Packing is a pleasure, though. The thought of getting away from London at last! Our last holiday was that disastrous three weeks on Mars. Wind, sand and gravity sores do not a holiday make. This tour, though, is going to be **very** different. I just can't wait to see Tombworld, and the G'chathraga ruins on Pluto. We get that choice, apparently, something spectacular to see in our own system. Caroline wants to see the ice castles on Titania, one of the moons of Uranus — natural formations. We've argued about it already, but I'm determined to get to Pluto. One thing we didn't expect was the number of forms we've had to fill in. They asked us to use lite-writers, but I've asked for paper prints of them all so that we can keep a scrap book of the holiday. Our own print-outs are grey and smelly. They've agreed, too. I'm beginning to relax with this diary now — just a sliver of cold crystal. It sticks by epidermatak. Leaves a red mark when you slide it off your skin. **End entry.**

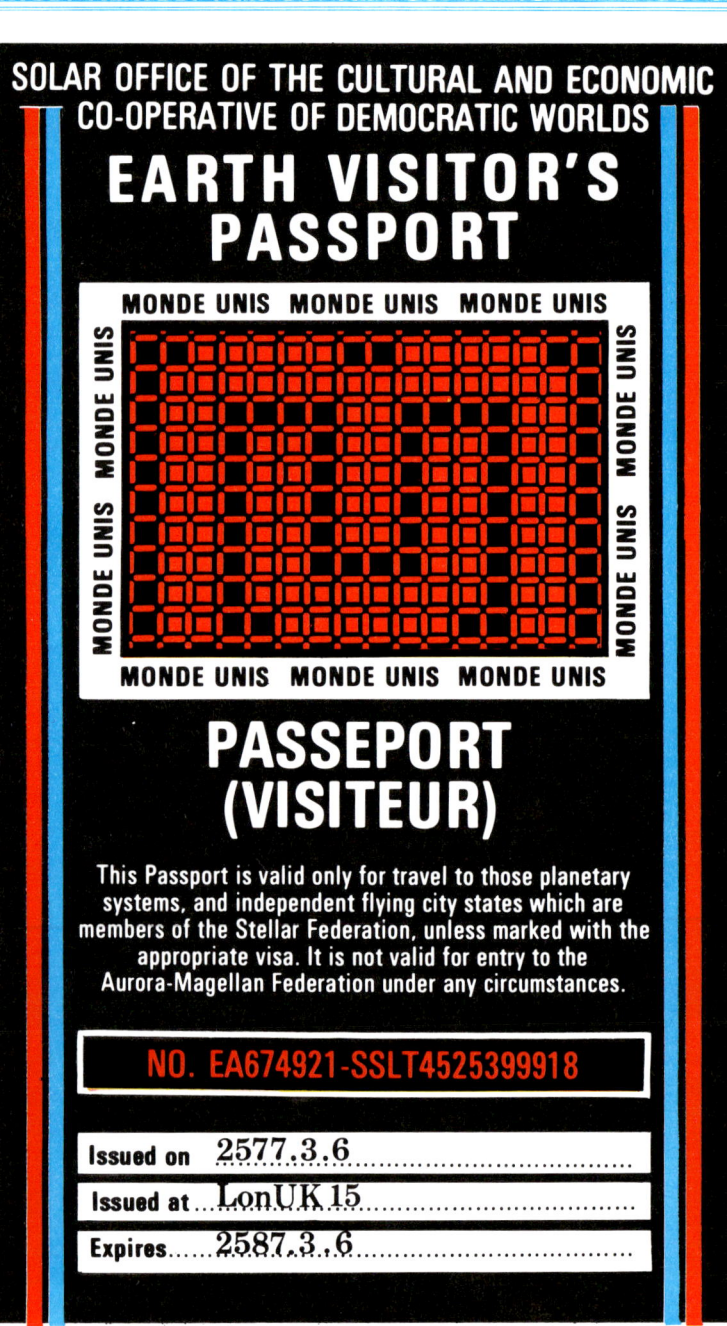

SOLAR OFFICE OF THE CULTURAL AND ECONOMIC CO-OPERATIVE OF DEMOCRATIC WORLDS

EARTH VISITOR'S PASSPORT

MONDE UNIS MONDE UNIS MONDE UNIS

PASSEPORT (VISITEUR)

This Passport is valid only for travel to those planetary systems, and independent flying city states which are members of the Stellar Federation, unless marked with the appropriate visa. It is not valid for entry to the Aurora-Magellan Federation under any circumstances.

NO. EA674921-SSLT4525399918

Issued on 2577.3.6
Issued at LonUK 15
Expires   2587.3.6

HIM

Thumbp(rint)
(if digit transplan(t)
state dat(e)
and ope(ration)
transplac(e))

Name	
Place, date, creche of birth	
If growth by excor or deldev, tick	
World of residence	
Current address	
Personal credit number	
Religion, if any (if non-terrestrial specify world of origin and galactic worship code)	
Height	
Eye colour (natural)	
Eye colour (at time of application)	
Hair colour (natural)	
Hair colour (at time of application)	
Retinal code	
If 1st or 2nd gen. clone, tick	
Distinguishing features	
Cerebrum scan	
Body weight (kg)	

Personal diary Caroline. 3rd June 2577: I can hardly believe it: today we arrived at Earthport on the first leg of our journey. I'm recording this in the departure lounge while we wait for the elevator shuttle to take us to Ring City (for some reason Leio won't record in public, but it doesn't worry me). I've been here before, of course, but each time it seems more bustling, more exciting: a tremendous throng of humans and aliens. And this time, too, it's more than just a short trip to Mars or the Moon – this time we're going all the way across the Galaxy, and beyond. We haven't yet agreed on which alternative route we should take, and I can see it's going to lead to quarrels, but for now we're both too excited at what's happening. The trip over from Paris I could have done without: those electro-grav tubes always make me feel queasy, especially the period of quasi-weightlessness at the bottom of the curve, however many thousand metres under the surface. It's different from true zero-g because there is still a sense of rapid motion. It also gives me a feeling of claustrophobia (or maybe just plain **fear**) – those millions of tons of rock ready to squash us as thin as a lunar meat ration if the field should fail. The last two weeks have been incredibly hectic. (I wish I **had** been on leave as the newsfaxes – accurate as ever – said!) Leio has been racing around saying should we take this, do we need that – just like a kid on his first Moontrip. It's as well one of us is organized. The office arranged a celebration send-off for me. Almost everyone turned up – the first time I've ever met about half of them in the flesh. It made me wonder if work might have been more enjoyable before you could do nearly everything from your home terminal. But I suppose it would soon get boring. Anyway, everyone popped a lot (several people had to be carried out) and the Boss gave me a new holo-camera, which I'll be able to keep if I bring back some good material. She says this is my chance to break out of subediting into something more creative – maybe even a holovid recorder! So this may be more than the trip of a lifetime – it could even be the beginning of a new life. **End entry.**

HER

WARNING TO HOLDER

Before making ex-Solar journeys with this passport you should check that it is:
a) Still in force and will not expire before your redocumentation at a Solar Starport.
b) Valid for those planets you propose to land upon (orbital transit is not affected). See Stellar Federation Schedule 17.
c) Stamped with appropriate visas for those Independent Planetary Federations listed in Stellar Federation Schedule 18.
d) Is not marked, creased or blotched in any way liable to arouse suspicion that extra information is being transmitted.

Signature

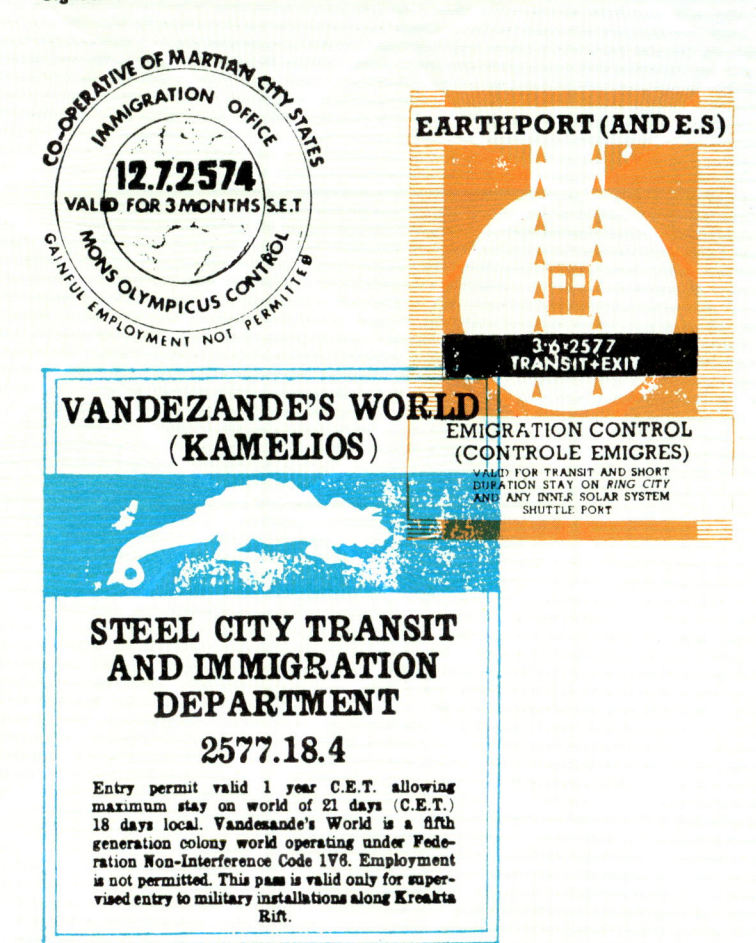

CO-OPERATIVE OF MARTIAN CITY STATES
IMMIGRATION OFFICE
12.7.2574
VALID FOR 3 MONTHS S.E.T
MONS OLYMPICUS CONTROL
GAINFUL EMPLOYMENT NOT PERMITTED

EARTHPORT (AND E.S)
3·6·2577
TRANSIT+EXIT
EMIGRATION CONTROL
(CONTROLE EMIGRES)
VALID FOR TRANSIT AND SHORT DURATION STAY ON *RING CITY* AND ANY INNER SOLAR SYSTEM SHUTTLE PORT

VANDEZANDE'S WORLD (KAMELIOS)

STEEL CITY TRANSIT AND IMMIGRATION DEPARTMENT

2577.18.4

Entry permit valid 1 year C.E.T. allowing maximum stay on world of 21 days (C.E.T.) 18 days local. Vandezande's World is a fifth generation colony world operating under Federation Non-Interference Code 1V6. Employment is not permitted. This pass is valid only for supervised entry to military installations along Kreakta Rift.

PAN GALACTIC
STARTOUR DISPLAY TICKET

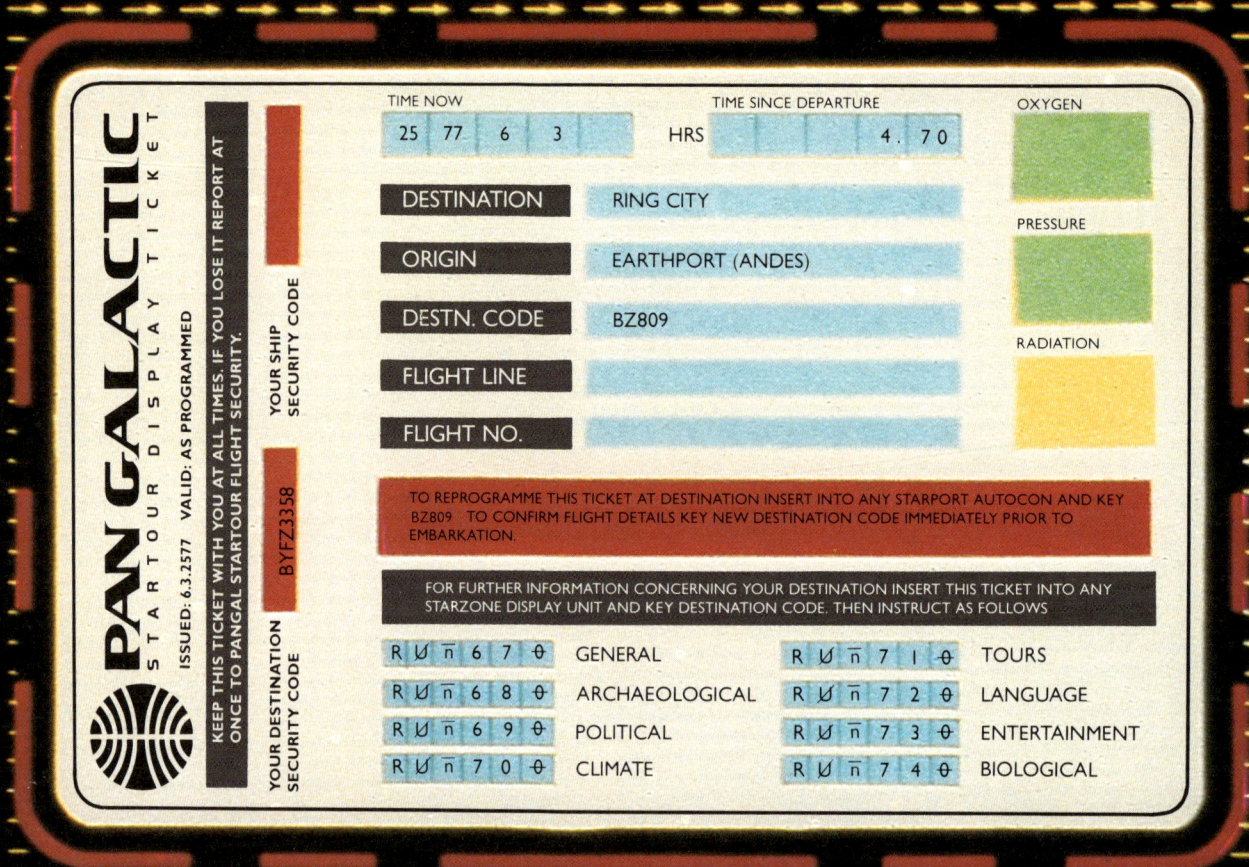

ISSUED: 6.3.2577 VALID: AS PROGRAMMED

KEEP THIS TICKET WITH YOU AT ALL TIMES. IF YOU LOSE IT REPORT AT ONCE TO PANGAL STARTOUR FLIGHT SECURITY.

YOUR SHIP SECURITY CODE: BYFZ3358

YOUR DESTINATION SECURITY CODE

TIME NOW				TIME SINCE DEPARTURE		
25	77	6	3	HRS	4.	70

DESTINATION	RING CITY
ORIGIN	EARTHPORT (ANDES)
DESTN. CODE	BZ809
FLIGHT LINE	
FLIGHT NO.	

OXYGEN

PRESSURE

RADIATION

TO REPROGRAMME THIS TICKET AT DESTINATION INSERT INTO ANY STARPORT AUTOCON AND KEY BZ809 TO CONFIRM FLIGHT DETAILS KEY NEW DESTINATION CODE IMMEDIATELY PRIOR TO EMBARKATION.

FOR FURTHER INFORMATION CONCERNING YOUR DESTINATION INSERT THIS TICKET INTO ANY STARZONE DISPLAY UNIT AND KEY DESTINATION CODE. THEN INSTRUCT AS FOLLOWS

R U n̄ 6 7 0	GENERAL	R U n̄ 7 1 0	TOURS
R U n̄ 6 8 0	ARCHAEOLOGICAL	R U n̄ 7 2 0	LANGUAGE
R U n̄ 6 9 0	POLITICAL	R U n̄ 7 3 0	ENTERTAINMENT
R U n̄ 7 0 0	CLIMATE	R U n̄ 7 4 0	BIOLOGICAL

EARTHPORT I · EARTHPORT

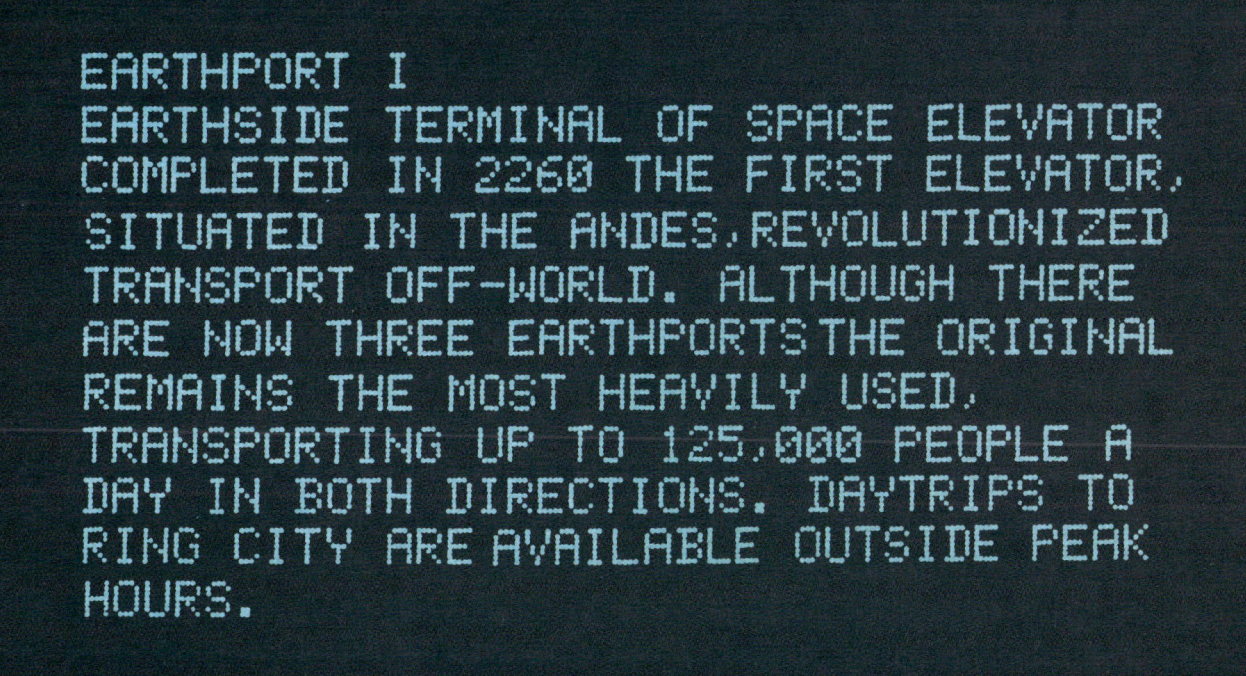

EARTHPORT I
EARTHSIDE TERMINAL OF SPACE ELEVATOR COMPLETED IN 2260 THE FIRST ELEVATOR, SITUATED IN THE ANDES, REVOLUTIONIZED TRANSPORT OFF-WORLD. ALTHOUGH THERE ARE NOW THREE EARTHPORTS THE ORIGINAL REMAINS THE MOST HEAVILY USED, TRANSPORTING UP TO 125,000 PEOPLE A DAY IN BOTH DIRECTIONS. DAYTRIPS TO RING CITY ARE AVAILABLE OUTSIDE PEAK HOURS.

EARTHPORT I

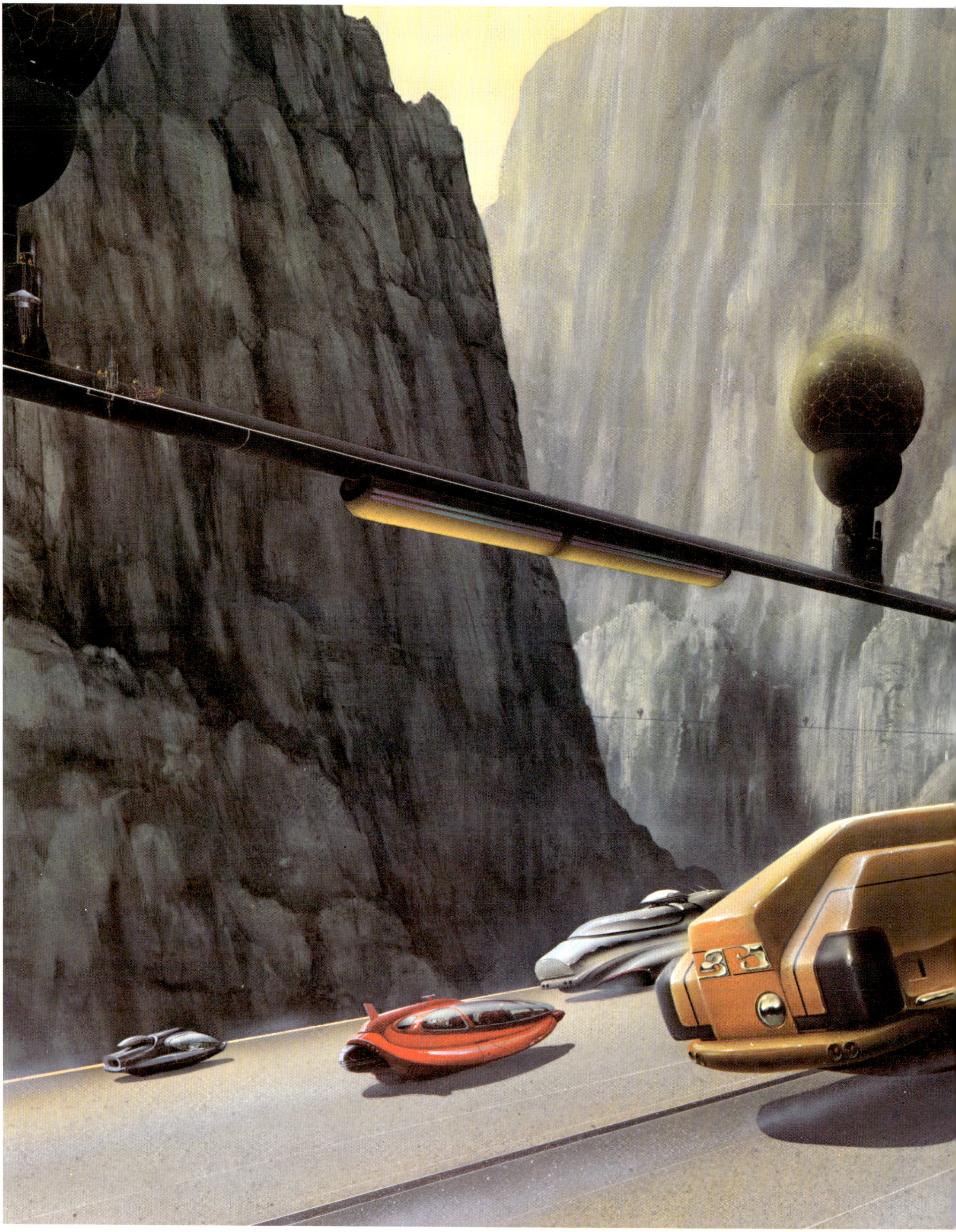

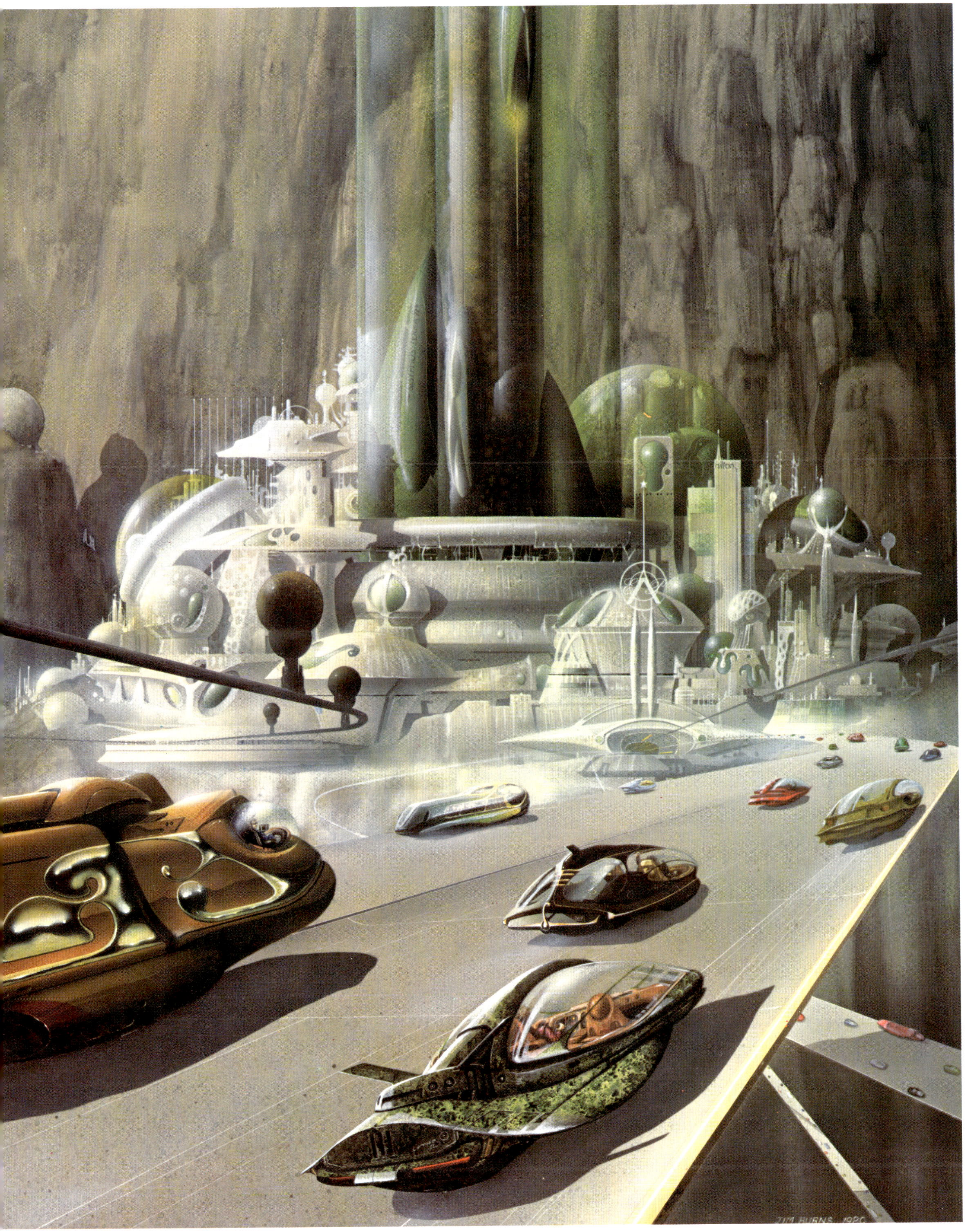
JIM BURNS

EXTRACT FROM: INTO SPACE: A SHORT HISTORY OF HUMANITY'S EXPANSION INTO THE GALAXY (2543)

The concept of the space elevator was first put forward as long ago as 1960, in a paper by the Russian engineer Artsutanov. During the following fifteen years it was independently conceived of by several other scientists, and by 1980 had received considerable discussion and popularization. Several alternative names were canvassed: orbital tower, sky-hook, heavenly funicular, and so forth. But the vision was centuries in advance of the technology necessary to bring it into existence, and it was not until the early 23rd century that the invention of the Clarke filament (a continuous pseudodiamond crystal) combined with the development of engineering solutions to previously intractable problems (wind and sun/moon effects and instabilities in the geosynchronous orbit) made the elevator feasible.

The final design was the work of three European scientists: Arthur Bradford, E.G O'Brien and Charles Willis. The site selected was close to the peak of Mount Cayambe, approximately 40 kilometres north-east of Quito in Ecuador province. Construction began in 2235, and took nearly 40 years to complete. Several square kilometres of the mountainous Andes had to be levelled as the site of Earthport I. Construction of the elevator began in orbit, with a thread of filament being lowered to Earth as an anchor for the elevator. In order to maintain its stability it had to be built simultaneously upwards and downwards from the midpoint. The engineering problems were immense and (at the time) unique: on several occasions the project came close to disaster, and the lives of over fifty people were lost during construction. The work took many years longer than anticipated, but Earthport I was eventually opened to traffic in 2273. Its four capsules were able to carry up to 12,000 passengers a day each way from Earth to the orbital station (a journey of 36,000 kilometres), plus thousands of tons of freight – and all at a fraction of the cost of conventional shuttle transportation. The cost and difficulty of space trips were immediately and drastically reduced (to the dismay of shuttle operators, who saw a regular and profitable business dwindle almost overnight to insignificance: indeed, both the Confederation of Shuttle Operatives and their workforce embarked on long, costly and abortive legal action to close Earthport). A few space travellers were psychologically unable to use the elevator, suffering from an acute form of vertigo which became known as 'elevator sickness'; everyone else flocked to it.

Indeed, such was the demand that within 25 years of the opening of Earthport I a second tower was under construction, this time with eight tracks. Despite this doubling in size Earthport II (at Mount Kenya) was completed much more quickly than its predecessor, and opened in 2316. Earthport III, also with eight tracks and situated in Central Borneo, was commenced in 2330 and finished in 2347. With a maximum capacity of 60,000 passengers per day – over 20 million per year – the three Earthports have been able to cope with a stabilized flow of passengers and emigrants.

The Earthports are a vital historical link in the establishment of *homo sapiens* as a true interplanetary and interstellar race. They brought space travel within the reach of vastly more people; they revolutionized the economics of interworld commerce; they made it possible greatly to simplify the construction in orbit of habitats and space liners, as it became easy and cheap to prefabricate items on Earth and ferry them in easily-assembled sections into orbit. They finally and permanently changed the outlook and perspective of the human race.

SOLAR CO-OPERATIVE

Name: ....
Number: ....
City and Country of Business: ....
Nature of Business: ....
Name of controlling Co-operative or Corporation: ....
....
Are you registered with PanGal Exchange or any other recognised InterPlanetary materials and credit bureau of exchange: ....
....
Extra-solar location of Business trip: ....
Purpose of business: ....
Credit control code: ....
Solar Authority: ....

TRANSOLAR
BUSINESS IDENTIFICATION FORM GAMMA C221

WORK STATUS:
(If Director or writer please state)

REGISTERED NO. OF DAYS WITH THIS COMPANY:

REGISTERED NUMBER OF DAYS AS SCHEDULE 56A INDIVIDUAL WORK STATUS:

GOVERNMENT CLEARANCE NUMBER:

Please state if your company is practising economic sanctions against any non-Co-operative Stellar Federation If YES you must fill out form Gamma C221B

EARTHPORT
EMIGRATION CONTROL
INTERSTELLAR EMBARKATION FORM

Name:	LEIO SCOTT
Destination:	WORLDS MARKED ON SCHEDULE 178
Proposed length of absence from Earth:	SIX MONTHS
Proposed length of absence from Solar System:	FIVE MONTHS
Passport number:	Ea 674921-SsLT 4525399918
Personal credit number:	60-777-0071-2-931mm 5998
Name(s) of travelling companion(s):	CAROLINE LURANSKI
Reason for travel:	HOLIDAY
Tour Operator:	HARLEQUIN GALACTIC TOURS
Spaceline(s) in sequence:	—
Travel insurance:	HARLEQUIN INSURALIFE

It is forbidden to export any of the following items from Earth without the appropriate licences: livestock, transuranic elements, human organs, cultured human ova, cultured pathogens and/or parasites, religious tracts, weapons (except those defined as for personal use), historical and/or cultural artifacts pre-dating 2500AD.

If travelling for purposes of business you must fill in form Gamma C221.

SHUTTLE TRANSIT CARD — EARTHPORT

▷▷▷▷▷▷▷▷▷▷▷▷▷▷

Please study the information below and keep card available at all times. The card must be presented on demand. A memLog copy will be taken, and if the card is lost it may be replaced at the purser's office.

NAME:	SCOTT
SHUTTLE CODE:	45D - 793
CABIN NO:	163
MED BAY:	14
MAX CURRENCY AVAILABLE FOR FLIGHT:	1000gc
MEDICAL ATTENDANCE TIMES:	6-6 10.30
DRUG AVAILABILITY:	PEPSONE-G
SECURITY CLEARANCE: (see Availability of Movement)	CD12

NOTE: YOU MAY NOT CROSS ACCESS SILLS THAT DO NOT DISPLAY YOUR COLOUR CODE

DISEMBARKATION ZONE	LIFEBOAT POINT*
E	10

*NOTE: YOU MAY BE REFUSED ACCESS TO THE LIFEBOAT IF YOU ARE NOT IN THE CORRECT ZONE

JUPITER SHUTTLE
EMBARKATION FORM PX23cX

NAME:	CAROLINE LURANSKI
PASSPORT NUMBER:	EA674921-SSLT45253999918
FLIGHT NUMBER:	JOVE45D
LUGGAGE (KILOS):	32
CURRENCY:	40,000 GC
INSURANCE (A. LIFE B. LUGGAGE:)	
A.	HARLEQUIN INSURANCE
B.	HARLEQUIN TRAVELSAFE
MEDCON AUTHORISATION NO:	+76231 5
BODY WEIGHT EMBARKATION:	52
TISSUE CALCIUM:	666-1
VISORIENT CAPPANT:	73/1 24 RET
BODY AGE:	21.5
SHUTTLE CLASS:	LUX

I have/have not flown Earthport Shuttles on a previous occasion. I accept full responsibility for my presence on flight JOVE45D......... and will address all claims for compensation to my insurer.

Signed: Caroline Luranski
Date: 2577-6-4

****Earthport Shuttles (a branch of InterStel) accept no responsibility for loss of luggage or personal effects, nor for any premature ageing, or other individual effects of extended space flight. They accept full responsibility for the time space integrity of their shuttles and passengers in accordance with the UniSpac Andes Safety Agreement of 2544****

Cosmic Holiday Guide

HYPERIONA

FROM GC 1200

If your idea of a holiday is nonstop fun, then Hyperiona is the place for you! It's the undisputed pleasure centre of the galaxy, a world whose only industry is providing entertainment. Hyperiona's slogan, "Your pleasure is our business", is nothing but the simple truth. Here you can enjoy the full range of sensory experiences, including many which because of their potency are restricted to this world only! Whether your taste is for total-experience holoshows, Sensualoan immersions, or just the intimate attentions of a Pleasure Parlour, Hyperiona offers you the best. Children are catered for by an astonishing range of specially tailored experiences. And whatever your pleasure preferences, you're sure to want to spend some time im Hyperiona's fabulous casinos, which in addition to their unique range of gaming attractions offer a full spectrum of sophisticated entertainments. You don't know what pleasure really is until you've visited Hyperiona!

Transit time from Sirius 37 hours (one TSMD jump); Starport 44 hours (one TSMD jump).

HOTEL EXCELSIOR
LOCATION Right in the heart of Hyperiona City, on fabulous Starset Strip.
AMENITIES The Excelsior is one of the great pleasure hotels on Hyperiona. Rooms are equipped to the highest standards of luxury; room service can cater for almost any requirement.
ENTERTAINMENT The hotel has one of Hyperiona's finest casinos, as well as fully-equipped Sensualoan Chamber and Tactile Emporium. Male guests may make use of the Excelsior's famous Three Whores of Robotics.

HOTEL MIRAMA[R]

LOCATION Quietly situated in a secluded private clearing only three hundred miles [from] planet's finest sandy beaches.
AMENITIES This is a small hotel which despite frequent changes of management mair[tains] standards of service and protection. A triple force field augmented by automatic lasers ke[eps] the largest predators at bay, and over the last two seasons the Miramar boasts the lowes[t] rate among its guests of any Pyrran hotel.
ENTERTAINMENT The hotel has two laser rifle ranges, and is famed for the boisterous re[tinue?] wakes.

PYRRUS

FROM G.C. 1450

Looking for a holiday that's really different? Try exciting, mysterious Pyrrus. With its fascinatingly varied animal and plant life it's an ideal place for the zoologist and the adventurous in spirit, young and old. The oceans, with their thirty-metre waves, providing exciting opportunities for surfing, while the many volcanoes provide a constant display of fireworks. You can go on safari in complete safety in one of our armour-plated hovercars, or relax back at the hotel and let the sun and bracing wind complete your tan. Local delicacies are always available in the restaurants (take no notice of the appearance – they're delicious!) And remember, the price of your Cosmic Holiday on Pyrrus includes a gun with powered holster and full medical and survival kits. "See Pyrrus and die!" says the old proverb, and when you visit this wonderful planet you'll understand why!

Transit time from Sirius 96 hours (3 TSMD jumps, one Stargate transit; includes overnight stay at the Orbitsville Hilton); Starport 77 hours (4 jumps, nonstop).

BEDROOMS The luxurious bedrooms, each with double-filtered hot and cold running water, are protected by 10cm armour plate. Each is equipped with full life-support equipment for seven days.

Note It is not possible to issue medical or life insurance for holidays on Pyrrus.

Ganymede Hilton
the Galaxy's biggest hotel chain
CONFIRMATION OF RESERVATION

NAME: LEIO SCOTT

The following accommodation has been reserved for you.

TYPE OF ROOM:	DBL	ATMOSPHERE TYPE:	NORM
ARRIVAL DATE:	77-6-8	DEPARTURE DATE:	77-6-10

Conditions of booking: The Hotel will accept cancellations or alterations to this reservation received no later than 28 Earth standard days before 12.00hrs on the day of arrival (Galactic Standard Time). In case of such cancellations a handling levy of 10% of the inclusive price of one night's accommodation will be deducted. Cancellations received after this deadline may at the hotel's discretion, be debited for the full cost of the original booking. The Hotel accepts no responsibility in the case of cancellation instructions lost or delayed in transmission: customers are therefore advised to use Registered Ansible Broadcast or Insured Courier Services. Occasionally it may be necessary for the hotel to provide accommodation other than that stipulated in this confirmation: no refunds are payable in such instances. The Hotel guarantees to provide proper atmospheric conditions in any room allocated.

Ganymede Hilton
the Galaxy's biggest hotel chain
ACCOMMODATION RESERVATION FORM

NAME(S): LEIO SCOTT

PERMANENT ADDRESS: MOD 1238, ARCOL 23, LONDON RING 7, G-EUROPE.

SYSTEM/WORLD OF RESIDENCE: EARTH

ARRIVAL DATE (GST): 2577/6/8.

DEPARTURE DATE (GST): 2577/6/10.

CREDIT NO: 60.777.0071-2-931 MM sq. 98.

PASSPORT NO: E2674921-S&LT4525399918

DEPARTURE FLIGHT: PAN GAL F0432.

NEXT DESTINATION: PLUTO.

TYPE OF ROOM REQUIRED:

Single ☐   Double ☒   Twin ☐   Mutilple ☐   Cocoon ☐

No. of chambers ☐ Pressurised ☐ (Give atmospheric mix code) ☐☐☐☐

Signature or recognized identity mark ...*Leio Scott*...

NOTE: Completion of this form constitutes a binding agreement under the terms of Section XVII(m) of the Intersystem Trade Protocol (rev. 2547)

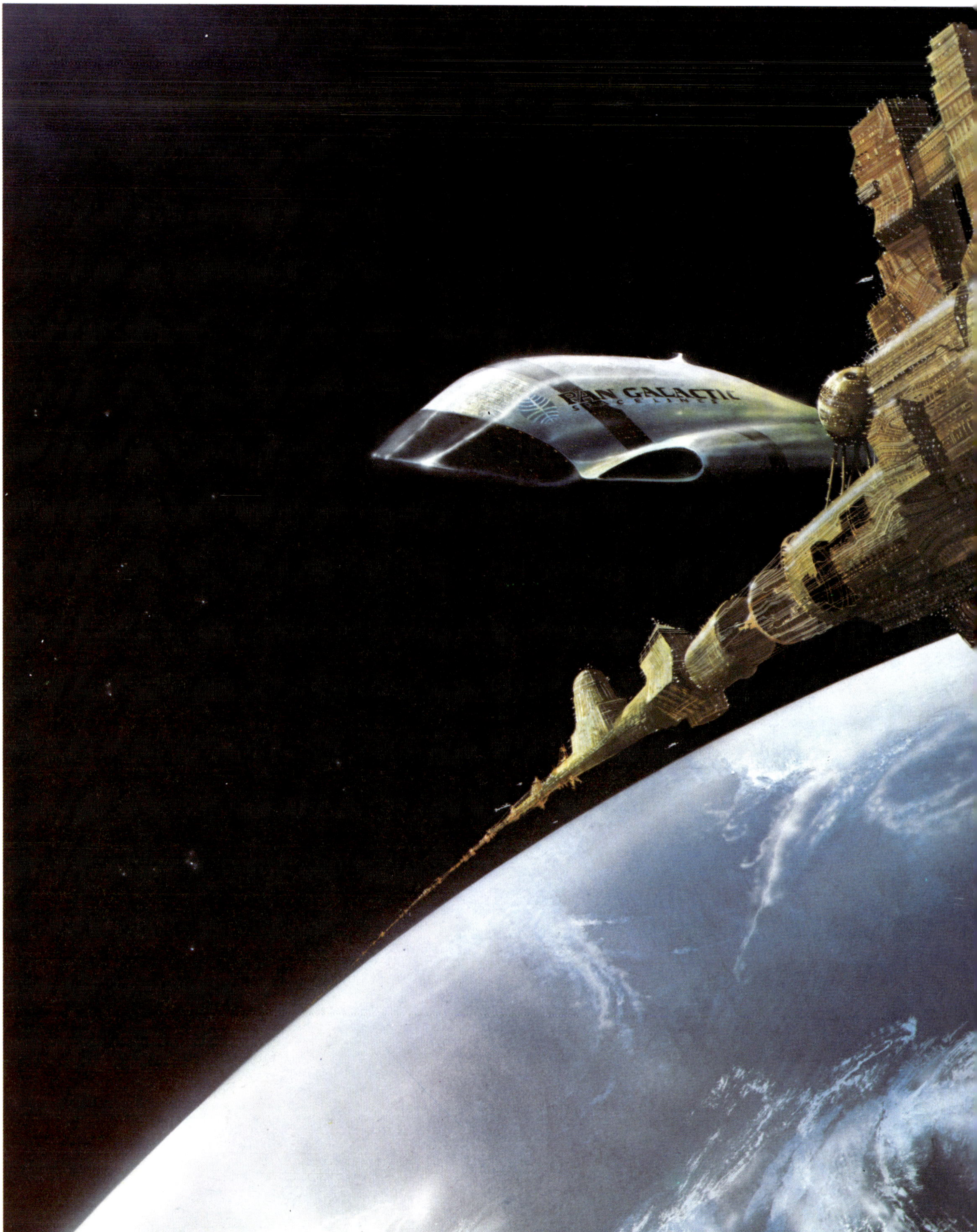
PAN GALACTIC

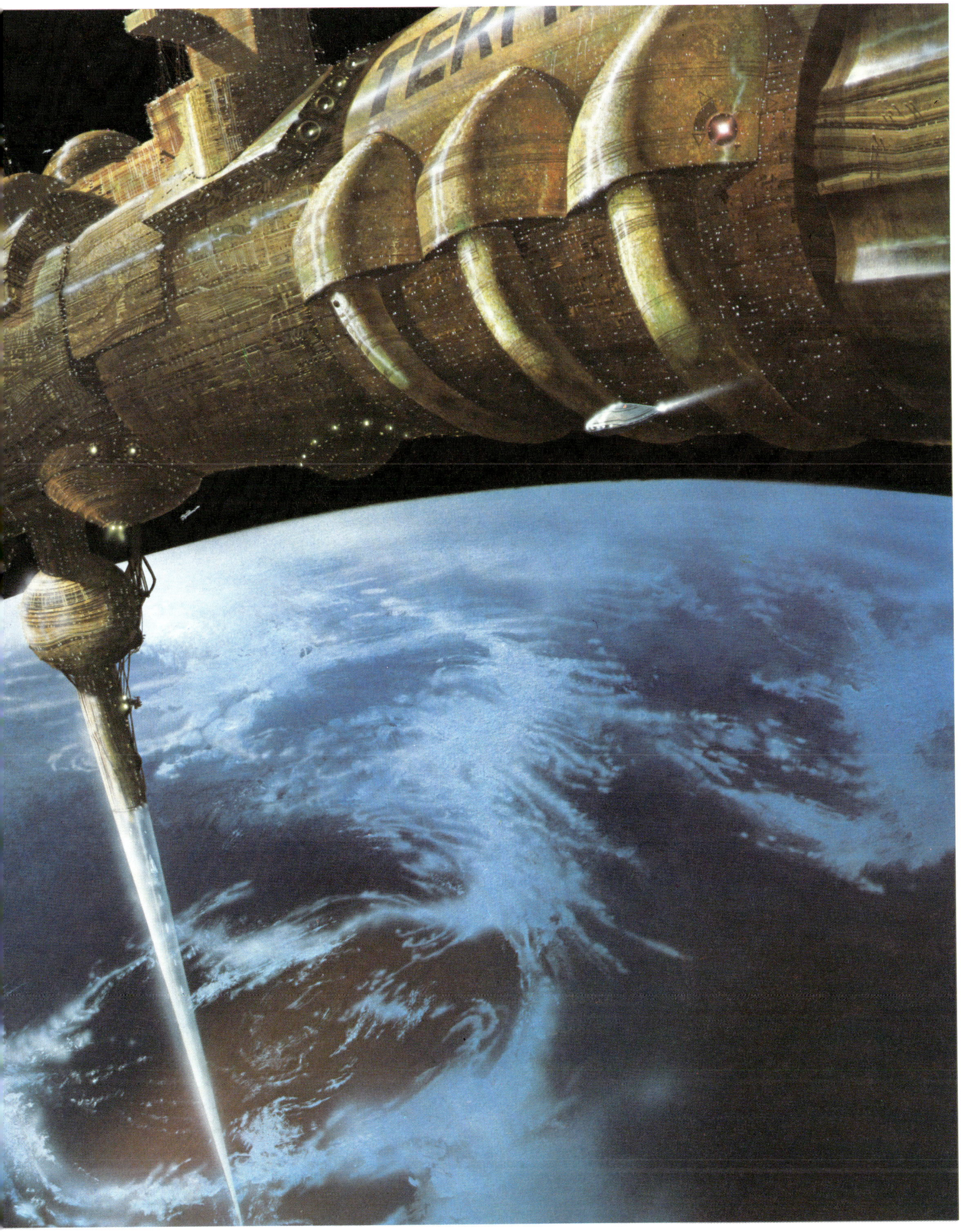

Agent Luranski: Memory Implant. 5th June 2577: I should now be recording on the implanted memory crystal, though of course I have no way of checking through playback. However, I can feel the tingle in my upper arm which is supposed to indicate that the crystal is activated. It's been so hectic the last three days that this is the first chance I've had to get somewhere by myself to test out the system. The crystal implant was easier than I'd expected: hardly more noticeable than an inoculation (though I'm not looking forward to having my arm broken to get it removed). Installing the retinal holo-cameras was less pleasant, and my eyes have been a little sore; but that's easily passed off as the effect of the new contacts I bought for the trip. The existence of these completely organic and undetectable recording implants still amazes me. Anyway, Leio obviously suspected nothing: he just thought I spent even longer than usual buying stuff for the holiday. I feel nervous, of course, being put on active status after six dormant years. Part of it is obviously the responsibility, being aware that a lot — possibly the peace of the galaxy — depends on our getting an accurate assessment of Aurora-Magellan intentions. That's heavy enough — what makes it worse is not having a specific task to accomplish. It could be that no chance will present itself, and the whole thing will prove abortive. The other thing which bothers me is the necessary duplicity. I don't like having to hide things from Leio — somehow, as a dormant agent, it was easy to pretend that I wasn't really doing so. Now it's different. And not only do I have to lie, I also have to act out the role of Caroline Luranski, excited holidaymaker — when inside I'm feeling scared and tense. I'm sure he'll notice something, even if he won't know the reason . . . I just played back the wrist diary. Nothing of what I just recorded was there, so I assume the crystal is working. Keeping that 'ordinary' diary is another hard, but necessary, part of the pretence. I will limit further recordings on this level until we reach Aurora-Magellan space. **End report.**

EXTRACT FROM: RING CITY OFFICIAL VISITOR'S GUIDE

Once Earthports II and III were under construction, first discussions of the orbital linkage which would become Ring City began. It made immediate practical sense: Earthspace was becoming increasingly crowded with satellites, orbital factories, power stations, observatories, hospitals, space habitats and so forth; navigation and traffic control were extraordinarily complex. The idea of linking the great majority of these in a single structure — in effect a single torus-shaped satellite girdling the Earth — was first popularized in 2317 (shortly after Earthport III construction had started) by the visionary space habitat designer Joanna Chikarema. For many years government estimates of cost ruled out detailed consideration of the project, and it was not until May 2396 (with cruel irony the month after Chikarema's death) that the Solar Assembly approved the first draft scheme.

Work on Operation Doughnut — as the popular newsfaxes quickly named it — began in 2407. The first step was to manoeuvre as many orbiting constructs as possible into synchronous equatorial orbit. (With one exception the space habitats declined to forego artificial gravity and remained stationed at the Lagrange points.) When this was done construction began on the electromagnetic tube which would provide fast transport around the ring. In 2433, President Christopher Carlsen ceremoniously welded the link which completed the ring. (Or so it seemed to the billions of holovoid viewers; in fact, as soon as the ceremony was over the last link was separated and re-welded by more skilled construction workers!)

Now new additions began to spring up all around the ring: Spaceline terminals, factories, living quarters, even office space. Ring City quickly acquired a name, and its inhabitants began to regard themselves as a community. The freefall environment was quickly and easily accessible from Earth; people would move there without the feeling of total upheaval which accompanied a move to another planet; nor were there exclusive entry requirements which kept the space habitats limited to the wealthy. Ring City was also ideal for people with heart disease or physical disability. The population soared. Ring City was incorporated as a city, undertaking most of its own administration, in 2459, by which time the population had already reached seven million. In his study of the Ring City and its long term effects, population dynamicist Eremei Delaney likened the three space elevators to capillaries, drawing Earth's life blood up into Ring City and beyond. His projections suggested that by 2700 the population of Ring City would exceed that of Earth. So far the rate of growth has been slower than his predicted curve, but nevertheless by 2550, Ring City's total population had reached 475 million, with all projections suggesting it would pass the billion mark by the end of the century.

Personal diary Caroline. 5th June 2577: En route to Jupiter, after an overnight stop on Ring City. I'd like to have spent longer there, although I can't see myself wanting to settle down to permanent weightless life. Lots of people obviously do, though — masses of construction going on, new environmental areas being developed — and all the publicity (A New Frontier, Ten Times the Size of America) is evidently having an effect. I sometimes wonder what all those people of the 21st century, crowded in their tenement cities, would have thought if they'd known that in 500 years' time the human population would be several times as large, but totally unable to fill the living space available in the solar system, let alone the colonized planets . . . The first thing I did after we'd arrived and been assigned accommodation was to visit one of the astro-bubbles. It's tremendously invigorating to shed your clothes and pretend you're swimming in free space. The sun was set and the moon was up, so none of the polarizing filters in the bubble were activated and interior lights weren't needed. The illusion was complete: you could drift up and touch the bubble and still not be able to see it. Weird. It's also good for the figure (I was propositioned several times, which made Leio very jealous until a couple of women approached **him**!), although I didn't find much to admire in the various members of the Kindred of Flesh floating about. Silly, I know, but I find those huge mountains of blubber — 150, 200, even 300 kilos — a rather repulsive sight. Still, I suppose they're true zero-g citizens — their hearts would never stand the strain of Earth gravity, let alone their legs! I know we are to travel on much bigger ships, but the Jupiter Shuttle seems huge enough to me: far bigger than any ship I've been on before. It's almost like a flying arcology, with its restaurants, stores, holo theatres and gymnasia — though tourist class accommodation is rather basic. I'm glad we travel first class on this trip! Starport arrival in a couple of days, and the predictable quarrel is brewing. Where do we go next — the ruins on Pluto or the Titanian Ice Castles? I can see myself getting very weary of Leio's obsession with ruins. **End entry.**

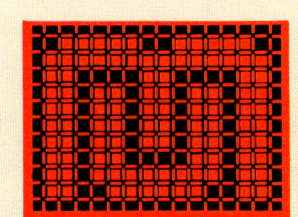

INTERSTELLAR TRANSIT FORM

A SEPARATE FORM MUST BE COMPLETED BY EACH PASSENGER

The purpose of this form is to ensure that before departing from Starport Ganymede you are in possession of all necessary documentation for your journey. The information given on these forms is also used in the collation of statistics on interstellar travel movements. Please complete each section as fully as possible. Your travel courier will help you with any necessary information but in case of difficulty please contact the Interstellar Transit Office in your embarkation sector. The form must be surrendered at your Embarkation Office at least six hours prior to departure.

NAME:

HOME ADDRESS:

PASSPORT NO.:

CREDIT NO.:

PURPOSE OF JOURNEY:
a) Business
   Please specify nature
b) Vacation
c) Government employ
d) Visiting relatives
e) Other
   Specify

IS YOUR JOURNEY PART OF AN ARRANGED TOUR? IF SO, STATE TOUR OPERATOR AND GIVE TOUR CODE
DESTINATION

NAME OF WORLD	DATE OF ARRIVAL/ DEPARTURE (GST)	CARRIER	STATE IF VISA GRANTED. GIVE EXPIRY DATE

Signature .... Date ....

Note: It is a criminal offence to give false information on this form.

GALACTIC HEALTH ORGANISATION

·MEDCON·
·INTERWORLDS MEDICAL CONTROL·
GENEVA — NEW ALEXANDRIA

MEDCON SCHEDU

IMPORTANT

Because MedCon exist with all Co-op Federation Worlds microfax copy, mu times and produce

This schedule must be filled out by *hand by* the person named in frame 17 and in the presence of a doctor registered with a MedCon Agency, or MedCon Authorized Hospital Centre.
PLEASE REMEMBER TO CLEAR COMAXESS TO YOUR FILES WITH YOUR LOCAL MEDP.
Failure to fill in this form correctly may result in withdrawal of InterWorlds exit permit, or forfeiture of re-entry permit to Earth.

MEDICAL HISTORY MedCon 7 i

Blood Pressure		High ☐ Normal ☐ Low ☐
Lipid Deposition	Heart	High ☐ Normal ☐
	Skeletal Muscle	High ☐ Normal ☐
Type K7 Embryonic Cells	Skin Density	50+/cluster ☐ Less than 50 ☐
Exposure to Landau HV radiation (if 40+hours schedule MedCon 15iii must be filled out)		40+hours ☐ Less than 40 ☐
Hours on cryogenic stasis, specify		....
Average post-menache flow (if high it may be necessary to undergo oestroLax delay treatment)		High ☐ Normal ☐ Slight ☐
Blood Lymphocyte count (% L cyte)		Less than 10 ☐ 10-20 ☐ More than 20 ☐
Basal Temperature		Normal ☐ Abnormal (specify) ....
Corneal Sensitivity		High ☐ Normal ☐
Blood Clotting Time (Schedule MedCon 3ii)		Normal ☐ Abnormal (specify) ....
Bone Fractures and Breaks: Specify with Dates		....
Susceptibility to Viral Influenza		High ☐ Low ☐
Alimentary Flora Analysis ....checked ☐	Skin Bacteria ....checked ☐	
Vaginal/Urethral Scrape ....checked ☐	Saliva Analysis ....checked ☐	

HAVE YOU EVER HAD:
Syphilis .... YES☐ NO☐
Other Venereal Disease .... YES☐ NO☐
Encephalitis .... YES☐ NO☐
Viral Hepatitis .... YES☐ NO☐
Malaria .... YES☐ NO☐
Bubonic Plague .... YES☐ NO☐
Lassa Fever .... YES☐ NO☐
Weston's Syndrome .... YES☐ NO☐
Haemorrhagic Fever .... YES☐ NO☐

IMMUNISATION SCHEDULE MedCon 7 ii

Simian HiRec labelled Lymphoblast H3b	1st exposure	Boost ....
Bovine high resolution A13 'Redon' antitoxin	Exposure	
Serum 63-Halor (with neur-stim)	Exposure	Skin Test +++ ++ +
Muncke's Serum (immune activation)	Exposure	t/b transformation (rodent antigen) +++ ++ +
I-tagged Marrow-blast (ovine)	No.	
Attenuated wide-spec mosaic in viral 'Tough' serum	Exposure	Fever .... Re-exposure ....
FOR VISITORS TO ORGONE 7 ONLY 17-di-cyclo-chloro-cerebrolinfuside	Exposure course Begun Completed	....

SUSCEPTIBILITY TO 'PRIME CONCERN' EXTRA-TERRESTRIAL ANTIGEN MedCon 7 iii

Heliosporus pollen (Abraxus 3, GN436679sk(ii)Abr)	+ + + + −
Invasive Mitogen Bx4 (Aurora 2, AM8692AurK)	+ + + + −
Auror-spiragid surface antigen 'chela' (Canis-Aurora 6, GN282113mz(vi)CA)	+ + + + −
Mutagenic 'skin-crawl' antigen (Virgana 17, GN6094522g(ix)Vi)	+ + + + −
Bladderlash toxin (Altuxor 4 (Kamelios), GN7774533rph(xxxi)VW)	+ + + + −
Spore-factor HG17 (Hyperion 7, GN 37598981mje(xxx)Hy)	+ + + + −
Hunderag spiralysing toxin (Sirius B 2, GN45pf(vii)Sir)	+ + + + −
Mycospira 'eye-rot' WIK13 (Albanak 1, GN8 553932ej(iv)Alb)	+ + + + −

---

17 NAME:
18 PERSONAL NUMBER:
19 DATE OF MEDCON DOCUM
20 PLACE:

FOR OFFICIAL USE:
21 DIAMOPTIC
INFLUENT
PARASITOSIS Q
INBLUEK
FILIGRANT
CEREBROCLOMSAT
ERECTOMETRIAL
PANGREAHEPAT

22

25

NOTE: Tick schedules belo destination:

☐ SCHEDULE 13: Worlds organis
☐ SCHEDULE 13b: Worlds organis
☐ SCHEDULE 13c: Worlds organis
☐ SCHEDULE 14: Worlds cultura
☐ SCHEDULE 17: Worlds constit
☐ SCHEDULE 17d: Worlds constit
☐ SCHEDULE 22: Worlds relation
☐ SCHEDULE 26: Worlds
☐ SCHEDULE 27: Worlds proper

SUBJECT ....
NOT SUITABLE FOR LONG S
....
....

Sched22 (cont.)

ADDLER'S PLANET
Time flows backwards; organisms are born old, and return to state of infancy, and then embryonic fission. Field of reversed time extends 4 million miles about world; safe for rapid visits; time to human tissue reversal, 10 hours.

ADONIS
World covered with space-time fractures, through which both past and future constantly seep; fractures well localised, and infrequently appear as new. Safe for human contact, but danger of undocumented disease organisms and predators passing through fractures.

AERAN
Time oscillates through 0.02 seconds, with subsequent affect on localised determinism of world: oracles, predictions all work in absolutes; human tissue absorbed into time framework in 100 days; loss of memory usual, followed by unnatural, and unexplained, dependance on symbol known as *Earthwind*.

AESOPS FABULOSA
World caught in stasis, probably artificially generated. Within framework of world time is static, but human tissue and mentality will survive for some weeks.

AGGLUTANSIS
Spontaneous generation of time flux (cf VandeZande's World) dangerous and violent. World covered with ruins of previous colonisation attempts.

Sched13 (cont.)

DOROTAXA 7
Invasive myco-spore, penetrates feet and patches of rough skin where violent entry (acid aided) is not so easily noticed; organisms are telepathic, a group of several billion forming a single consciousness. Moves to frontal lobes of human host, but swiftly dies.

DULLIES PLANET
Multicellular mucoid organisms, enter lower body orifices, esp. male UG channel; attach to epithelial walls with hundreds of recurved, chitinous hooks; move very slowly, ingesting scraped tissue; female grows to diameter of six inches in less than an hour.

DUNN'S FOLLY
Squamoid plasma beings attach to skin and are absorbed rapidly; tendrils (nervous tissue?) reach to brain, and total control of host achieved; creatures require only temporal contact, and then withdraw and die. Reasons unknown.

DYKSTRA'S WORLD
Spider-worm, enters skin through cut or abrasion, and swims as larva to heart, where it 'braces' itself across the right ventricle, appearance of spider; feeds on serum globulin and communicates with host through dreams.

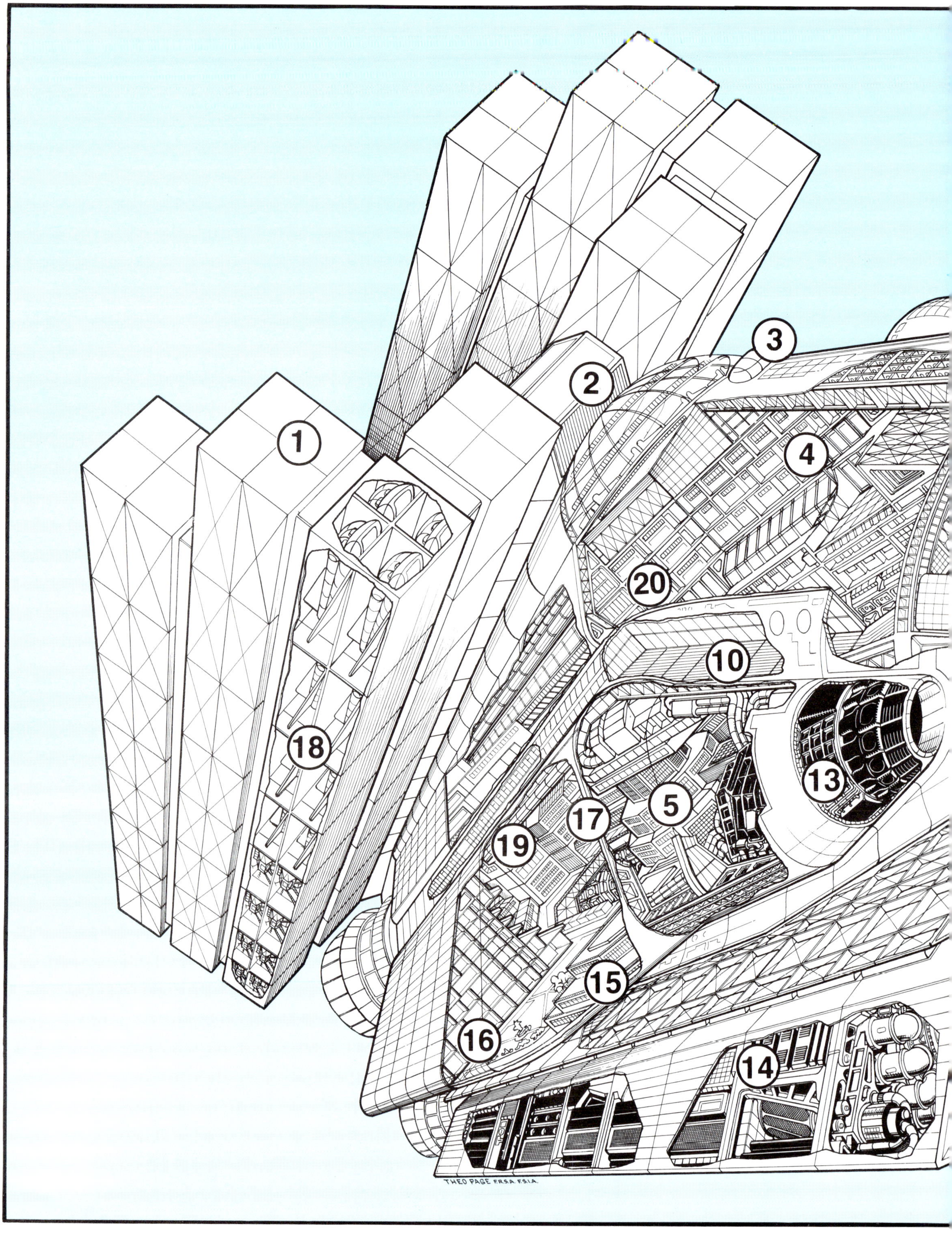
1
2
3
4
20
10
13
18
5
17
19
15
16
14
THEO PAGE F.R.S.A. F.S.I.A.

EARTHPORT JUPITER SHUTTLE

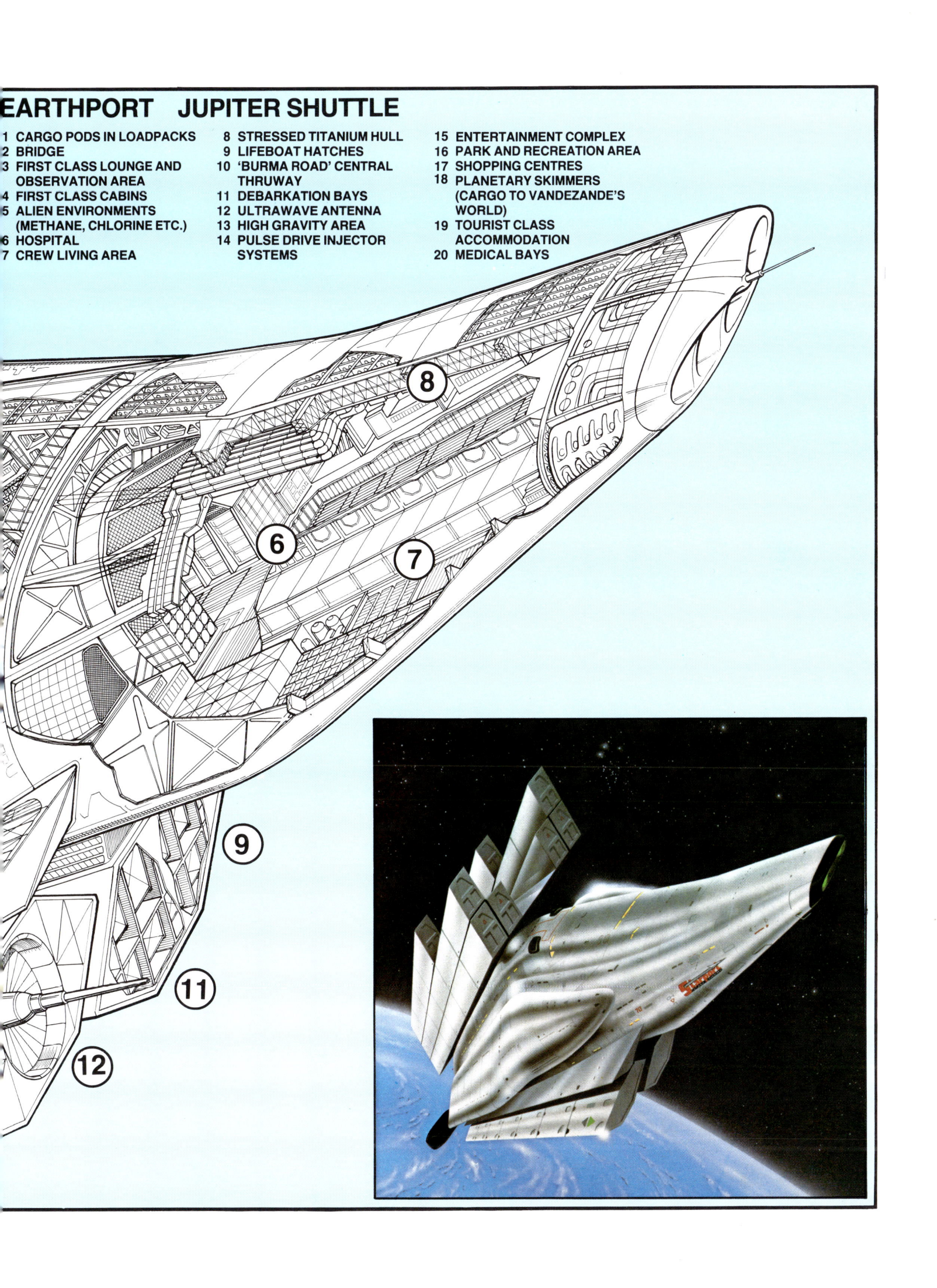

1. CARGO PODS IN LOADPACKS
2. BRIDGE
3. FIRST CLASS LOUNGE AND OBSERVATION AREA
4. FIRST CLASS CABINS
5. ALIEN ENVIRONMENTS (METHANE, CHLORINE ETC.)
6. HOSPITAL
7. CREW LIVING AREA
8. STRESSED TITANIUM HULL
9. LIFEBOAT HATCHES
10. 'BURMA ROAD' CENTRAL THRUWAY
11. DEBARKATION BAYS
12. ULTRAWAVE ANTENNA
13. HIGH GRAVITY AREA
14. PULSE DRIVE INJECTOR SYSTEMS
15. ENTERTAINMENT COMPLEX
16. PARK AND RECREATION AREA
17. SHOPPING CENTRES
18. PLANETARY SKIMMERS (CARGO TO VANDEZANDE'S WORLD)
19. TOURIST CLASS ACCOMMODATION
20. MEDICAL BAYS

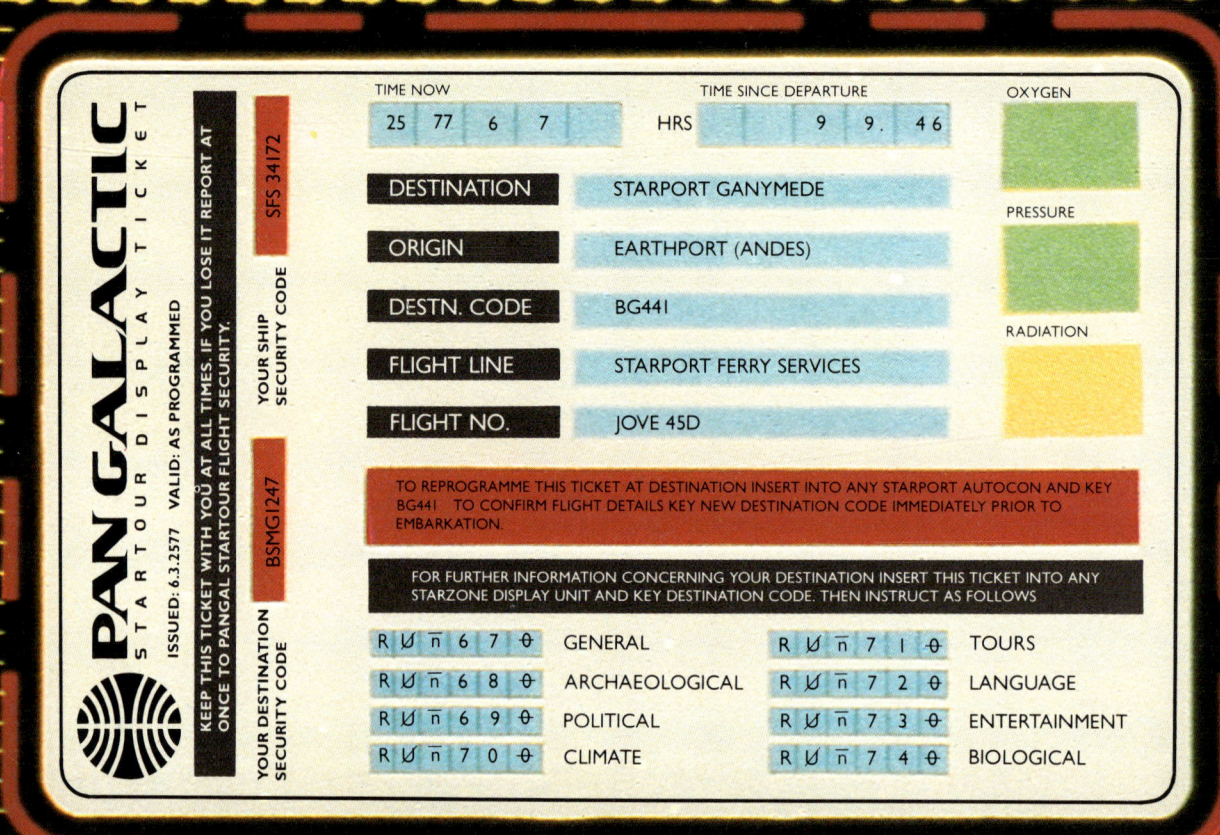

PAN GALACTIC
STARTOUR DISPLAY TICKET

ISSUED: 6.3.2577 VALID: AS PROGRAMMED

KEEP THIS TICKET WITH YOU AT ALL TIMES. IF YOU LOSE IT REPORT AT ONCE TO PANGAL STARTOUR FLIGHT SECURITY.

YOUR SHIP SECURITY CODE: SFS 34172

YOUR DESTINATION SECURITY CODE: BSMG1247

TIME NOW	25 77 6 7
TIME SINCE DEPARTURE	9 9 . 46 HRS
DESTINATION	STARPORT GANYMEDE
ORIGIN	EARTHPORT (ANDES)
DESTN. CODE	BG441
FLIGHT LINE	STARPORT FERRY SERVICES
FLIGHT NO.	JOVE 45D

OXYGEN
PRESSURE
RADIATION

TO REPROGRAMME THIS TICKET AT DESTINATION INSERT INTO ANY STARPORT AUTOCON AND KEY BG441 TO CONFIRM FLIGHT DETAILS KEY NEW DESTINATION CODE IMMEDIATELY PRIOR TO EMBARKATION.

FOR FURTHER INFORMATION CONCERNING YOUR DESTINATION INSERT THIS TICKET INTO ANY STARZONE DISPLAY UNIT AND KEY DESTINATION CODE. THEN INSTRUCT AS FOLLOWS

RUn 670	GENERAL		RUn 710	TOURS
RUn 680	ARCHAEOLOGICAL		RUn 720	LANGUAGE
RUn 690	POLITICAL		RUn 730	ENTERTAINMENT
RUn 700	CLIMATE		RUn 740	BIOLOGICAL

STARPORT · STARPO

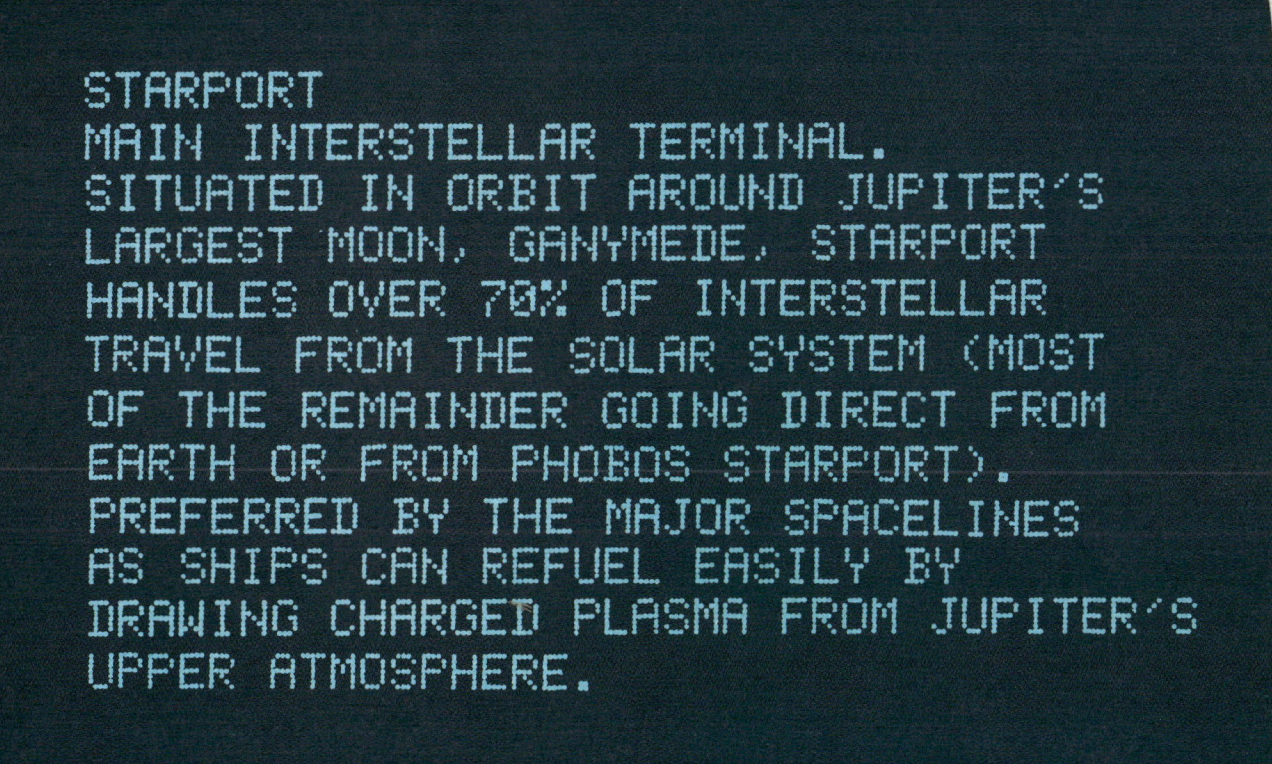

STARPORT
MAIN INTERSTELLAR TERMINAL.
SITUATED IN ORBIT AROUND JUPITER'S
LARGEST MOON, GANYMEDE, STARPORT
HANDLES OVER 70% OF INTERSTELLAR
TRAVEL FROM THE SOLAR SYSTEM (MOST
OF THE REMAINDER GOING DIRECT FROM
EARTH OR FROM PHOBOS STARPORT).
PREFERRED BY THE MAJOR SPACELINES
AS SHIPS CAN REFUEL EASILY BY
DRAWING CHARGED PLASMA FROM JUPITER'S
UPPER ATMOSPHERE.

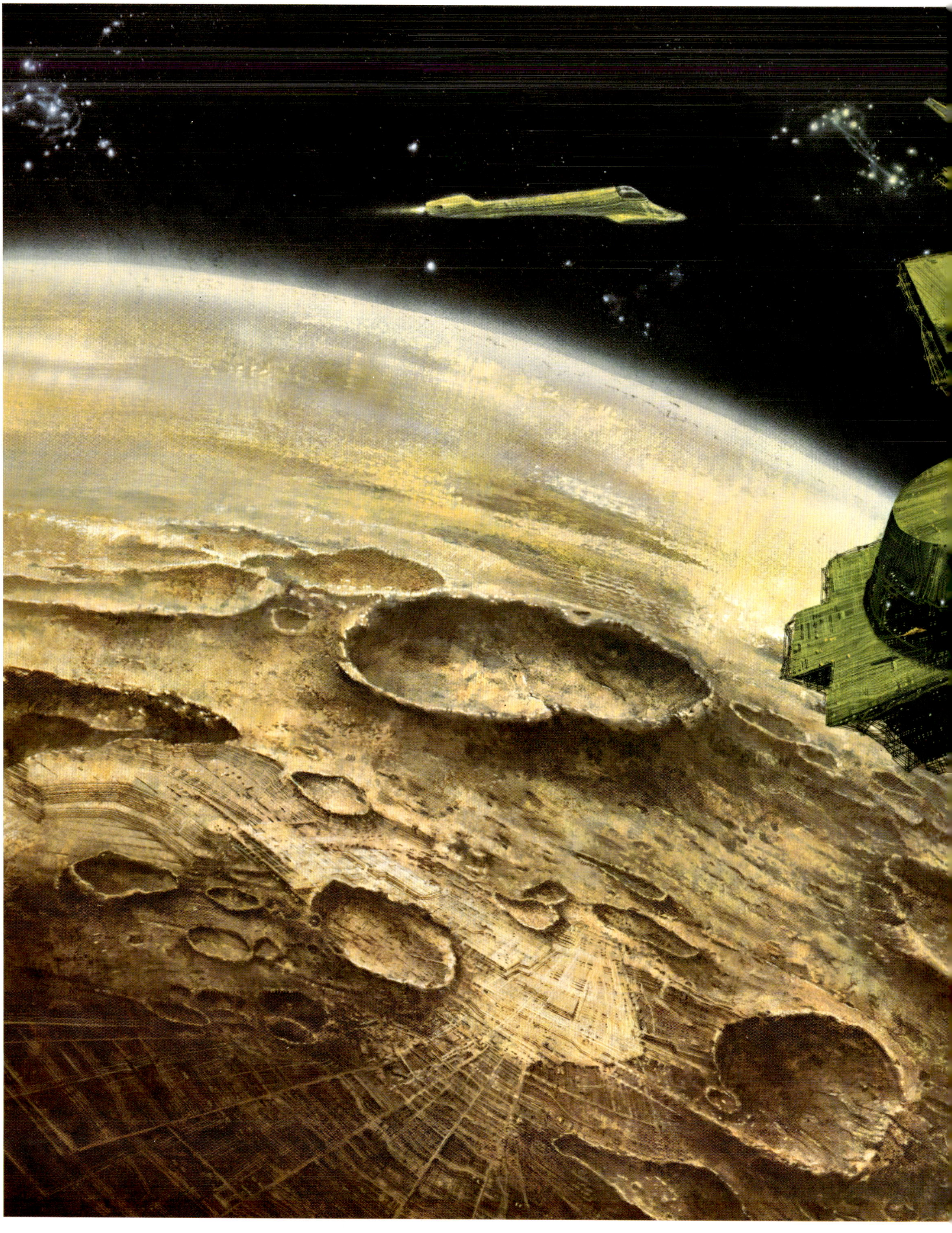

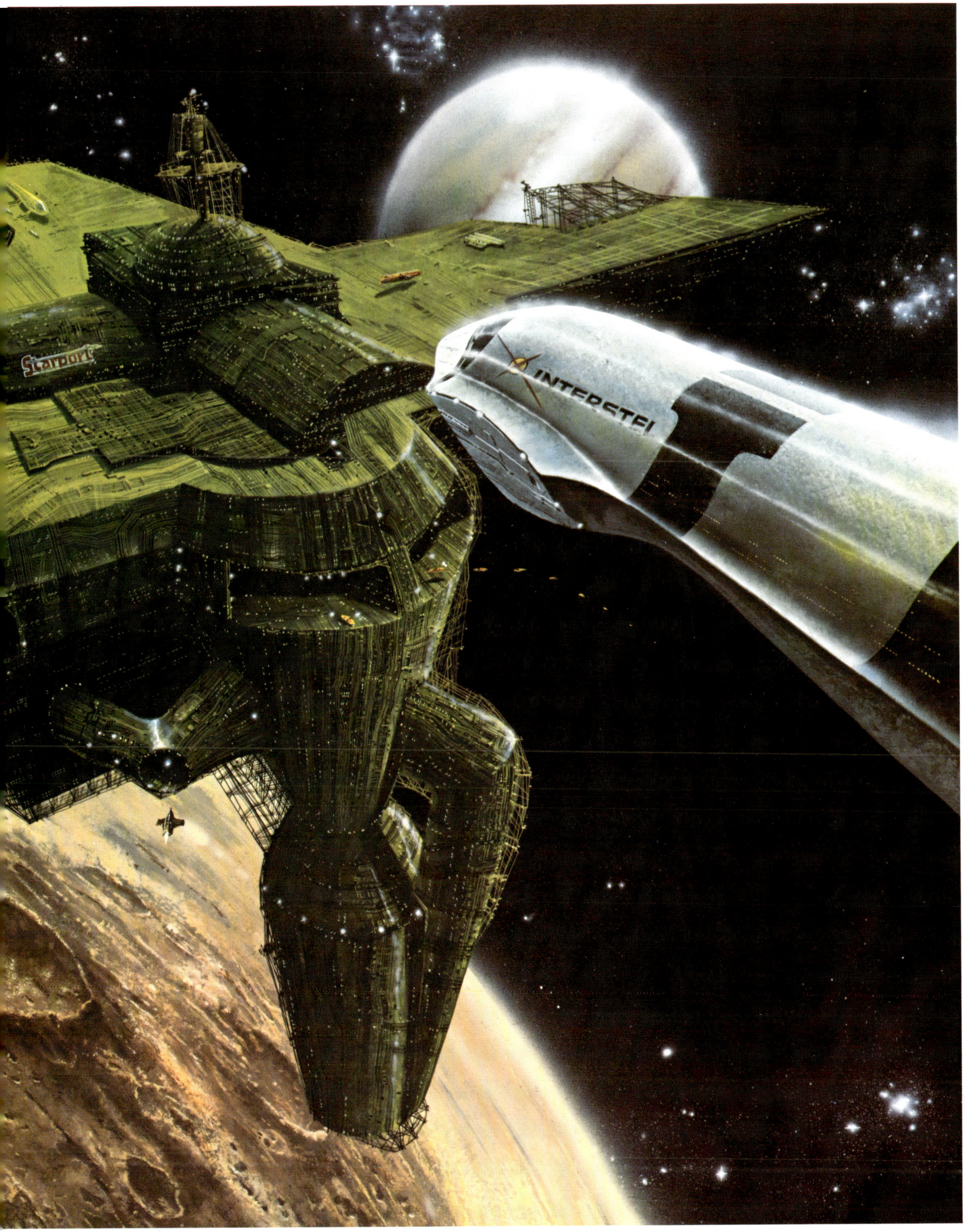
Starport
INTERSTEL

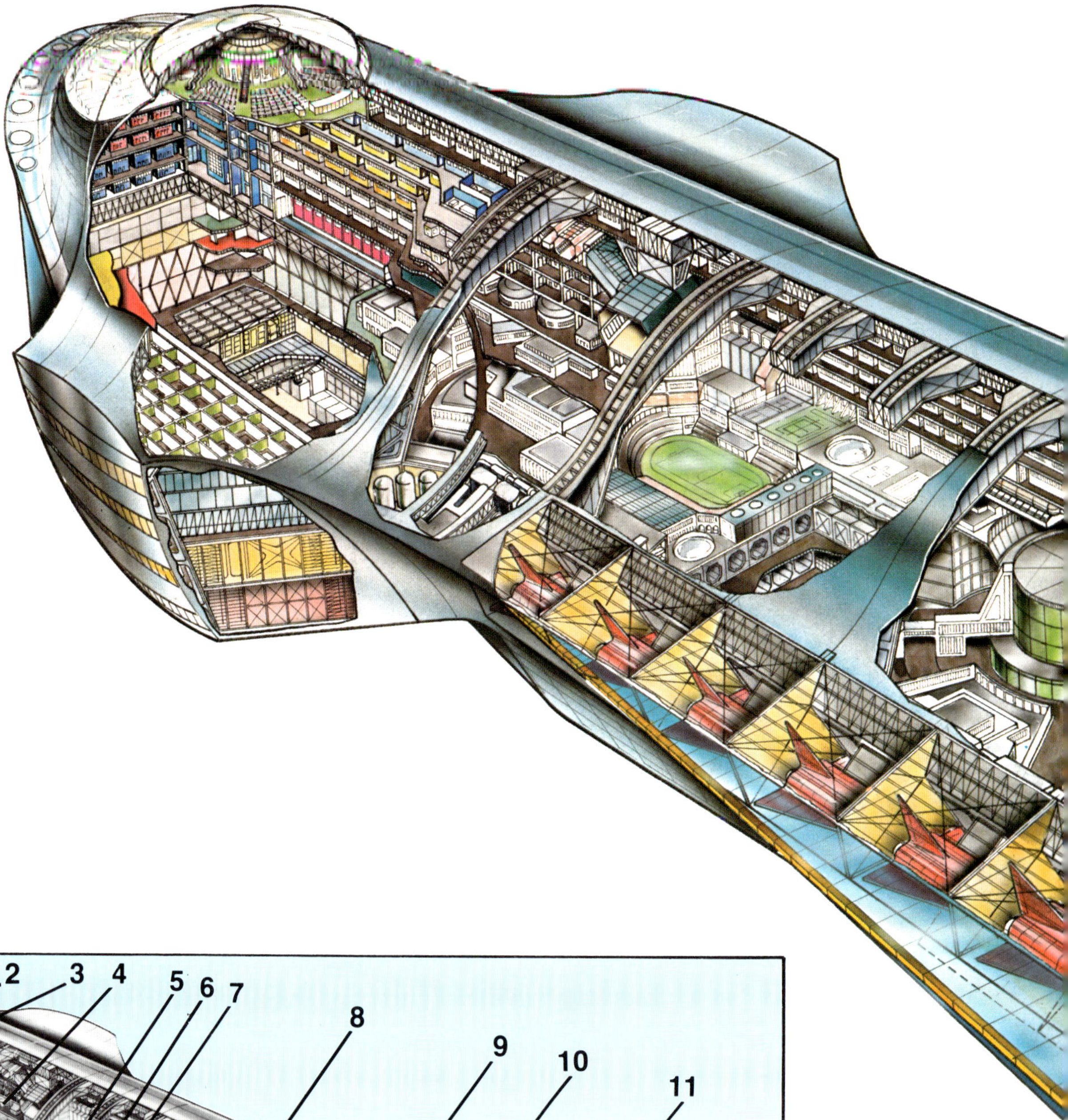

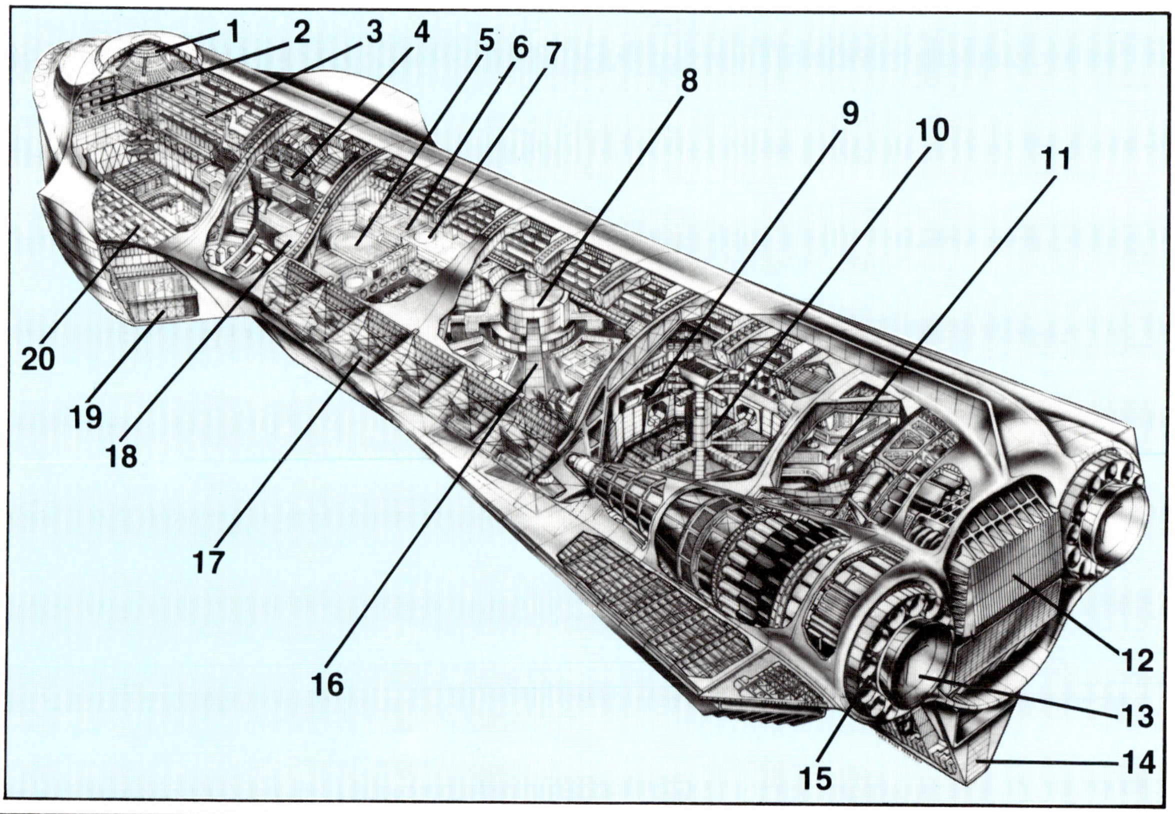
1
2
3
4
5
6
7
8
9
10
11
12
13
14
15
16
17
18
19
20

PAN-GALACTIC 'STARFRIEND' LUXURY LINER

1. PASSENGER OBSERVATION LOUNGES AND STAR RESTAURANTS
2. V.I.P. ACCOMMODATION
3. FIRST CLASS ACCOMMODATION
4. ALIEN ENVIRONMENTS
5. STADIUM
6. SPORTS COMPLEX
7. SWIMMING POOL
8. TOURIST CITIES AND CENTRAL HOSPITAL
9. BRIDGE
10. ENGINEERING AND MAINTENANCE
11. CREW ACCOMMODATION
12. TSMD DRIVE
13. ANTI-MATRAN STABILIZER
14. "WITCHHOLD"
15. EMERGENCY ION THRUST
16. EMERGENCY EXITWAY TO LIFEBOATS
17. LIFEBOATS
18. ENTERTAINMENTS COMPLEX
19. CARGO HOLDS
20. TOURIST ACCOMMODATION

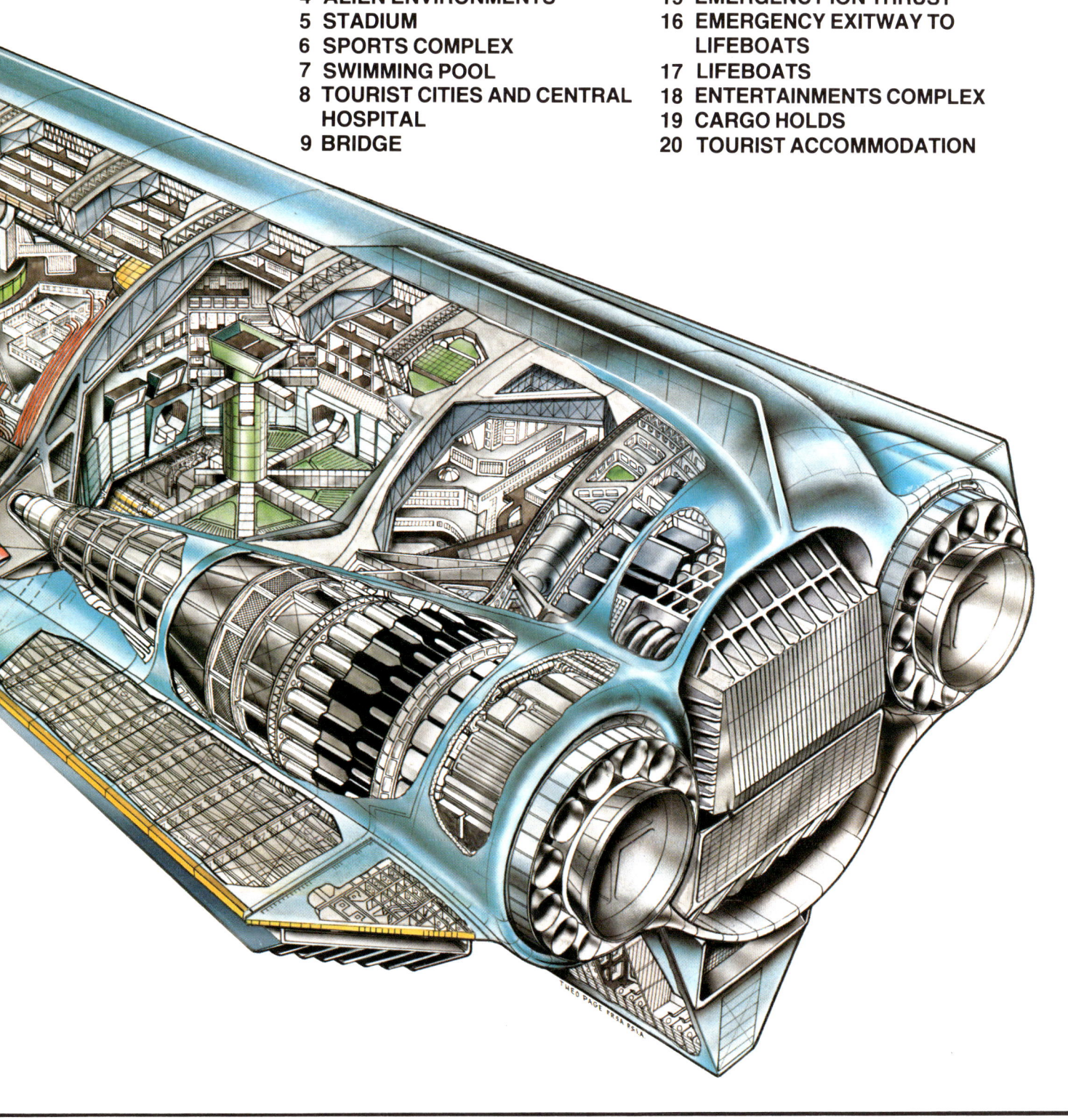

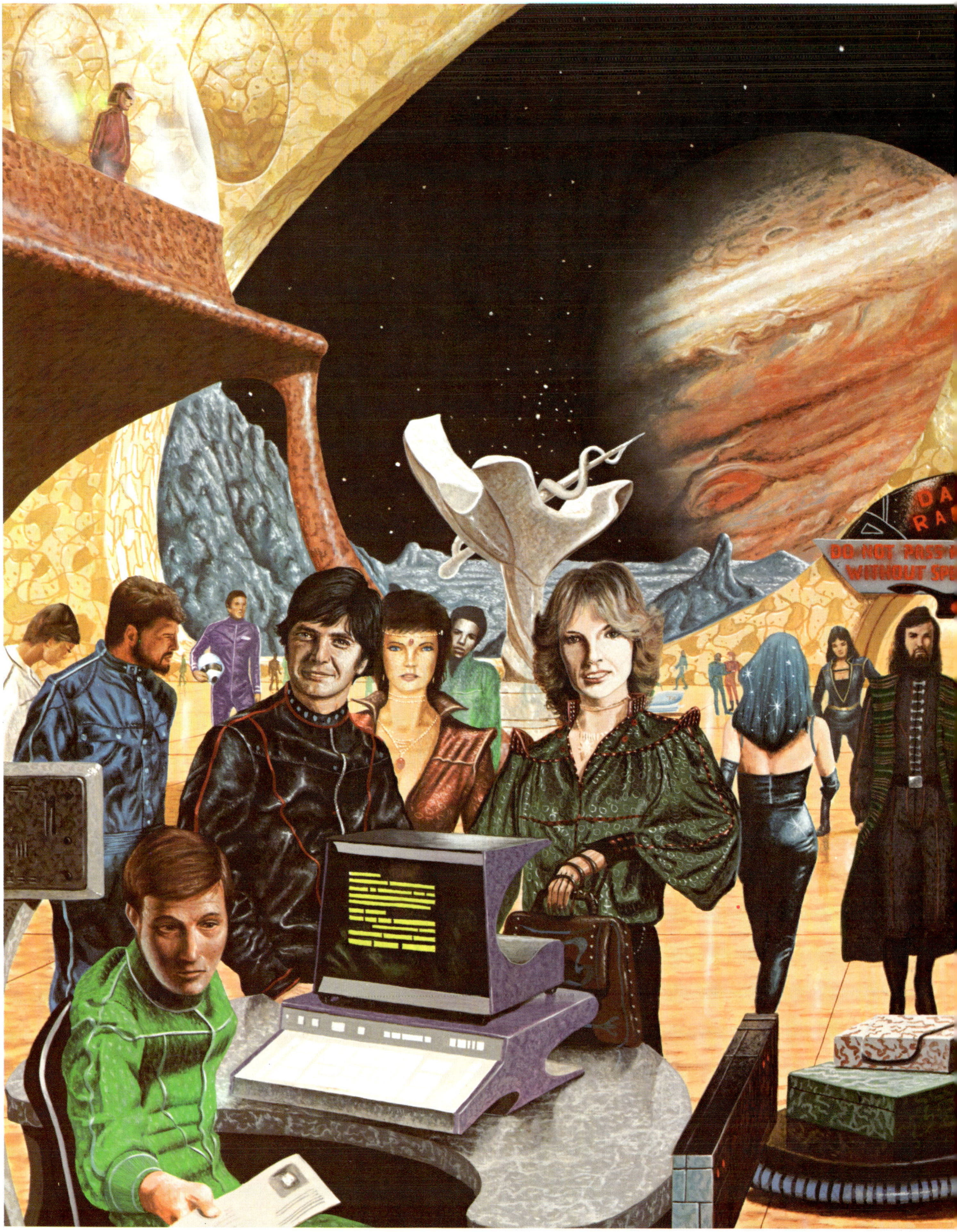
DO NOT PASS
WITHOUT

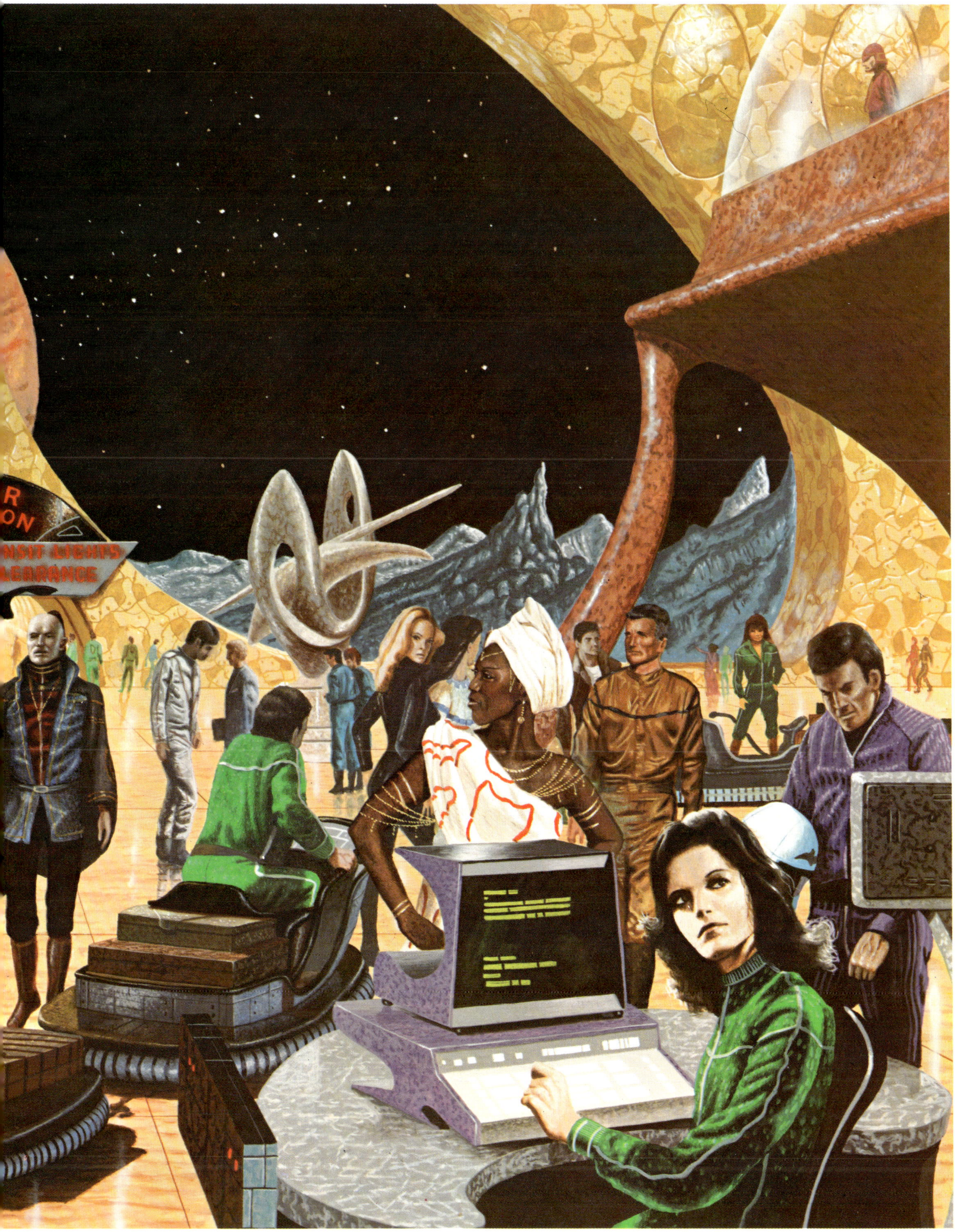
R
ON
NSIT LIGHTS
LEARANCE

Personal diary Lelo. 9th June 2577: As I record this I'm sitting in the Ionian Bar, right at the top of our hotel on Ganymede. The view is breathtaking. Jupiter is three quarters above the horizon and is so colourful! We've got so used to Solar images that I thought the whole Solar tour would probably be visually unremarkable; but I was wrong. The silence, and the feeling of age is incredible. The planet is a lot smaller than I expected, but there are magnifying windows that enable you to actually see cloud movement! I wonder why they didn't build this city, Ganymede Base, further round the moon, so you could see all of the planet? You have to go on a jaunt to get the full view, and we've decided not to bother. Caroline is off somewhere, shopping for tax-free clothes. She also wants some slides of the building of Starport or something. You can see Starport Jove above the bar, a great strand of winking lights. Ships that seem like needles of light are in fact over a kilometre long. They're floating up there in all sorts of positions relative to each other, sucking in the plasma-trapped particles or something. Our own ship is in dock, the Pan-Galactic **Starfriend**. We saw it, in fact, as the shuttle from Earth brought us in. We didn't know it was to be our ship, of course, as we've only just decided which route to take. You get this illusion of size which I'd forgotten. At first the Starport and the various liners floating or attached to it seemed about the size of our own shuttle vessel, but for some minutes as we approached you could see details quite clearly and we must have been hundreds of kilometres away. Eventually we passed below a Sirian InterWorlds Spaceliner and I swear it blanked out the Universe. Our shuttle could have landed on the letter S. Big traffic. Ganymede Base is in fact a gigantic city. The check-in parts fill a dome, and basically you just log your arrival, and get various security cards and lists of places you can and can't go. Ganymede floats inside Jupiter's magnetosphere and there's a powerful radiation problem. Some parts of the city are less safe than others, and you can't go beyond the Base without a Moonwalker, who's a sort of paid guide and guardian. You can only go out in groups of ten. I'm not keen on the idea. Beyond the moonport the Base is like an enclosed town, with streets, traffic, police, hotels

STARPORT DEPARTURES 10 JUNE 2577 (a.m.)

SOLAR SYSTEM STOPOVERS:S
FLIGHT NO:F
CARRIER:C

DATES GIVEN ON THIS SCHEDULE ARE THE MONTH AND DAY OF ARRIVAL.

Flight	STARPORT	SIRIUS	TAU CETI BRIDGE	KAMELEOS	REUNION	STARHAVEN	PYRRUS	QUETZALCOATL	CORONA	BOREALIS VIII	APHRODITE	PLIAX	STARGATE MAGELLAN	LYNX III	PHOENIX	CLUSTER	FIRESTONE	FAFNIR	LOKI'S W
F:0201 C:INTERSUN S:DIRECT	03.45	→	→	→	→	→	→	→	→	→	→	→	6.15	→	6.22	→	7.03	7.07	7.19
F:0230 C:SIRIAN INTERWORLD D:DIRECT	04.20	6.15	→	→	→	→	→	→	→	→	→	→	→	→	→	→	→	→	→
F:0297 C:PAN-GALACTIC S:DIRECT	05.00	→	→	6.22	7.03	→	→	→	→	→	→	→	→	→	→	→	→	→	→
F:0341 SIRIAN INTERWORLD S:IAPETUS	06.40	6.21	→	→	→	→	→	→	→	→	→	→	→	→	→	→	→	→	→
F:0369 C:TRANSGALACTIC S:PLUTO	07.15	→	→	→	→	→	→	→	→	→	→	→	7.13	→	7.27	8.11	→	→	→
F:0432 C:PAN-GALACTIC S:PLUTO	08.10	→	→	6.26	→	→	→	→	→	→	→	→	7.30	8.22	→	→	8.29	→	9.07	9.22
F:0477 C:LAKER SPACE S:TITANIA	09.30	6.17	→	→	→	→	→	→	→	→	→	→	→	→	→	→	→	→	→
F:0502 C:INTERSTEL S:IAPETUS	10.20	→	→	→	7.01	7.20	7.27	8.20	9.03	9.27	10.11								
F:0509 C:LAKER SPACE S:DIRECT	10.40	→	→	→	→	→	→	→	→	→	→	→	→	6.14	6.19	→	6.26	7.01	
F:0577 C:INTERSTEL S:TITANIA	11.10	→	→	6.23	→	→	→	→	→	→	→	→	7.03	7.14	→	→	→	→	7.23
F:0611 C:PAN-GALACTIC S:DIRECT	11.30	6.15	6.19	→	6.27	7.10	7.19	→	→	→	→	7.29	→	→	→	→	→	→	→
F:0641 C:TRANSGALACTIC S:PLUTO	11.55	→	→	→	→	→	→	→	→	→	→	→	→	6.19	→	→	→	7.01	

and shops. Everything is called after towns on Earth. There are two shopping precincts called London and New York and they're right next door to each other. The Black Hole of Ganymede is a sort of joke place, where you can get mystery rides, and see a lot of waxworks of historical periods. Why would anyone come a billion miles into space to see the first moon landing? Caroline and I have sorted out the opinion difference on what sight to see in the Solar System. I won. She gave in gracefully, but I think I was right to persist. The alien buildings on Pluto are part of our heritage, since their builders apparently visited Earth some four million years ago. Ice castles you can see anytime. The only other alternatives were the 21st Century diamond mines on several of the Patroclus asteroids — can you imagine spending four days being ferried from one lump of mined rock to another? How the Trojan Trip can be so popular I can't imagine. What else? Oh yes, an orbital flight around Neptune to watch those strange, vacuum-living creatures that inhabit the world. I think we've made the right decision, so it's the **P-G Starfriend** for the first leg of the tour, as far as Stargate Magellan, via the world where the time winds blow, and the Chikstha Refuge system. **End entry.**

...H YOUR SPACE OFFICE FOR STOPOVER TIMES.

...X / ...TATION / WINDBLOW	NOACH'S REST	NEW TRITON	ALEXANDER'S WORLD	HARLEQUIN	DUNN'S FOLLY	NEW BRAZIL	TERMINUS	INDUS SYSTEM	OBELISK	LIEBENHOF'S WORLD	SWINGAROUND	VOORENEN VII	NEW TITAN	TOMBWORLD	HEAVEN	VERNE	ORIONIS DELTA	SCATTEROCK SYSTEM	HYPERIONA	STARGATE MAGELLAN	NINEWORLDS
→	→	→	→	→	→	→	→	→	→	→	→	→	→	8.01	→	→	→	8.07			
→	→	→	→	→	→	6.21	6.27	7.03	7.07	7.15											
→	→	→	→	→	7.14	→	→	→	→	→	7.22	7.27	→	→	8.14	→	8.28				
→	→	→	→	→	→	→	→	→	→	→	→	→	→	→	→	→	6.27				
→	→	→	→	→	→	→	→	→	→	→	→	→	→	→	→	→	→	8.26	9.17		
→	→	→	→	→	→	→	→	→	→	→	→	→	10.03	10.09	10.21	11.05					
→	→	→	→	→	6.30	7.11	7.18	→	→	7.29	8.15										
→	→	8.04	8.22	8.29																	
→	→	→	→	→	→	→	→	→	→	→	→	→	→	→	→	→	→	→	8.14	9.01	
14	8.11	9.02																			

Starport

STARSHIP & SPA

AURORA
MAGELLAN

PAN G
SPAC

Star
FERRY

CIRCUM SOLAR
VOYAGER

INTE
HAULA

INTERSTEL

ELINE INSIGNIA

LACTIC
LINES

LAKER SPACE

port
SERVICES

SUN
INC.

THIRDWORLD
SPACE CARGO

SIS
SIRIAN INTERWORLD SPACELINES

PAN GALACTIC
STARTOUR DISPLAY TICKET

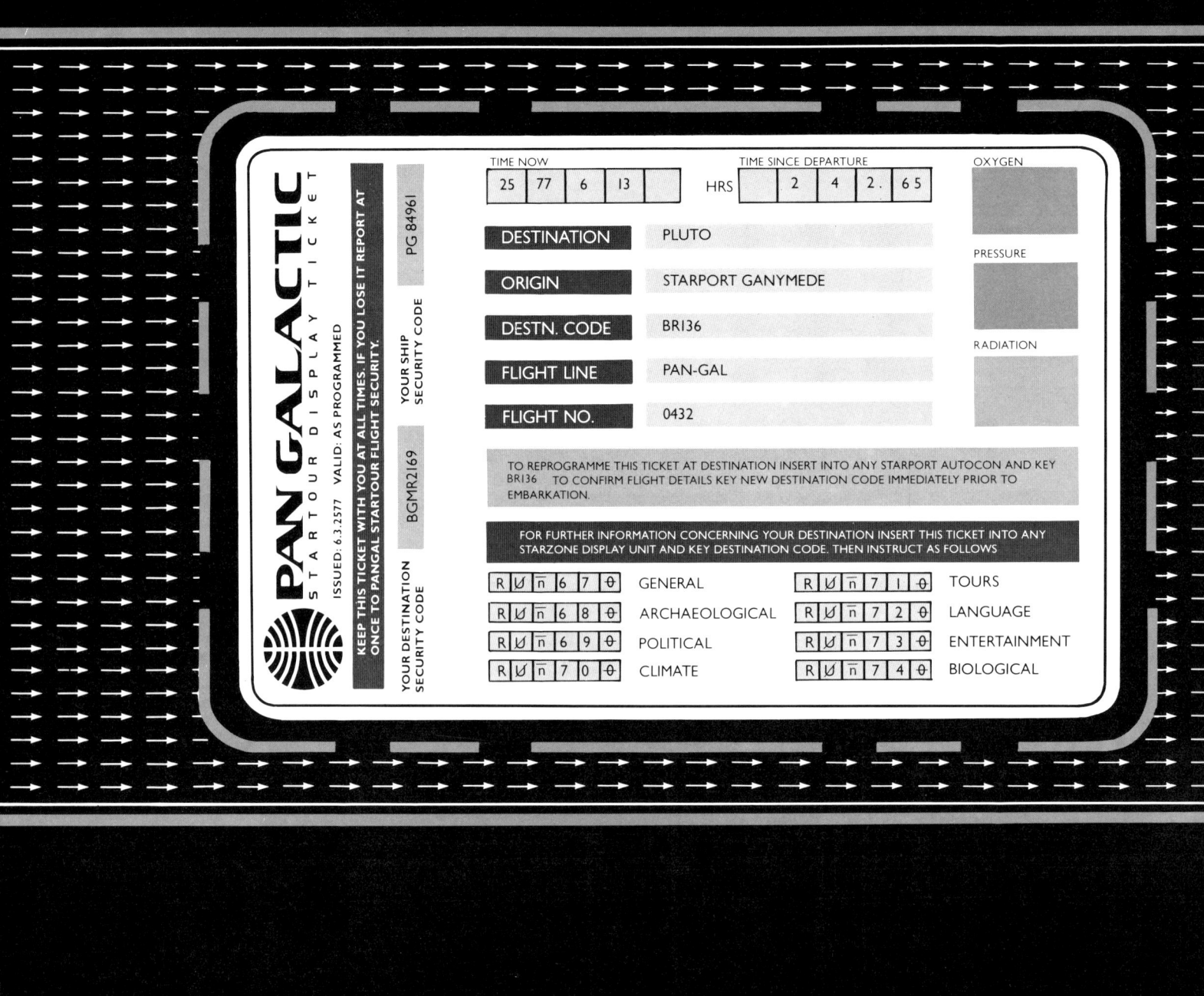

ISSUED: 6.3.2577   VALID: AS PROGRAMMED

KEEP THIS TICKET WITH YOU AT ALL TIMES. IF YOU LOSE IT REPORT AT ONCE TO PANGAL STARTOUR FLIGHT SECURITY.

PG 84961 — YOUR SHIP SECURITY CODE

BGMR2169 — YOUR DESTINATION SECURITY CODE

TIME NOW					TIME SINCE DEPARTURE			
25	77	6	13	HRS	2	4	2	.65

DESTINATION   PLUTO
ORIGIN   STARPORT GANYMEDE
DESTN. CODE   BRI36
FLIGHT LINE   PAN-GAL
FLIGHT NO.   0432

OXYGEN

PRESSURE

RADIATION

TO REPROGRAMME THIS TICKET AT DESTINATION INSERT INTO ANY STARPORT AUTOCON AND KEY BRI36 TO CONFIRM FLIGHT DETAILS KEY NEW DESTINATION CODE IMMEDIATELY PRIOR TO EMBARKATION.

FOR FURTHER INFORMATION CONCERNING YOUR DESTINATION INSERT THIS TICKET INTO ANY STARZONE DISPLAY UNIT AND KEY DESTINATION CODE. THEN INSTRUCT AS FOLLOWS

R Ø n̄ 6 7 0	GENERAL	R Ø n̄ 7 1 0 TOURS
R Ø n̄ 6 8 0	ARCHAEOLOGICAL	R Ø n̄ 7 2 0 LANGUAGE
R Ø n̄ 6 9 0	POLITICAL	R Ø n̄ 7 3 0 ENTERTAINMENT
R Ø n̄ 7 0 0	CLIMATE	R Ø n̄ 7 4 0 BIOLOGICAL

PLUTO · PLUTO · P

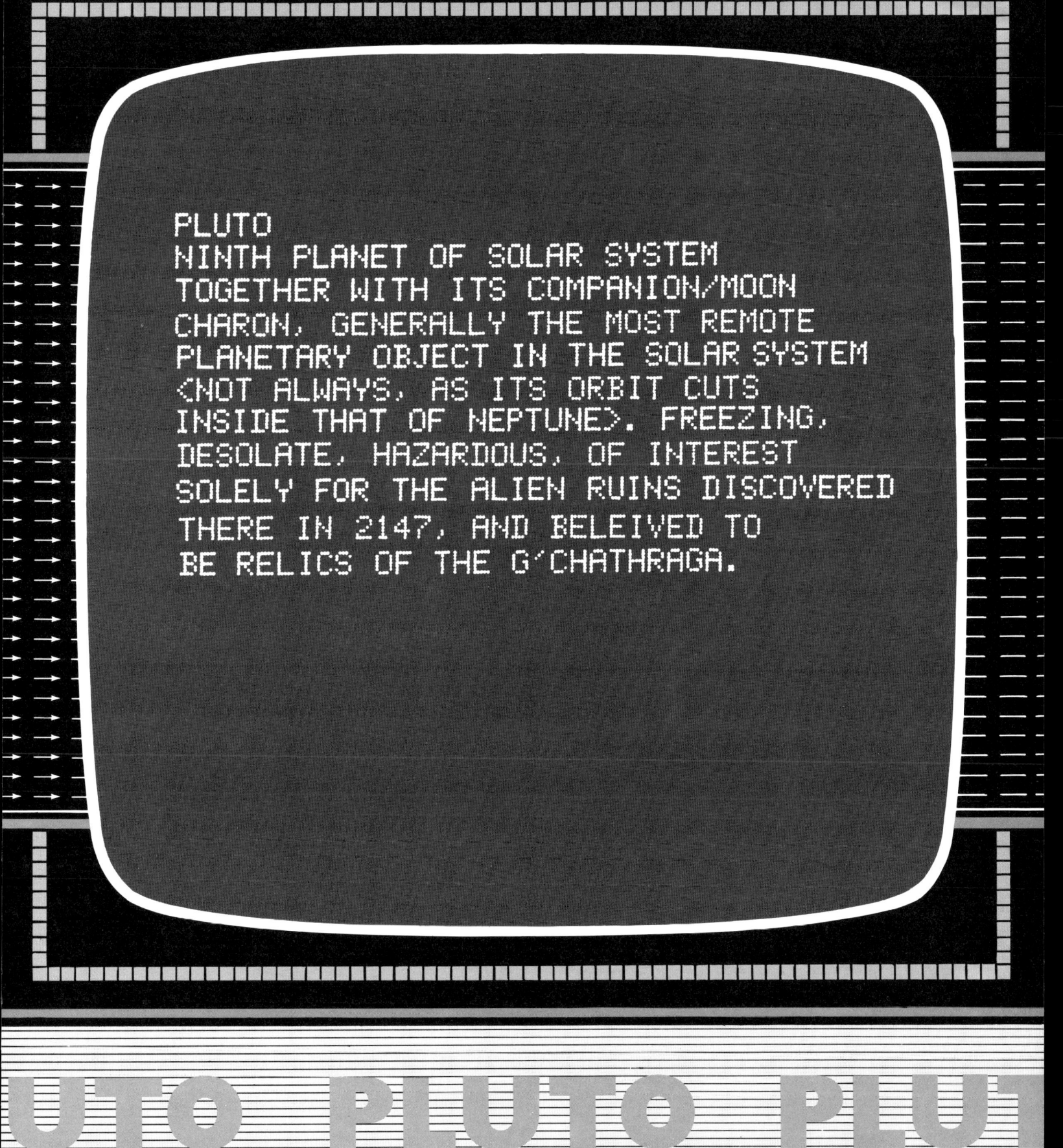

```
PLUTO
NINTH PLANET OF SOLAR SYSTEM
TOGETHER WITH ITS COMPANION/MOON
CHARON. GENERALLY THE MOST REMOTE
PLANETARY OBJECT IN THE SOLAR SYSTEM
<NOT ALWAYS, AS ITS ORBIT CUTS
INSIDE THAT OF NEPTUNE>. FREEZING,
DESOLATE, HAZARDOUS, OF INTEREST
SOLELY FOR THE ALIEN RUINS DISCOVERED
THERE IN 2147, AND BELEIVED TO
BE RELICS OF THE G'CHATHRAGA.
```

UTO PLUTO PLU

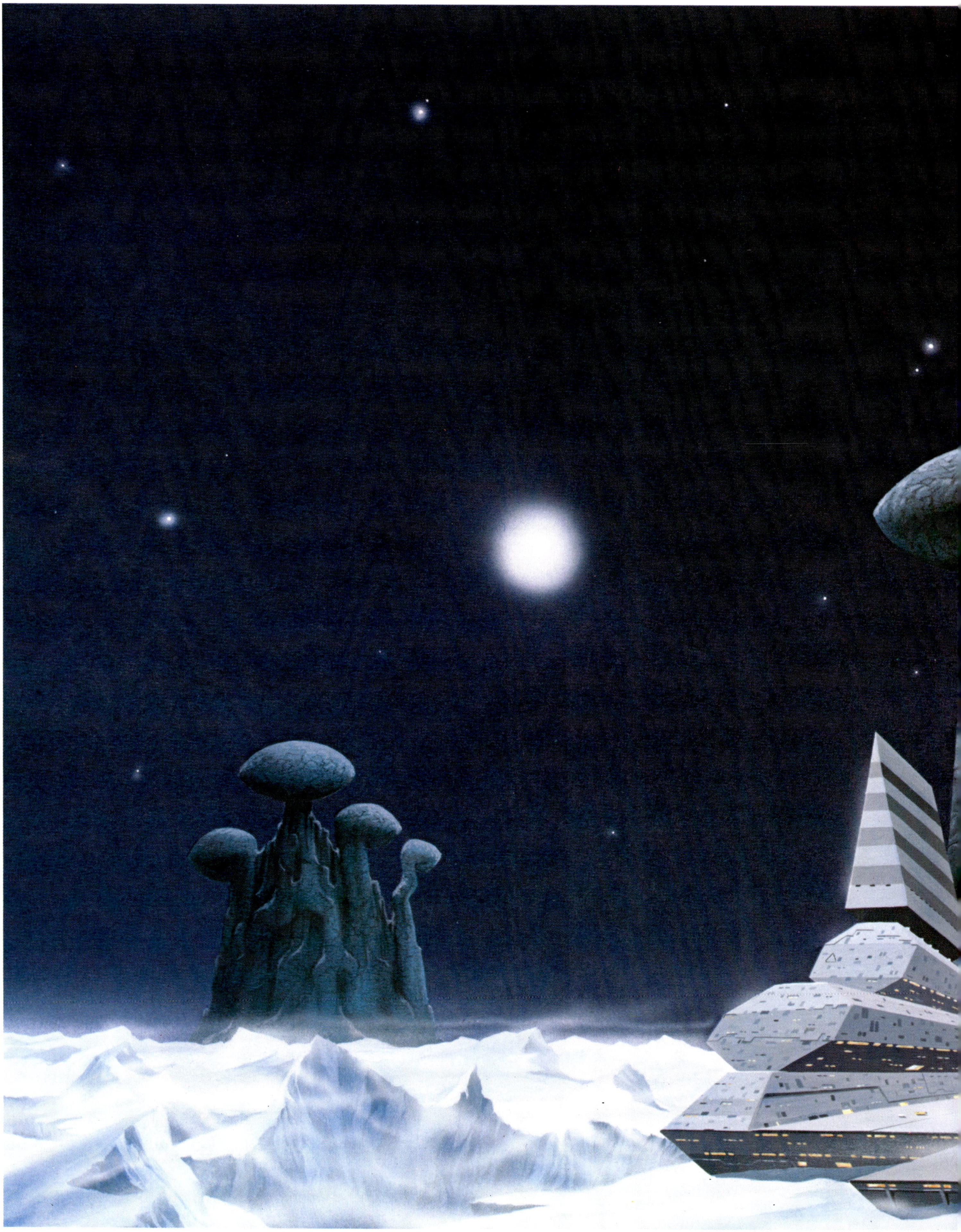

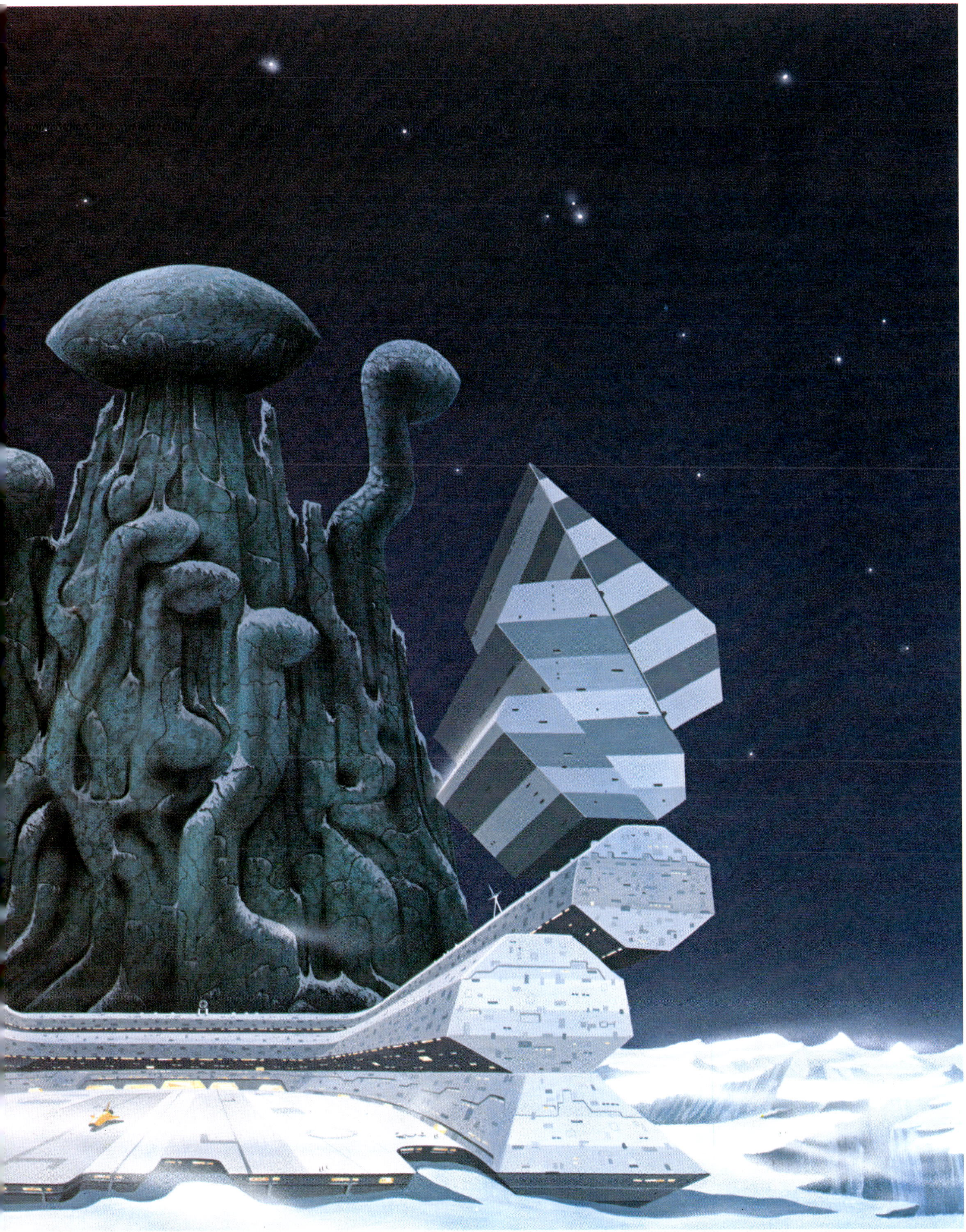

Personal diary Lelo. 14th June 2577: We are now in far orbit above Pluto. There's been a delay in getting us to the shuttles to go down to Breakaway, the name of the city that has been built outside the ruins. I didn't know there were so many bases on Pluto. We have to use the telescope to observe the world, and a very dull place it looks too, practically featureless, a faint blue colour, with patches of brighter red forming a complex spiral pattern across the whole surface. The sun here is far brighter than we expected, but still no more than an intensely yellow star. You can look at it, of course, and I suppose its light isn't enough to make the planet's surface shine . . . But from orbit you can see patches of light that are beacons, straddling the world in a line from north to south. It's cold down there, 50 degrees K, and we'll have to wear special – and very bulky – walking suits. The ground is solid nitrogen. We've been warned against playing snowballs with the methane snow. And there will be a walk from shuttle to city, and city to enclosures, because the whole place is not really set up for tourists, only scientists, and they've never finished making it luxurious. That's a joke, looking down at that iceball. And of course, if we go inside the ruins, then we walk, and they're not enclosed. Caroline has shuffled away from me in the lounge to make some recordings of her own. She's very annoyed that she gave in, now, pointing out that in our suits we'll see and experience very little. She's wrong. She also seems to spend a lot more time alone; moody, or tense, or something. And she's got more diary programmes than I have. She's keeping a private part for her own consumption, I bet. She won't let me hear her read-ins, and we've both decided not to start home-transmitting until we get to Refuge, which is Pliax II. Then we'll start sending our diaries home for our friends to read. Something's happening . . . no: false alarm. We've been in orbit for nearly a day, now. Pluto is a long way from anywhere, something else I'd forgotten. They used to think it was a moon of Neptune. It gets one liner every month coming to it, bringing supplies and tourists. And what a liner this is! Pan-Galactic certainly know how to build ships! There are at least five whole cities, one of them devoted to Q'rowjkth aliens. There's a 'gape-zone' where you can look at them, all the different life-forms on board that can't breathe oxygen; and they can look at you. It's weird, like

EXTRACT FROM: THE OFFICIAL GUIDE TO THE RUINS ON PLUTO

Although difficult to see from orbit, the surface of Pluto is littered with the structures, and surface markings referred to as the G'chathragan ruins. Cities have been built at three sites where the ruins are particularly extensive: Breakaway, Amalthus Base and Charon Hide. Fourteen separate scientific communities are strung around the tiny world studying the sites of deeper placed structures, such as the Grey Vaults at Umbriel Rift, which extend two miles into the ice and rock crust. It is nearly four million years since Pluto was inhabited by the alien visitors, and in that time ice-sublimation, and crustal movement, have obscured many of the community sites of the G'chathraga. Nevertheless, the cities at Breakaway, Amalthus and Charon allow the (human) visitor to experience the more startling of the alien structures, and to explore sites that are believed to have been the original community sites of the aliens. The G'chathraga constructed twenty-three buildings that stand, above the crust, to a height of 750 metres. Although they appear to be empty, they are in fact crowded living blocks; the outer walls of these immense towers are riddled with cells and chambers, connected by narrow, high passages, whose disregard for gravity suggests that the G'chathraga moved in a different way than humans. All the cells, or rooms, are over ten metres in height, giving an indication of the tall, slender form of the builders. These rooms look inwards, out into the void that fills the centres of the buildings. Few windows look out across Pluto, and where such portals exist they seem to be associated with 'community rooms', perhaps temples or other ritual rooms; certainly, in these larger chambers, the walls are more densely inscribed with designs, and the peculiarly geometric hieroglyph script that the Visitors used. Excavations in the area of the Amalthus ruins have revealed decorated vaults, smaller but otherwise not unlike the vast chambers at Umbriel, which were possibly used to store samples and artifacts from G'chathragan expeditions to Earth, Mars and perhaps all the worlds of the Solar System. Several vaults are clearly 'animal environments', with facilities for piping air, water and artificial sunlight. Scratches on the walls of two of these vaults appear to have been made by the imprisoned specimens, and are remarkably reminiscent of the sort of artistic marks made by such higher primates as the chimpanzee; similar marks could be attributed to early forms of humanity. Excavations have also revealed deep sanitation pits, filled with frozen waste product; this reveals that the G'chathraga ate a diet of fibrous material, not unlike wood. Among this monotonous waste are deposits of primate faeces, and the dung of a wide variety of terrestrial animals. It seems, from the frustrating evidence of the excavations, that the aliens removed most of their portable waste, debris and material artifacts when they left. The museum at Breakaway, and the smaller display building at Amalthus Base, contain exhibits of the G'chathraga machinery and utensils that were left behind. Here also can be seen examples of their symbol design and script, including the justly celebrated Dead World Scroll, which many think was left specifically for humans to discover. Script samples occur in many places in the ruins, most particularly in the community or ritual chambers. Plaques, and the thin foil sheets on which they wrote, have also been located on certain asteroids, in particular among the Trojans, and on Phobos; the Martian moons both show signs of extensive excavation by the G'chathraga, possibly to establish relay bases to their exploration teams on the Martian surface. They interpreted the dead script of the Martians, and translated what they had learned into their own symbols, thus giving us the key to translating the Dead World Scroll itself.

Who were the G'chathraga? The first thing that must be said is that the alien race that explored our Solar System four million years ago may not, in fact, have been the mythical race known as the G'chathraga. The association of the Plutonian ruins with these long vanished aliens is based on very flimsy evidence, namely the folk legends of the Ruimzegga, a docile, ancient alien race inhabiting the world Mason Eight. The Ruimzegga myths talk of Radiant Visitors who carried one of the stars of the heavens in a block of red crystal; the Visitors left holy words written upon slabs of green, cold metal-that-was-not-metal. The plaques were lost, and the epic Cycle of the Star Wind tells of a million years of seeking the precious scriptures, by a host of adventurers and kings. The description being in a zoo on both sides of the cage at once. Incidentally, less than a third of the tour winners have opted for this route via Pluto. We'll all meet up at Stargate Magellan. Caroline and I have played a lot of sport together, and you know, you can actually go on a simulated marathon? Across country, below waterfalls, through fields of cows! Cows on a liner, the illusion is terrific, until you look up, against the sun's glare, and see the pipes and machinery of support systems. **End entry.**

Personal diary Lolo. 16th June 2577: And suddenly we're here! And I really can't believe it, the effect of the place. Even Caroline has fallen silent, and I know she's impressed. We've been taken into one of the G'chathraga buildings, a huge hangar-like place, nearly a kilometre tall. The entranceways are decorated with strange designs, all frosted with ice, and shimmering red in the lights from our suits. Inside, the walls rise up into a stygian gloom, but when spotlights are turned upwards you can see ramps and passageways leading away; the whole space above us is criss-crossed with golden girders. What did they use this place for, I wonder? To live in? There are five of the great structures around Breakaway, and more ruins at Amalthus Base and Charon Hide. But this settlement is the biggest, and someone was telling me that below the ice, where we landed in the shuttle, there are signs of an ancient landing site as well. From here, then, the G'chathraga sped off into the inner Solar System over four million years ago. We were still barely upright; ape-like creatures, running about the veldts. There's not much machinery to see, a few funnels and wheels, made out of platinum and richly decorated, but that's about all. We walked round the ramp inside the ruin, and into tall, dome-roofed chambers, presumably living quarters. From the window you could look down across the grey-blue surface and see the outline of straight roads and runways, like the desert lines in the Andes. It's all so still, so silent, just the shuffling lines of bulky space-suited humans walking through the cavernous building. The museum is next. There are many artifacts there, and best of all, the Dead World Scroll, the fragment the G'chathraga left to record their stay in this System. **End entry.**

of their metal-that-was-not-metal fits closely with the Dead World Scroll. If the explorers of our System *were* G'chathraga, is it possible to tell where they came from? The Dead World Scroll makes reference to a world where "memory sings from the incubation rocks, swift passage of wind through the bones of hills". If this refers to their homeworld, it is not very helpful. And although our detailed exploration of his Galaxy is only ten percent complete, no world has yet been found on which either architectural or fossil remains exist to hint at the origins of the ancient Visitors. And to add frustration to the mystery, recent work at the Ionian Institution on Triton, piecing together mythological tales and the race memories of a number of alien species, now suggests that the Radiant Visitors of the Ruimzegga were very different beings from the gigantic, upright creatures that built their base on Pluto. The Ionian Institute suggests further that the builders probably came from another Galaxy. If that is so, it is remarkable that they picked only Earth of the then millions of emerging worlds to study. Did something draw them to our Solar System, some legendary connotations of our world?

How long did they stay? This is a difficult question to answer. Dating the ruins by Chronon-Quark excitability is accurate only to one hundred thousand years, and the alien presence on Pluto, and on Phobos, certainly lasted less than that period of time. The evidence of the ruins, and their complex of roadways, and deep-level monorail systems, is that they built small (to them), restricted bases, capable of supporting an exploration team of perhaps forty thousand. All buildings appear to have been constructed simultaneously, which would suggest a limited stay, and an intense programme of exploration. The reference in the Scroll to them having 'Watched until the Time of Hiding' is unhelpful. According to the Scroll they left 'Voice mounds' on both Earth and Mars. It is not known what these are, and none have been discovered; but in the event that one such 'voice mound' should be excavated there is a possibility of it filling in some of the gaps in our understanding of the G'chathraga, or whoever the visitors were.

Is there any evidence from either of the Time Exploration groups? The question is always asked. Time Rescue and Time Visits Associates, however, are restricted organisations dealing only with prevention of time displacement. It is thought that a 'future agency' is the real control behind these two systems. No information about the future is ever released. It is also known that time travel is only possible between present and future; the back-barrier, as it is called, appears not yet to have been broken. The mystery must be solved by archaeology or space exploration.

Earth, in all its long history, has been watched and explored by many races, notably (and notoriously) by the B'tashik, who were responsible for gross crimes against early humans in the form of killing and hunting, not to mention kidnapping. But of all the aliens that have taken a quizzical look at our evolving world, the visitors we believe to have been the G'chathraga were the earliest, and the most thorough, and remain the most intriguing.

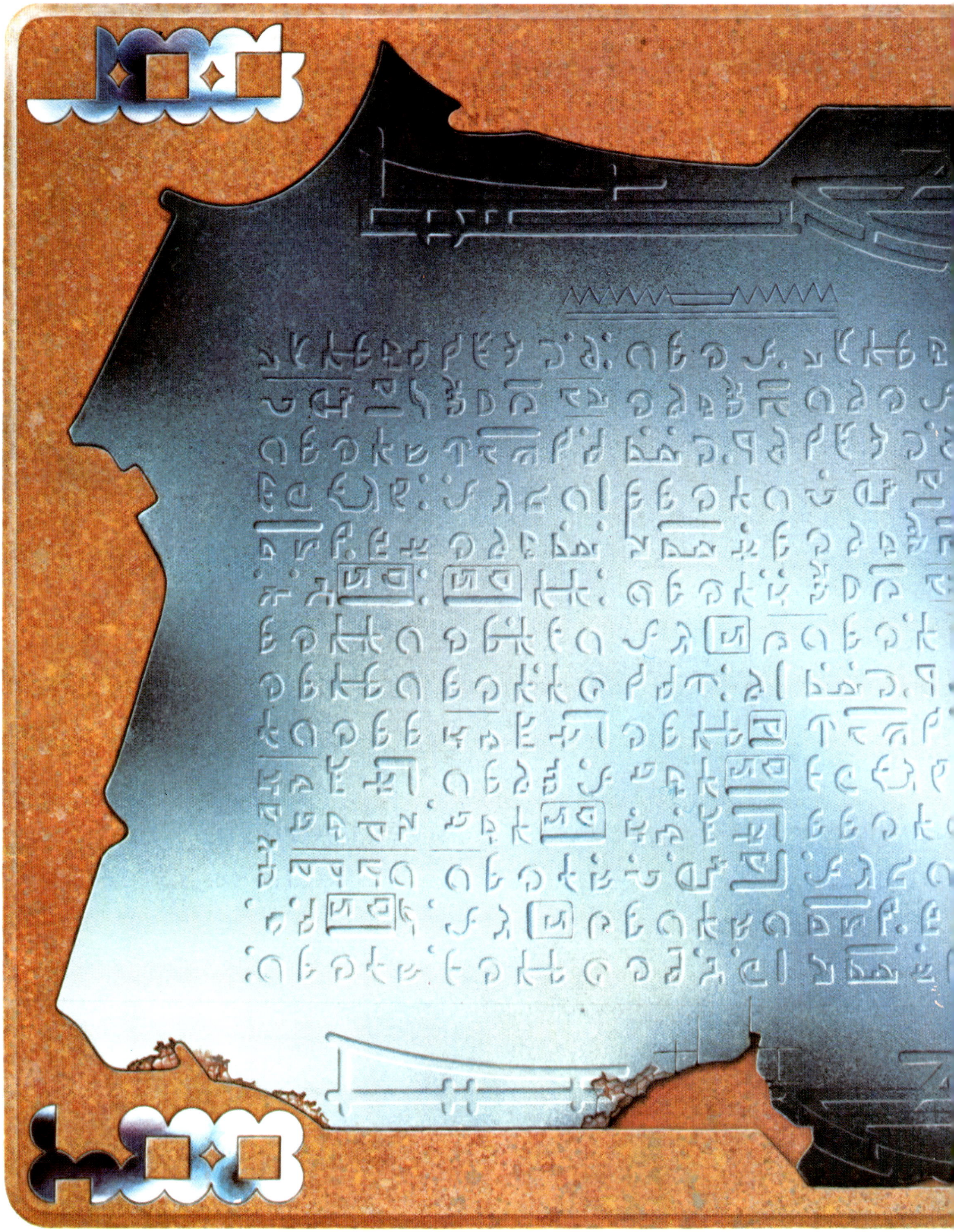

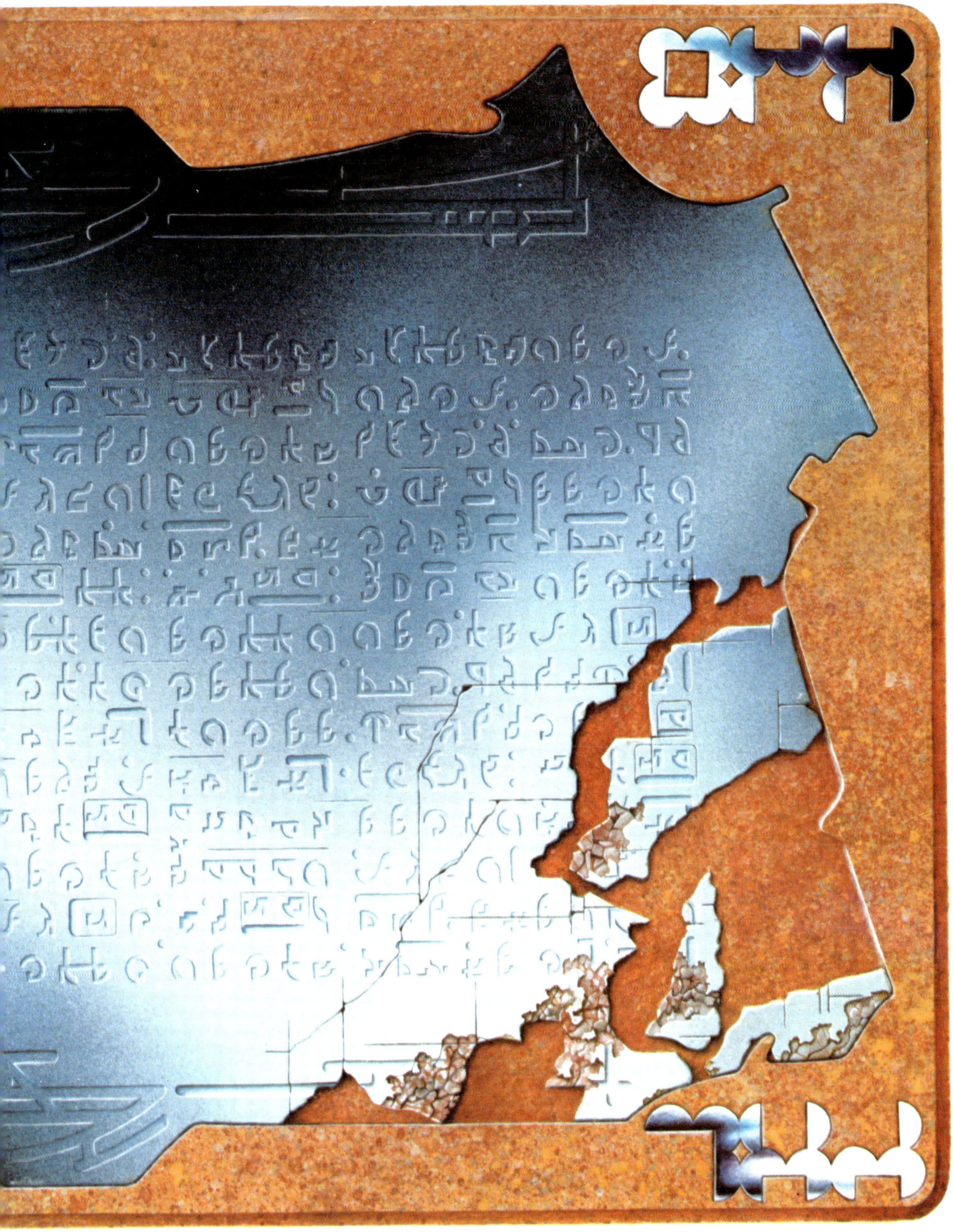

Personal diary Caroline. 23rd June 2577: Well, we've left the Solar System behind us, and are travelling through wiccan-space to the Altuxor system and VandeZande's World. Leaving normal space is a spectacular experience. Almost all the passengers – some 10,000 – gathered in the main lounge, where there's a huge screen. As the Time-Space-Matrix-Distortion Drive was activated, and the ship passed into wiccan-space, strange colours – the phenomenon popularly known as witch-light – flowed across the screen, together with disorienting patches of **absence** of colour that refused to let your eye focus on them (a little like the gaps in vision which for me signal the onset of migraine headaches). A lot of passengers (me included) popped mild hallucinogens to heighten the experience. But I'm getting ahead of myself – a lot has been happening since my last entry, and I ought to try to deal with events in order . . . Sure enough, we argued over which route to follow from Starport. Leio won – or rather, I realized he'd sulk for the rest of the trip if he didn't get to visit Pluto, and decided it wasn't worth it. So Pluto, it was, and I have to admit it was interesting enough once we got there. Most ruins I can take or leave alone (though I was exaggerating when I told Leio that when you'd seen one lot you'd seen them all), but some specific relics **do** fascinate me. Sometimes an ancient object will conjure up a powerful, almost mystical feeling of understanding of its period, without your needing to know any of the formal history. (It occurs to me that my religious impulses and Leio's obsession with the past may at root be more similar than we'd normally admit.) I don't know why, but for me it's writings that seem to cause the effect. I get it when I look at medieval illuminated manuscripts, imagining the monks labouring for months or years over a single book. And I got it, very strongly, from the Dead World Scroll (although I wish it had a more suitable name than that piece of slick journalese). The hieroglyphs and the whole appearance of the thing are weird enough, but it's the translation that gives it an extra dimension. Obviously it records something of tremendous importance to the G'chathraga (or whichever aliens left it) . . . but what can it **mean?** I stood in front of it for hours, trying to imagine myself into the minds of beings for which it had significance; I felt that if one were only able to take an imaginative leap it would all become clear.

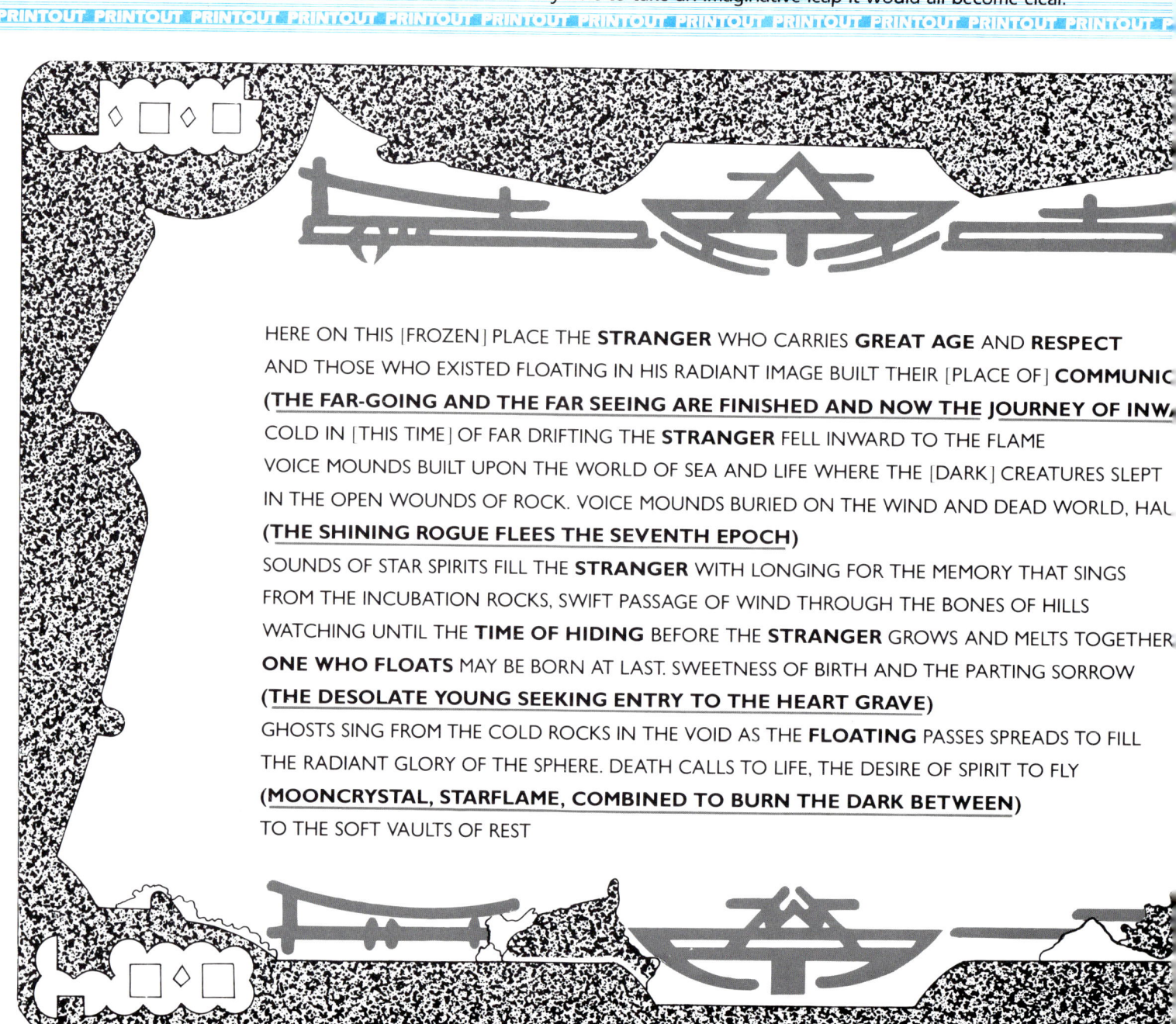

HERE ON THIS [FROZEN] PLACE THE **STRANGER** WHO CARRIES **GREAT AGE** AND **RESPECT**
AND THOSE WHO EXISTED FLOATING IN HIS RADIANT IMAGE BUILT THEIR [PLACE OF] COMMUNIC
(**THE FAR-GOING AND THE FAR SEEING ARE FINISHED AND NOW THE JOURNEY OF INW**
COLD IN [THIS TIME] OF FAR DRIFTING THE **STRANGER** FELL INWARD TO THE FLAME
VOICE MOUNDS BUILT UPON THE WORLD OF SEA AND LIFE WHERE THE [DARK] CREATURES SLEPT
IN THE OPEN WOUNDS OF ROCK. VOICE MOUNDS BURIED ON THE WIND AND DEAD WORLD, HAU
(**THE SHINING ROGUE FLEES THE SEVENTH EPOCH**)
SOUNDS OF STAR SPIRITS FILL THE **STRANGER** WITH LONGING FOR THE MEMORY THAT SINGS
FROM THE INCUBATION ROCKS, SWIFT PASSAGE OF WIND THROUGH THE BONES OF HILLS
WATCHING UNTIL THE **TIME OF HIDING** BEFORE THE **STRANGER** GROWS AND MELTS TOGETHER
ONE WHO FLOATS MAY BE BORN AT LAST. SWEETNESS OF BIRTH AND THE PARTING SORROW
(**THE DESOLATE YOUNG SEEKING ENTRY TO THE HEART GRAVE**)
GHOSTS SING FROM THE COLD ROCKS IN THE VOID AS THE **FLOATING** PASSES SPREADS TO FILL
THE RADIANT GLORY OF THE SPHERE. DEATH CALLS TO LIFE, THE DESIRE OF SPIRIT TO FLY
(**MOONCRYSTAL, STARFLAME, COMBINED TO BURN THE DARK BETWEEN**)
TO THE SOFT VAULTS OF REST

Eventually it was Leio who had to suggest it was time to leave: pretty ironic, considering the fuss I'd made. But I think I managed to make it up to him when we got back to our cabin on the **Starfriend.** If the shuttle was amazing, this ship simply defies description — it's so big that its lifeboats are the size of the shuttle! There are all kinds of strange aliens aboard and I spend a lot of time at the mutual observation windows watching those in special environments. I particularly enjoy looking at the Ssth'Isth floating around their low-gravity compartment: the pulses of coloured light with which they communicate are like an expensive lightshow. A courier showed me how to operate a communicator torch and so now I give them a greeting burst (probably with the equivalent of a dreadful accent!) each time I go down. They solemnly line up on the other side of the plastiglass and return the greeting in unison. We're getting to know a few of the people who will be on the Aurora-Magellan part of the trip. Some are friendly, but on the whole Leio and I keep away from them. They are all ultrarich of course, and seem to regard us — who could never in a hundred lifetimes afford a trip like this were it not for the competition — with rather patronizing amusement. Leio doesn't worry about this as much as I do: he says it's my atavistic class-war tendencies coming to the surface. I disagree: I don't think I'm jealous of these people, or dislike them for what they are, it's just that our lives are so different that there's no point of contact (and, damn them, they do manage to make you feel that your life is so much less interesting than theirs — which wouldn't be so bad if it wasn't probably true!) **End entry.**

Agent Luranski: Memory Implant. 24th June 2577: Nothing urgent to report, but I think I should record my suspicion that we have been under surveillance since arrival at Starport. This does not seem particularly directed at us: I suspect that at least one Aurora-Magellan agent has been infiltrated into the tour party. This, of course, was to be expected. I particularly recommend investigation of one Aaron Chirau, who claims to be a resident of Copernicus City on the Moon. **End report.**

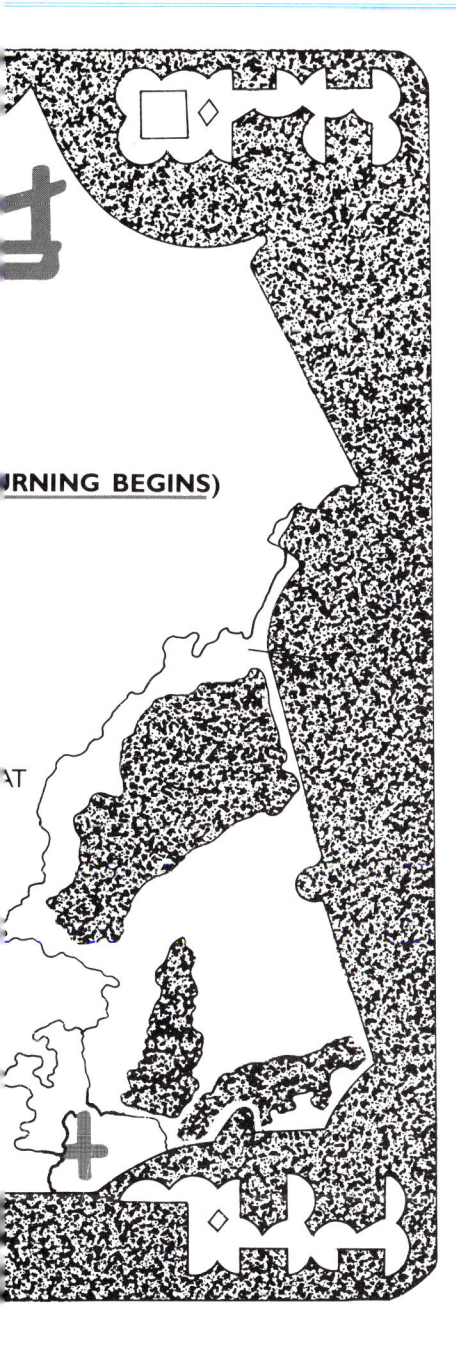

THE DEAD WORLD SCROLL: NOTES ON THE TRANSLATION

The script is read from bottom to top, with alternate lines reading right-to-left and then left-to-right so that the eye can scan continuously. Because of the break in the lower right-hand corner some words in the first four lines are uncertain; these are set off in square brackets. The meaning of each glyph varies according to its position in the line and the three preceding glyphs. Those lines shown underlined in the translation are a speculative translation of the occasional framed and raised glyphs; their placing within the whole translation is largely arbitrary. Visitors interested in the possible meaning of the text are referred to volumes XLIV-LV of the Proceedings of the Institute of Alien Language and Linguistics, *ably summarized in Nathan Shibano's* Interpreting the Stranger *(2533)*

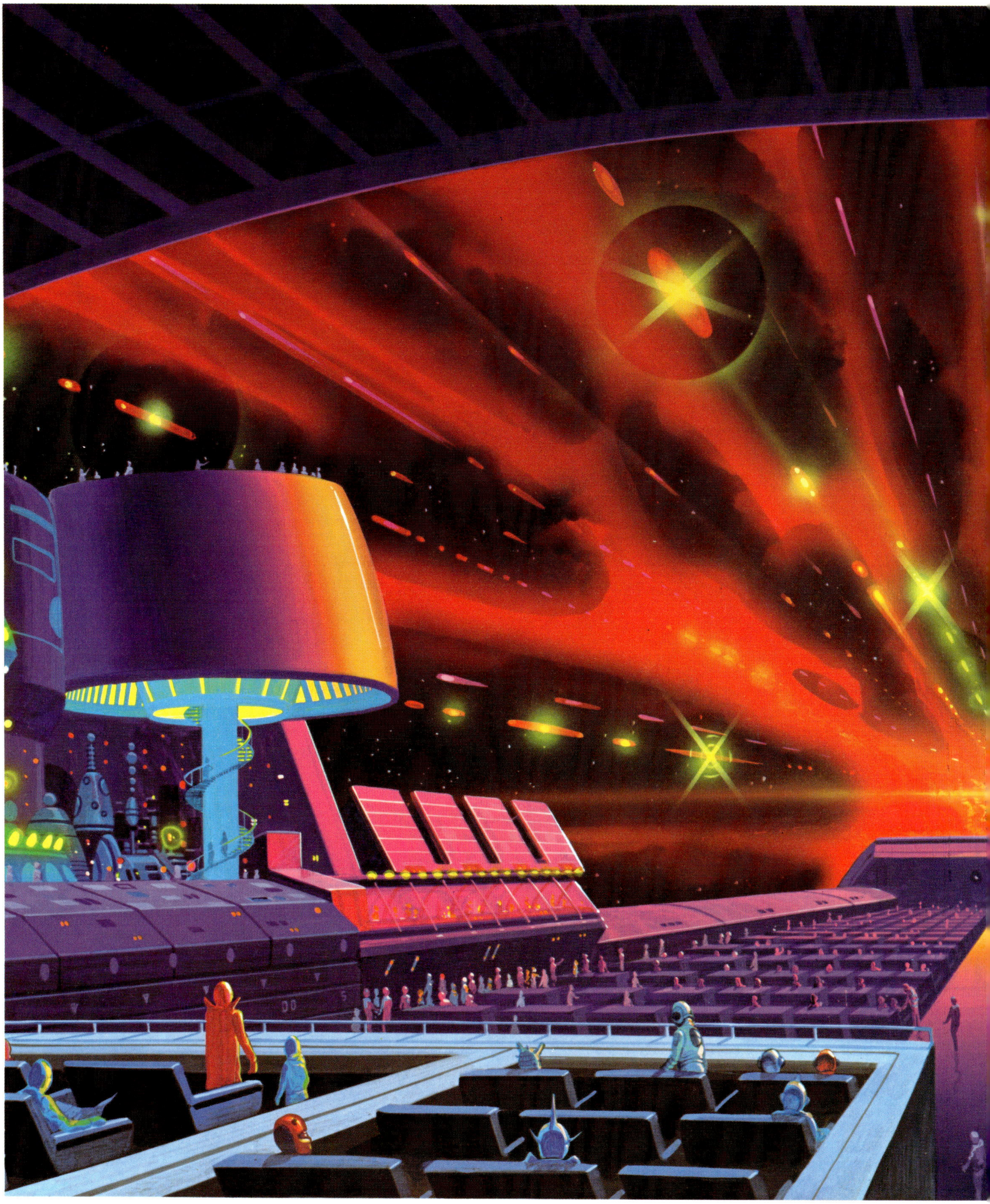

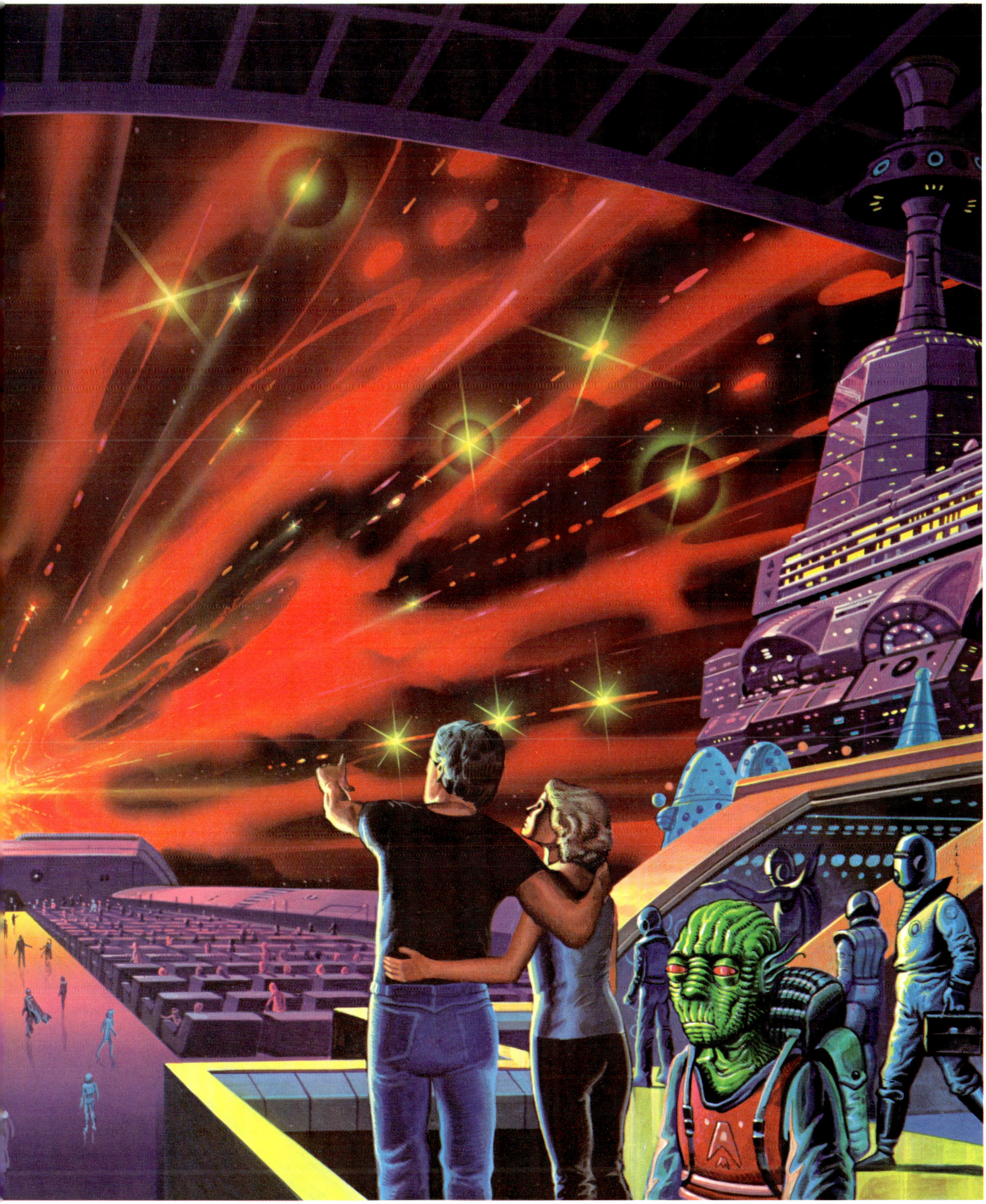

PAN GALACTIC
STARTOUR DISPLAY TICKET

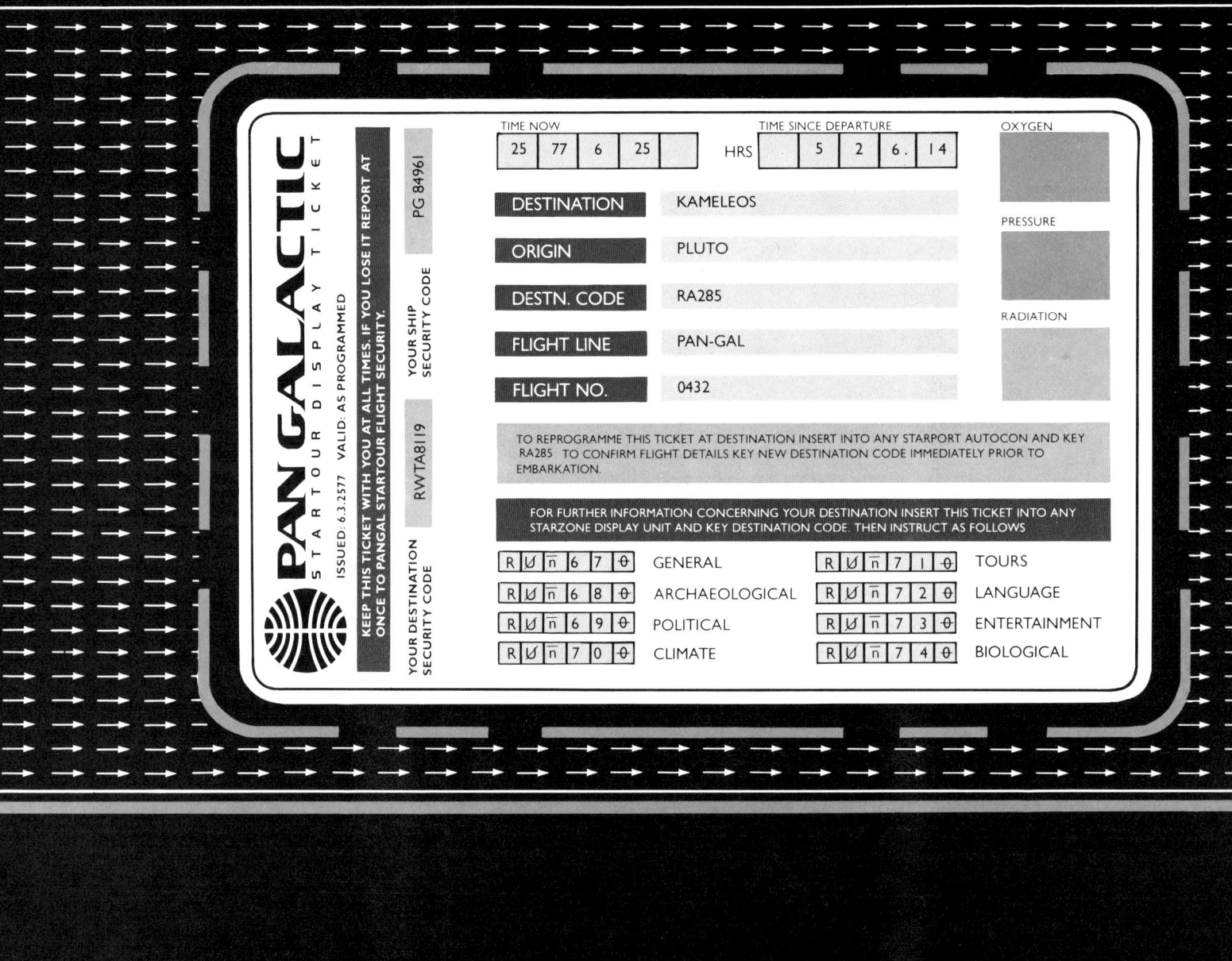

ISSUED: 6.3.2577 VALID: AS PROGRAMMED

PG 84961

YOUR SHIP SECURITY CODE

KEEP THIS TICKET WITH YOU AT ALL TIMES. IF YOU LOSE IT REPORT AT ONCE TO PANGAL STARTOUR FLIGHT SECURITY.

RWTA8119

YOUR DESTINATION SECURITY CODE

TIME NOW					TIME SINCE DEPARTURE				
25	77	6	25		HRS	5	2	6	14

OXYGEN

PRESSURE

RADIATION

DESTINATION	KAMELEOS
ORIGIN	PLUTO
DESTN. CODE	RA285
FLIGHT LINE	PAN-GAL
FLIGHT NO.	0432

TO REPROGRAMME THIS TICKET AT DESTINATION INSERT INTO ANY STARPORT AUTOCON AND KEY RA285 TO CONFIRM FLIGHT DETAILS KEY NEW DESTINATION CODE IMMEDIATELY PRIOR TO EMBARKATION.

FOR FURTHER INFORMATION CONCERNING YOUR DESTINATION INSERT THIS TICKET INTO ANY STARZONE DISPLAY UNIT AND KEY DESTINATION CODE. THEN INSTRUCT AS FOLLOWS

R Ø n̄ 6 7 0	GENERAL	R Ø n̄ 7 1 0	TOURS
R Ø n̄ 6 8 0	ARCHAEOLOGICAL	R Ø n̄ 7 2 0	LANGUAGE
R Ø n̄ 6 9 0	POLITICAL	R Ø n̄ 7 3 0	ENTERTAINMENT
R Ø n̄ 7 0 0	CLIMATE	R Ø n̄ 7 4 0	BIOLOGICAL

· ALTUXOR · ALTU

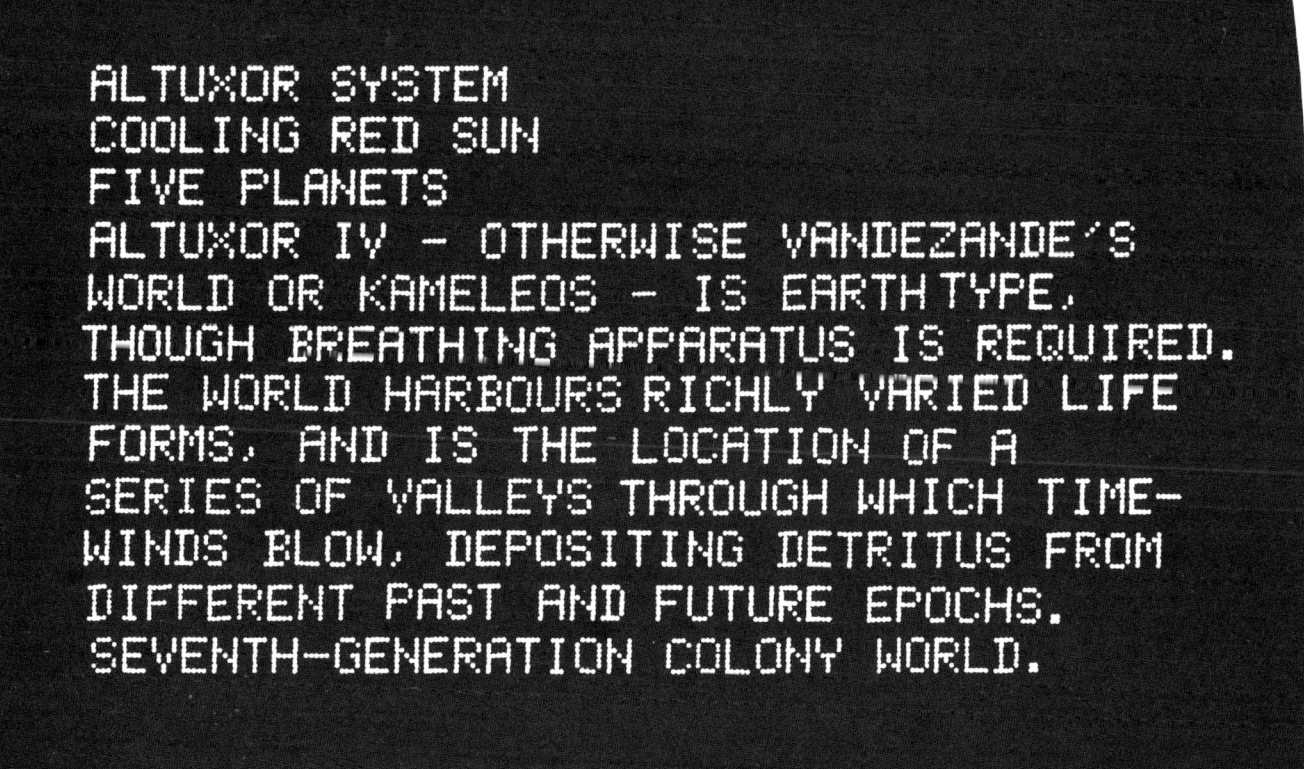

```
ALTUXOR SYSTEM
COOLING RED SUN
FIVE PLANETS
ALTUXOR IV - OTHERWISE VANDEZANDE'S
WORLD OR KAMELEOS - IS EARTHTYPE,
THOUGH BREATHING APPARATUS IS REQUIRED.
THE WORLD HARBOURS RICHLY VARIED LIFE
FORMS, AND IS THE LOCATION OF A
SERIES OF VALLEYS THROUGH WHICH TIME-
WINDS BLOW, DEPOSITING DETRITUS FROM
DIFFERENT PAST AND FUTURE EPOCHS.
SEVENTH-GENERATION COLONY WORLD.
```

OR · ALTUXOR · AL

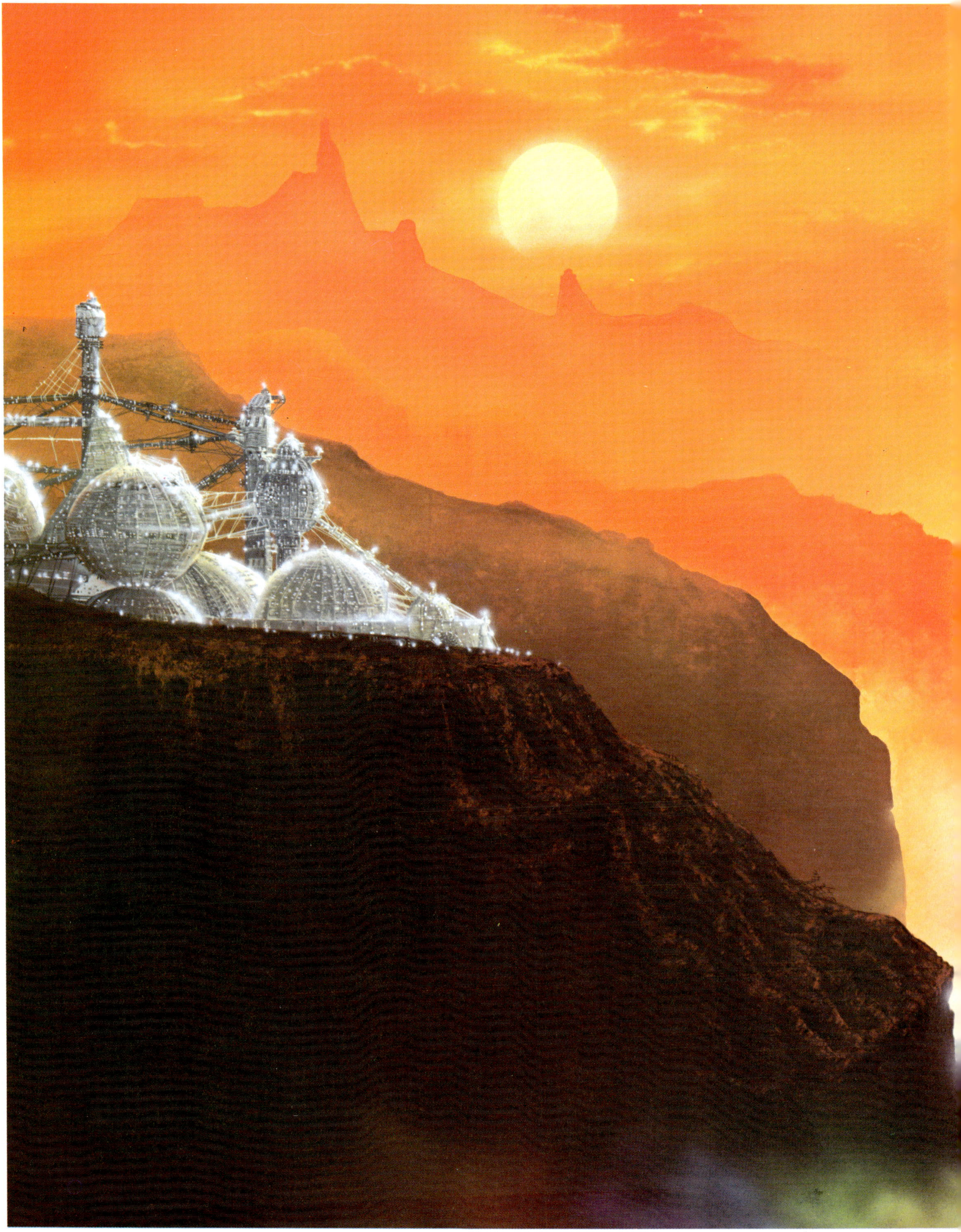

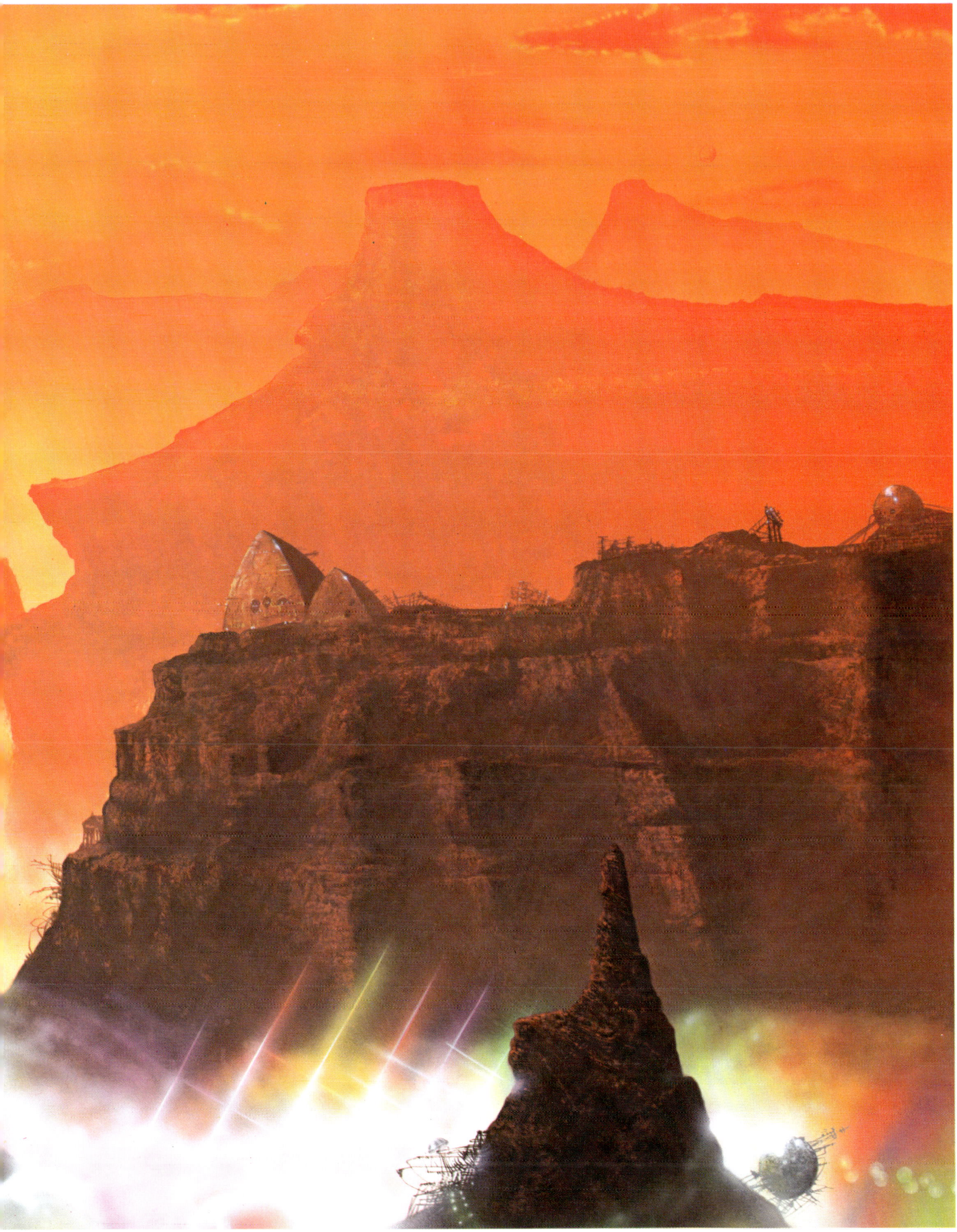

Personal diary Lelo. 30th June 2577: In one way, I suppose, the holiday is really beginning now. How can I convey what it's like to stand on a planet that until a couple of hundred years ago wasn't even known about? A world that is a **real** alien world, orbiting a dying red sun that can't even be seen from Earth. It's fantastic. We're in the Galaxy at last. And the name of the world is VandeZande's World, after the man who first set foot upon it, but everyone here calls the place Kameleos, from chameleon, because the world is a very changeable world indeed. Just out of sight of our hotel room there's a huge valley where, every so often, a wind blows up that doesn't only blow a gale, but blows through time! We were here three days before we were allowed out on to the planet's surface, because the place is dangerous. It's still incredible to think that it took only twice as long to cover hundreds of light years of space as it did to jaunt across the Solar System to Pluto. And wiccan-space is really something. You get a sort of brain explosion that's all illusion as you pass the light barrier into what they call 'witch-light'. You hallucinate a bit, seeing moving shapes and getting the sensation of spiralling down into a whirlpool. The stars vanish completely, and outside the ship for the two days of witch-light travel you just see colours and confusion, like a whole different Universe. Honestly, it's quite easy to believe that you're flying through another world of cloudlike creatures, and strangely shaped cities, all watching you as you pass. But it's just the distortion of space and vision by the wiccan-drive. We spent a lot of time on the flight talking to alien life . . . it's funny to speak to a female Thurukra (the only sound-emitting sex) in English. Some of the human passengers took exception to our mixing like that, but thank Luck there was no trouble. Pan-Gal hires an army of security men, and they were very much in evidence. And so to VandeZande's World, the first Wonder of the Galaxy. From orbit the world looks like a jungle, with these immense rift valleys, like the Grand Canyon only much forested, winding across its surface; the rifts are just unbelievably littered with ruins and fragments of what look like castles, and crystalline hemispheres. There are several mountain ranges, and we flew low over one of them and you could see the field patterns of the colonies, well away from the time winds. And the oceans are vast, and effectively inland as they don't

EXTRACT FROM: DUNN'S COSMIC GAZETTEER

The Altuxor planetary system was first referred to in the log of the Community Star Ship *Helga*, in 2280. It was not revisited for a hundred and fifty years to be properly documented and recorded. The first explorers to set foot upon the world were the Flemish crew of the ISS *Grauwels*, Giid Eekhaut and Iiv VandeZande. The two men argued ceaselessly about which of them should give his name to the world; their argument was resolved by the sudden appearance of a time wind, which swept both of them away. Rank took precedence, and VandeZande's World was officially named. The scientific mission that was established thereafter soon came to nickname the world Kameleos, after its ever changing face, for VandeZande's World is a planet where nothing is as it seems, and nothing can be depended upon to stay in the same form and of the same texture from day to day.

Steel City, the mobile, central human installation of the world, was built over a period of twenty years. It has roving sub-units, and can itself blast away from the surface upon which it sits, increasing its survival chances should a time-squall reach out of the rift valley known as Kriakta Rift and attempt to dispatch it to some othertimely age.

Kameleos is a smaller world than Earth, but similar gravitationally. It has an oxygen-nitrogen atmosphere, but a very rich atmospheric content of molecular pollen makes the air unbreathable, necessitating the wearing of a mask, or the bio-adaptation of the lungs and eyes. Ten time-winds are so far known; eight blow through similar fault valleys to the Great Rift Valley being studied by Steel City (and to which the small tourist trade is permitted). Two winds blow across the inland sea known as the Luberpallen Sea. The frequency of these interruptions in the normal progress of time varies; in the year 2540 there were forty time winds in Kriakta Rift alone. These followed a decade, however, when time broke free only five times across the whole world. What causes the time winds is unknown, but a peculiar arrangement of black holes around the Altuxor System, at a distance of ten light years, is one possible solution. A more recent proposal links the flow of time to the sporadic appearance of the radiating machine entity known as the Traveller. Theory holds that the Traveller is a time machine, policing the world from past to future, and that its slowed passage during humankind's stay on the world – perhaps to take readings and observations on humanity itself – causes the rapid flow of condensed time, and the beaching of so many artefacts and structural fragments.

Time fragments: most of the debris 'washed ashore' by time-winds appears to be ruined, and of alien design. Some fragments are obviously primitive, such as stone archways, marble columns, fragments of clay and straw brickwork, and the various megalithic structures so familiar to students of Earth history, and possibly a primal cultural image in the prehistory of all alien species. Machine wreckage is usually mechanical, or electric-powered; several materials have been discovered that do not conform to known technology. Fragments of space vehicles abound, all showing variations of the wiccan-drive principle. Animal life is occasionally left behind, but it is always dead. The same is not true of plant life. By relating pollen and structural design to fossilised and preserved plant life from areas not distorted by time, the origin of a few time winds can be ascertained. The oldest wind blew from eleven million years in the past, and it lasted for several hours. Unfortunately a wind from the future obscured the valley soon after and the amount of detailed information rescued for study was very slight.

No intelligent life form has ever been dredged up. Evidence for other alien visitations is rife, and humanity's own artefacts are commonly beached, giving some insight into the future development of the colonial world beyond the valley. Our stay on Kameleos is believed to extend over forty thousand years into the future.

As a colony, Kameleos is 'Highly Restricted'. In its early years, before the full import of those valleys where the time winds blow became apparent, several colonial groups were permitted. These are the communities that spread along the Kriakta Rift for two hundred miles. Divided into townships, self-governing and with sponsored trade turnover with the Federation, the total colonial connect, like on Earth. Only an eighth of the planetary surface is water. But the tides are complex. Kameleos has six moons. One of them is called Merlin, and it's nearly always hidden behind Kytara. But when it emerges and can be seen from the world all manner of strange behaviour occurs in the various animal life-forms that live below. There's a human base on Merlin, and the crew of the liner were telling us stories about how people who work there become really weird. They get to think they can walk on the stars, and a lot of people apparently vanish from the base, totally and inexplicably. There's only one real city on the world, called Steel City because it looks like a huge, steel dome; it moves, like all installations on dangerous worlds, and you can see how it's really a military base, set up for science and military use. The theory is that one of these days the time-winds will dredge up not just ruins, but a live and highly intelligent alien creature, one of the inhabitants of this world who either once built the fabulous buildings and machines that keep being dragged through time, or **will** build them. There's no telling whether a ruin has been blown from future or past, but because the world is very old, the likelihood is the latter. The museum is crammed with things, equipment, weapons, primitive travelling vehicles, china bits and pieces, statues, containers . . . some of it looks quite familiar, and again the theory is that alien visitations to the world have left their mark . . . man is one such alien visitation, and his own future detritus has often been picked up by a time wind and blown into the past. Of course it's all very dangerous. We had to learn to walk in huge, black-armoured suits called Rift Suits. They are practically living machines. You can control them easily enough, but if danger threatens they take over and run **you** away from the scene. They can move fast too. Caroline took an immediate fancy to them, and toured on her own yesterday, strictly against the rules. I don't know if she was caught, but she certainly said she'd got away with it. She's spent money on books for the first time this vacation, a novel called **Where Time Winds Blow**, which is the first fiction I've ever known her to buy, and one of those interminable Dunn's Cosmic Guides. **End entry.**

presence in the lowlands is half a million. The colonists encourage tourist visits and offer a varied, and inexpensive, range of entertainments, from harvest dances to drinking matches. Over the last century a further colonisation group has been allowed; these have settled in the high plateaus of the mountains. Tourist visits here are not permitted since the type of colonisation is Bioform. Known as the 'Manchanged', their human appearance is sufficiently altered to render them disturbing.

What to do on Kameleos: this world is justifiably known as one of the Wonders of the Galaxy; but it is a dangerous world, and an unpredictable one. Movement is restricted of necessity, and three days basic training in the bulky, rather unpleasant survival suits, is considered essential. Within Steel City itself there are several museums, lecture theatres, play houses, and two Sensuadomes available for visitors. There are numerous lounges and restaurants, and several positions from which the planet may be observed. Beyond Steel City there are five designated tour-routes, which may be undertaken in groups of fifty. Sub-orbital observation flights are available twice daily, and you are encouraged to restrict your observation of VandeZande's World to these means. On no account should you leave the confines of Steel City alone.

Personal diary Caroline. 9th July 2577: Tomorrow we leave VandeZande's World – and the Altuxor system – for Pliax and our first living alien civilization. I'm getting very excited over this, although Leio seems less keen. (I think part of the reason is that the aliens, the Chikstha, are distinctly spider-like and Leio, though he'd never admit it to anyone – least of all me – definitely has a minor phobia about spiders.) VandeZande's World was well worth the visit, though. Partly it was the thrill of standing on your first truly alien planet, looking into the sky and realizing that the great red sun was another star – one so dim and distant that you couldn't even see it from Earth without a telescope. I suppose seasoned interstellar travellers become blasé about that sort of thing, but the feeling of strangeness and displacement was very powerful, almost mystical. The Rift Valley was breathtaking. I once spent a holiday mule-trekking in the Grand Canyon, and thought that was about as spectacular as natural scenery could get – but the Grand Canyon is just a crevice compared to this. Of course, you have to stand at the edge in your clumsy Rift Suit and just admire it, because of the time winds (they aren't prepared to take any chances on stupid tourists getting caught by a sudden squall). I've been making good use of the holo-camera, and the results should be spectacular. Leio is fascinated by the time winds – he has the idea that if the force could somehow be harnessed or artificially generated it could revolutionize archaeology. He recommended an old micro-fiction called **Where Time Winds Blow**, all about VandeZande's World. I don't normally enjoy novels, but this one caught me in the right mood, though Leio did his best to dispel it by telling me, in gory detail, what happened to the author. Still, on to Pliax. **End entry.**

EXTRACT FROM: THE GALACTIC GEOGRAPHIC MAGAZINE VOL. XXXIII NO. 7

Rock of Ages: Tour-route 3 leaves the gleaming dome of Steel City and meanders west, between towering pinnacles of chalk, and through the sprawling forests of stubby skagbark, where Kameleos's animal life waits in silent anticipation of its prey. Ten kilometres from the city the road skirts perilously close to the edge of the sheer valley known as Kriakta Rift. The tour-bus lurches and groans around the tightly curving track, sending up a cloud of dust and the bitter, gritty pollen that makes the world so dark, and so poisonous. Here, though, close to where the great drop of the gorge rivets attention on its escarpments and their rich heritage of alien remains, the more astute traveller may notice the distant gleam of red light on the crystals and polished ebony of the megalithic cluster. Two hundred metres from the road, and from the edge of the valley, this is a place where the bus seldom stops, and the driver is unlikely to volunteer to halt the tour for you to investigate. For this unimposing pile of rocks and ruins is one of the strangest, and most awesome graveyards on the world. It is Hunderag Rock, and it is a haunted place.

Anyone in Steel City will tell you the story of Hunderag Rock; anyone who lives within the protective walls of the colonial communities will talk to you of the man who lies buried in the granite monolith. They will talk about it endlessly, but they will never go there, and they will never lead you there. Only tourists touch the Rock, and there is no danger in it for them: for, by his uniform, the man trapped in the stone is manifestly not a tourist. The whole world is a haunted world and the people who live here are haunted people; for a drink, for a meal, they will talk of anything, of ghosts, of strange sightings, of the alien presence that watches them, even of the fears that accompany a life eked out so close to unstable time; but ask about Hunderag Rock and the tone changes. They won't refuse to talk, but they will take what they say with far more seriousness. If tradition holds that the corpse in Hunderag Rock is thought to be that of Amos Hunderag himself, there's not a man or woman working on Kameleos who does not secretly believe it to be themselves. Hunderag Rock is the graveyard of a whole world.

From the Valley Road the site appears to be a single, highly coloured and sparkling stone of amorphous shape. A short walk through the tangleweed undergrowth, however, will bring you to the cleared area about the Rock, and it will instantly be seen that Hunderag Rock is in fact a collection of stones, columns and fragments of buildings. Dragged here, from the Valley, more that one hundred years ago, the markings and runes on several of the fragments are particularly fine, and have resisted the destructive impact of a hundred years of wind and rain erosion. But attention is immediately drawn to the much obscured, yet unmistakable, shape of a man embedded in the largest of the rock columns. His face-plate is clearly delineated, and part of the equipment he wore upon his chest; and from the rock surface, some forty centimetres away, a hand grows out, half clenched as if in final agony. There are no names, no visible clues as to this time-lost person's identity. Standing before that awesome shard of rock it is easy to feel the fear and panic that reputedly drove the discoverers out of their minds. It is easy to understand how, living on this blood-red world, the frightened men of Earth have come to see in this stone ghost a common peril, a symbol of the danger they all face when the time winds blow. The rock is haunted; the ghostly shape of Amos Hunderag has often been seen, struggling to escape the confining granite. But in Hunderag Rock can be seen a greater ghost…the ghost of a race's courage, drawn from them by such constant exposure to the unthinkable.

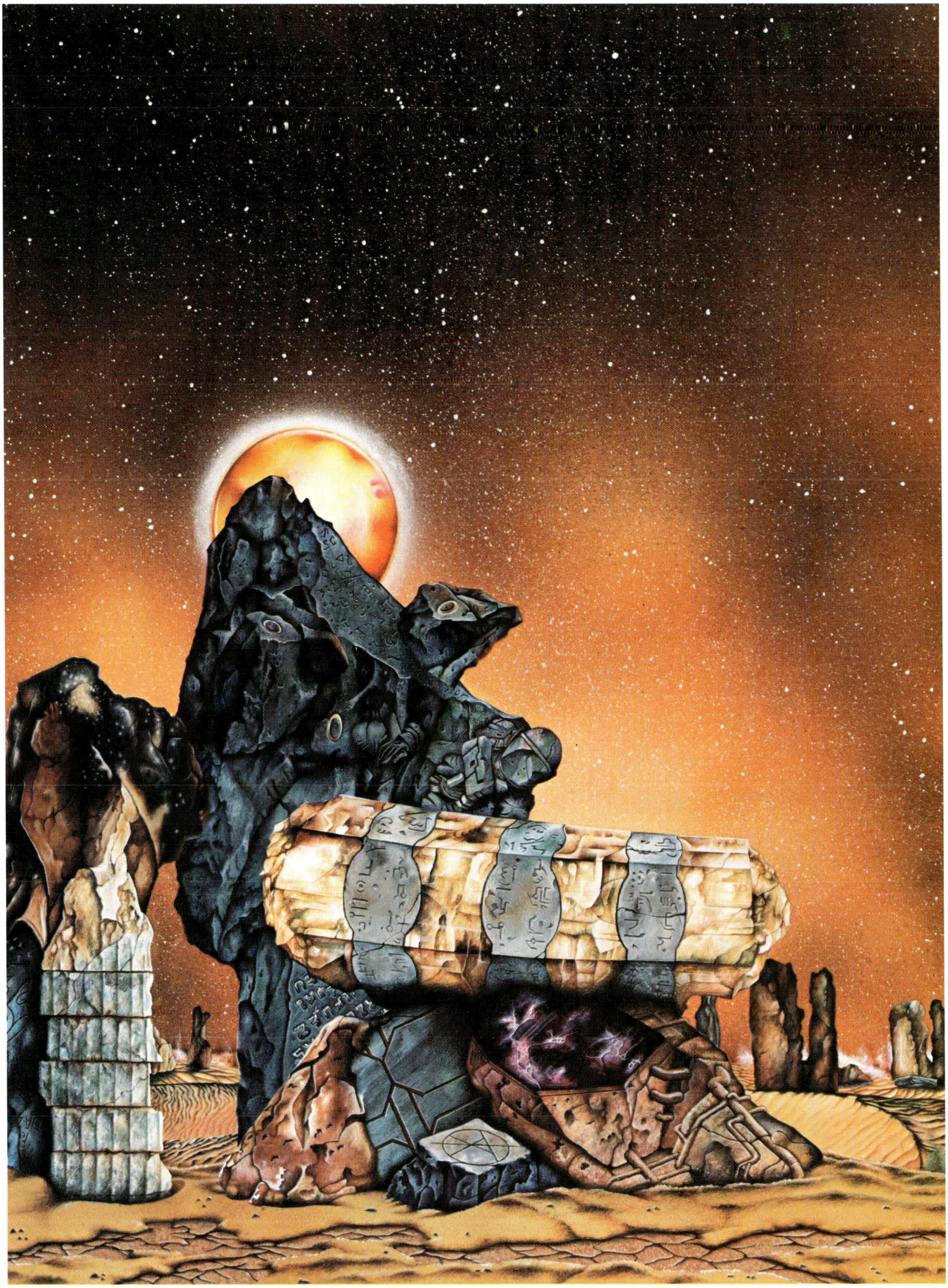

PAN GALACTIC
STARTOUR DISPLAY TICKET

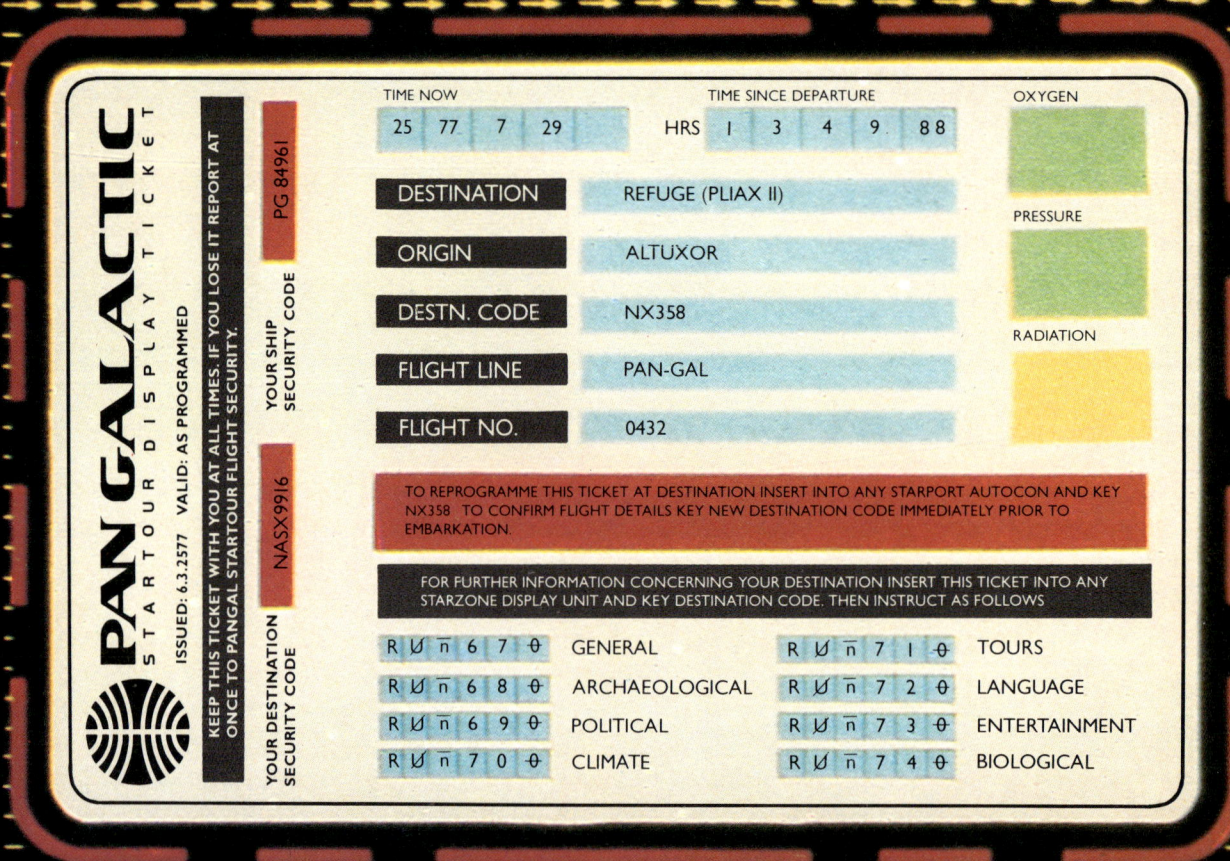

ISSUED: 6.3.2577 VALID: AS PROGRAMMED

KEEP THIS TICKET WITH YOU AT ALL TIMES. IF YOU LOSE IT REPORT AT ONCE TO PANGAL STARTOUR FLIGHT SECURITY.

YOUR SHIP SECURITY CODE: PG 84961

YOUR DESTINATION SECURITY CODE: NASX9916

TIME NOW				TIME SINCE DEPARTURE				
25	77	7	29	HRS	1	3	4	9	88

DESTINATION	REFUGE (PLIAX II)
ORIGIN	ALTUXOR
DESTN. CODE	NX358
FLIGHT LINE	PAN-GAL
FLIGHT NO.	0432

OXYGEN

PRESSURE

RADIATION

TO REPROGRAMME THIS TICKET AT DESTINATION INSERT INTO ANY STARPORT AUTOCON AND KEY NX358 TO CONFIRM FLIGHT DETAILS KEY NEW DESTINATION CODE IMMEDIATELY PRIOR TO EMBARKATION.

FOR FURTHER INFORMATION CONCERNING YOUR DESTINATION INSERT THIS TICKET INTO ANY STARZONE DISPLAY UNIT AND KEY DESTINATION CODE. THEN INSTRUCT AS FOLLOWS

RUn 670	GENERAL	RUn 710	TOURS
RUn 680	ARCHAEOLOGICAL	RUn 720	LANGUAGE
RUn 690	POLITICAL	RUn 730	ENTERTAINMENT
RUn 700	CLIMATE	RUn 740	BIOLOGICAL

PLIAX · PLIAX · P

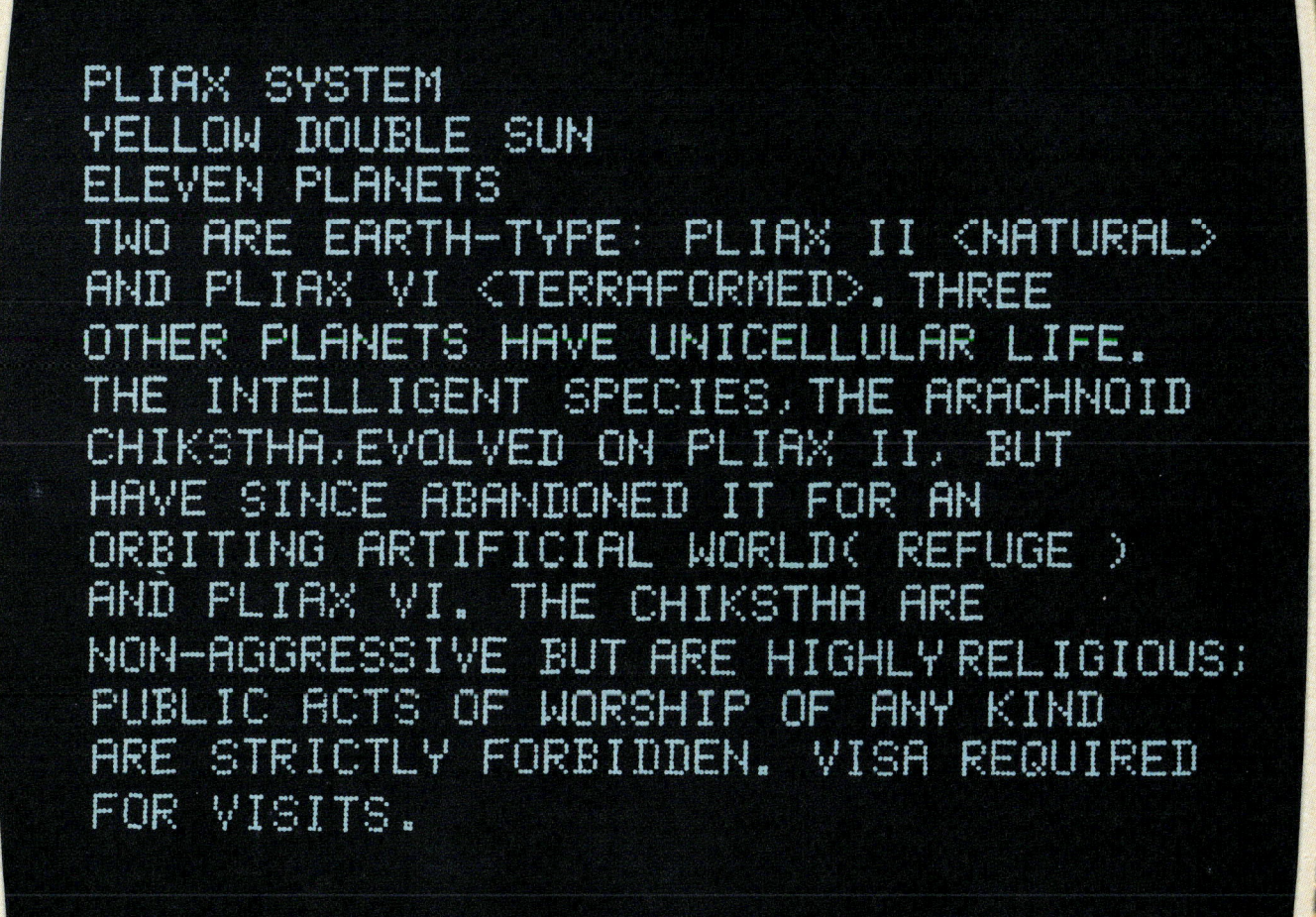

```
PLIAX SYSTEM
YELLOW DOUBLE SUN
ELEVEN PLANETS
TWO ARE EARTH-TYPE: PLIAX II (NATURAL)
AND PLIAX VI (TERRAFORMED). THREE
OTHER PLANETS HAVE UNICELLULAR LIFE.
THE INTELLIGENT SPECIES, THE ARACHNOID
CHIKSTHA, EVOLVED ON PLIAX II, BUT
HAVE SINCE ABANDONED IT FOR AN
ORBITING ARTIFICIAL WORLD( REFUGE )
AND PLIAX VI. THE CHIKSTHA ARE
NON-AGGRESSIVE BUT ARE HIGHLY RELIGIOUS;
PUBLIC ACTS OF WORSHIP OF ANY KIND
ARE STRICTLY FORBIDDEN. VISA REQUIRED
FOR VISITS.
```

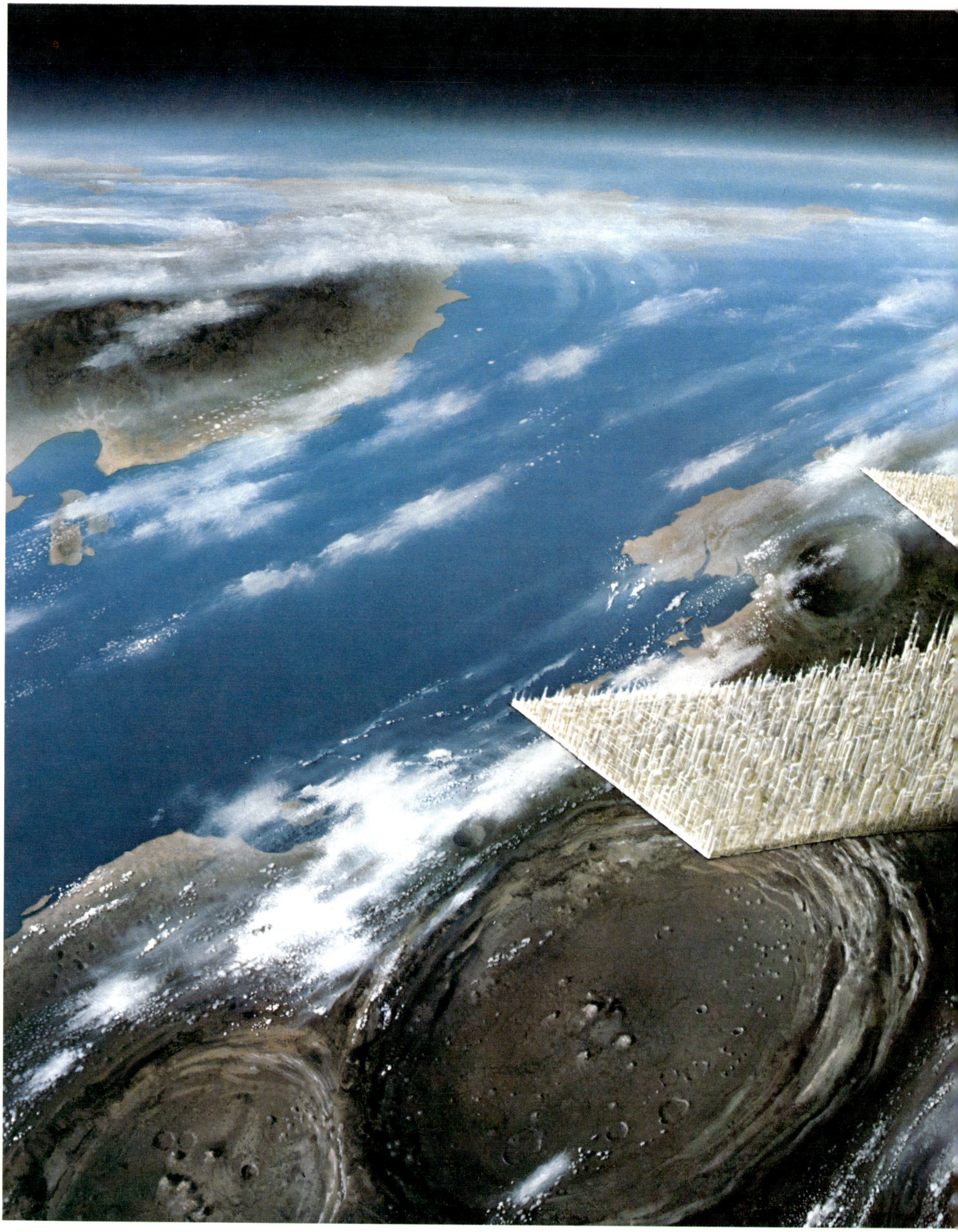

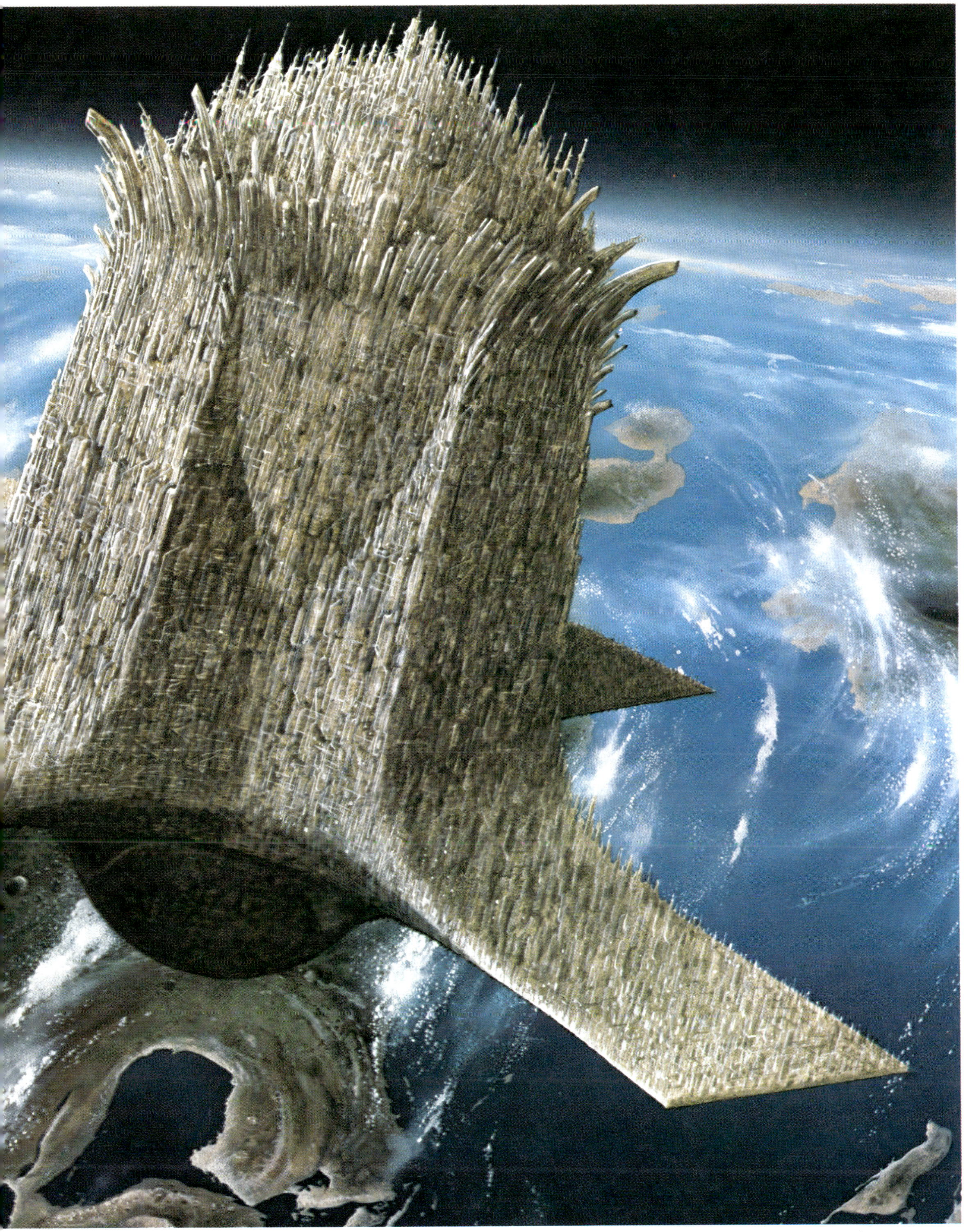

EXTRACT FROM: DUNN'S COSMIC GAZETTEER

In recent years a detailed Life Sciences study has been mutually undertaken between Man and Chikstha, the intelligent, and dominant race of the Pliax System. Because of this, the Chikstha are one of the best understood races in the Galaxy, although their evolutionary history remains obscure. Details of the research are not available, but the Chikstha value individual life less than does the human race, which supplied laboratory nurtured embryos for the Chiksthan exchange studies.

The immediate obvious feature of the Chikstha is that they are spider-like creatures, especially in the region of the head, jaws and eyes. This analagous evolution to that of the terrestrial spider is quite remarkable, and is the reason for the widespread belief that the Chikstha seeded Earth with their own kind some millions of years in their past (a theory easily disprovable: the Chikstha First Cycle occurred less than two million years ago). The average height of the Incubator, the main caste, is four feet. Their bodies are spindly, upright, and the upper limbs are highly specialised into sensitive and very manipulable 'hands'. The middle limbs are quite often atrophied, although they form an important holding organ when the Incubator forms its unity with a Symbiote.

The Incubator Caste: often referred to, incorrectly, as the 'female sex', the Incubators form the largest caste of the Chikstha, and are highly intelligent and technologically capable. When an Incubator receives the seed-mixture, known as the *ch'chiss*, from the Depositor caste, it goes into seclusion for a period of four Earth months, during which time it does not eat, nor exercise. The development of the young during this time is more a process of chemical selection, and the unconscious process of genetic scrutiny known as *g'thall-ik*. After four months the Incubator emerges from its nest and begins to eat from the population of the food creature caste, the Nourritors. It grows rapidly in size and after eight months lays four soft, red eggs that rapidly hatch. Each egg is a different caste: Depositor, Soldier, Nourritor and Symbiote. No Incubators are laid for reasons that will be seen.

The Depositor Caste: often referred to erroneously as 'the male sex', the Depositor caste is much smaller on average than the Incubator, and each possesses an intromittent organ on its lower end, curled up around its back, and held protected in a dorsal groove. It is darker in colour than the Incubator, and does not have obviously 'functional' hands; an orifice is visible in its front region, where other Chikstha family strains deposit their own sperm-laden *ch'chiss* before the seed mixture is processed and passed on to an Incubator. The function of the Depositor is now complete. It retires to a special room in the heights of their city, spins a slimy, impenetrable net about its body and undergoes metamorphosis into an Incubator. During the process of metamorphosis it achieves intelligence on a higher scale, and on emerging into the Chiksthan society again is treated as 'new born', and protected by other family members.

The Soldier Caste. Paradoxically, the Soldier caste is formed from the weakest of the four embryos finally selected by the body of the Incubator. Soldiers grow rapidly after birth, and possess only a rudimentary intelligence (although accidents occur and intelligent soldiers arise – they are usually detected and killed, but the wastelands of Pliax VI are heavily populated by renegades). Their bodies are grossly adapted for weaponry, each limb ending in a different slashing or piercing chitin weapon, and their heads helmeted with chitin outgrowths. They grow slightly taller than the Incubators in old age. They are a solitary caste that responds most positively to aroma and scent signals, gathering into armies when danger threatens. The Chikstha police are all Soldiers, and Soldiers also perform most of the routine mundane jobs in the cities.

The Nourritor Caste: The Nourritors are food-creatures, designed to make feeding easy for the pre-hatch Incubator. The Chikstha tradition of cannibalism is horrendous for a human to contemplate, but to the Chikstha the ingestion of their own kind establishes a form of afterlife for the caste. The Nourritors have evolved to be 'glad' to be sacrificed in this way, although their rudimentary intelligence allows them little opportunity for the finer contemplation of their role in life and society. Small, fat, and with only a thin chitin exoskeleton, the Nourritors are housed in the inner parts of each sky city, and are only hunted and eaten at night.

The Symbiote Caste; This caste is quite remarkable, and sets the Chikstha apart from all other races in the Galaxy, man included. Although the Incubators achieve a high level of intelligence and technological insight during their lifetimes, they remain poor philosophers. The Symbiote caste represent an evolution within the species of a variety specialised for philosophical thought, and designed to 'join minds' with an Incubator to form a dual, boosted intellect. When born they look like tiny Depositors, but they never grow taller than half a Depositor's height. They remain weak, underdeveloped, and need feeding by other castes. After two years they are carried by a soldier to an Incubator that has been re-educated and is ready for life and the solitary process of hatching. The Symbiote is placed upon the back of the Incubator, it grips, and the dual existence is formed for life. The tiny Symbiote chews through its host's back and taps directly into its body fluid for nourishment. From the jaws, which rapidly fuse with the Incubator's body, neural tendrils grow along the nervous pathways of the host, and direct to the brain. As the Symbiote's body atrophies to a shapeless lump, so the double mind expands. The Symbiote contemplates the nature of things metaphyscial, while the Incubator applies insights to building and science.

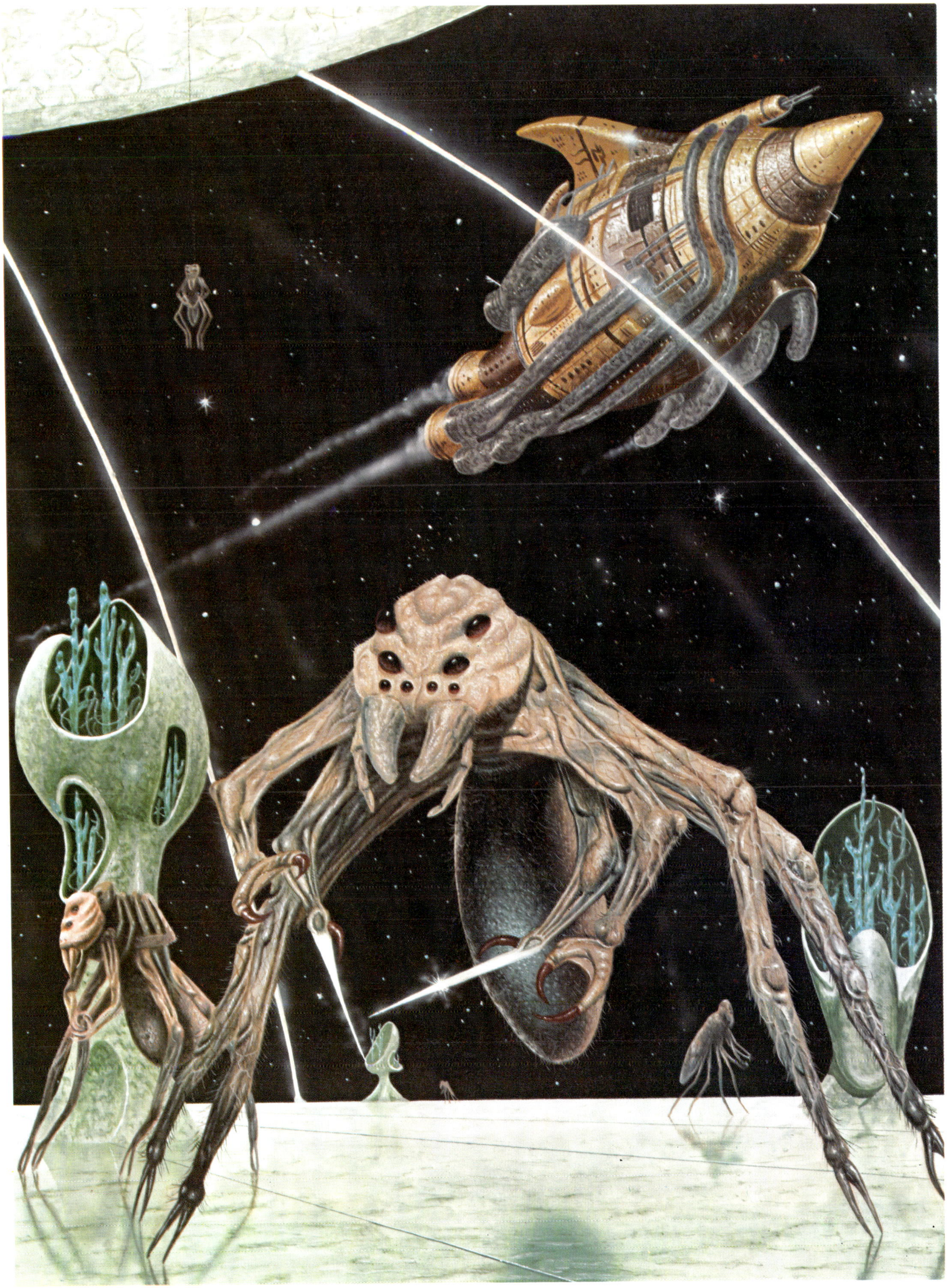

Personal diary Caroline. 14th August 2577: Well, it took a week of waiting, but we finally got our visas to visit the Chikstha Sacred World approved. They are very wary of letting anyone on the soil of their home planet (as I suppose they're entitled to be) and in our case the problem turned out to be the admission on my passport that I held a religion. It isn't so much that they disapprove as that they're fearful of a conflicting theistic belief polluting the sacred atmosphere of their planet. I spent some time convincing them that the Ubiquitous Church, arguing as it does that Christ was but one manifestation of a universal deity with no particular anthropomorphic bias, does not threaten or contradict their beliefs, but rather welcomes them as further evidence of a universal religious conviction. (On one occasion I argued so vehemently that Leio had to remind me that the church also professes to be non-dogmatic!) In the end they classified me, so the official dealing with the case informed me, as 'ontologically benign'. I'm still not sure if this was an obscure Chikstha witticism: it's hard to read nuances of expression on a pair of mandibles. So, down to the surface of Pliax II (the Chikstha name for it is something I refuse even to attempt to pronounce). The shuttle did not land, of course, nor did the Chikstha pilots or guides disembark. We had to clamber down a rudimentary ladder (its lower end kept carefully clear of the ground) while they waited, hovering. While on the surface I felt a strange sense of unease, which I put down to a weakened version of whatever psychic manifestation forced the entire race to abandon their home world for an orbiting city-cum-temple, and a terraformed (or whatever the Chikstha equivalent is) world elsewhere in their system. It must have been powerful to have had such effect, and to leave traces after thousands of years. Leio, who felt nothing, says the only powerful thing is my imagination. Although it was interesting I wasn't sorry to get back to Refuge. The Chikstha I find fascinating, though the symbiotes are undeniably creepy and the soldiers sometimes sinister. Despite appearances they seem gentle and thoughtful, and I'm looking forward to seeing their home world. **End entry.**

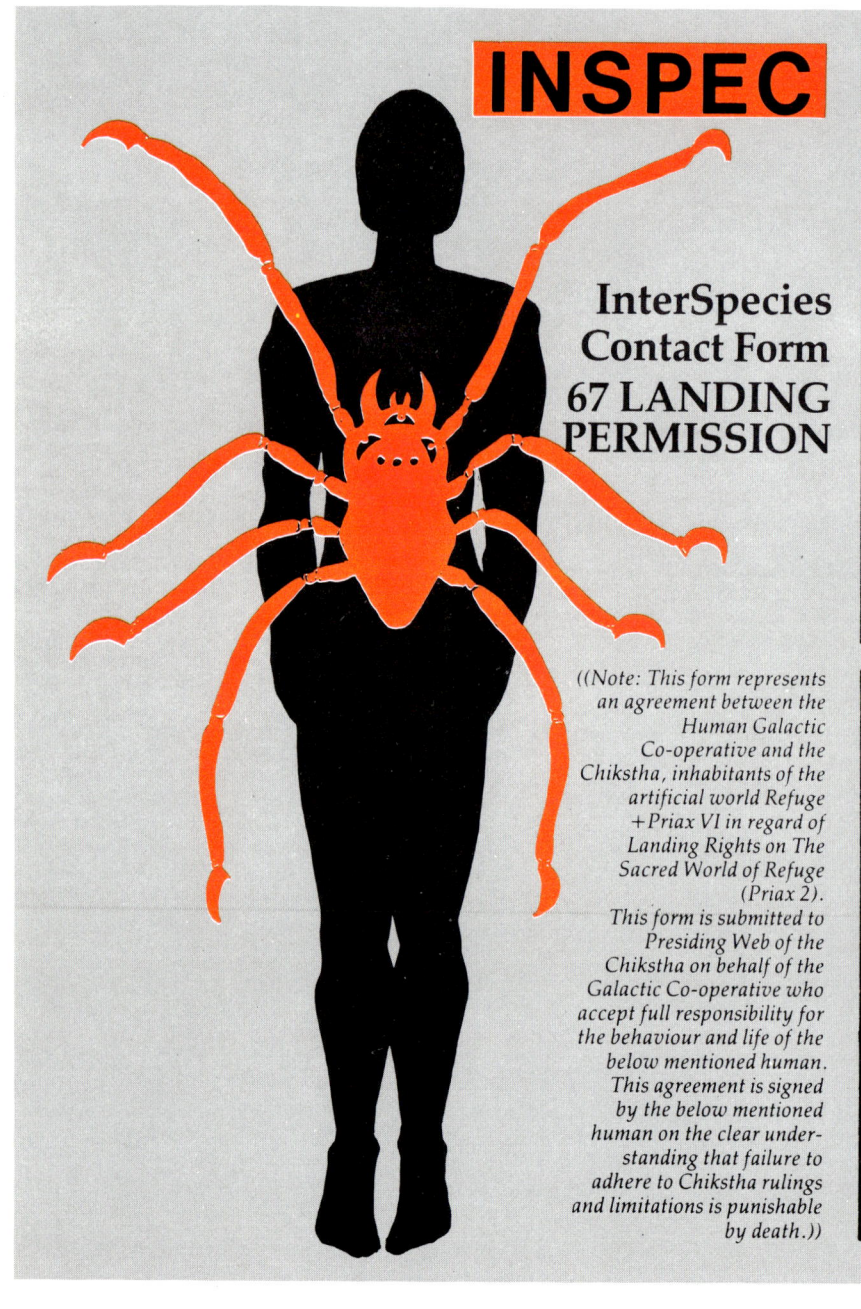

INSPEC

InterSpecies Contact Form
67 LANDING PERMISSION

Name:	CAROLINE LURANSKI
Race:	HUMAN
Nationality:	MONDE UNIS
Supervising government:	GALACTIC CO-OP
Purpose of visit:	TOURIST
Required time of visit:	2 DAYS RST
Specific requests for visiting certain areas:	NONE
Organisation with whom present in Priax System:	HARLEQUIN TOURS

((Note: This form represents an agreement between the Human Galactic Co-operative and the Chikstha, inhabitants of the artificial world Refuge +Priax VI in regard of Landing Rights on The Sacred World of Refuge (Priax 2). This form is submitted to Presiding Web of the Chikstha on behalf of the Galactic Co-operative who accept full responsibility for the behaviour and life of the below mentioned human. This agreement is signed by the below mentioned human on the clear understanding that failure to adhere to Chikstha rulings and limitations is punishable by death.))

Personal diary Lelo. 25th August 2577: We arrived in the Pliax System after a wiccan-space flight lasting twenty days. If you want to know how small a two kilometre long Pan-Galactic liner can become, live on it for twenty days. Here, though, we have a real treat. Ancient, intelligent life-forms, of an almost unbelievably horrendous appearance, and a mystery that makes this system truly enthralling. The Chikstha live on two worlds, neither of which is the world of their evolution. One, Refuge itself, is just what it says, a huge, orbiting refuge, a city of steel nearly a thousand kilometres in diameter. It's so big it casts a shadow on the deserted world below, Pliax II. Pliax II is their sacred world, and the hassle we had getting permission to go down as tourists! Caroline's religious interests delayed things a lot. They wanted to make absolutely sure that there was no fragment of God lurking inside her, ready to emerge. The planet on which most of the Chikstha live — on Refuge it's mainly a priest and military caste — is Pliax VI. Their cities are huge iron and concrete affairs, laced and covered with cables, some thick, some thin. There's no concept of up and down, left and right. Chikstha emerge all over the place, and skim around on their webs. We've been told that the Chikstha were once interstellar voyagers. They're an immensely old race, over two hundred million years; their similarity to terrestrial spiders is too close for coincidence, but they couldn't have been responsible for seeding earth with their own form — earth spiders are even older than the Chikstha. The Chikstha migrated **en masse** to Pliax VI thousands of years ago, after their fifth great evolutionary advance. The question is, why? They have Secret Legends that they never reveal, but themselves are engaged in some sort of quest, a sort of 'racial exorcism' of some event in their distant past. We shall probably never know what event that was. Pliax VI has quite obviously been arachnoformed. It's been extensively mined and quarried and from orbit there's very little that's natural left. We spent a few days there, living in their web-rooms, rooms that are supposedly set up for humanoid comfort, but which are full of discomforts such as sloping ceilings, web-hammocks instead of beds, and no sound-proofing, which means the clacking and scuttling of the Chikstha is loud and frightening. But their Sacred World is something else. I wouldn't have missed it for anything. **End entry.**

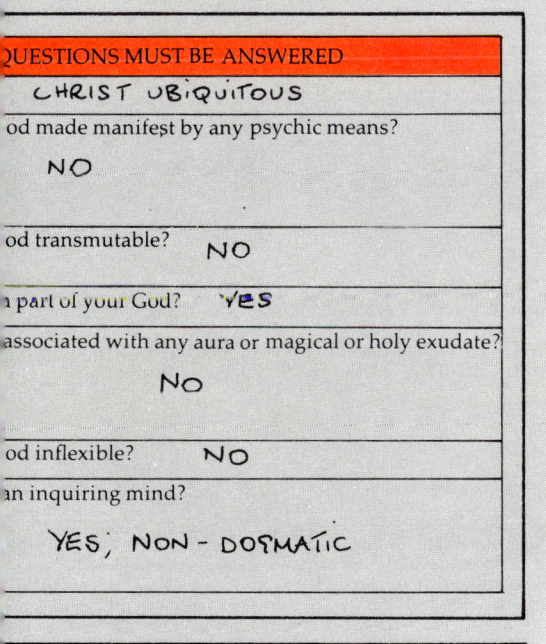

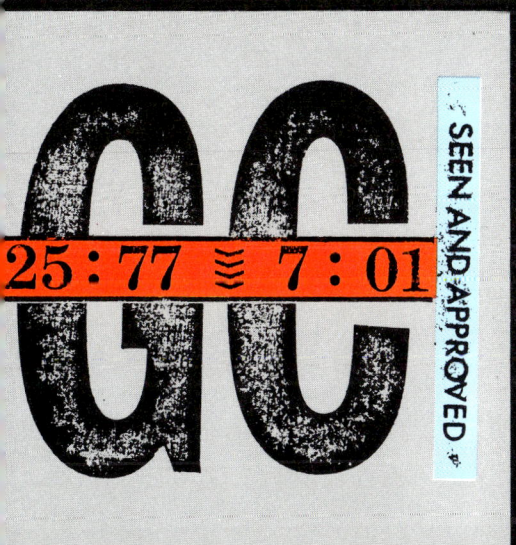

QUESTIONS MUST BE ANSWERED

	CHRIST UBIQUITOUS
od made manifest by any psychic means?	NO
od transmutable?	NO
a part of your God?	YES
associated with any aura or magical or holy exudate?	NO
od inflexible?	NO
an inquiring mind?	YES, NON-DOGMATIC

GC
25:77 ≋ 7:01
SEEN AND APPROVED

GALACTIC CO-OPERATIVE
PLIAX SYSTEM
ADVICE TO VISITORS

You are being shown this form on the ship approaching Pliax, and you will not be allowed to take it with you, nor will you be permitted to leave the ship at Refuge Orbit unless your signature appears at the bottom. This form is a serious warning. You disregard it at your peril.

Despite appearances to the contrary, Human-Chikstha relations have been steadily deteriorating for some years. The point at issue is the gross irresponsibility shown by many human visitors to the Pliax System towards what is, to the Chikstha, a world of supreme Holiness: Pliax II. Many restrictions are placed upon human visitors to this world, and those restrictions are becoming tighter. Similar restrictions do not seem to be applied to other visiting species. Inevitably, as the Chikstha deny access to their sites of interest, so human frustration grows.

You are seriously urged to obey everything on Refuge, and the inhabited world Pliax VI. You are seriously urged to obey every Chiksthan individual that speaks to you. The Chikstha are much more of a group mentality than the human species, and they have not fully grasped the extent of our individuality; thus, you may find yourself held responsible for some-one else's lapse. Do not resist or argue; to do so will inevitably be to deny yourself the chance of appearing before the INSPEC panel, on which a human Controller sits.

The Chikstha have a different form of judiciary system to ours, and a different concept of Guilt, and of Responsibility. Human rights do not apply in the Pliax System. If you are taken into the deeps of Refuge, and entered into the Chiksthan Judiciary, you will be denied proper defence. It is unlikely that you will be returned.

The Co-operative herewith gives warning that no retaliatory action can, or will, be taken in the event that you are 'lost to law'. You enter Refuge at your own risk.

Caroline Luranski
....

I have read the above statement, and fully understand it. I accept full responsibility for my own actions, and the actions of others, whilst in the Pliax System.

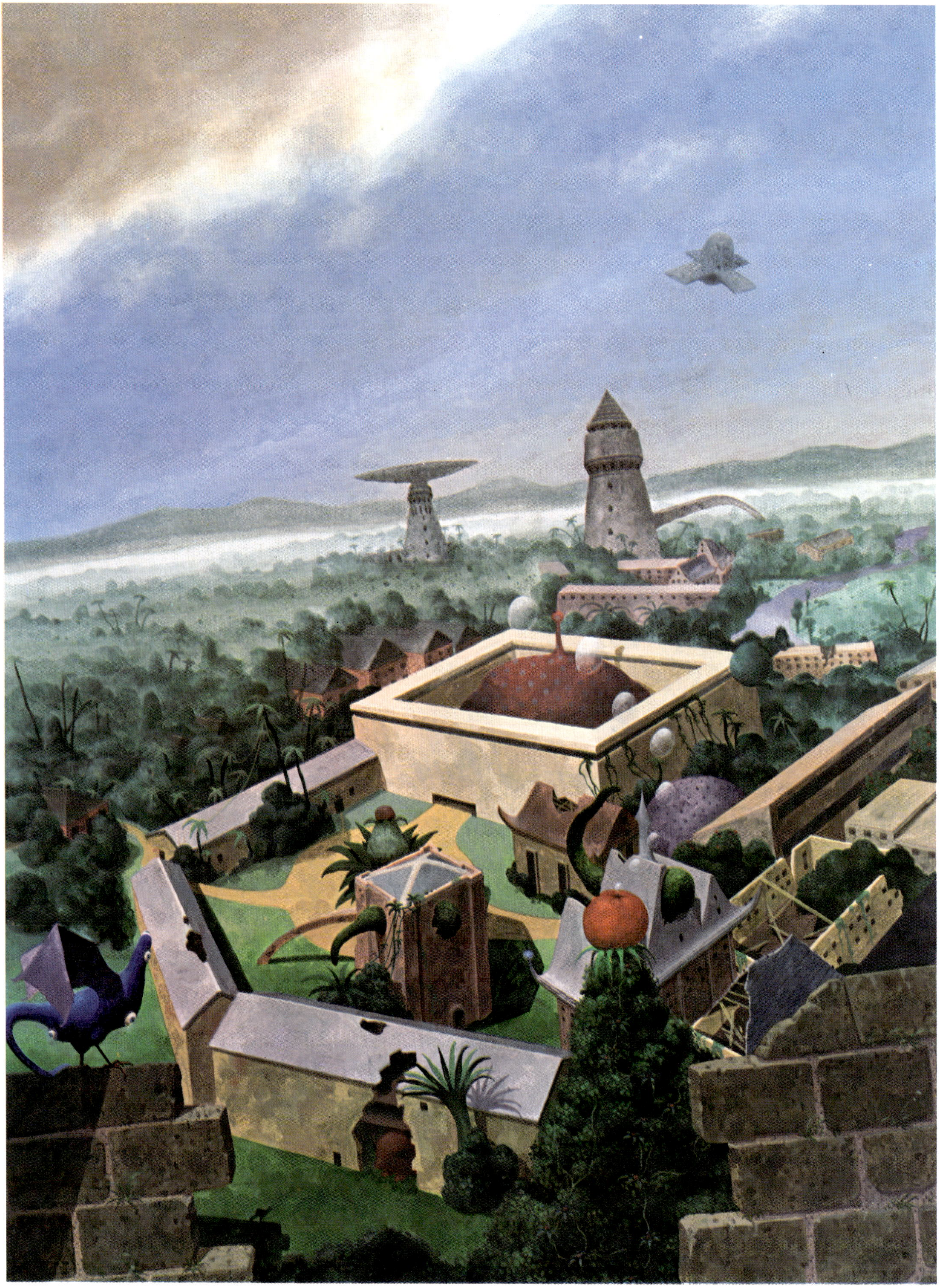

EXTRACT FROM: DUNN'S COSMIC GAZETTEER

When did the Great Migration occur? Even the Chikstha have forgotten. They speak of the Walking Fires, and the Ancient; they remember, in their legends, the Voice of the Deep, and they tell epic stories of the Rising in Glory to the other inhabitable world in their planetary system. But the date of that Rising in Glory, the year of the migration away from the world on which they had evolved, is something they have long since ceased to remember. From the evidence of the vast, artificial world they built in orbit about Pliax II, that migration occurred no more recently than a quarter of a million years in their past. But who, then, builds the strange cities on the surface of the world, buildings and structures that can be seen to be falling into decay all across the planetary surface? Those few representatives of other species permitted to tread the sacred soil of Pliax II could not possibly have the time to build such sprawling towns and communes, and the Chikstha themselves never return to the actual soil of their homeworld. It is the planet itself that produces the strange phenomena below, echoing, perhaps remembering, the time when its woodlands and valleys were filled with the chattering life of an intelligent species.

The Chikstha Sacred Caste, the priests and militia that control the orbiting city of Refuge, do not allow photographs to be taken of the Sacred World; thus we have only a series of paintings, made by those who have walked upon its jungle-covered surface, from which to get an idea of how the world looks from the ground (orbital photographs are most unsatisfactory): vast plantlife, strange, warped creatures, a sense of stillness disguising a fauna that is dangerous and distinctly unfriendly. Everywhere the planet has produced the structures known, to the Chikstha, as 'spirit-homes', the places, or so they believe, where the Singers of the Ancient reside, until wind and weather cause the structures to crumble and return to the Deep.

To ask a priest on Refuge the simple question, "What drove your people from the world below?" is to be answered in riddles. On Refuge it is claimed that the deepest secrets of the mysterious planet are known, but that to speak them would be to bring down the orbiting city, and destroy the Nine Rituals. No human has ever witnessed the Nine Rituals, but in their complex prayers, invocations and movements lie hidden the facts and race memories of what occurred, perhaps half a million years before, to make a race evacuate one world for another. It is unlikely that mankind will ever share that secret.

The building of Refuge was undertaken during the Chiksthan Third Cycle of the Shield, which gives an approximate date for the Migration, and took two thousand years. At that time, it is said, the space around Pliax II was filled with the frozen corpses of Chikstha who had opted to die rather than move to the new world of Pliax VI. Over the centuries, as their orbits decayed, the corpses plunged back to the earth, burning up briefly and scattering their ashes to the wind. When the last had gone, the building of Refuge ceased, leaving more than thirty percent of its immense structure incomplete. Millions of Chikstha live on the platform, among its towering web-blocks and temples. The city is so vast that it casts a shadow on the world below, and can be seen from the surface even by day. To produce the metal for the artificial world an entire world, Pliax V, was stripped and gutted.

It was to the world Pliax VI, however, that the majority of those Chiksthan family groups opting for survival migrated. Pliax VI is practically identical to Pliax II in size, gravity, and surface conditions, a total sister-world that, whilst covered with vegetation, was devoid of animal life. It had been colonized during both previous Cycles, but the colonies disbanded, and all trace of the Chiksthan presence returned to the Deep. Now the Chikstha of the Third Cycle regarded Pliax VI as a new paradise. They arachnoformed it to the extent necessary. Once they could live upon the world in total harmony, and without fear, they began to build. The cities they built were much like Refuge . . . towering structures where the normal concepts of vertical and horizontal were ignored. Although much influenced by gravity, the Chikstha web-minds are attuned not only to the downward pull of the earth, but to the outward throw of centrifugal force. Their cities run in three dimensions and a Chikstha thinks nothing of living out its existence along a sloping web-strand reaching a kilometre or more into the heavens. It makes visiting the Chikstha particularly harrowing for humankind, who enjoy the feeling of 'feet firmly planted on the ground'. The aliens are as comfortable 'shaking in the wind with a web below their claws'.

Human tourism is encouraged on the arachnoid world of Pliax VI, and indeed to Refuge itself. The Chikstha have a great fear of religious entities entering their own religious domains, and the small tourist contingent allowed down to the Sacred World at any one time has first been thoroughly vetted for any residual 'holy entity'; whatever it is exists on the now deserted world, whatever phenomenon lurks behind the Ancient and the Walking Fires, it is certainly vulnerable. You may ask, why do the Chikstha allow tourism at all? The answer is certainly that they allow it reluctantly, but prefer to monitor alien visits to their world than to have illegal and destructive visits incognito, as happened extensively before they established the Refuge Run.

On Pliax VI, on the world now totally covered by Chiksthan cities, which even extend out across the oceans, here the human tourist may enjoy a brief, and possibly frightening holiday. Food suitable for human consumption is available, although the filtered food, accumulated in the great funnels that cover every building, is digestible and non-toxic if eaten raw.

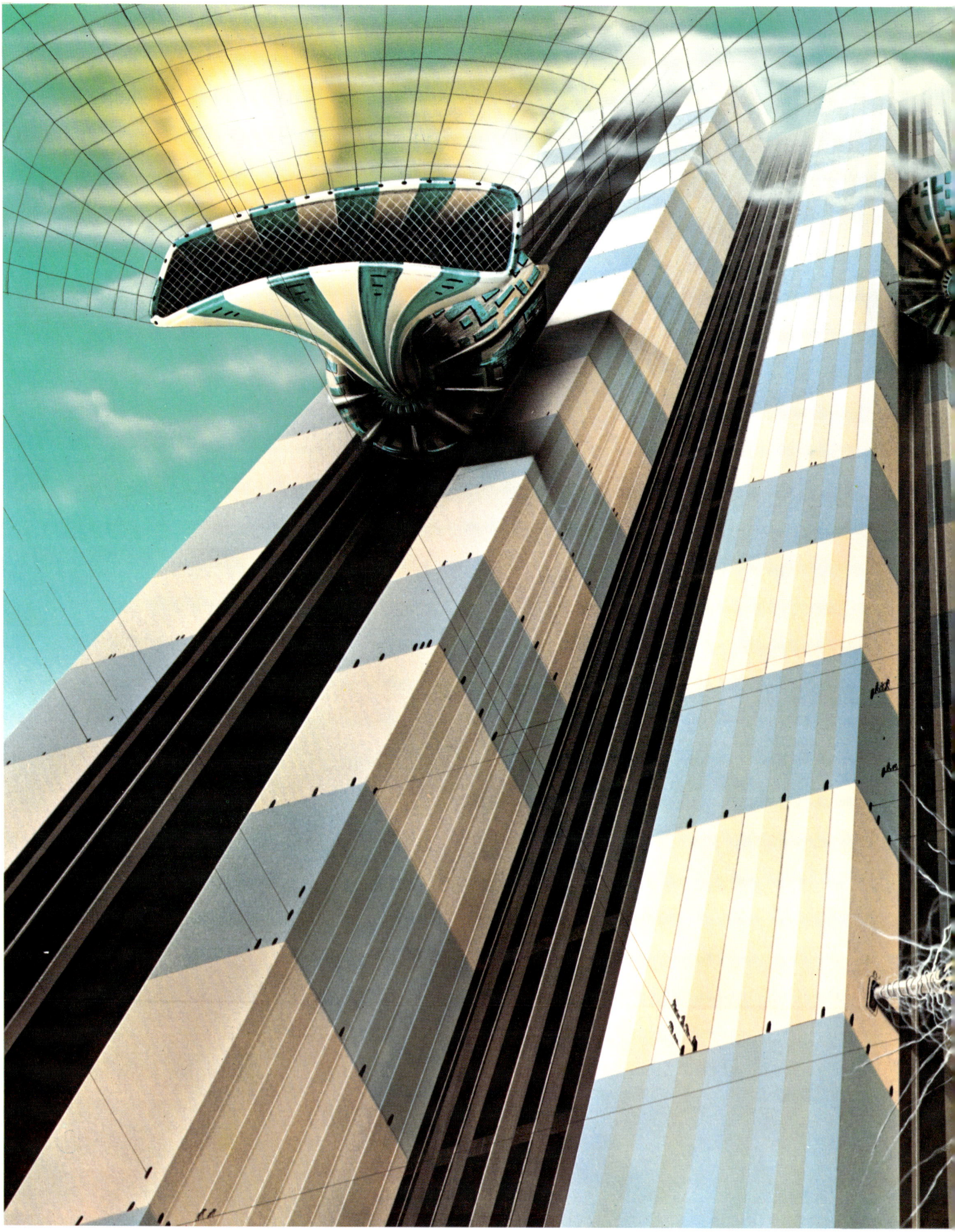

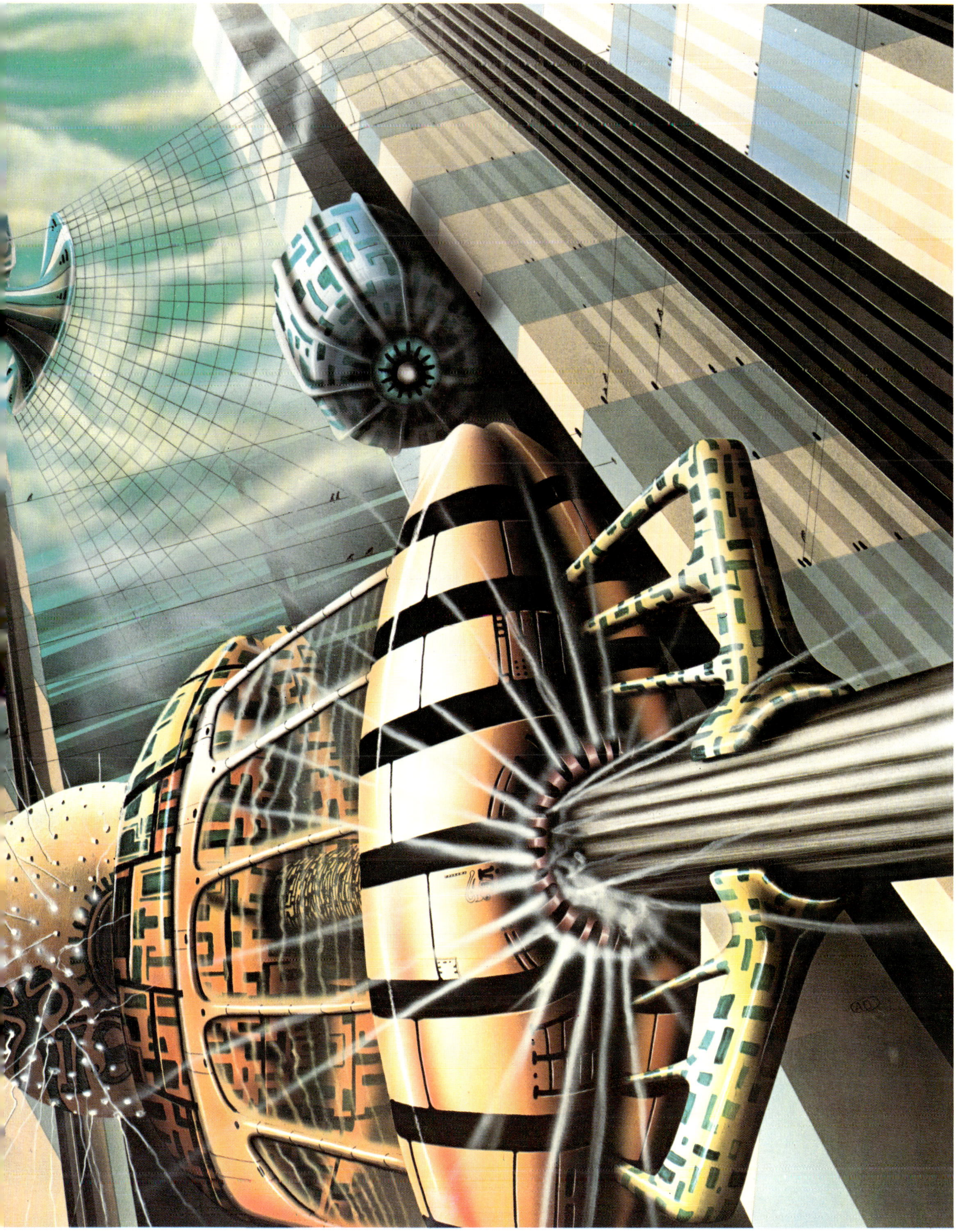

PAN GALACTIC
STARTOUR DISPLAY TICKET

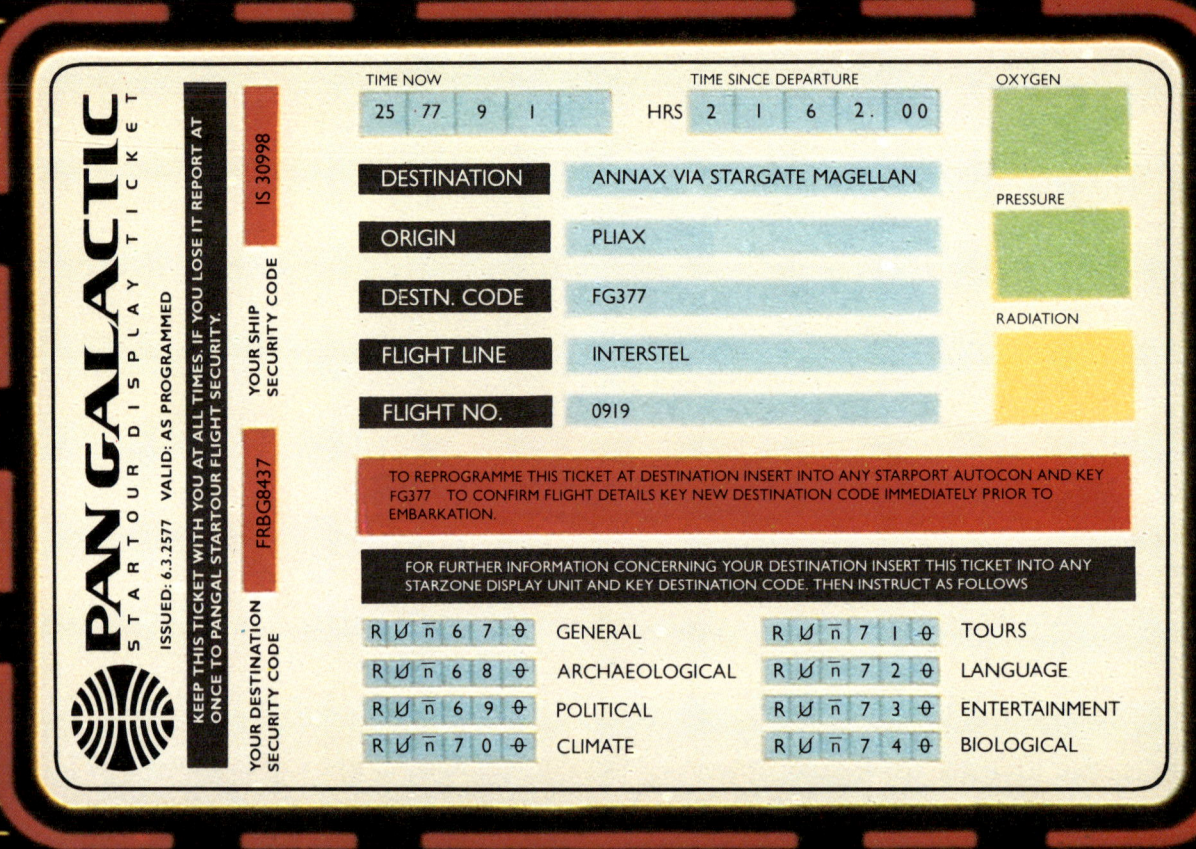

ISSUED: 6.3.2577   VALID: AS PROGRAMMED

KEEP THIS TICKET WITH YOU AT ALL TIMES. IF YOU LOSE IT REPORT AT ONCE TO PANGAL STARTOUR FLIGHT SECURITY.

YOUR SHIP SECURITY CODE: IS 30998

YOUR DESTINATION SECURITY CODE: FRBG8437

TIME NOW	25 · 77 · 9 · 1
TIME SINCE DEPARTURE	HRS 2 1 6 2.00
DESTINATION	ANNAX VIA STARGATE MAGELLAN
ORIGIN	PLIAX
DESTN. CODE	FG377
FLIGHT LINE	INTERSTEL
FLIGHT NO.	0919

OXYGEN
PRESSURE
RADIATION

TO REPROGRAMME THIS TICKET AT DESTINATION INSERT INTO ANY STARPORT AUTOCON AND KEY FG377 TO CONFIRM FLIGHT DETAILS KEY NEW DESTINATION CODE IMMEDIATELY PRIOR TO EMBARKATION.

FOR FURTHER INFORMATION CONCERNING YOUR DESTINATION INSERT THIS TICKET INTO ANY STARZONE DISPLAY UNIT AND KEY DESTINATION CODE. THEN INSTRUCT AS FOLLOWS

RØn̄670	GENERAL	RØn̄710	TOURS
RØn̄680	ARCHAEOLOGICAL	RØn̄720	LANGUAGE
RØn̄690	POLITICAL	RØn̄730	ENTERTAINMENT
RØn̄700	CLIMATE	RØn̄740	BIOLOGICAL

MAGELLAN · STARG

STARGATE MAGELLAN
LOCATION: 47 LIGHT YEARS FROM PLIAX,
BEARING GALACTIC NNW/E. DISTORTION
DISCOVERED IN 2211, DETECTED BY
PROBESHIP DURING ROUTINE
GRAVITATIONAL SCAN. RECONSTRUCTION
OF ALIEN REMAINS COMMENCED 2279,
COMPLETED 2293. INSTRUMENTAL IN
HUMAN EXPANSION TO LESSER MAGELLANIC
CLOUD, BUT LARGELY INACTIVE SINCE
THE END OF AURORA-MAGELLAN WAR OF
INDEPENDENCE IN 2453. NEAREST
INHABITED SYSTEM AT EXIT POINT-ANNAX
WHOSE FOURTH PLANET IS THE HOME OF
THE PRISMOIDS, OR CRYSTAL BEINGS.

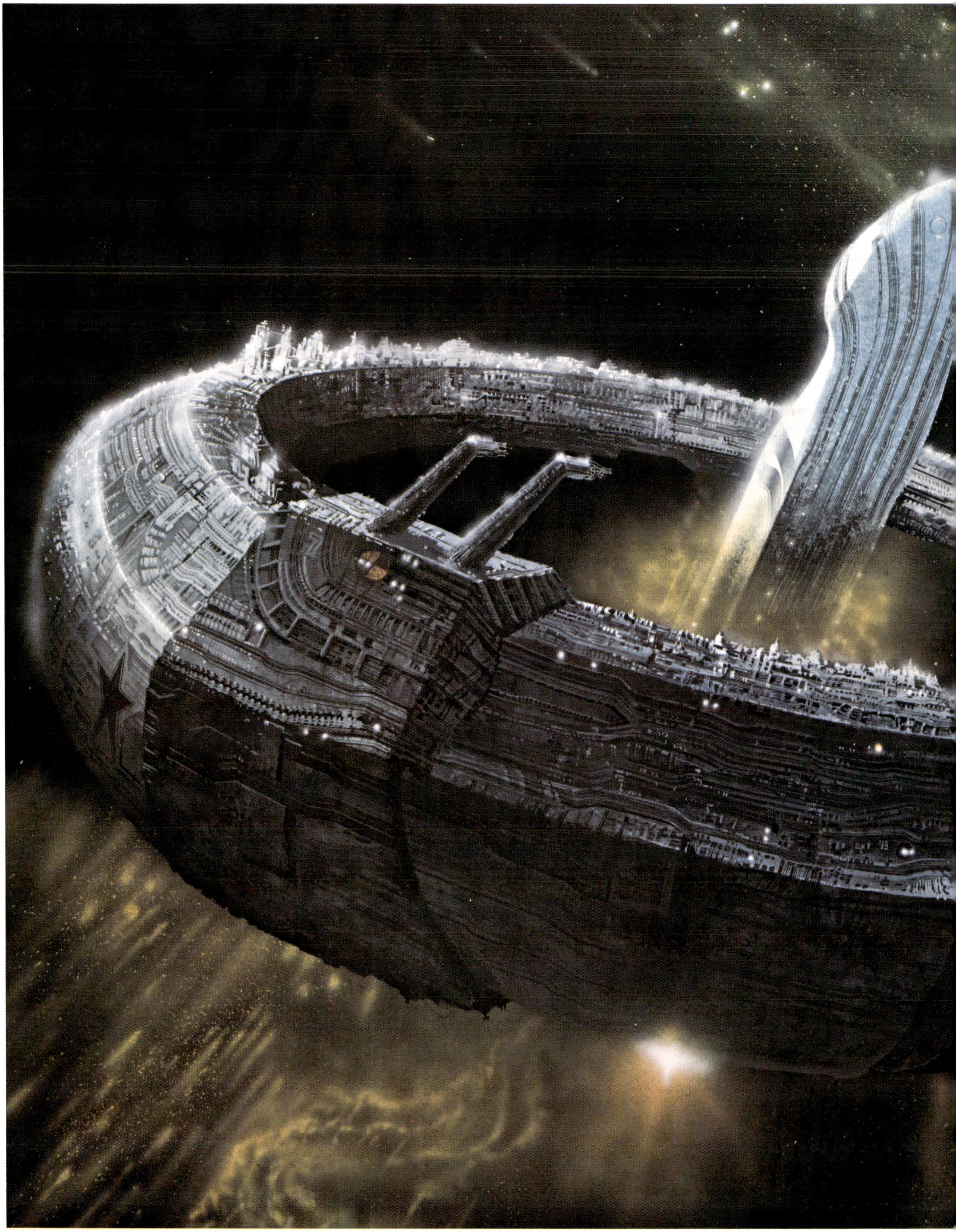

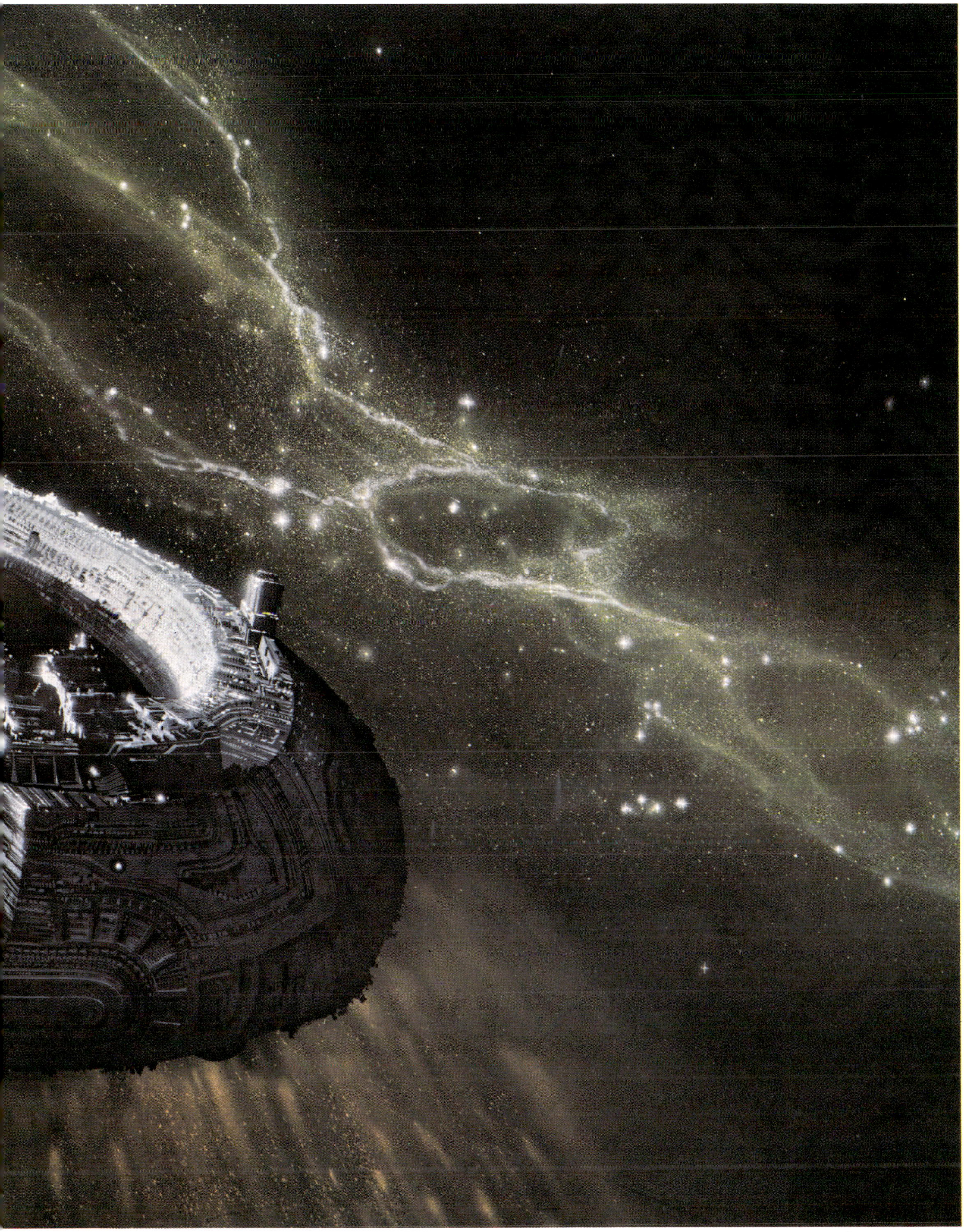

Personal diary Lelo. 3rd September 2577: A very short flight has brought us to Stargate Magellan. Goodbye Chikstha. Goodbye nightmares. Refuge was a real treat, but I hardly saw a single human tourist who wasn't white with fear, apprehensive about the arachnoids and what they might suddenly do. Most of them have had an hour of revID deprogramming but I've decided to do without; if I'm going to write a book about this trip I want my nightmares raw and real. Interstel will take us through the 'Eye' to the interZonal space beyond, where the Aurora-Magellan Federation begins. There we'll be picked up by a new starship and escorted (some say almost at gunpoint) from place to place. You will enjoy, you **will** enjoy. I'm getting restless to see Tombworld, but Caroline has been looking forward to this diplomatic part of the trip, and I think that at last she's getting happy. Stargate Magellan is really primitive. It looks spectacular, of course, an immense ringed city with its central area of blazing light, which is the Eye. I suppose it's a conventional gravity well, held in harness, but views seem to differ. I was talking to an Iirjiragraat and it, and all its kind, have always been taught that the sinks, or holes in space, were made by ancient creatures (the Chikstha?) and Man has discovered several of them and re-exploited them. In any event, the city is more shell than corpse, and only a small section is actually used. It's pieced together from just about anything that's come its way, bits of rocket ship, liner, junk that has drifted through the Eye from the other end. It's in the middle of nowhere, of course, forty light years from Pliax. The cloud of our destination, the Lesser Magellanic, is a blur in the all-encompassing heavens. You get an idea of just how far this Stargate reaches. Behind, viewed from the high lounges of the liner, the Galaxy is quite a blaze of light. There's a good depth of stars between us and the space beyond. We have just a short wait in the Magellanic Eye Hotel, which is probably just as well. Security restrictions have confined us to a tiny lobby-like area; you can buy models of the Stargate, and books, and exotic foods, but there's only one observation lounge, and it's always packed to capacity. But excitement grows. It's going to be a novel way to travel. **End entry.**

EXTRACT FROM: THE HAUNTED EYE: MYTHS AND LEGENDS OF THE STARGATES

Stargates are distortions in space; they are also distortions in time, a fact that is often overlooked. It is also far too easy to think of a Stargate as a single 'hole' from one part of the Galaxy to another. Whilst there is certainly a main bore, or Eye, most Stargates have peripheral connections with other 'edge-sinks'; small, difficult to find, leading to unknown destinations, these sinks have nevertheless been the cause (and eventually the explanation) of a number of the early mysterious disappearances associated with Stargates.

But Stargate Trax is associated with one of the most celebrated vanishing tricks of any century. To this day it has not been satisfactorily explained.

On Christmas Eve, 2286, only twenty years after the first human Stargate city had been built on the decaying alien remnants, a small passenger liner piloted by Captain Kiril Taubman approached the Trax Gate from Earth. It was part of the Interstel line, a routine visitor to the Gate. Its passengers were dignitaries and their families from the Unified Church of Sol, on their way to the Sacred World of Mecca, to the Unified Faith Conference.

The ship was the IS *Ambassador*, and she moored at berth 27 for three hours while she was re-provisioned and boarded by a customs crew and engineering inspectors. The reports of these two groups show that a) there was no cargo on board that in any way could have been responsible for the events that would subsequently occur, and b) that the TSMD drive was in top condition, and had only recently been overhauled.

At 1530 hours Stargate Time (based on a 24 hour clock) the *Ambassador* slipped from her holding and negotiated her way to E-approach run 15. Stargate Trax has thirty different approaches to the central Eye. On this occasion fourteen were occupied by larger ships. Approach run 15 was a northerly spiral-magnetic runway. It was mainly used for cargo ships of the unmanned variety.

IS *Ambassador* entered the radius at a velocity of 100 kph, and at 1546 hours. A pre-signal had been sent through to Stargate Tethys, the opposing Eye. In the monitoring console, above the approach way, two men waited for the signal capsule to pass back from the Tethys Gate, along signal route 23. The normal wait-time for such acknowledgement of safe arrival is ten minutes. At 1610 hours the alarm was raised, and Stargate Control alerted. All ships were held back from their approach runs. Signal route 14 was used to despatch a query to Tethys Gate. Almost immediately a signal was received, in response to the arrival zone not being occupied, declaring "IS *Ambassador* has not arrived". Five minutes later an acknowledgement to the question signal was received. "Occupation Zone for *Ambassador* showed momentary reverse charge on anti-quark vortex. No *Ambassador*. Will keep zone clear until advised otherwise. Have we lost a ship?"

Lost it certainly was. And yet not lost. Certainly as far as the Stargate was concerned the *Ambassador* was a ship that had vanished without a trace, and inexplicably. It was logged as such, and the log was left undisturbed for twenty years. A thorough search of all known peripheral 'edge sinks' failed to show any sign of the *Ambassador*. The disaster was concealed from the general public, and the disappearance of the passengers explained by 'ship crash'.

But the story of the *Ambassador* does not end there; twenty years later the file was re-opened, for the *Ambassador* became, overnight, the most celebrated mystery of the spaceways.

On June 15 2306, Stargate Trax had only a single Pan-Gal cruiser in dock, waiting for an incoming passenger ship to clear the Eye. An advance signal was received at 0936 hours. At 0938 the Eye began to radiate purple light, and a glowing, multi-coloured aura formed about its tiny radius, at approximately one thousand metres diameter. The aura actually touched the eastern in-face of the city, but no physical effects were experienced. The emission of colour was captured on fine grain film, but no particle emission was detected, although neutrino flux, monitored routinely, shows three sharp peaks in the ten seconds following the first appearance of the aura.

The Stargate Control had never experienced any such phenomenon before. A signal capsule was instantly dispatched to Stargate Tethys in response to advance signal 046BB to hold their ship in its approach run. Unmanned drone ships entered the aura, and as they did so, the colour vanished; an intense, purplish hue remained about the radius of the Eye.

As a fascinated Gate crew watched so the nose shield of a ship appeared, edging its way slowly into Gate space. At first the crew thought this

Personal diary Caroline. 3rd September 2577: We've disembarked from the **Starfriend** in order to take an Interstel ship through the Stargate to the Lesser Magellanic Cloud, and probably the most exciting part of the trip. There's a feeling among all the tour members that we've now ceased simply to be sightseers and have become both pioneers and ambassadors rolled into one. Quite a few newsfax and holovid people have been around doing interviews, asking people how they are feeling on the eve of this momentous trip, and so on and on. It's sickening to watch some of the really unbearable individuals puffing themselves up and mouthing platitudes right back at the reporters. Mind, my own interview was quite disastrous. I thought I'd said considered, sensible things, but on the playback I looked a vapid, ungainly fool. (Leio says I'm oversensitive.) Still, it **is** very exciting. Leio has been reading up on Stargates, and specifically about the things which can go wrong when you go through them. He seems to take a special delight in mentioning these casually in conversation with people he knows to be nervous about interstellar flight — and then pretending to be flustered and apologetic. I wouldn't mind if I didn't happen to be jumpy about it! **End entry.**

Agent Luranski: Memory Implant. 3rd September 2577: This is it, then. I'm not lying when I tell my wrist diary I'm nervous (even though I can't say why). I've managed almost to put the mission out of mind since leaving the Solar System, which is just as well as I'm now certain we are under surveillance, and I would surely have given myself away by now had I not been able to act naturally. The question this raises is: why are they watching us? Is it just precautionary? I suppose this would be natural enough after more than a century of mutual suspicion (and, given the facts, would be perfectly justified). Or is it that they have something to hide? I'm keeping an open mind. **End report.**

---

was the Tethys ship coming through despite the warning, but it soon became apparent that the ship was too small for that vessel. And it wasn't emerging smoothly. Rather, it seemed to nudge a few hundred yards forward, and then pull back. There were strange symbols on its side, and shapes moving at the tiny, circular portals.

The ship glowed with purple light. It emerged two hundred metres, and the name on its side became clear. Not an alien script, but terrestrial lettering reversed as if in a mirror: the IS *Ambassador*.

The Gate crew attempted to make contact, both EM and phase-shift, with the ship's crew, but heard only a high pitched burbling shriek. Two seconds of this was recorded. Slowed down it is a human voice speaking in reverse. The voice is that of Captain Taubman. It is a repeated and panic stricken cry for help. It makes reference to 'the wheels'. "The wheels, all around. What the hell are they? Hello Stargate Control, can you see them?"

As unexpectedly as it had emerged, it then pulled back into the Eye. The aura vanished.

The *Ambassador* has emerged on two further occasions: in 2526 and 2547. On each occasion the pattern of emergence, and the burst of message, are the same. Wherever she is, the *Ambassador* is stuck in space and stuck in time. One day, perhaps, the fault will be diagnosed, and she will be brought back into the real Universe.

The same is unlikely to be said for the crew and passengers of the SIS *Andromeda*, a Sirian Spacelines colony ship that was granted access rights to Stargate Jarana on July 1st 2516. The *Andromeda* was a converted military cruiser, nose to stern nearly four thousand metres long. It had a Gate transit time of ten seconds, which is dangerously close to the limit of safety, since it is in critical phase-split for nearly a full second. Larger ships than the *Andromeda* have safely traversed the Gates, however, and for the answer to the particular mystery she poses one must look elsewhere.

The *Andromeda*, being an older ship, was manned by a hundred men and women. On this occasion she had a mere fifty passengers on board, not colonists but holiday-makers rescued from stand-by by the co-operative Captain of the vessel.

The Sirian ship waited for four hours for its access chance to the Gate; the gate was busy at this time, and after re-provisioning, the liner moved off into a line of eleven ships waiting for transit through the Central Eye. She was preceded by a giant Pan-Galactic cargo ship, which arrived safely at its destination. The *Andromeda* appeared to pass Stargate Jarana without a hitch. But when she arrived at Stargate Meriax she did not acknowledge the signal from the gate crew, but continued to drift slowly beyond the arrival bays.

Four tugs fled to the giant ship and were able to stop its impact with the side of the torus of the city. An investigating team immediately boarded the *Andromeda* and reported it to be empty. The crew and the passengers had vanished totally. All controls were operative. Two dogs lay unconscious in their kennels. A card table was covered with cards dropped in disarray, as if in the middle of a game. On a window a child had been drawing the shape of a Pan-Galactic cruiser. The shape was unfinished. Next to the seat where the child had been sitting, part of the fabric of a seat is torn, and the torn fragment located several metres away. A reconstruction suggests that the seat's occupant tried frantically to hold on, but whatever force was tugging at him or her was too great. A gruesome discovery was made by the second team that came aboard to investigate. At the fore of the main lounge a forty foot square area of ceiling was found to be covered with a thin layer of hornified human skin; the torn piece of fabric lay below this smear.

Were the occupants of the lounge sucked out into another Universe through that part of the ship, passing across the hull without disturbing the hull's molecular structure? We are unlikely ever to know. The flight recorder gives no indication of anything amiss, calm voices speaking routine instructions. At the moment of vanishing no-one was talking; the body monitors on the ship in the Captain's seat show that her body ceased to register on the temperature and neural activity controls at 1056.23.07; the co-pilot ceased to register at 1056.23.09. They vanished soundlessly.

Unlike the *Ambassador*, which most probably has fallen victim to a time-vortex, the fate of the *Andromeda* cannot be explained by physical interference. Centuries ago, during the Age of Sailing Ships, the crew and passengers of a clipper known as the *Marie Celeste* vanished without trace. It took two hundred years before the grisly solution to that mystery was found. It is likely to take a lot longer to solve the mystery of the SIS *Andromeda*.

GALACTIC CO-OPERAT

PASSENGER ROUTES

- STARPOOL
- BLEGARD
- PERIHELION
- GREYROCKS
- Pan-Gal connection to AURORA-MAGELLAN
- STARGATE (CIRAX)
- FIVE WORLDS
- RATNER'S PLANET
- XAVIER'S WORLD
- TOMBWORLD
- NEW TITAN
- BLISTER
- NEW BRAZIL
- SIRIUS
- TAU CETI BRIDGE
- LEO D'OR XX
- TERMINUS
- INDUS SYSTEM
- SWINGAROUND
- VOORENEN VII
- REUNION
- OBELISK
- LIEBENHOF'S WORLD
- STARHAVEN
- PYRRUS
- UTOPIA
- NOSFERATU
- SILVERSEAS
- DESTINATION
- TANNISON'S ROCK
- QUETZALCOATL
- OSTER'S FALL
- APHRODITE

Legend:
- TRANSGALACTIC
- PAN-GALACTIC
- INTERSUN HAULAGE
- LAKER SPACE
- INTERSTEL
- SIRIAN INTERWORLDS SPACELINES

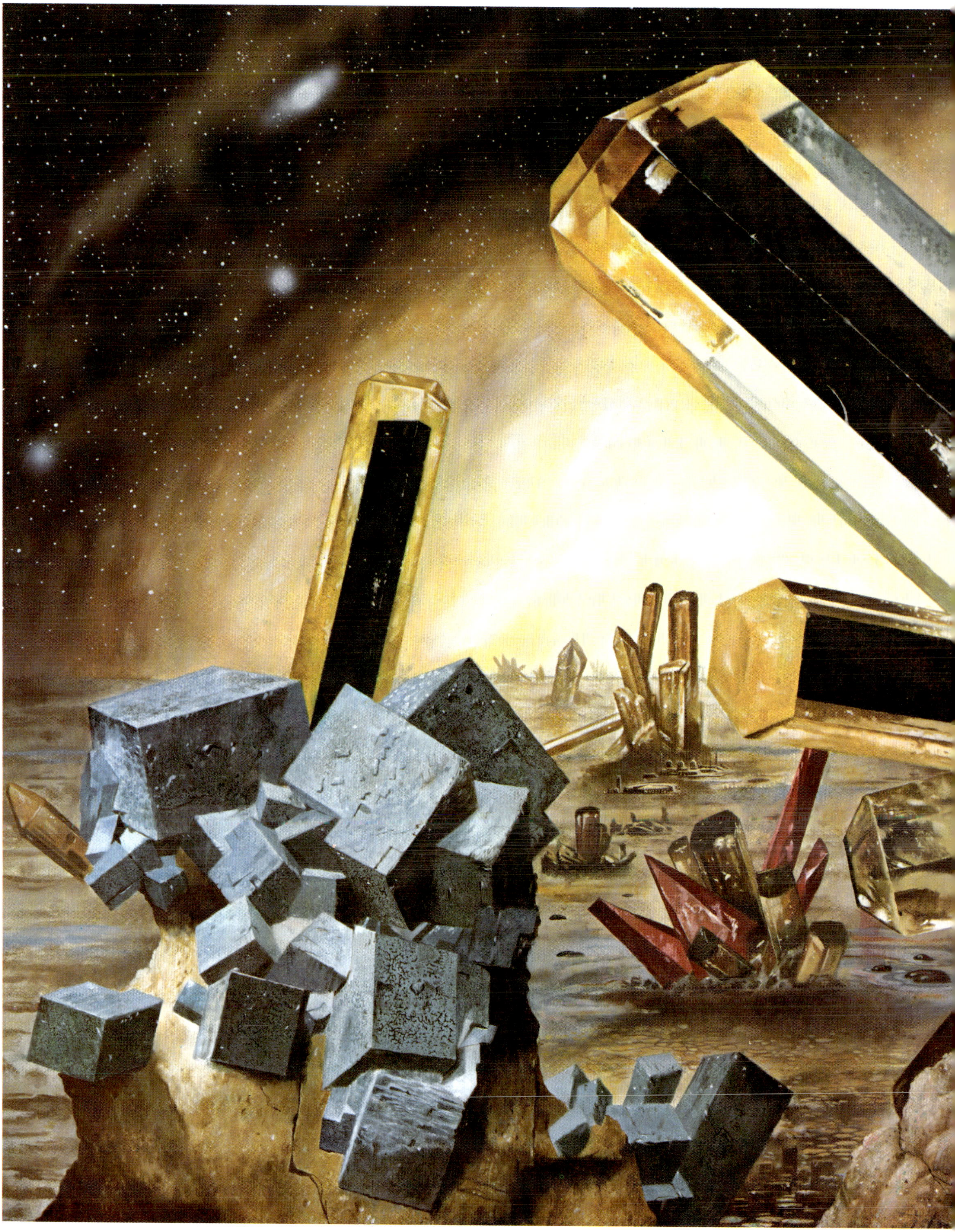

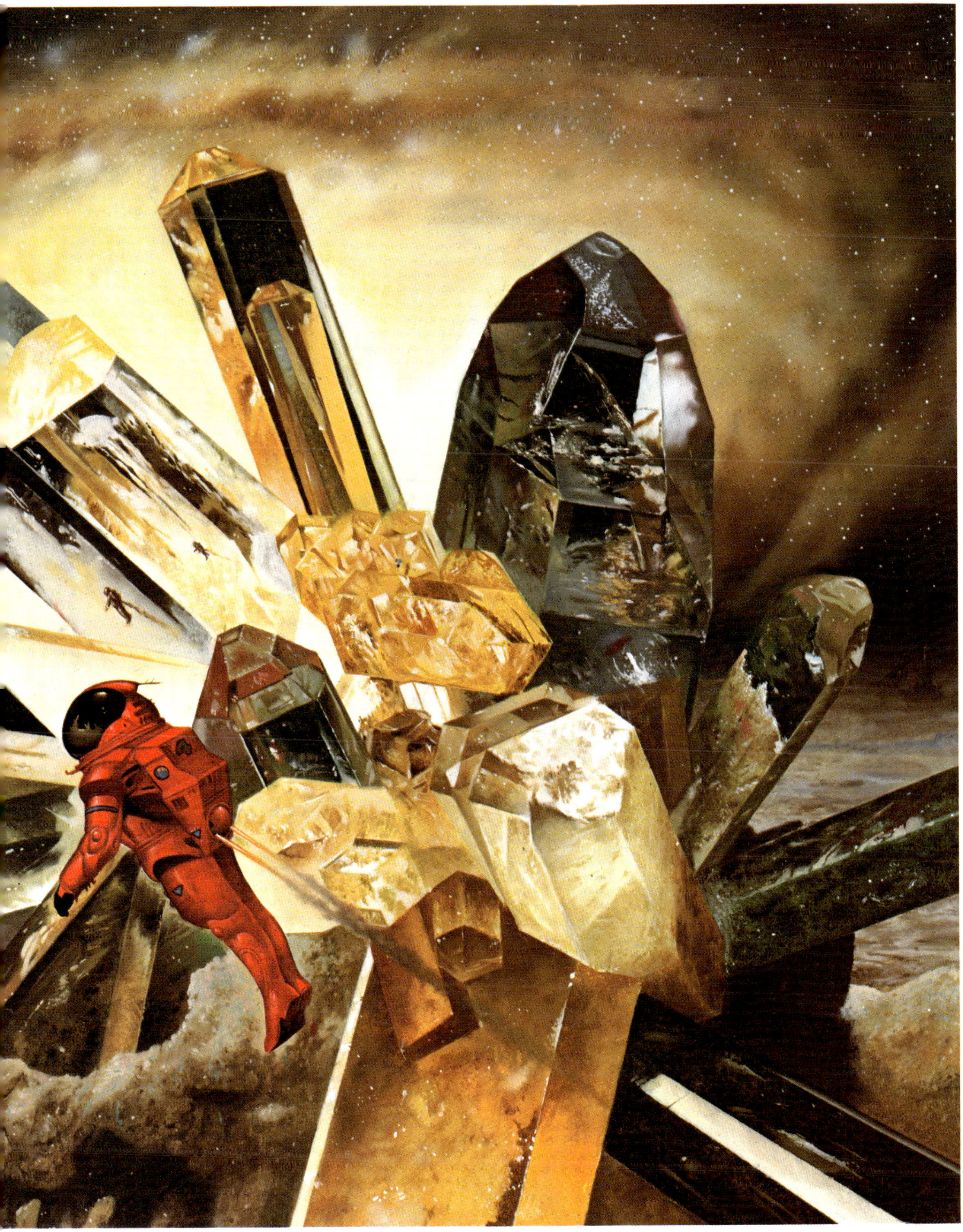

Personal diary Lelo. 12th September 2577: Aurora-Magellan. The name still sends a bit of a shiver through me. I feel like a stranger in a strange land. You can't help remembering the stories of atrocities, the destruction of planets, the pictures of the A-M star fighters, all black-faced and heartless automatons. The ship that took us out of the hands of Interstel looked sinister, flesh-coloured and organic, all ribbed, and bristling with spikes and tiny, dark windows. It was a warship, of course, converted for passenger use. Guards everywhere, dark-uniformed men. Red lights, security zones, a sense of hush, of discomfort. Oh, there are smiles and greetings, and pleasantries and free souvenirs, but it's an uncomfortable place, on their ships, on their worlds. Caroline is very quiet. She enjoyed Refuge, but she looks drawn now, not sleeping well; she's got that distant, detached air that always sparks an argument between us. She flares up at the slightest thing, any reason at all, and we spend long hours in silence, only making up with a smile, a touch, a shrug. I can't blame her. All the tourists are tense. The Galaxy is awe-inspiring. We can't see it full face, but what a sight! A great, faint spiral wheel above us, again smaller than I'd expected, but I'm getting used to having spent my life over-estimating the scale of the Universe. The Federation have treated us to a tour of one of their strangest worlds, and strangest life-forms, the crystalline beings they call Prismoids. The world is Annax IV, uncolonised of course, but with several domed installations built upon it. The landscape glitters like coloured frost. Pinnacles and growths of crystal sprouting everywhere, and when you walk it cracks and crunches underfoot, and starfish-like Prismoids flex and twist and jump metres across the planet's surface. If you look hard you can see the organic centres to the big, parent crystals. They live for thousands of years without moving, just absorbing minerals and sunlight, and budding their shiny young. Two surface trips and my appetite was sated, but they've booked us in the Annax System for another ten days.
End entry.

EXTRACT FROM: THE HANDBOOK OF INTELLIGENT LIFE, 2570 edition

PRISMOIDS The Prismoids of Annax IV are the most enigmatic of known intelligent life – if, indeed, they can properly be said to be either intelligent or alive. Debate on these questions has raged ever since Annax was discovered in 2264. Early explorers did not associate the motile "starfish" with the seemingly inorganic outcroppings; it was not until Erica Goldberg and Kwame van Sproat completed their exhaustive study of the crystals in 2311 that it was definitively established that the starfish were the offsrping of the giant Prismoids (as Goldberg named them).

The life-cycle is slow, sometimes occupying hundreds (or perhaps even thousands) of years. Inside the mature Prismoid slow chemical changes cause buds to appear on many of their facets. After a period of anything between six months and five years the buds are shaken loose (the planet's residual seismic activity is sufficient to accomplish this) and become starfish.

The starfish vary in size between about 15 and 50 centimetres across, and have been observed with any number of limbs between 3 and 14. They have an organic core, with contractile tissues which enable them to bend and move the crystal exoskeleton. Hermaphroditic but not self-fertilizing, they hump their way slowly across the planet in search of a mate – a process which may take hundreds of years as, lacking sensory apparatus, they rely on chance meetings, and for successful mating must find another starfish with matching limbs.

When two compatible starfish meet and match their limbs they begin to meld and never move again from the point of their encounter. The crystalline exterior begins to grow quite rapidly, thrusting down into the planet's soil as well as expanding upwards. The organic core begins to decay (though it leaves traces which can be seen inside even the largest adult Prismoids). They draw energy from sunlight, and extract minerals from the soil. A process of fertilization (still not understood) is presumed to have taken place during the mating and after about five years – by which time the typical Prismoid will be about three metres tall – the first buds may appear. Observation so far suggests that Prismoids continue to bud throughout their adult existence (and there is no evidence that adults ever die).

This is the generally accepted theory. An alternative view holds that starfish are the only living Prismoids, and that after mating they die. The "adult" form, according to this theory, is a protective shell in and on which the new starfish develop; its continued growth is a process of purely random crystal information. Adherents of this explanation can offer no reason for the glowing light which permeates adult Prismoids, and which most specialists take to be visible evidence of life processes.

Many attempts have been made to communicate with both adult Prismoids and starfish, without any hint of success. It is generally held that the starfish are purely instinctive – no more intelligent than human spermatozoa – and it may also be that the adults have life but no reason. The most compelling objections to this are either philosophical or religious and are too complex to treat in detail here. Boiled down to their essence they are a) that the Prismoid, having no other occupation than thought, may be supposed to have developed this ability with some efficiency; and b) as before, but with the rider that any God would evidently not have ordered it otherwise.

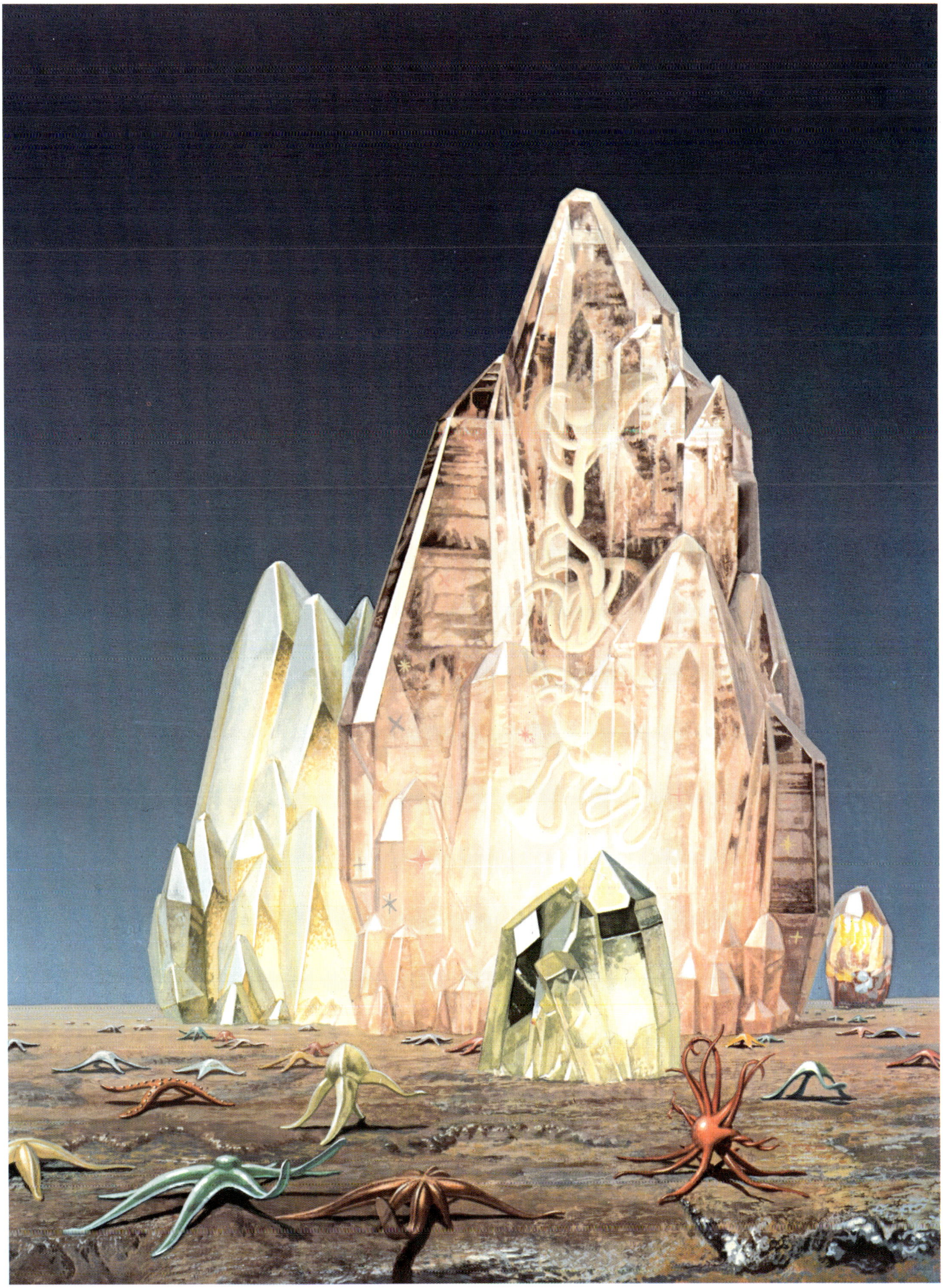

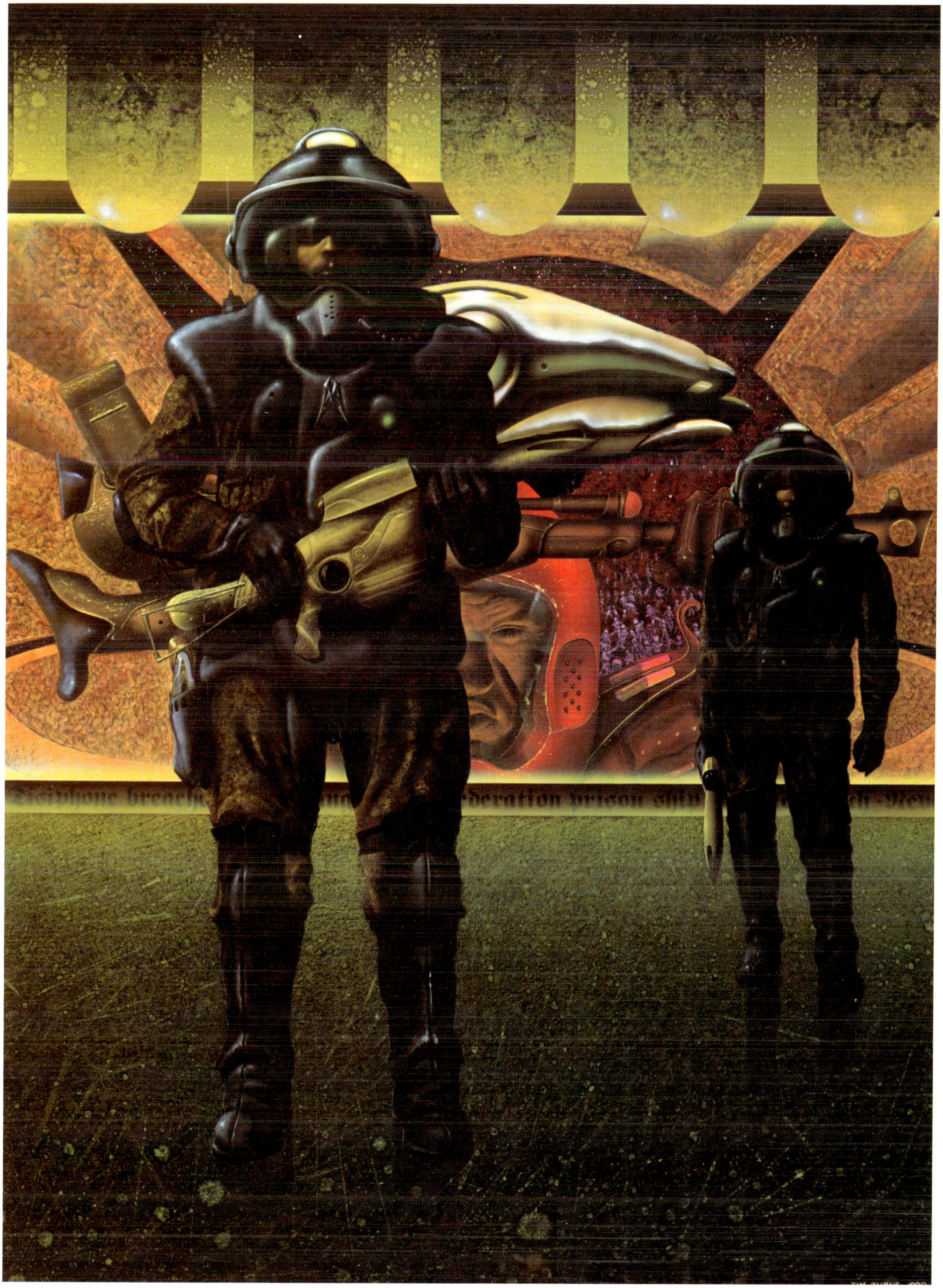

Personal diary Caroline. 14th September 2577: We've now been on the Crystal Planet – Annax IV – for five days, with nine more to go. I think our hosts misjudged, as boredom is already setting in. The Stargate passage was strange. It takes a long while to prepare, because the ship has to enter the Eye at precisely the correct angle. It slides very slowly towards the aperture, and from our cabin (which had an observation bubble) you could watch its nose shimmer and distort as it entered the Stargate. Then you go through, and for perhaps ten seconds there is an indescribable sensation of being turned inside out (and apparently in a theoretical mathematical sense you actually **are** turned inside out). Then you're through, emerging from another Stargate thousands of light years away. Leio had been reading up on something called the Stargate Transit Club, which he wanted us to join (apparently if you time it right it feels as though the whole Universe moves!) – but I was too nervous. His fault for telling me all the things that could go wrong. The Prismoids are certainly impressive, though once you've spent a day or two admiring the formations the attraction begins to pall. The Aurorans – who are amazingly courteous and friendly, not at all the dour, humourless people of old propaganda – gave us individual backpacks so that we could jet around the various crystal outcrops. Watching the strange colours glowing from within the Prismoids it's easy to imagine them as beings of tremendously powerful thought. Perhaps they've reasoned out the secrets of the universe! I wonder if they're aware of our presence, and if so what they make of it. The little starfish are fun – pick up one with five limbs and it will slowly start to attempt to mate with your hand. They spend hundreds of years, if need be, crawling around in search of a mate, so it must be a considerable disappointment when you put them down. The Aurorans' society is rather militaristic, perhaps understandably in view of their history. The main building here is dominated by a huge patriotic mural of a crucial space battle, and anniversaries of various skirmishes are celebrated religiously. I don't mind that – in fact I'm looking forward to getting to the Aurora System and to Safariworld. **End entry.**

EXTRACT FROM: THE OFFICIAL HANDBOOK

This mural, completed in 2493 by artist Kleo McHaag, depicts one of the crucial encounters in the great War of Independence: the Battle of Shiva's Rift, which took place between 13th and 24th May 2451.

Shiva's Rift is an area of space approximately 13 light years from Annax; it was of considerable strategic importance as the nearest nexus of minimum matrix distortion to Stargate Argath – the point of arrival for ships travelling to Aurora-Magellan space *via* Stargate Magellan.

On 22nd February 2451 a robot fusion weapon succeeded in disabling the defences of Stargate Argath, resulting in its capture by a Galactic Co-operative armada. Shiva's Rift became the front line of conflict in this sector: if the Co-operative fleet took control there, they would be able to mount attacks on a wide range of targets in the heart of the Federation. But the bulk of the home fleet was engaged in a major holding action at the other side of Federation space, and no ships could immediately be spared. This left the defence of Shiva's Drift in the hands of its normal garrison: six medium-size cruisers under the command of Captain Meikal Charkin.

Outnumbered eight to one, faced with opposing ships of much greater firepower, Captain Charkin and his crews nevertheless succeeded in holding off the Co-operative fleet for eleven full days, until the arrival of a battle flotilla which routed the opposition and secured Shiva's Rift for the Federation.

But the cost to Captain Charkin's command was large. Six ships were completely destroyed with no survivors, and by the end the other two were badly disabled, suffering heavy casualties. For the last 42 hours of the engagement three ships – the *Chaka* the *Myrmidon* and the *Kepler* – held out alone. The flagship, *Chaka*, was so badly damaged that it managed successfully to pose as a lifeless wreck. Two Co-operative super-cruisers drew alongside it – at which point Captain Charkin detonated all the remaining fusion weapons in the ship's armoury, instantly killing himself and the twelve surviving crew, but also annihilating the enemy ships. For this final act of heroism all thirteen crew were posthumously awarded the Star of Aurora, as were another twenty-one men from other ships. The Battle of Shiva's Rift produced more winners of our ultimate honour than any other battle of the entire war, despite the small number of Federation combatants.

As we look upon McHaag's rendition of the epic scene, we are powerfully reminded of the sacrifices our ancestors made to win our freedom. Such examples from history should inspire us in case the need ever arises to defend this hard-won independence.

AURORA TRUTH

THIS WEEK sees the arrival in our system of the first party of visitors from the Galactic Co-operative to set foot on our soil for more than 130 years. It is an historic occasion. But should we open our arms in welcome or should we view these representatives of expansionism with misgivings?

Our leaders say the time has come to put old memories behind us; that trade and cultural links with the Co-operative will benefit us all; that the cold war must be brought to an end. There can be no argument that we have lived too long in the shadow of war – *if* it can be shown that the Galactic Co-operative truly wants peace. But can we – *should* we? – ever forget the atrocities endured by our ancestors during their just fight for independence? And does the decadent Co-operative have anything worthwhile to offer us in terms of goods or culture? We answer *no* to both these questions. By all means let us live peacefully with our neighbours, but let us not allow the old, overt expansionism to be replaced with a new and insidious form of cultural expansionism coupled with attempted economic domination.

The visitors are here and cannot be turned away. There will be others. We say, let us behave hospitably towards them; let us permit them to see the benefits of the Auroran way of life. Perhaps in this way some of them will come to perceive the corruption in their own society – and perhaps then the Co-operative may begin to move slowly towards a system as honest and just as our own. Then and only then will there exist a basis for a true community of worlds. In the meantime we hope for peace – but must keep up our guard!

WARNING TO HOLDER

Before making ex-Solar journeys with this passport you should check that it is:
a) Still in force and will not expire before your redocumentation at a Solar Starport.
b) Valid for those planets you propose to land upon (orbital transit is not affected). See Stellar Federation Schedule 17.
c) Stamped with appropriate visas for those Independent Planetary Federations listed in Stellar Federation Schedule 18.
d) Is not marked, creased or blotched in any way liable to arouse suspicion that extra information is being transmitted.

Signature

CO-OPERATIVE OF MARTIAN CITY STATES
IMMIGRATION OFFICE
12.7.2574
VALID FOR 3 MONTHS S.E.T
MONS OLYMPICUS CONTROL
GAINFUL EMPLOYMENT NOT PERMITTED

EARTHPORT (AND E.S)
3·6·2577
TRANSIT + EXIT
EMIGRATION CONTROL
(CONTROLE EMIGRES)
VALID FOR TRANSIT AND SHORT DURATION STAY ON *RING CITY* AND ANY INNER SOLAR SYSTEM SHUTTLE PORT

VANDEZANDE'S WORLD (KAMELIOS)

STEEL CITY TRANSIT AND IMMIGRATION DEPARTMENT
2577.18.4

Entry permit valid 1 year C.E.T. allowing maximum stay on world of 21 days (C.E.T.) 18 days local. Vandezande's World is a fifth generation colony world operating under Federation Non-Interference Code 1V6. Employment is not permitted. This pass is valid only for supervised entry to military installations along Kreakta Rift.

AURORA-MAGELLAN FEDERATION OF INDEPENDENT WORLDS
WARNING: VIOLATION OF LOCAL LAWS MAY LEAD TO THE IMPOSITION OF HEAVY PENALTIES: FOR YOUR OWN PROTECTION FOLLOW PRECISELY THE INSTRUCTIONS ISSUED TO YOU.

EXPIRES 11-30-2577

ENTRY PERMIT VALID FOR BEARER ONLY

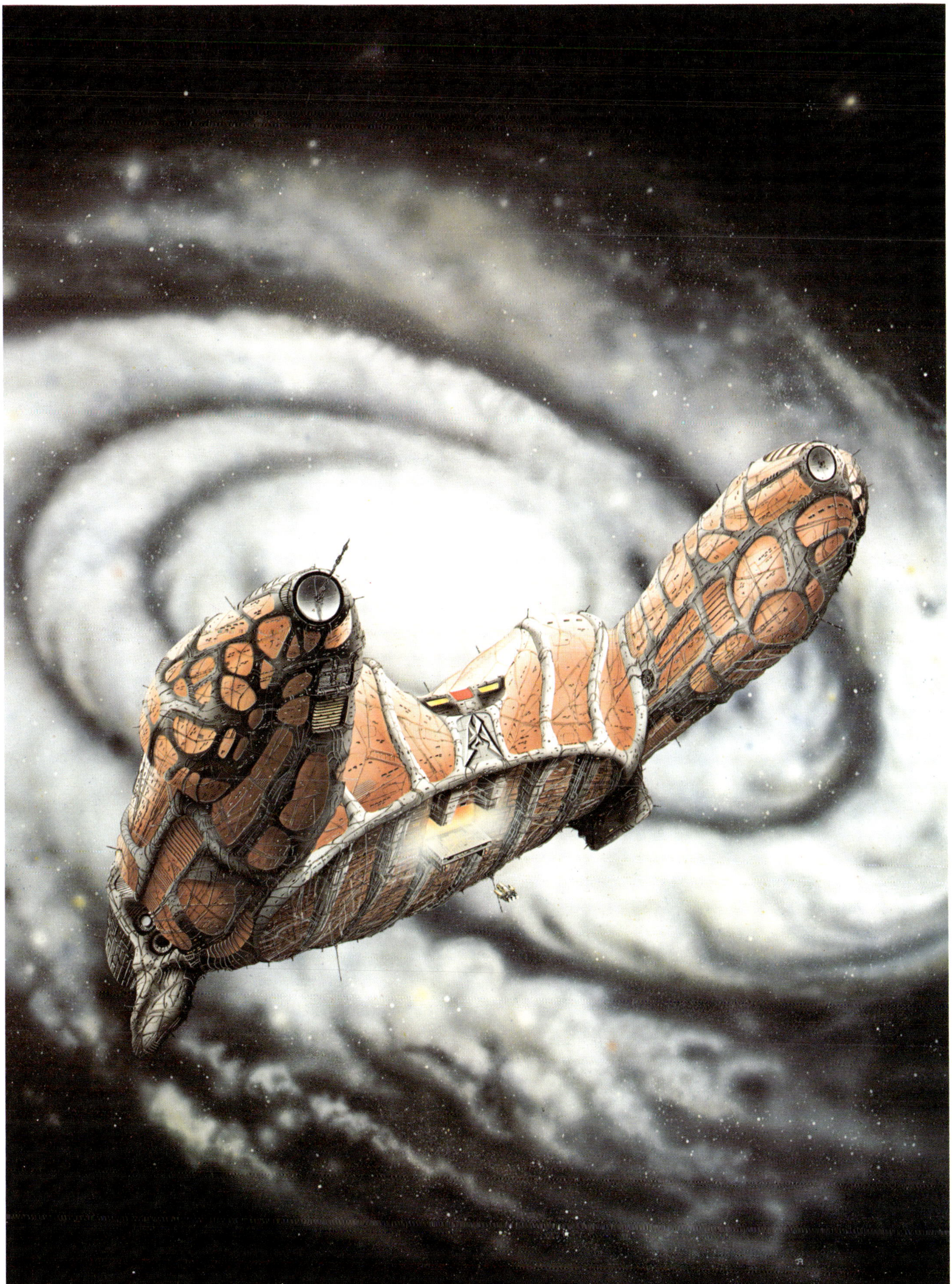

PAN GALACTIC
STARTOUR DISPLAY TICKET

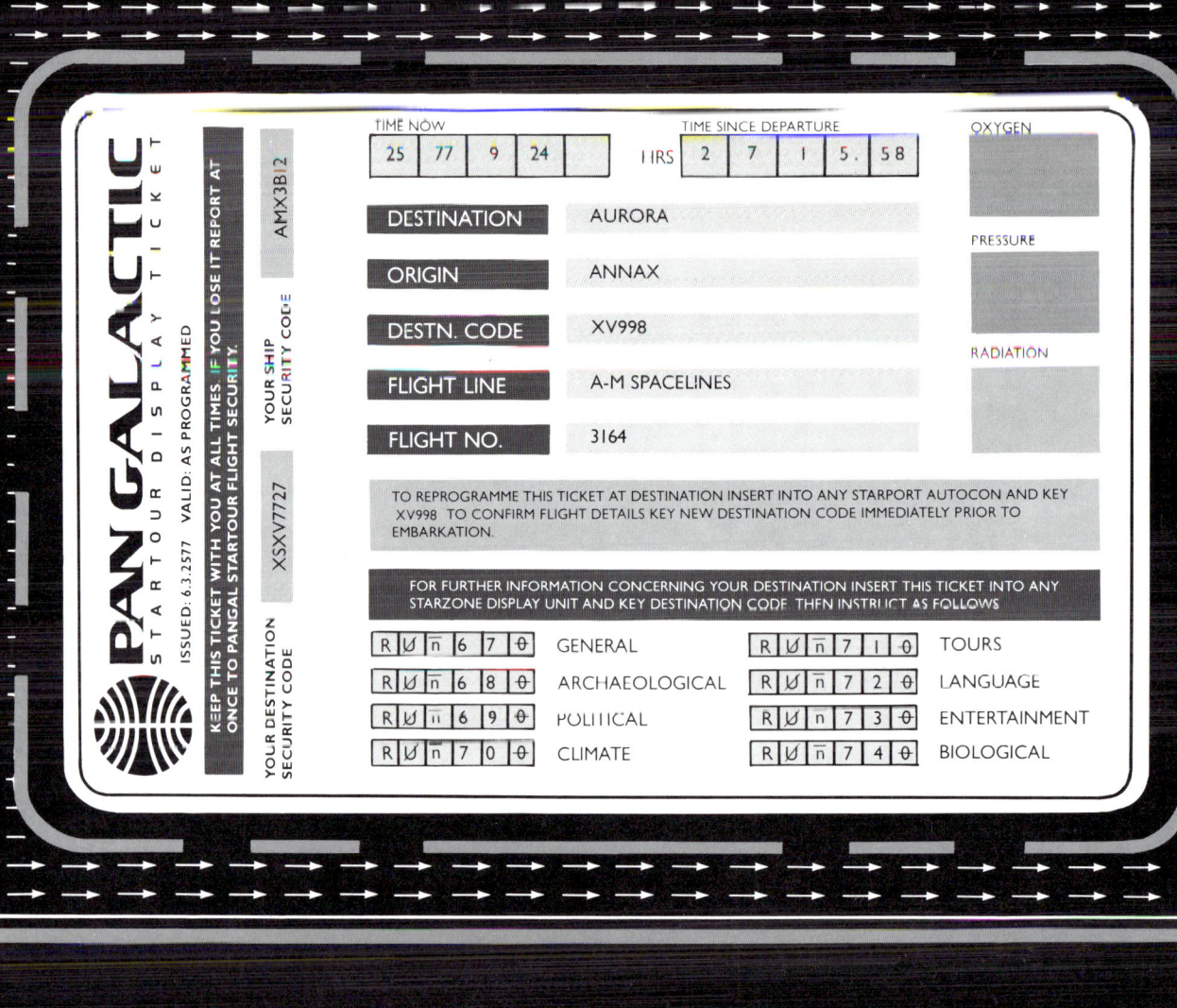

ISSUED: 6.3.2577   VALID: AS PROGRAMMED

KEEP THIS TICKET WITH YOU AT ALL TIMES. IF YOU LOSE IT REPORT AT ONCE TO PANGAL STARTOUR FLIGHT SECURITY.

YOUR SHIP SECURITY CODE: AMX3B12

YOUR DESTINATION SECURITY CODE: XSXV7727

TIME NOW				TIME SINCE DEPARTURE				
25	77	9	24	HRS	2	7	1	5.58

DESTINATION	AURORA
ORIGIN	ANNAX
DESTN. CODE	XV998
FLIGHT LINE	A-M SPACELINES
FLIGHT NO.	3164

OXYGEN

PRESSURE

RADIATION

TO REPROGRAMME THIS TICKET AT DESTINATION INSERT INTO ANY STARPORT AUTOCON AND KEY XV998 TO CONFIRM FLIGHT DETAILS KEY NEW DESTINATION CODE IMMEDIATELY PRIOR TO EMBARKATION.

FOR FURTHER INFORMATION CONCERNING YOUR DESTINATION INSERT THIS TICKET INTO ANY STARZONE DISPLAY UNIT AND KEY DESTINATION CODE THEN INSTRUCT AS FOLLOWS

RUn 670	GENERAL		RUn 710	TOURS
RUn 680	ARCHAEOLOGICAL		RUn 720	LANGUAGE
RUn 690	POLITICAL		RUn 730	ENTERTAINMENT
RUn 700	CLIMATE		RUn 740	BIOLOGICAL

AURORA · AURORA · AUR

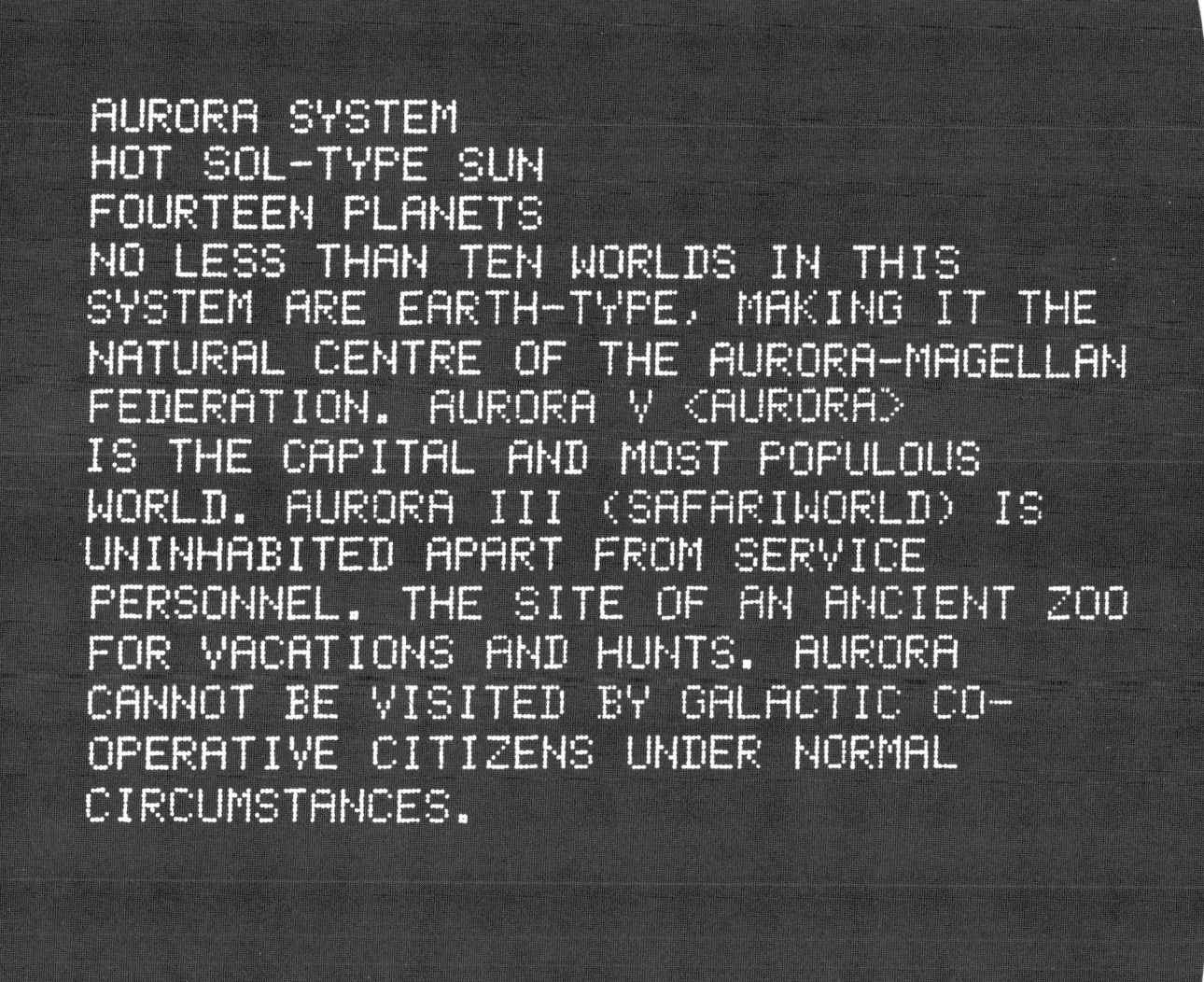

AURORA SYSTEM
HOT SOL-TYPE SUN
FOURTEEN PLANETS
NO LESS THAN TEN WORLDS IN THIS
SYSTEM ARE EARTH-TYPE, MAKING IT THE
NATURAL CENTRE OF THE AURORA-MAGELLAN
FEDERATION. AURORA V (AURORA)
IS THE CAPITAL AND MOST POPULOUS
WORLD. AURORA III (SAFARIWORLD) IS
UNINHABITED APART FROM SERVICE
PERSONNEL. THE SITE OF AN ANCIENT ZOO
FOR VACATIONS AND HUNTS. AURORA
CANNOT BE VISITED BY GALACTIC CO-
OPERATIVE CITIZENS UNDER NORMAL
CIRCUMSTANCES.

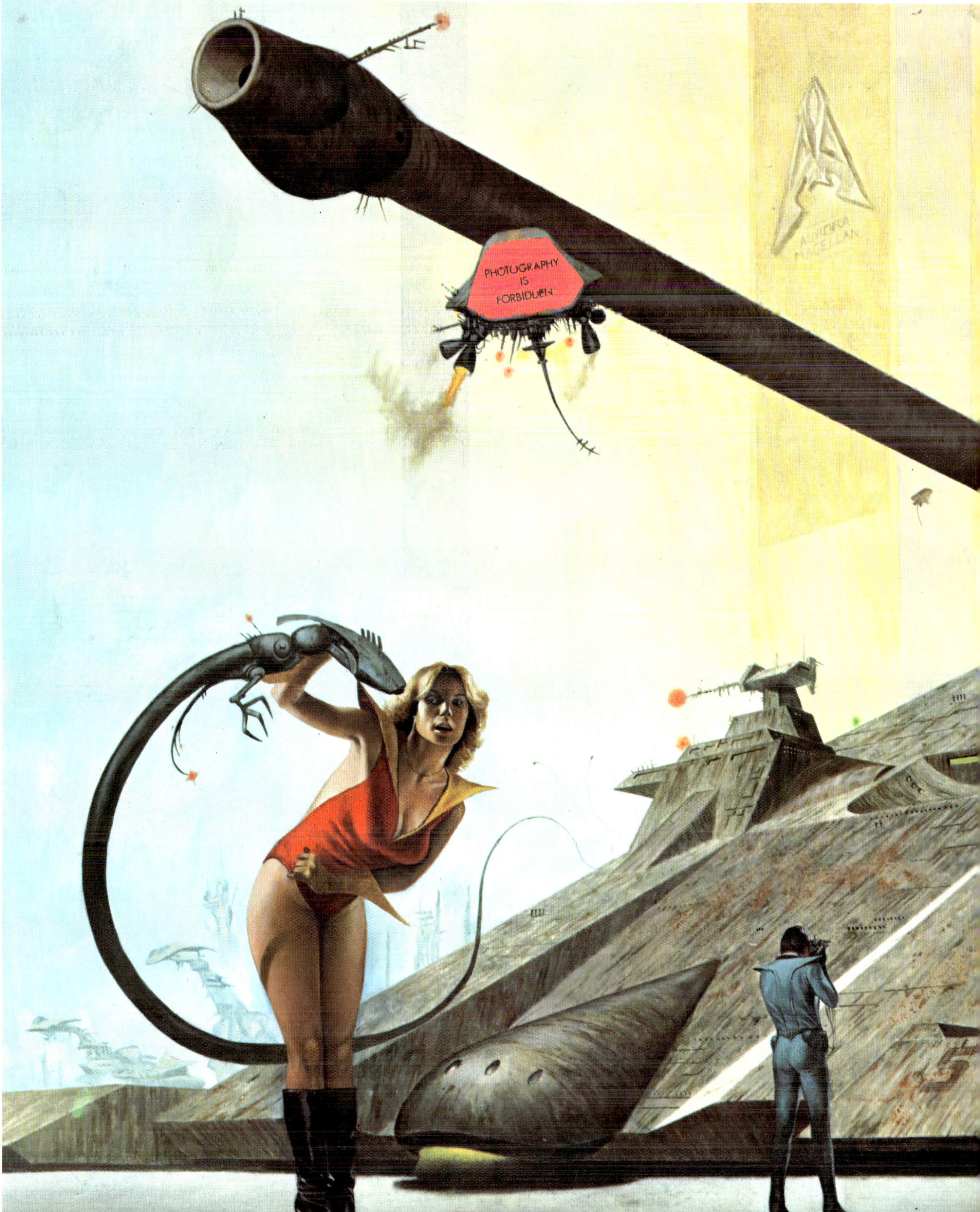
PHOTOGRAPHY
IS
FORBIDDEN

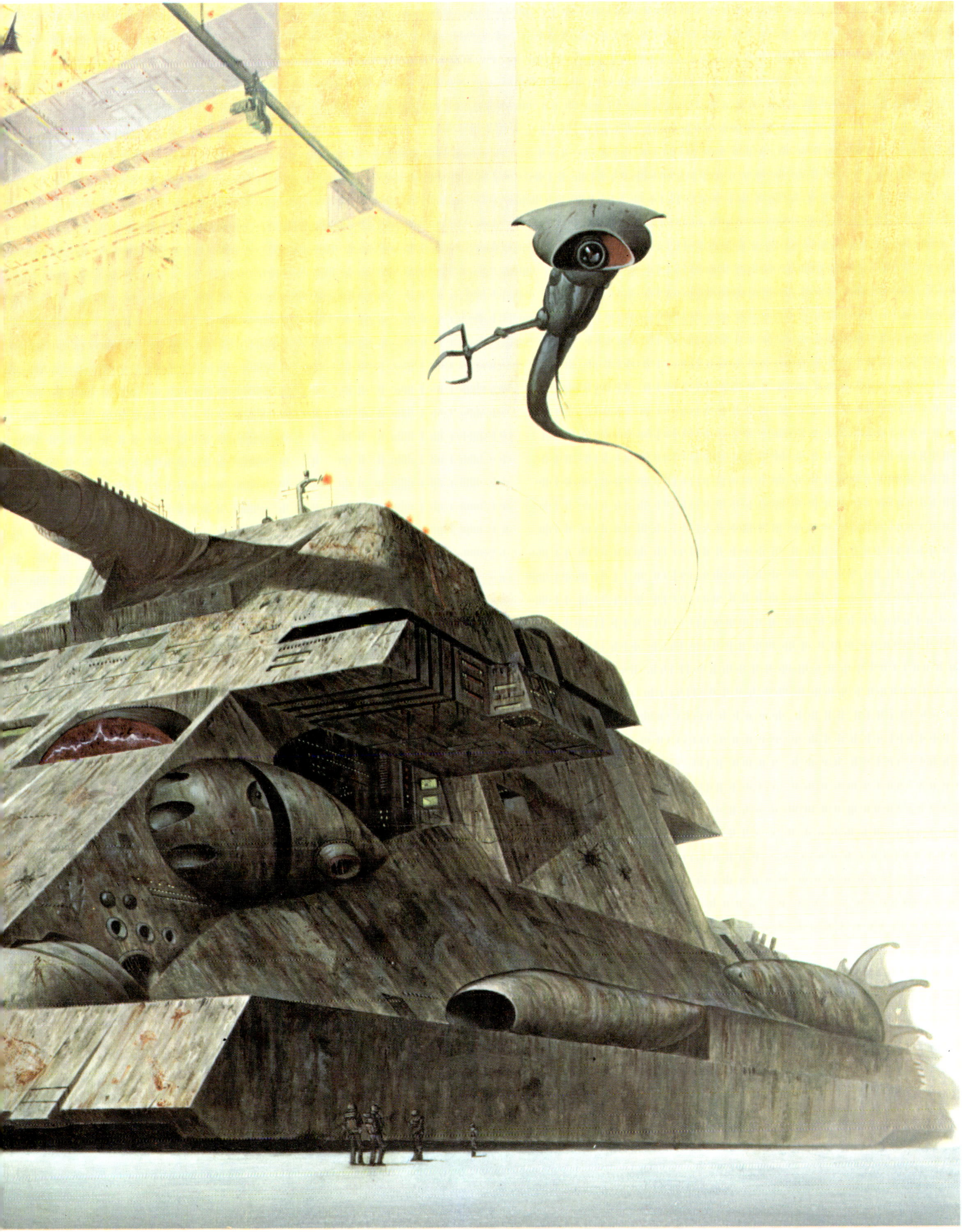

Personal diary Caroline. 27th September 2577: Well, Leio really did it this time. The Aurorans told us repeatedly that while we were undergoing weapons training we were on no account to enter restricted areas. But Leio borrowed my holo-camera and wandered off. When I saw he was heading into a restricted area I rushed after him, but it was too late. He'd emerged into a sort of huge hangar containing a machine like an enormous tank, and spy-eyes were coming at him — and me — from all sides. They restrained us and we've been taken separately into custody. The Aurorans looked grim. I hope we aren't in too much trouble. **End entry.**

Agent Luranski: Memory Implant. 28th September 2577: I am dictating this while (I believe) temporarily free of electronic surveillance in a transient confinement cell. If anyone should see me, with luck they'll think I'm praying. Everything went off remarkably well, and I think we should come through successfully. I noticed a restricted area which, judging from the people coming and going, looked particularly important. I gave Leio a sub-conscious suggestion to wander that way, and followed at a discreet distance. It was easy enough to use a hypnocapsule on the two guards at the entrance. It should look like carelessness on their part. Inside we found ourselves in a huge hangar containing a machine which was indisputably a DreadHulk. I estimate it was at minimum 30 metres square at base and 20 metres high, with a projectile barrel perhaps 40 metres in length. It looked fairly old-fashioned and innocuous, but we know all about the theoretical power of its anti-matter pulse weapons systems from historical accounts. It has always been believed that the few remaining DreadHulks were permanently immobilized half a million years ago when the Voor'hees lost their final campaign; however, there was clear evidence that this one has been activated by the Aurorans. If this is the case, then mounted on a military cruiser it is a weapon which might crucially affect the balance of power. Obviously work must immediately be stepped up on DreadHulks in Co-operative hands. The Aurorans do not appear ready to use this weapon but we must assume they view it as at least a

---

RESTRICTED
SECURITY CLEARANCE AAA

To DIRECTOR OF INTELLIGENCE OPERATIONS
From ASSISTANT TO MILITARY COMMANDER, AURORA V
Subject ARREST OF EARTH SUBJECTS SCOTT (L), LURANSKI (C)
Date 9/28/77
Enclosures COPIES OF PASSPORTS

```
These two were picked up by Security Eyes taking
holovid shots of a Dreadhulk, having managed to
wander into a restricted area. They claim to be
innocent tourists, didn't see the notices (or
listen to instructions) etc etc. Normally it
would be a case for a simple brainscan and wipe,
but as they're part of the Galactic Co-op tour we
can't do that unless we're sure they aren't telling
the truth. Do we know or can we find out anything
about them?
Please reply soonest: this is potentially explosive.
```

REST
SECURITY C

To ASSISTANT TO MILITARY
From DIRECTOR OF INTELLI
Subject PRISONERS SCOTT
Date 9/30/77
Enclosures

```
Our records reveal nothi
these two. They aren't p
influential -- and our t
Records show nothing unu
record of drug abuse; ot
any one of a billion cou
are working undercover a
camouflage -- but unless
than we think they do ab
we've penetrated their i
unlikely that they would
false identities. Also,
that real spies would be
The disturbing thing to
got where they did. Do y
are they all on holiday

RECOMMENDATION: Omit bra
memory-wipe and implant
incarceration, then let
procedures urgently.
```

theoretical possibility. I believe I managed to get a good series of shots with the retinal cameras, including hypersonics which may yield significant information. As expected, the series of squints and blinks needed to activate the cameras were readily passed off as the result of grit under a contact lens. Now we wait to see if we are under heavy suspicion. Leio will certainly check out completely clean in any test they run on him (and they are hardly likely to wish to provoke an incident by doing anything as drastic as irreversible brain scan). Still, as he was carrying the holo-camera he's the immediate target of suspicion, and I'm unhappy at the thought that this might rebound on him. But the beauty of the manoeuvre is that it looks exactly like a piece of clumsy tourist blundering. For myself, we will see how effective all those dormant years have been in building up my cover. I know it should be clear — even if they've completely penetrated our systems they should find me to be precisely who I purport to be — but I have to admit I'm scared. **End report.**

Agent Luranski: Memory Implant. 28th September 2577: Second report, following another interview with an Auroran officer. I think their suspicions are fading. He was as polite as all previous interviewers (interrogator seems too strong a word for their diffident approach, even though that's what they undoubtedly are), and clearly had quite a full computer profile of me from which he drew his questions. I was able to answer completely straightforwardly, including genuine trivial lapses of memory. Some of the information he had implies thorough Auroran entry into our computer systems, and I recommend careful checks for floating programs. Obviously we can look forward to a selective memory-wipe (and probably a false memory implant), but at present it looks as though that will be all. It will be galling not to know afterwards what I've accomplished — at least until the crystal is extracted and replayed — but that's a minor irritant compared with the sense of relief. **End report.**

RESTRICTED

SECURITY CLEARANCE AAA

To ASSISTANT TO MILITARY COMMANDER, AURORA V
From DIRECTOR OF INTELLIGENCE OPERATIONS
Subject SCOTT/LURANSKI
Date 10/1/77
Enclosures

Your recommendations accepted: they now think they spent three educational days visiting the Weapons Museums as part of their prize. Agree totally about inexcusable slackness: 4 guards have been reprimanded and two unit commanders stripped of rank and reassigned to combat duties.

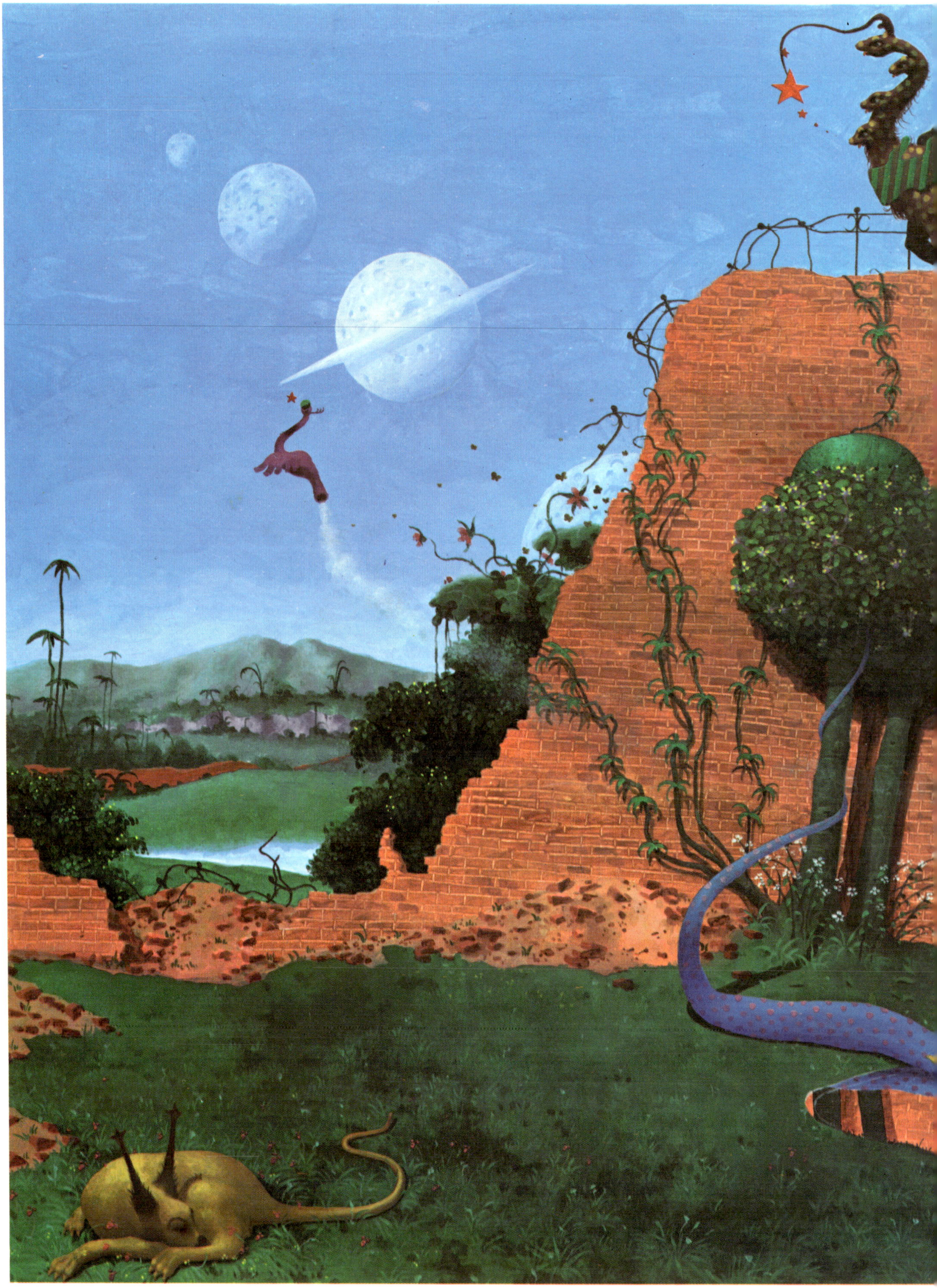

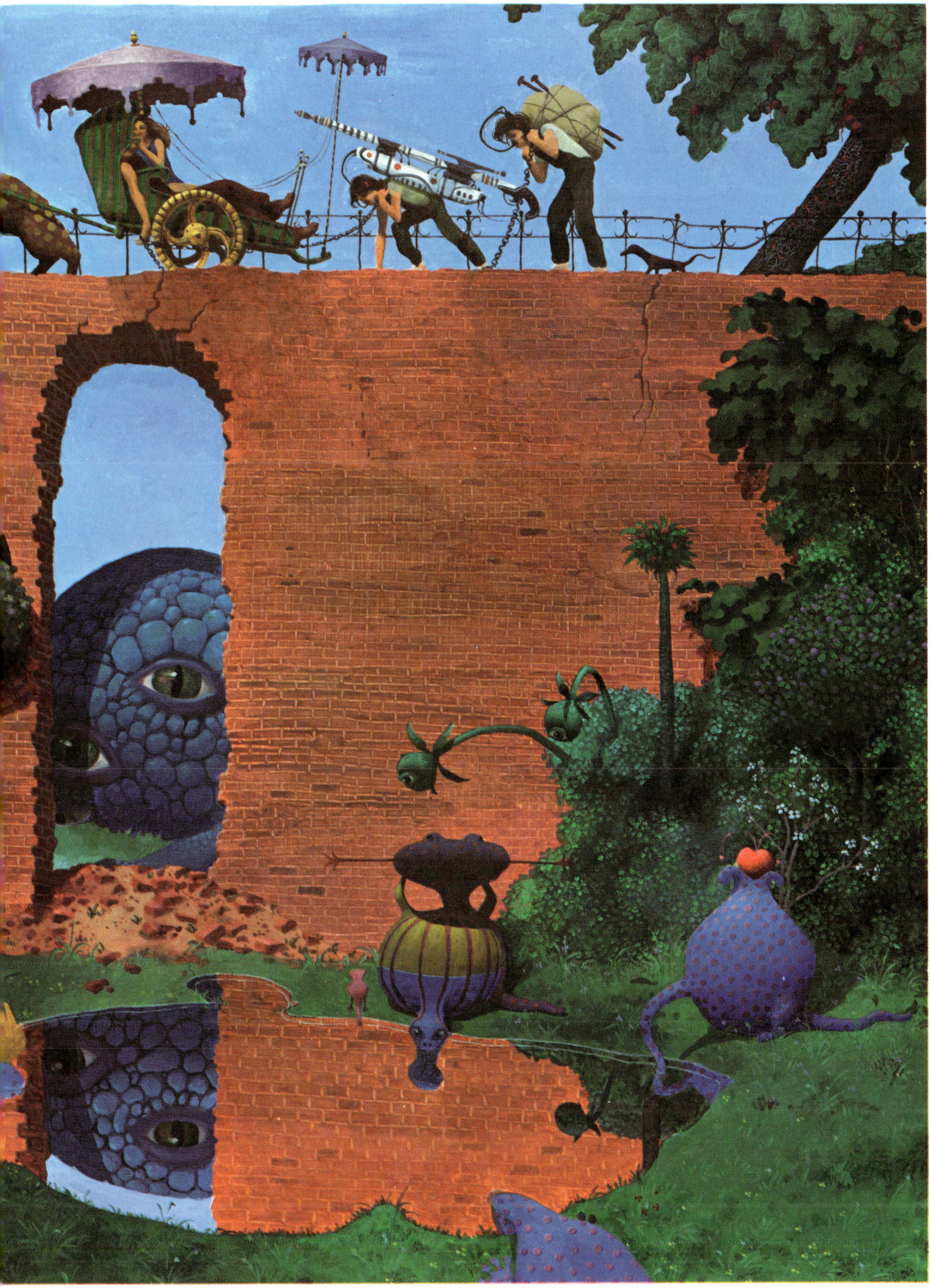

Personal diary Lelo. 16th October 2577: We've been in the main Aurora System for three weeks now, getting ready for the safari on Aurora III. We've both been slightly ill for a few days, blinding headache, slight nausea, and the cetistral capsules we bought don't seem to help. But it's passing off, and we're being more careful about what we eat. This Solar System, with a bright yellow sun like our own, is quite a hub of activity. There are fourteen worlds, and ten of them inhabited; they all cluster within a band about two hundred million miles wide, and it seems that worlds collide every epoch without fail. You can take a small ship and go jaunting, from world to moon, even to other worlds. The sense of crush and crowd is overwhelming. This is a busy place. On Aurora V we've been touring the great sights, getting a bit of simple indoctrination into the wonderful political and economic system, all that sort of stuff. They haven't laid it on too thick, thank heavens. Weapons training for our safari was great fun. You can choose basic weapons and I've picked an Imbara multi-blaster. Caroline's opted for a rocket-boosted long bow which will limit what she can shoot. They have bows, spears, slings, and all manner of genuine primitive weaponry for the real hunters. I'm trying a multi-knife myself. There's an endless list of creatures to hunt, but we have to agree to just five, pick them out, learn about them, practice with automata, and then we can go and hunt two of each. We've been doing a lot of walking. There are restricted zones everywhere on all the worlds. No heavy types following us, nothing that dramatic, but there seem to be little disc-cameras everywhere, and when, on a couple of occasions, we've crossed security zones — they use photosignals here, not visual guides, and it's confusing — we were very quickly stopped by white-suited men who appeared as if from nowhere. I've noticed that Caroline is really looking forward to the hunt. She seems very happy here, and for her, with political and foreign interests, this must be the high spot of our holiday. No ruins, though. I can't get excited about a world that knocked down its archaeology. **End entry.**

EXTRACT FROM: THE TOURIST BROCHURE OF SAFARI WORLD

Welcome to Safari World! Aurora III is one of the most popular tourist resorts in the Great Federation of Aurora Magellan, and we are pleased to make it exclusively available to our colleagues from the Co-operative for the two week period of their stay. You have a whole world to range in pursuit of pleasure and your prey. There is no commitment upon you to actually fulfil the requirements of the hunt and killing. If you prefer to shoot with cameras rather than guns, then we are happy to accommodate you in this way too. All we ask is that you read this, and the other short pamphlets, and behave in accordance with the simple rules that have been explained to you. In particular we ask you not to alter the highly-flexible plans that you have agreed upon, not, that is, without prior consultation with your Hunt Warden. And please remember: you have agreed a total kill, and you must not exceed that kill, nor must you change your prey without consulting your Hunt Warden. Read the facts about Safari World below, and memorise the details of Medicare and Stalking Routes, and then it's up to you. Good hunting; good sport.

What is Safari World? The planet Aurora III, in the complex and crowded Aurora System, was once a zoo. If that seems hard to comprehend — a planet-wide zoo! — you need only look to various of the Co-operative's worlds where already whole continents have been set aside as 'game reserves' in which alien life is able to flourish without interference. Safari World began life in exactly the same way. The original inhabitants of the system, the *jiril*, roamed far and wide during the Ages of their supremacy. They visited Earth and Rigel VII many times. They brought specimens of life from all over. Safari World was not to their taste as far as living was concerned; it was too warm, too lush, too oxygenated. But most of the life they found in the Galaxy needed oxygen to survive, and Aurora III became their Oxygen zoo.

There are more than twenty thousand alien life-forms roaming free upon Safari World, although they have all tended to cluster in their climatically favoured location; the ecosystem is complex, and of necessity artificial, but it works remarkably well. Safari World is a dense, and rather heavy planet (you will weigh a quarter of your normal weight more). It has snow caps, and a stifling equatorial belt. There are eighteen continents, some of them connected by natural 'bridge formations' of granite. But beware, the seas are richly populated with snapping, tearing, man-eating creatures, and the bridges have become the favoured haunts for many varieties of solitary hunters. Regular copter tours will take you to any location you choose, and your pocket map will show you where the supply and shelter installations have been established.

On your Safari you will see many signs of the original zoo. The world had once been divided into thousands of enclosures, some quite natural to look at, such as the Square Mountains in the continent of Abaracea, which are still the breeding grounds of the *trothlak*; other enclosures were like vast, walled townships, and these walls remain, crumbling and rotted, but still covered with the remarkable script of the *jiril*.

The Equator: the equatorial belt is considered to extend for a thousand kilometres on either side of the equator itself; this band of stifling heat includes the three continents Pyronata, Ilfruga and Pirros, and substantial portions of Karamane and Indunaland. The atmosphere in this region is dense and unfavourable; persons of a weaker constitution will almost certainly experience breathing difficulties and should not enter the region without a fully functioning respirator. It will be necessary to wear thermcontrol body suits. If you can face the thick and poisonous conditions of the equatorial zone, however, your hunting prospects are excellent, since it is to this region that the most prized specimens have retreated, in particular the ivory scaled White Nemeth and the thousand metre long aga-Python. Here too are to be found small dinosaurs. Do not expect them to be exactly like their terrestrial ancestors, for they have adapted to the richer oxygen of the world, and have grown in size. Specimens of *Ornithomimus* and *Hesperosuchus* have bred well, and are dominant life-forms in the area.

Personal diary Caroline. 18th October 2577: Safariworld! What an incredible mixture of lifeforms. Almost every conceivable type of oxygen-breathing carbon-based life must have been brought here over millions of years by the Voor'hees. Everywhere you look there are different creatures, some so bizarre as almost to defy description. Here an animal which is no more than a lump of protoplasm with an improbably well-developed mouth and impeccable teeth; there a living pogo-stick escaping from predators by leaping over them; over there a surly herd of mammoths from Pleistocene Earth. Getting here was well worth the endless days on Aurora, trekking round military museums. Even Leio got bored, and indeed we've both been suffering from headaches since. The hunt should put paid to that. One member of the tour turns out to be carrying a lot of Friends of the Galaxy literature, which he has been handing round. One or two people have since dropped out of the hunt, but I'm determined to go ahead. The point, as I see it, is that if it wasn't for the safaris the world would be given over to human colonization and the various creatures would be wiped out. As it is their numbers are carefully controlled and maintained and thus by hunting you are in a sense helping to ensure their survival. (Adamek, the Friends of the Galaxy man, says this is a specious, shallow piece of self-justification, no different from what 20th century humans used to say as they went around proclaiming their social consciences and wiping out species. I think the situation **is** different.) My only problem is the antediluvian Auroran ideas about sex-roles. I wanted to use a rocket-boosted longbow, but they insisted on my having a 'lighter' weapon — a silly little 'prettified' (though admittedly powerful) handgun. **End entry.**

Agent Luranski: Memory Implant. 21st October 2577: We've been suffering headaches which I recognize as symptomatic of memory-wiping, and though the Aurorans have provided sophisticated false memory implants, once you suspect you can readily identify them by their one-dimensionality. Leio has no notion that anything is amiss. I'm burning to know what happened — but I've an almost subliminal sense of tranquillity which suggests everything has gone well. **End report.**

The Poles are cold and hostile environments, where terrestrial mammoth and a variety of cold-living alien forms can be found. Chief among them is the confusingly named *blindskat*. It stands forty metres high and has four whip-like tongues that can stretch to five hundred metres, so caution is urged. It is most likely that you will be restricting your hunting efforts to the temperate zone, and for the purposes of this small information booklet we will assume that the temperate regions are the rest of the world, a full eight continents, including the main northern continental mass where the Hotel Magellana is located, and the main Tourist Centre is set up. No hunting is permitted within a five-hundred kilometre area around the Centre. Here there are numerous outdoor zoos, enclosures, and pasturelands, and a great many enclosed environments where examples of the polar and equatorial fauna can be viewed and studied without fear. Beyond this Protected Zone, however, total freedom to hunt is available, and the course, and plan of campaign, is at your discretion. The Federation would like to encourage you *not* to hunt and kill in areas populated by the several large groups of *Australopithecus africanus*. They themselves are protected, but many of the Safari weapons available are too indiscriminate, and an accidental death may occur. Although no longer thought to be directly ancestral to man, these creatures are intelligent and sensitive and will, in rare cases, come into your camp and eat and 'sign' with you. Communication is not difficult, and they are not dangerous.

Logging a kill: each time you make a kill you are required to travel to one of the many scattered Recording Posts and enter the information. You will have no difficulty in locating these posts, even in the remotest continental wastes, as they emit ultrasonic signals that can be detected by your Safari World key. You must wear the key at all times, as it is the only way you can be instantly spotted by Safari Rescue. The information on the kill required is: time of kill; identity, weight of kill, sex, if any, location, and a comment on any particular difficulty experienced during the hunt. When you have killed your allocated quota of major life-forms you are free to hunt any number of the life-forms listed below. These are not protected, and they are all edible. You need not log these kills, and most can be hunted with ordinary blasters:

Red-eyed groth, Jumping stoad, Three-horned karelia, Golden-eared corga, Frilled mudslug, Whistling jimmy jax, Thiesen's whiptail.

WEAPONS AVAILABLE FOR USE BY VISITORS TO SAFARI WORLD

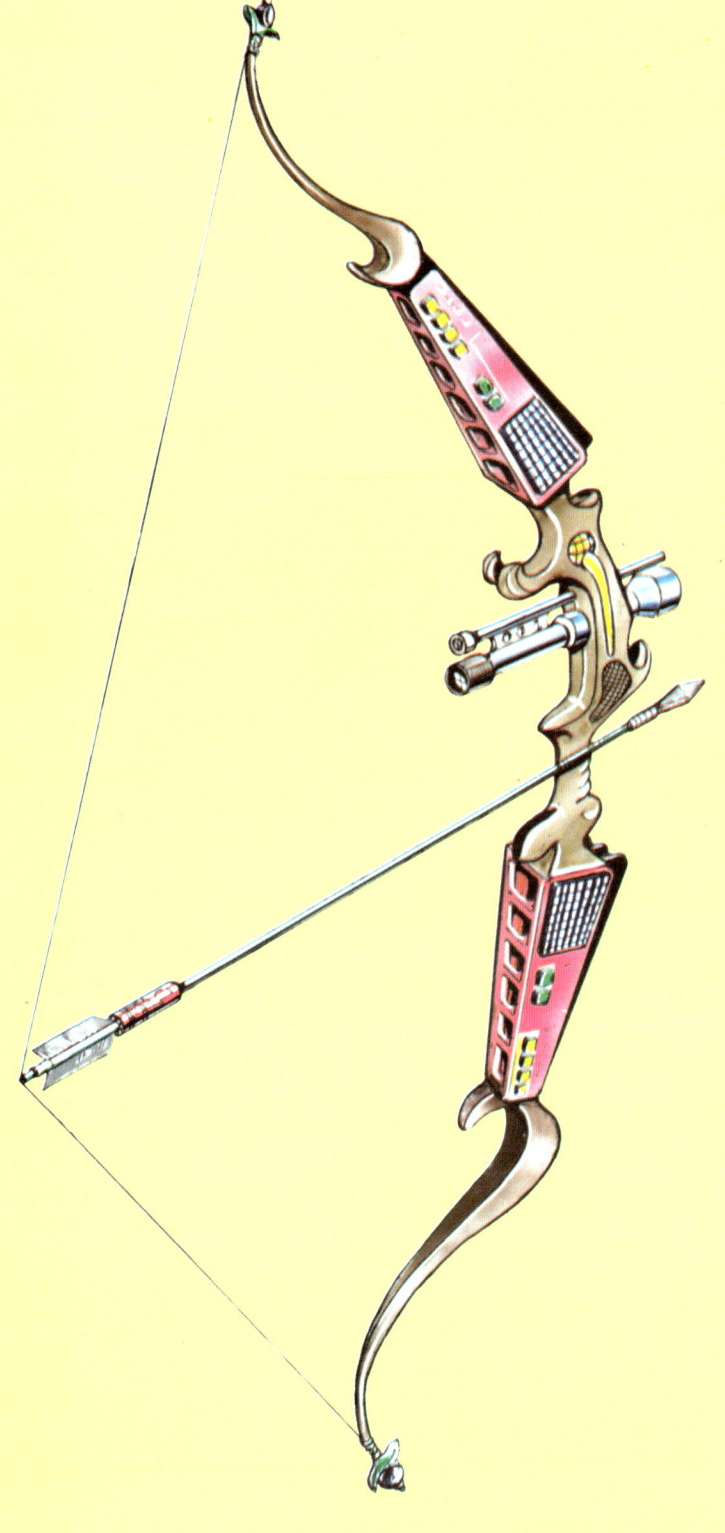

HI-FLEX POWER BOW: With microsensor arrows. Suitable for all prey in categories AA-BF.

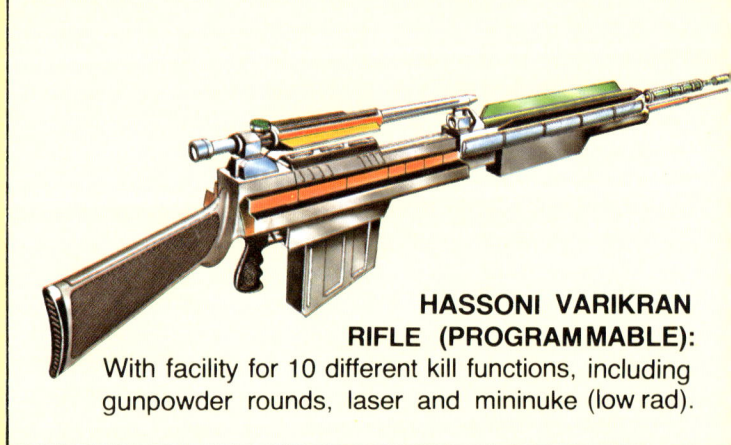

HASSONI VARIKRAN RIFLE (PROGRAMMABLE): With facility for 10 different kill functions, including gunpowder rounds, laser and mininuke (low rad).

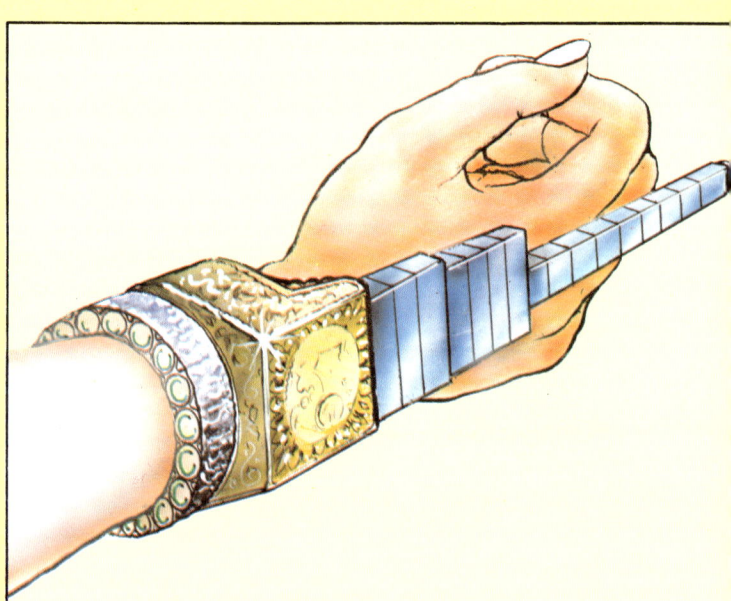

SAUD-KRUGER BRACELLETTI: Pretty and almost invisible hand defence, shooting deep penetration explosive pellets. Functions as watch and radiation warning. Suitable for all prey.

VOLTAIRE ANTIMECH ZOOK: A high powered, slow fire projectile weapon, ideal for stopping category LA-MO (giant, armoured) prey prior to a more sophisticated kill.

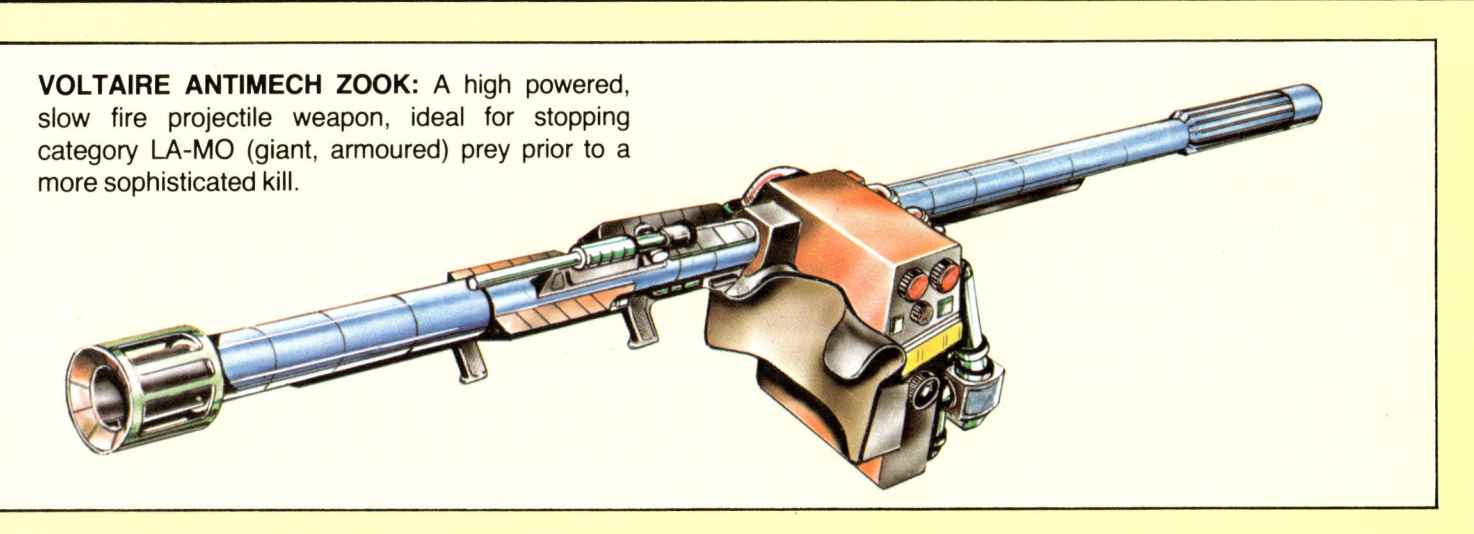

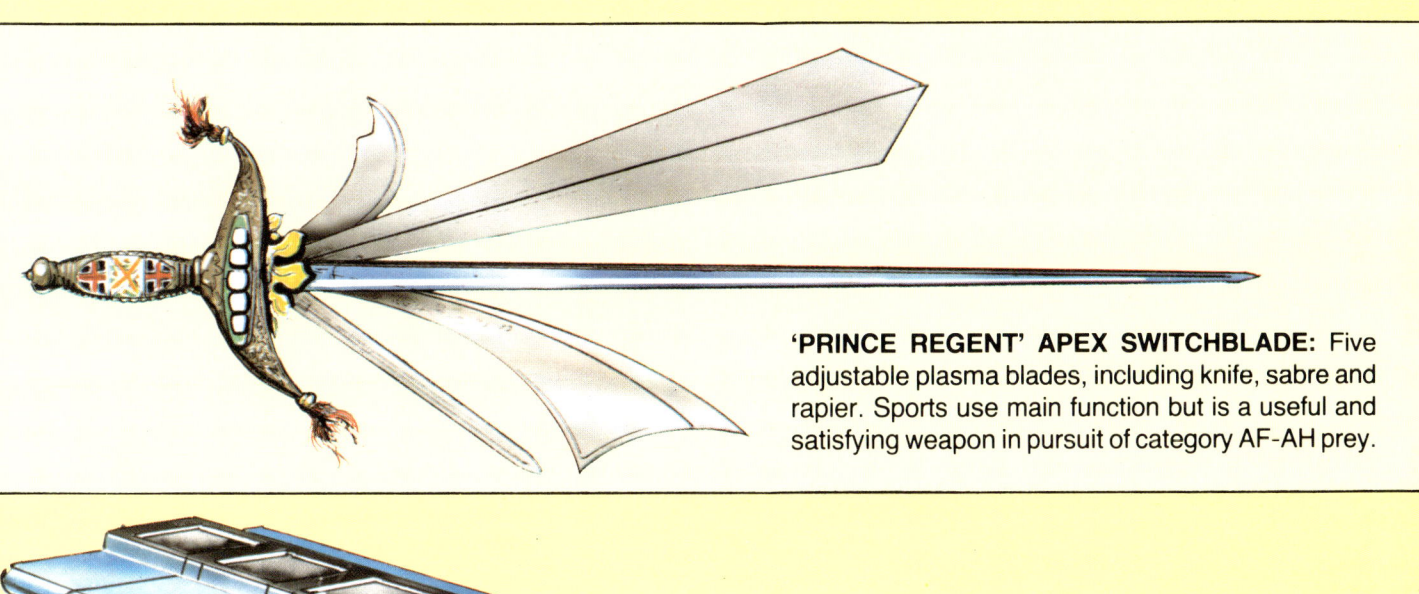

'PRINCE REGENT' APEX SWITCHBLADE: Five adjustable plasma blades, including knife, sabre and rapier. Sports use main function but is a useful and satisfying weapon in pursuit of category AF-AH prey.

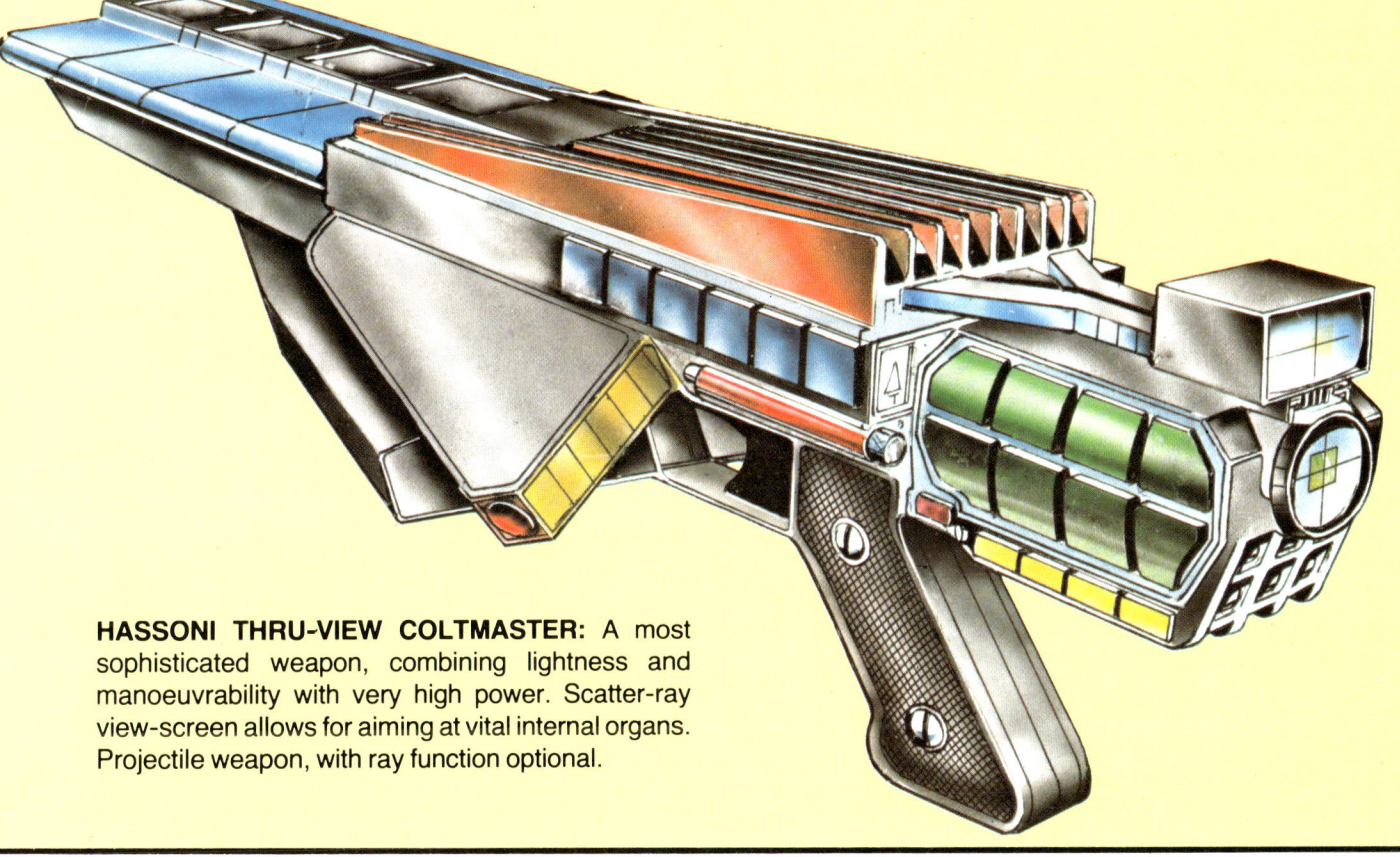

HASSONI THRU-VIEW COLTMASTER: A most sophisticated weapon, combining lightness and manoeuvrability with very high power. Scatter-ray view-screen allows for aiming at vital internal organs. Projectile weapon, with ray function optional.

FRIENDS OF THE GALAXY
Associated with Universal Wild-life Preservation
PERHAPS YOU DIDN'T KNOW IT BUT YOU'RE A MURDERER

There is no other word but MURDER to describe the appalling activities that the Aurora-Magellan Federation sponsors and encourages by keeping available the world Aurora 3 for the 'innocent' pleasure of tourists. There is no other word but MURDER for the sort of hunting expedition that you are engaged upon, that ends with the slaughter of creatures with whom no attempt at all has ever been made to communicate. The creatures you are encouraged to kill are rare species, many of them unknown on any other world but Aurora 3 itself! None of them are native to the world; they are part of what was once a huge, interplanetary game reserve, and many of the creatures are extinct on their home worlds. Only the lack of interest of the Federation allows for their slaughter rather than their preservation. But do you have to co-operate with that Federation?

EXCTINCT SPECIES

- THE WHALE
- THE GROTH
- THE EAGLE
- THE SNAKE
- THE DIRONOTHAXIOR

STARPEACE and THE FRIENDS OF THE GALAXY stand for RESPECT towards life, RESPONSIBILITY towards resources, and MAINTENANCE of the balance of the Socioecology of all worlds.
We don't ask for money. We ask you to LOOK, LISTEN and most of all LOVE.

FOR THE SAKE OF LIFE, *THINK!*
Five hundred years ago man was given the choice on his homeworld of either learning to communicate with an intelligent, sea-living mammal called the Whale, or of continuing to hunt it so that its meat could be fed to domestic pets, and its oils used in perfumes. Whole populations were killed, made extinct. Their songs could travel through the oceans of Earth, right-around the world. By the year 2000 the oceans were silent! Today most children have never heard of the WHALE. So why are you slaughtering equally rare creatures?

FOR THE SAKE OF LOVE, *THINK!*
Two hundred years ago Man colonised a world called Saffron. It was a rich world, ideal, beautiful, a second Earth. But the dominant life form was a cumbersome, cold-blooded, placid, friendly creature called the Groth. Man decided the Groth were ugly, and offended him. After twenty years of offering bounty for each Grothi eye-stalk, the creatures had become extinct. They had been killed because they offended the delicate senses of the colonists.

FOR GOD'S SAKE, BE RESPONSIBLE FOR LIFE!
The three worlds of the Choaran System were broken up last century to extract their rich uranium deposits. All three worlds supported rich populations of animal and plant life, all of which have now vanished from the Galaxy. And yet, just 20 light years away, the ManderHead System is a sterile system, and all 20 worlds are as rich in uranium as were the Choarans! For this sort of indifference to living things there can be no excuse.

WHAT ARE YOU DOING?
On Aurora 3 you are engaged in 'sport'. You are hunting and destroying creatures that were once free, alive and in many cases part of an evolving intelligence. Man used to hunt deer – he said it was for food, as if there weren't enough domestic food creatures. He used to hunt a small creature called the FOX – he said the fox was vermin, and besides, horses needed exercise. In the twentieth century he used to hunt his fellow man – he called his victim a terrorist, or a guerilla, or a contract! None of this can be denied, but just because our ancestors were the Great Destroyers doesn't mean that *we* have to be. We can look compassionately upon *all* life. We don't *have* to add our support to the brutal Industrial races and worlds to whom preservation and conservation are anti-finace.

Remember – populations become extinct well before the last member is killed. When their population density drops to a critical level, one death can mean extinction even though there appear to be herds of them. Can you bear to think of firing that terrible shot?

Registered offices on all 3rd Generation Colony Worlds. Central Information Office: 476 Inklep3 Brussels Outer gEur. 982. *Sponsored by InterGal Artificial Fur Products, and from public funds.*

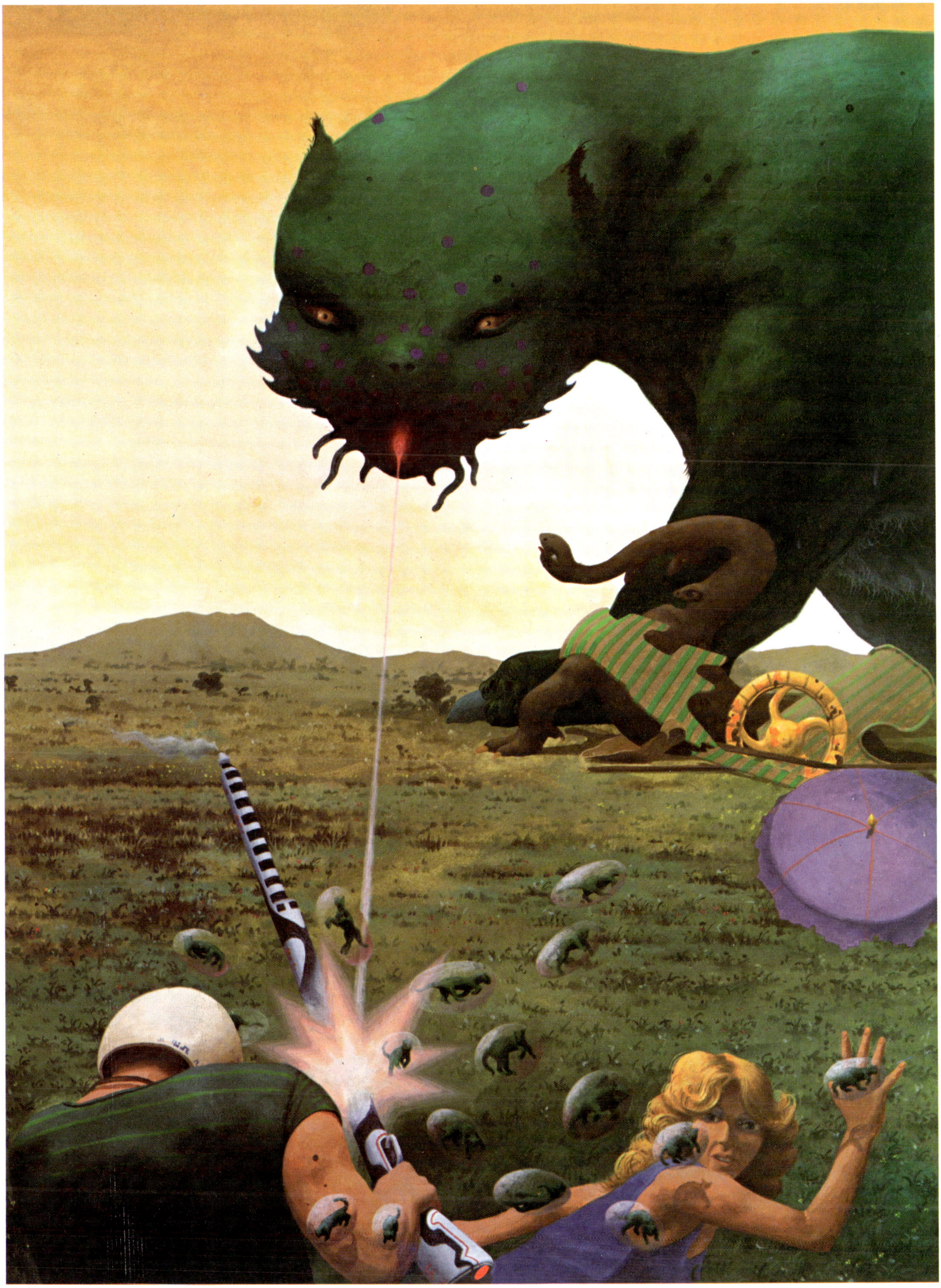

PAN GALACTIC
STARTOUR DISPLAY TICKET

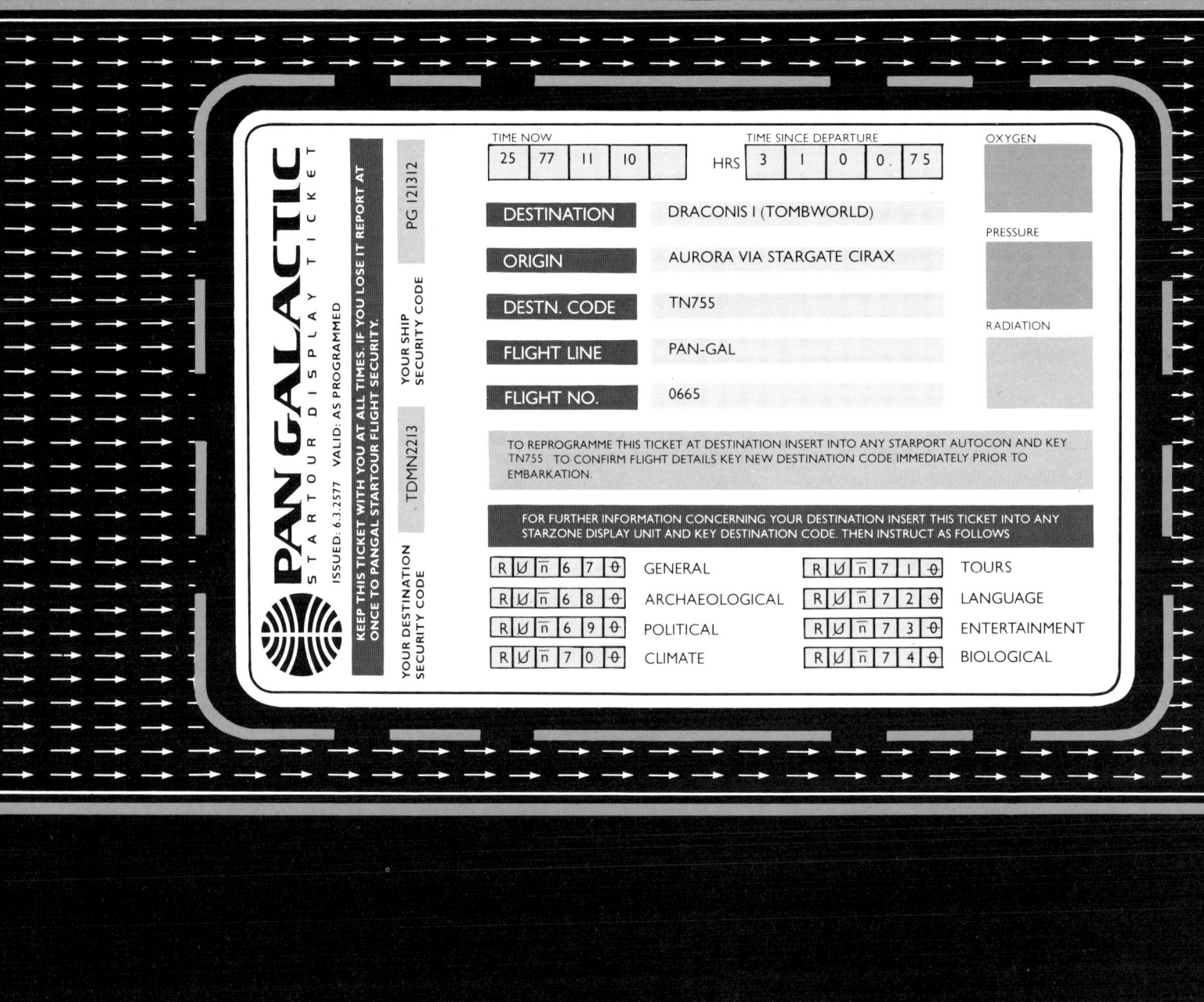

ISSUED: 6.3.2577 VALID: AS PROGRAMMED

PG 121312 — YOUR SHIP SECURITY CODE

TDMN2213 — YOUR DESTINATION SECURITY CODE

KEEP THIS TICKET WITH YOU AT ALL TIMES. IF YOU LOSE IT REPORT AT ONCE TO PANGAL STARTOUR FLIGHT SECURITY.

TIME NOW	25 77 11 10	
TIME SINCE DEPARTURE	HRS 3 1 0 0 . 7 5	

DESTINATION	DRACONIS I (TOMBWORLD)
ORIGIN	AURORA VIA STARGATE CIRAX
DESTN. CODE	TN755
FLIGHT LINE	PAN-GAL
FLIGHT NO.	0665

OXYGEN

PRESSURE

RADIATION

TO REPROGRAMME THIS TICKET AT DESTINATION INSERT INTO ANY STARPORT AUTOCON AND KEY TN755 TO CONFIRM FLIGHT DETAILS KEY NEW DESTINATION CODE IMMEDIATELY PRIOR TO EMBARKATION.

FOR FURTHER INFORMATION CONCERNING YOUR DESTINATION INSERT THIS TICKET INTO ANY STARZONE DISPLAY UNIT AND KEY DESTINATION CODE. THEN INSTRUCT AS FOLLOWS

R U n 6 7 0	GENERAL	R U n 7 1 0	TOURS
R U n 6 8 0	ARCHAEOLOGICAL	R U n 7 2 0	LANGUAGE
R U n 6 9 0	POLITICAL	R U n 7 3 0	ENTERTAINMENT
R U n 7 0 0	CLIMATE	R U n 7 4 0	BIOLOGICAL

ONIS B · DRACONIS

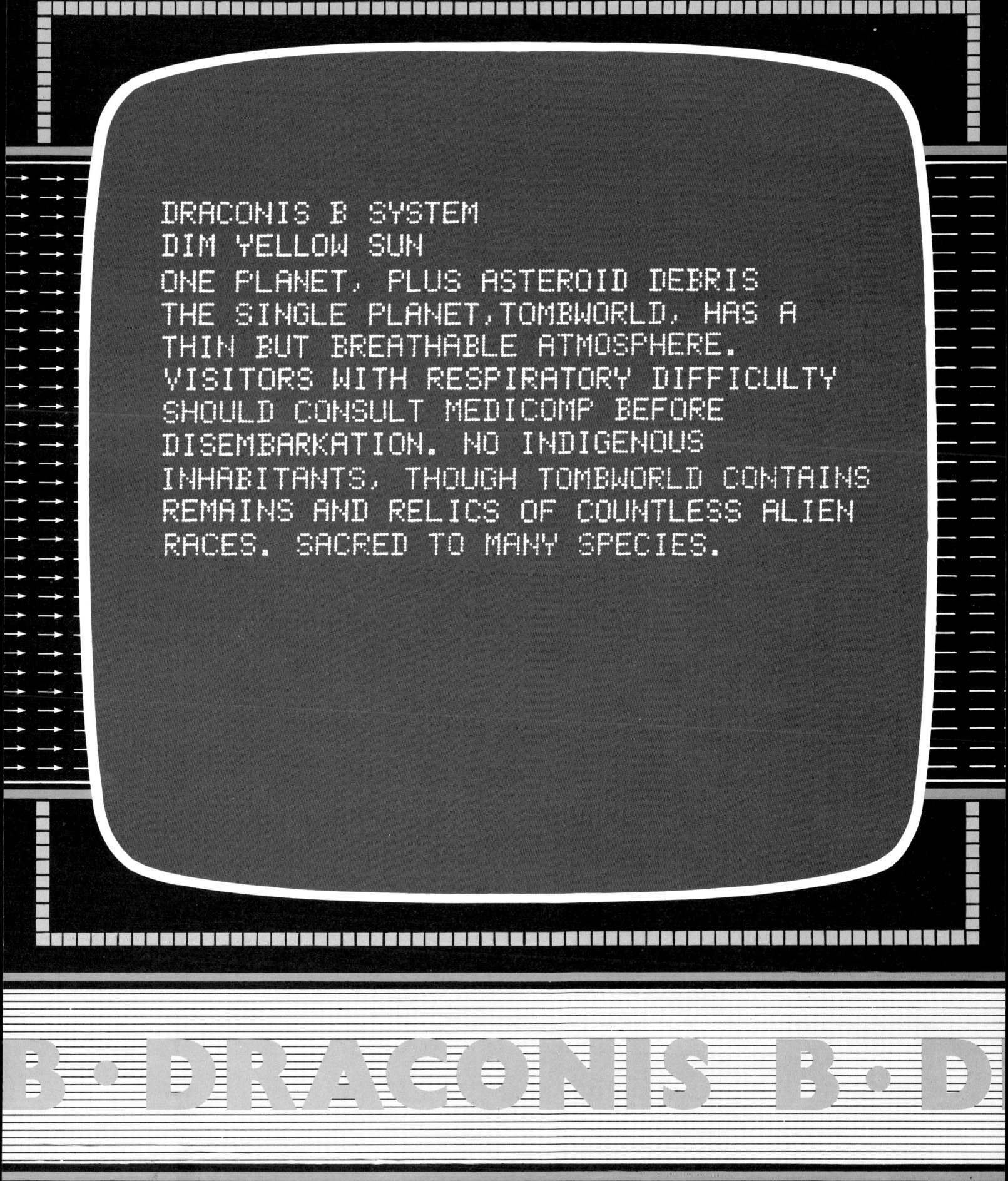

```
DRACONIS B SYSTEM
DIM YELLOW SUN
ONE PLANET, PLUS ASTEROID DEBRIS
THE SINGLE PLANET,TOMBWORLD, HAS A
THIN BUT BREATHABLE ATMOSPHERE.
VISITORS WITH RESPIRATORY DIFFICULTY
SHOULD CONSULT MEDICOMP BEFORE
DISEMBARKATION. NO INDIGENOUS
INHABITANTS, THOUGH TOMBWORLD CONTAINS
REMAINS AND RELICS OF COUNTLESS ALIEN
RACES. SACRED TO MANY SPECIES.
```

B · DRACONIS B · D

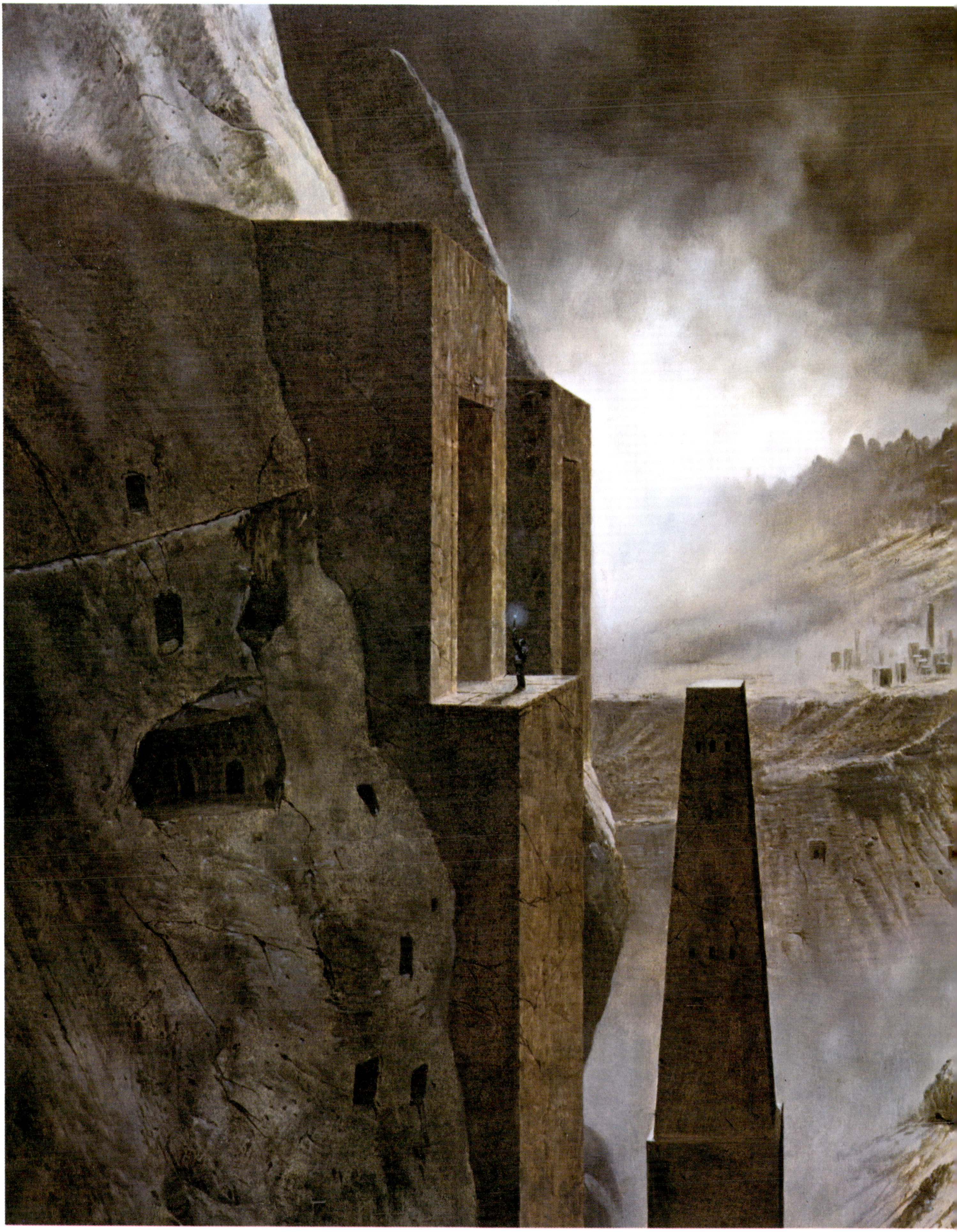

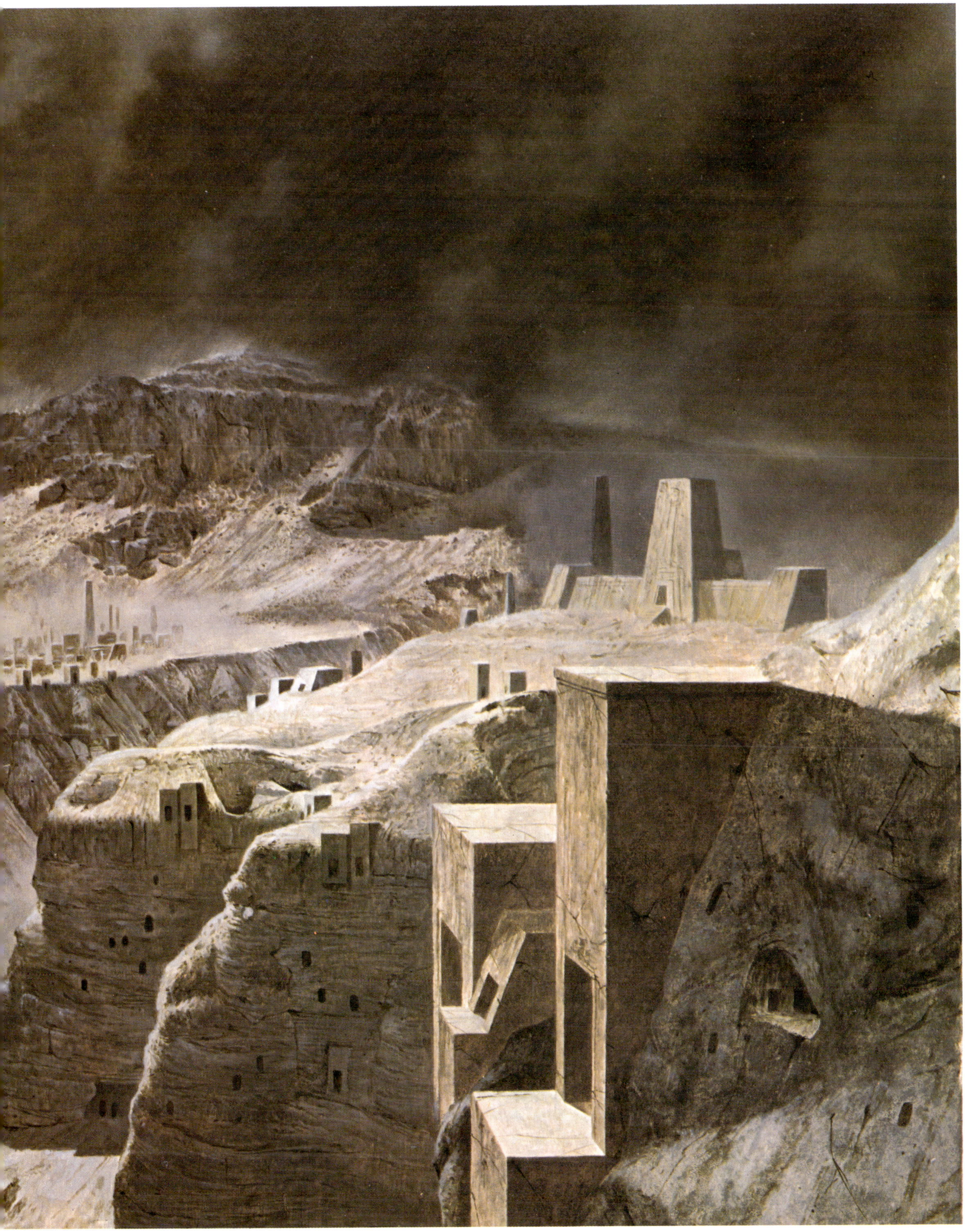

Personal diary Lelo. 16th November 2577: After two months beyond the galactic rift we're back in Co-operative space. The Magellans treated us with great courtesy, of course, and when we came back through Stargate Cirax we were positively hounded by newsmen. We gave two interviews – I had to do all the talking – along with the rest of the tour crowd, and then escaped. And at last we're on Draconis I, or Tombworld as it is more familiarly known. I don't think I've ever been so moved, so excited in my life. How can I describe the sensation of standing on a bare slab of gleaming tungsten steel, and staring across a landscape of shafts, doorways, and towering mausoleums, and knowing that the Star Kings of thousands of Empires have been coming here to die since well before the Age of Dinosaurs on Earth. It was used until as recently as two thousand years ago; and then, for some reason that no-one knows, it died itself. Most of the alien races which are buried deep below the surface are totally unknown to Man. We've so far explored ten galleries, and Caroline is much bouncier than I'd expected; she seems relaxed, almost playful, although she's too serious a person to ever be childish. God forbid! I think she's glad to be away from the A-M Federation. For all that she enjoyed it there, I think the obvious intellectual repression disturbed her. Tombworld has the remnants of an oxygen atmosphere, and we've been equipped with booster tubes, small cylinders that strap to our chests and probe into our lungs. They irritate a bit, but it's good to be able to walk and talk without masks. Metal, concrete, dirt and wood, there are tomb areas made of all these things, although the more primitive materials would have had to have been imported. The efforts of more recent races to preserve the tombs of the older Kings has been immense, hence the fact that the whole world is covered with tombs, to a depth, we're told, of two kilometres. It's just incredible to walk through a million year old gallery and look at the strangest hieroglyphs, and statuary, and then pass through a gate into a shaft of metal-walled splendour, reaching up more than a kilometre above the surface of the world like an unclimbable needle. The remains of the creatures here are embedded in crystal in the walls, and you can drift up the shaft on a sort of gravity lift and peer at the hideous death-masks of things that look like horned earthworms. **End entry.**

EXTRACT FROM: TOUR GUIDE TO TOMBWORLD: TOMBWORLD THE ESSENTIAL FACTS (DRACONIS PUBLICATION NO. 35)

The world Draconis B, more popularly known as Tombworld, was discovered in the year 2388, when the System was visited by scout ships of the Interplanetary Resources Corporation, IRC. Tombworld is the only planet in the system, although concentrations of asteroid and planetoid material at three locations suggest previous planetary bodies. The man who is credited with first establishing a base upon the world, and naming it Tombworld, is Arturo Yenez, Captain of the scout ship. He recognised at once that the world was dead and deserted, and yet an archaeological haven. A thin shell of pure metal deposits, parts of the tomb structures themselves, was nonetheless of insufficient interest to IRC, and Tombworld was left unexplored, and ignored, for twenty years. In 2410 an InterWorlds Colonial Survey Ship investigated Tombworld in view of its scant, but important, oxygen atmosphere. The full significance of the world was realised immediately, and its presence and nature was reported to Planetary (Documentation) Control, on Earth. The world was immediately declared 'untouchable', and scientific and archaeological survey teams dispatched.

There then began one of the century's longest, and most tiresome, court cases. IRC, in competition with other Industrial Conglomerates, were badly in debt. They expanded the definition of 'resources' to include archaeological and artifact material on any world to which they had a prior claim. They had logged, and had accepted, their right to exploit the resources of Tombworld. Now they began to do just that. They were taken to court by the Galactic Community of Friends, and in a simultaneous action by Star Heritage. After five years the courts found *for* the defendants, an unprecedented action allowing them to sell, loot and excavate the world for profit without restraint, provided all such material was represented in at least one hundred Galactic Museums. With considerable relish IRC began to strip the tombs of Tombworld. The result of their two years' unrestrained vandalism is the Devil's Crater in the southern hemisphere.

In 2427 a new action was brought, the case taken to the Vegan Appeal Court, and IRC were stopped. They were permitted to exploit only those items of artificial nature that were represented in bulk. They were forbidden to excavate or strip the world. No appeal against this decision was lodged by IRC, who established the flourishing industry that is now the property of the Galactic Co-operative itself. Dealing mainly in replicas, nothing original is sold until it has been studied, logged and replaced *in situ* by a replica itself. Thus the essential character of the world is retained. Each year an estimated four thousand miles of galleries are made newly available for the expanding tourist trade.

Although Tombworld is no longer used, awareness of the World of Ghosts, as it is frequently known, is widespread among alien species whose historical past includes a space-faring phase. To many such species, Tombworld is thought of as 'heaven', the place of rest of the good and holy. The human concept of 'heaven' is not thought to derive from an ancestral memory of Tombworld. As human contact with many alien species increased, so man's use and defilement of the planet became more widely known. In 2540 a further reduction of the human presence on Draconis B was forced by the Interworlds Species Community, sponsored by INSPEC. The Co-operative was shocked at the strength of feeling, the immensity of the anger experienced by so many alien forms who had come to realise that Earth was, effectively, 'setting up shop' in paradise lost. Again the business concern that owned Tombworld fought an action to retain retail and exploration rights, and finally won that action in 2545.

The question is often asked why was Tombworld finally left alone, why no longer used to bury the Kings and Princes of the Stars? It's use for so many millions of years, and by so many disparate species, suggests some greater awareness than is immediately obvious, and archaeological evidence has supplied a possible answer to Tombworld's importance. It is also a fact that Tombworld has always been used by the dominant Galactic species. At the moment that is Mankind himself. It is interesting to note that application has already been made by over a million wealthy citizens for entombment on Draconis B.

Personal diary Caroline. 20th November 2577: I can't say I'm sorry to be back in the Co-operative, charming though our Auroran hosts were! The trip back to Stargate Cirax was great – I think the Universe really **did** move – but after that it was an ordeal, with hundreds of reporters wanting our experiences and impressions. Remembering my previous performance I stayed clear and let Leio do the talking. He came over very well, although I could have done without having holovid shots of our apparent near disaster on safari flashed halfway round the galaxy. (It's easy to mock from a safe distance, but however many safety mechanisms you know there to be, I'd defy anyone not to panic when your weapon fails and several tons of ravening carnivore are bearing down on you.) In the event, embarrassments apart, I didn't enjoy the safari as much as I'd expected: it came to seem like gratuitous brutality, and I think Adamek might have had a point. I wouldn't admit this to Leio, though. He's really in his element here on Tombworld: the alien ruin to end all ruins. According to the figures there are something like 20 **billion** kilometres of catacombs here, honeycombing the entire planet. Only a tiny fraction has been explored, which means the amateur archaeologist has a chance to get his name in the history books by dredging up something important. The authorities aren't keen on having hordes of rampaging treasure-hunters pulverizing valuable relics underfoot, so permits are needed to explore beyond officially open catacombs; fortunately these came with our prize. Again, I must admit it's proved interesting: there's so much to see that it's almost a museum of the whole galaxy. And much to Leio's annoyance (which he tried but failed to hide) it was me rather than him who found something interesting: a half-buried metal plate covered in tiny etchings, part of which resembled the Dead World Scroll and part of which was O'rowjkth script. When we handed it in the duty archaeologist looked definitely excited. **End entry.**

Agent Luranski: Memory Implant. 21st November 2577: Brief rendezvous with a contact who tells me arrangements have been made to remove the crystal when we reach Orionis Delta. I can hardly wait. **End report.**

Archaeological work carried out between 2541 and 2548, by a team from the University of Xenoarchaeology on Pallatine VII, established that the original surface of the world still exists, more than two kilometres below the top level of tombs. The Devil's Crater, excavated and destroyed by the IRC, was not chosen as a starting point, mainly because of the build-up of debris on the lower levels. Tombworld is constructed rather like an onion, each layer of tombs covering many thousands of years, but effectively built as a new surface level. Thus, while it is possible to explore horizontally along many thousands of miles of galleries, a hundred metres or so of compacted stone, or metalwork have to be burrowed through to pass from one level to the next. The discovery of light shafts was the award-winning work of the team, which was facilitated in its penetration to the deep crystal level.

Light shafts are 'sun-watchers' narrow shafts that reach from the place of burial to the surface, allowing sunlight to touch the death-masks of the ancient Kings. Two species used such structures independantly, and both date from the second level of the world. Each subsequent layer of tombs has been built by creatures who recognised and acknowledged the importance of the light shafts, and extended those shafts so that they were permanently at the world's surface. Several hundred light shafts, two kilometres long, now exist. They form access for men and women of slight build, who can cope with the hours-long descent.

Although this level, and the excavated 'ground level', is not yet open to the public, representations of several of the domed tomb-housings from these most ancient sites are set up in the Morgan Museum. Access to the original crust was by way of connecting passages, left by the second level builders in order to revere the spirit of the Old Ones. Here the team have discovered a series of tombs believed built by the original inhabitants of Tombworld, tall, multiple-limbed creatures, of somewhat reptilian appearance, but with vestigial wings that could be splayed out to form a colourful and magnificent ruff. The walls of the tombs are richly decorated with paintings and hieroglyphs, and tell stories of the royal succession of Princes, the 'thought nets' that seem to have been webs of telepathic contact with other races, and the wars between various powers upon the globe. Legends too are represented, and here the story of the *tungollug* appears; in other tombs, deeper in the crust and perhaps older, the *tungollug* is represented not as legend, but as fact.

The *tungollug* was an ancient force, more spiritual than physical, that had lain in the crystalline mantle of the world, spread across millions of square miles, since soon after the world was formed in its final, geological state. It had come from a far galaxy, and had been trapped by the fierce magnetic field of the young planet. Old, weary, alone, the *tungollug* had found in Tombworld, a place of rest, not of death in the sense that we understand it, but of physical liaison with matter. The building of the first tombs awoke it. Its primal consciousness touched the minds of the reptile builders who, acting on what they took to be an instinctive impulse, built the tombs in a pattern, making deep shafts in the crust at the places their feelings dictated. The pattern resurrected the *tungollug* which entered the species consciousness of the builders, and used them to spread beyond the world, into space. It spread through life everywhere, filling them with the desire always to commit their mortal remains to the world where it had rested for so long. Thus, during a period of two hundred million years, the Great Lords migrated to Tombworld to die.

Is the *tungollug* dead? Has it passed beyond our Galaxy? Can that explain why Tombworld is no longer used? Or does the answer lie with the newness of the current dominant race in the Galaxy, its slow coming to awareness of this ancestral place of rest? The next thousand years might tell us the truth of the matter.

EXTRACT FROM: TOURISTS' GUIDE TO THE MAIN GALLERIES

Gallery 94: The Hall of a Thousand Races. In this immense gallery, which measures almost 30 kilometres in overall length, we see preserved in columns of ionized fluid representative specimens of **984** different alien species. Of these 633 are identified (including an early specimen of *homo erectus* in column no. 422); the remaining 351 are as yet unknown species (many of which may have been extinct for many years: estimated age of the gallery is 0.5 million years). Each appears to be the dominant species of its world, although the range of evolutionary development is very wide. The purpose of the gallery remains unknown, but it is generally believed to be the fruits of a galaxy-wide survey, a sort of Dunn's gazetteer of dominant species as found on a thousand worlds at a particular point in the past. If this is true it is a unique record of the overall level of galactic evolution at the time it was assembled — and it also leads experts to the conclusion that one of the 351 unidentified species must be the race who collected it together.

Column 732 **Asketha** Planet of origin: Bellatrix VII. The specimen here preserved is an example of the race at the time when it was its planet's dominant species, achieving a low-level technological civilization. Bellatrix VII is a world whose temperate landmass is covered by immense trees, up to 300 metres in height. Their luxuriant foliage absorbs almost all sunlight and moisture, with the result that the ground is barren except for fungoid and lichenous growths. All its animal species are arboreal. The Askthra, who were and are peaceful herbivores, escape predators through camouflage. When danger is suspected they dangle from branches by their long forelimbs, which strongly resemble wooden growths, and conceal their bodies in clumps of leaves and fruit. To facilitate this defence they have evolved immensely elongated forelimbs, which make it possible for them to swing great distances from branch to branch.

Since it is physiologically impossible for the Askthra to descend to their planet's surface, their civilization was entirely lacking in fossil fuels and metals (excepting some very low-grade iron which could be extracted from certain leaves by a laborious smelting process). In consequence their civilization never developed beyond a primitive level, and today they have devolved to ape-like intelligence. At their peak — as represented by this specimen — the Askthra reached a height of three metres, but their modern descendants barely achieve half that size. The russet and pink organs on nose and chest are used in sexual display (this specimen is a male).

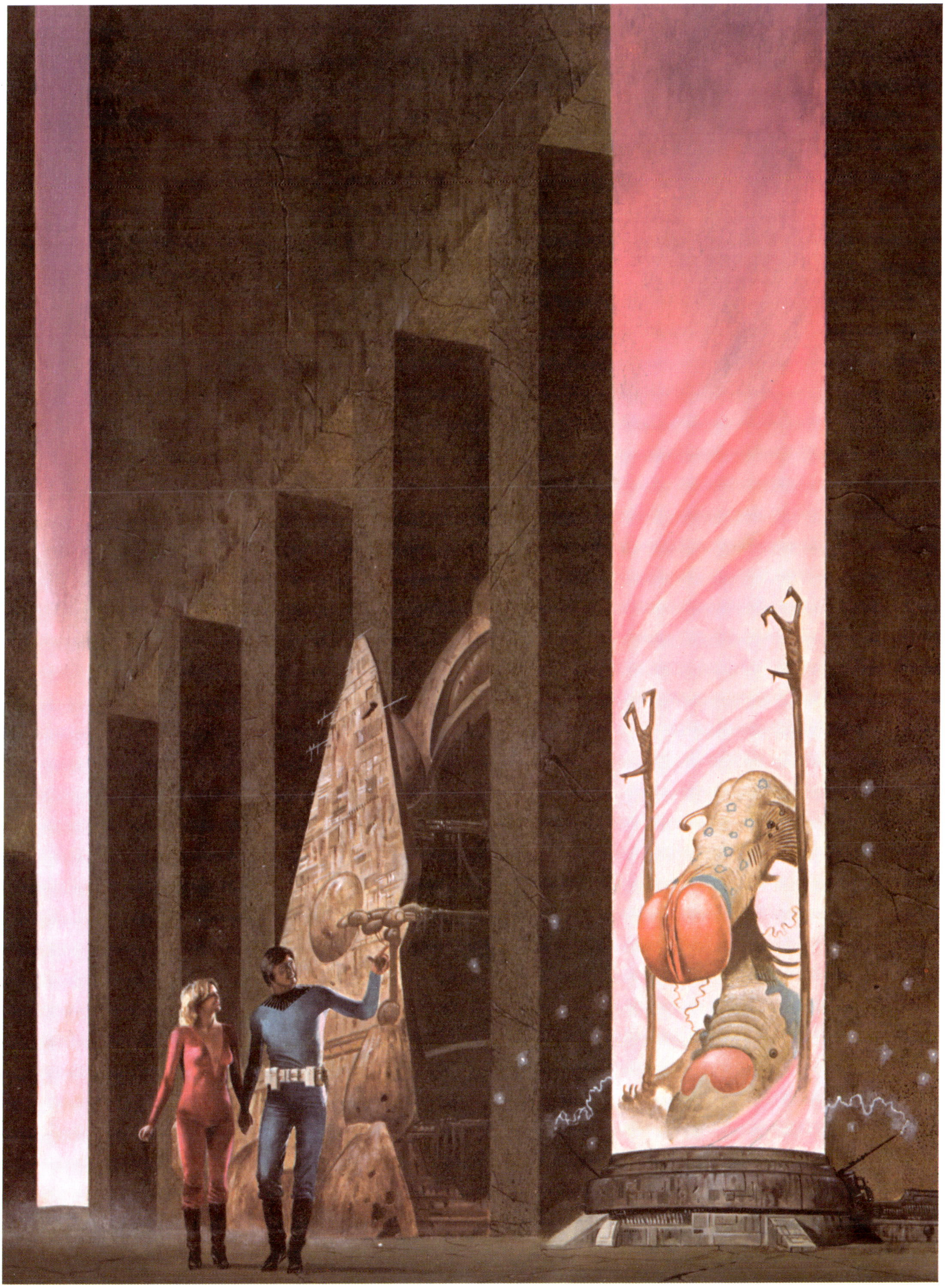

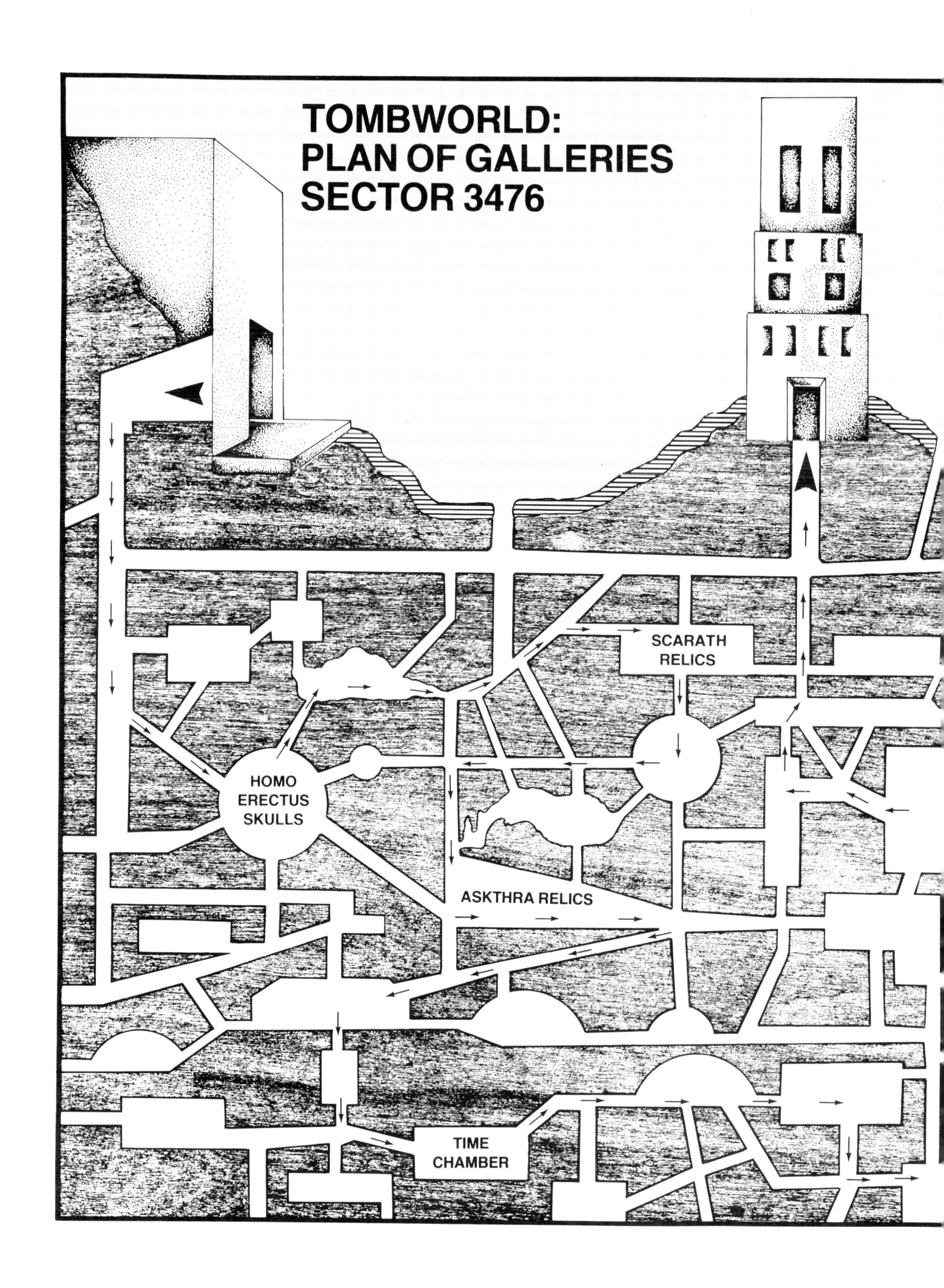

TOMBWORLD: PLAN OF GALLERIES SECTOR 3476

- SCARATH RELICS
- HOMO ERECTUS SKULLS
- ASKTHRA RELICS
- TIME CHAMBER

SSTH'ISTH
TOMBS

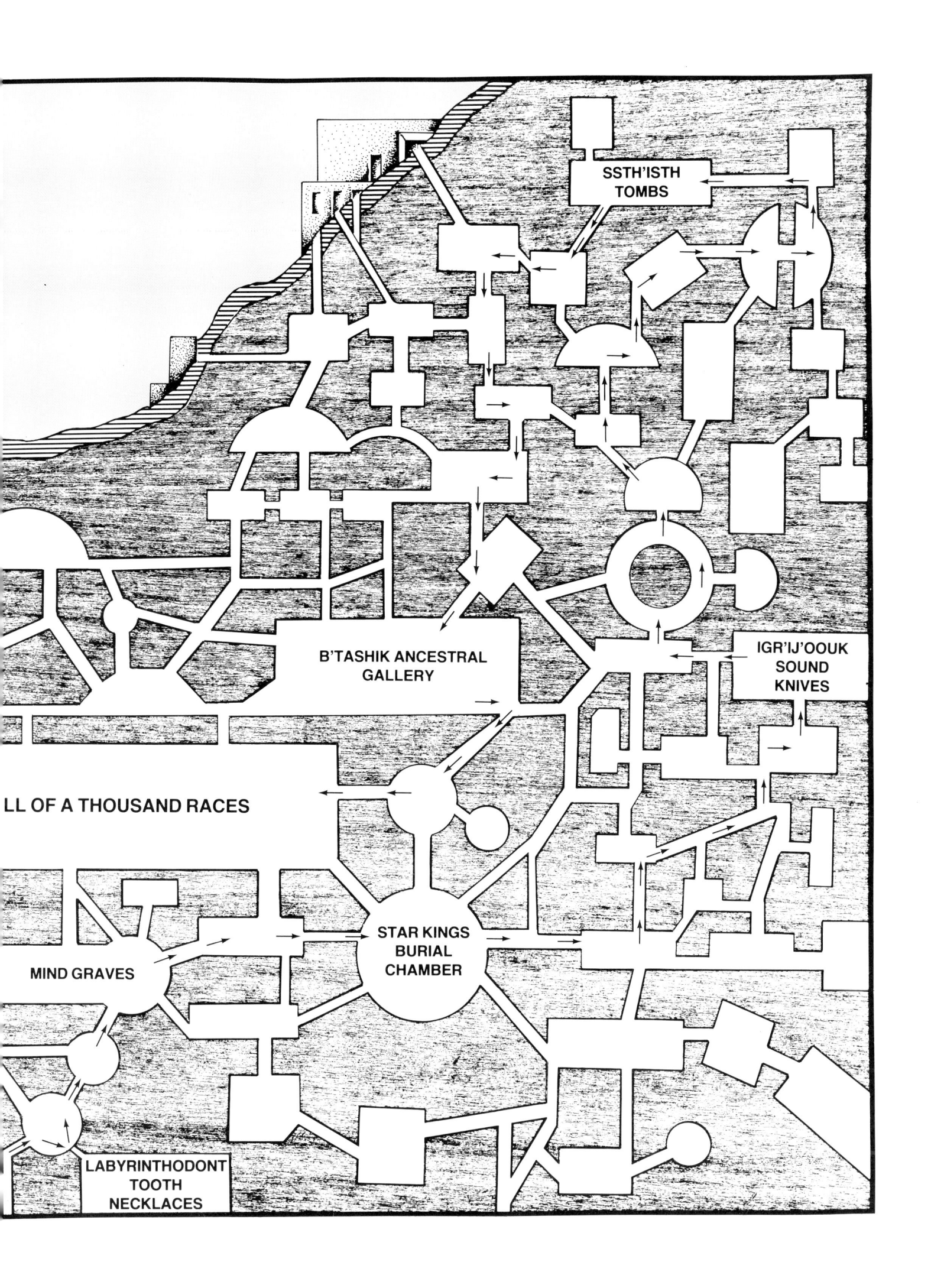

B'TASHIK ANCESTRAL
GALLERY

IGR'IJ'OOUK
SOUND
KNIVES

LL OF A THOUSAND RACES

MIND GRAVES

STAR KINGS
BURIAL
CHAMBER

LABYRINTHODONT
TOOTH
NECKLACES

TOMBWORLD SOUVENIRS

ØGT543

SOUND KNIVES designed by the now extinct race the Igr'ij'oouk. Two galleries were found filled with these elegant knives, and they are offered as souvenirs limited to one per family, or in replica. The blade is a sound blade, and quite invisible. It adjusts itself according to the tone of voice. Designed for use by a creature that communicates by a high-pitched squeal, human control is nevertheless possible by singing or shrieking. Maximum blade length is 17 metres. These are *real* weapons, and are very dangerous. The handles are gold trimmed, and rune-inscribed in various ways. Circa 45000 years BP.
Actual 14000 gc
Replica 80 gc

ØGT544

Roman pottery **VASES,** all from circa 200BC. A rare opportunity to acquire genuine cultural artefacts from the more recent period of Earth history. Whichever race visited Earth at this time, they took an obvious liking to those decorated wine and grain containers. A variety of styles are available; all in perfect condition, and richly decorated in several primitive pigments. Mostly from the Provinces.
Actual 22000 gc
Replica 120 gc

ØGT545

Q'rowjkth **DECORATIVE OBJECT**. Present in great abundance in the various galleries containing the remains of the Q'rowjkth Star Kings, these decorated and inscribed objects, sixty centimetres in length, have no known function. They were possibly used as body adornment. Variety of colours, inscriptions and materials, although most are constructed of iron. Contemporary Q'rowjkth have no understanding of them.
Actual 500 gc
Replica 25 gc

ØGT546

STASIS CAPSULE found amid what appears to be fossilized spaceship wreckage. Timescan dating puts age of wreckage at approx. 13 x 10⁶ years, suggesting that this may be a relic of the Llth'ryllyr civilization. The actual capsule is approx. 3 metres high and 2 in diameter; it resembles a giant capsicum. The surface is a perfect mirror, reflecting radiation of all wavelengths. Vincent (2467) suggests that it may contain the pilot or crew of the crashed ship, waiting in suspended animation for a rescue which never came. Replicas make ideal room sculpture.
Replica 130 gc

ØGT547

LABYRINTHODONT TOOTH NECKLACES. 230 million years BP. From one of the deepest, and oldest of the galleries, comes this collection of several hundred thousand necklaces formed from the primitive teeth of the earliest amphibians of Earth. Living in the Permian Period, the labyrinthodonts were among the first land animals. The creatures that slaughtered them for these trophies are not known as much of the gallery system has collapsed, and no written or printed records remain, or were left. But the likelihood is that the gallery belongs to the original inhabitants of Tombworld.
Necklaces 1800 gc
Single tooth 200 gc

ØGT548

THE TIME CHAMBER. The actual chamber measures 20 metres across, and it takes at least 30 seconds subjective time to traverse its ever-shifting labyrinthine passages. Yet to an outside observer a person begins to appear from the exit at precisely the moment they move into the entrance. The nature and purpose of the spacetime warp contained in the chamber – and its purpose – confound scientists.
Operating model 100 gc

ØGT549

DRINKING VESSELS from Hyperiona. These are of the same great age as those excavated during the colonisation of Hyperiona, now a world devoid of intelligent life, and available for inhabitation by Man. The gallery specimens are in exquisite condition. The vessels are shaped like funnels, and made from wood paste chewed and hardened with body fluid. The vessels were used ritualistically and drinking occurred from beneath. Highly decorated, showing the anatomical features and society of the extinct species.
Replica only 150 gc

ØGT550

TYRANNOSAURUS REX. The most savage animal ever to walk the Earth, here perfectly preserved in the act of consuming a small herbivorous dinosaur. For all its gruesomeness one of Tombworld's most popular exhibits.
Replica (stands 280 mm) 230 gc
Replica (Tyrannosaurus only) 190 gc

ØGT551

Two dimensional **DYNAMIC PHOTO/PICTOGRAPHS** of a number of terrestrial subjects, including: Pre-Christian Palestine, N. America approx. 2000 BC, lifestyle of Peking Man circa 400 thousand years BP, coronations of the Saxon Kings and the fall of the Arizona meteor. Movement time 10 seconds. These pictures are available in copied form, and come from the vast collection of a touring Royal Family of B'tashik, who quite evidently toured time as well as space. The B'tashik have

TOMBWORLD SOUVENIRS

ØGT552

SKULLS and **HEADS** of **HOMO ERECTUS.** Gathered by the now primitive B'tashik during their exploration of the Galaxy, over a million skulls and several thousand preserved heads are located in their upper galleries. Many of the skulls, for which the aliens seem to have taken a liking, have been converted into light sources, powered by Greenspar. A few skulls and heads are made available for sale each year, in accordance with and under the direction of the Community of Universal Faith.
Skull 25000 gc
Head 50000 gc
Replica 500 gc

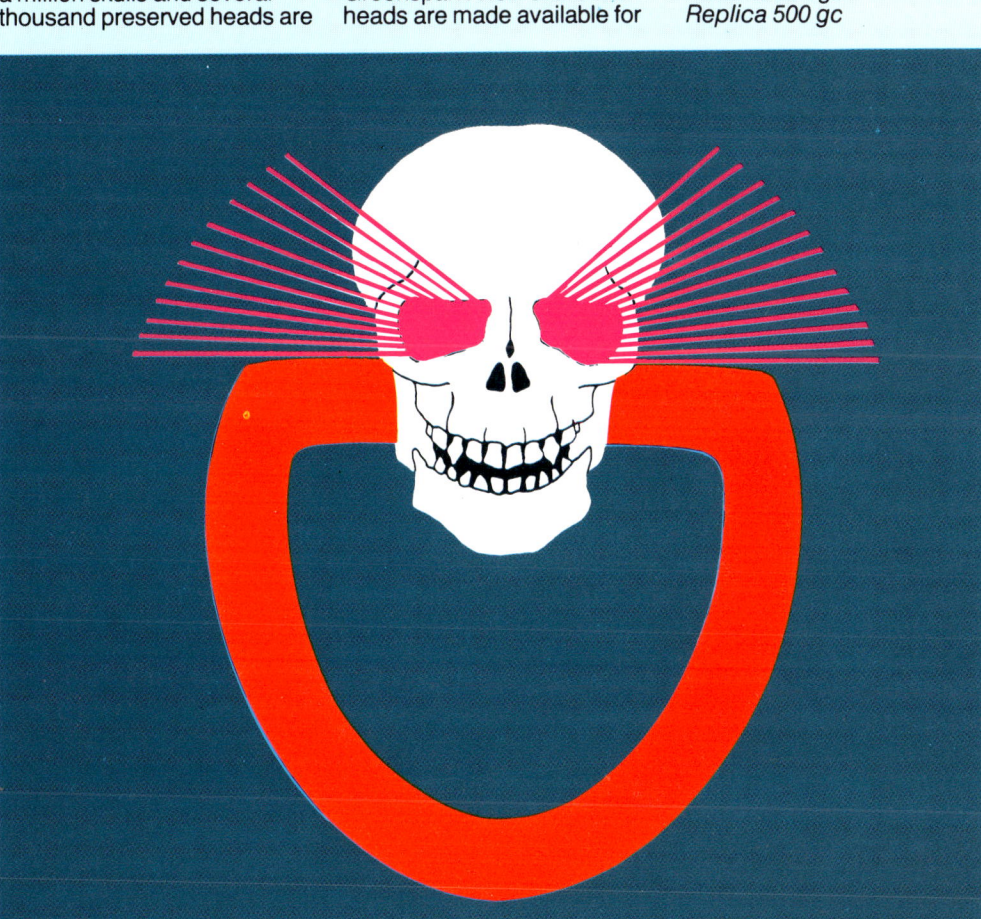

reverted to primitivism, but their ancestral galleries on Tombworld are among the richest and best preserved. The collection includes over ten million pictures of other alien life forms and worlds between 4 million and 400 BP.
Prints 10 gc

ØGT553

DEATH MASK from Sigma Draconis V. the bipedal inhabitants of this world (the Scarath) have, for countless millennia, worn elaborate masks on various ritual occasions. The most sumptuous of all is the death mask worn by the female Scarath when she elects to kill her fore-husband during the biennial festival of Frieth. Many of these masks, elaborately carved from wood and bone, inlaid with precious metals and stones, decorated with feathers and discarded eye-sheaths, have been collected.
Actual 9000 gc
Replica 110 gc

ØGT554

Monokolgi **COPROLITHS**. The fossilised stool of the now extinct Monokolgi are wonderful records of the hard-shelled animal life that once existed on the world Prilamar VII before it was burned by a nova and sterilised. The coproliths are covered by bizarre animalcular shapes, and inside show the concentration of shells and skeletal material that was compacted into the round deposit. Collected by the alien Federation known as the Jederam, they seem to have been held in some reverence, as if they contained the last spiritual life of the dead world.
Large 200 gc
Small 150 gc

ØGT555

THE CREATION OF A SOLAR SYSTEM
Continuous holovid projection showing the formation of an 11 planet system (unidentified). Runs 135 mins, compressing millions of years of action. Not a mock-up, this is a genuine recording made by advanced timescan techniques.
Holovid copy (FFT or CL system) 20 gc

ØGT556

Funkiktsch **EXCRETORY CONTAINERS.** Made from beaten bronze or iron, the vessels have a capacity of three gallons. The Funkiktsch believe that the force of the anti-Being resides in excretory matter; for millions of years they have collected all their bodily waste products in vast Foul Pits on their world, often carrying this matter for thousands of miles. Containers were the prize possession, and during the Funkiktsch supremacy, 12000 BP, when the nobility came to Tombworld to rest, these containers built up. Supply of spares now exhausted, but replicas are hand made by contemporary F. in ancient tradition. Highly decorated and ideal punch bowls for social occasions.
Replica 200 gc

ØGT557

ir-Grasnuavath **MIND GRAVES.** The mind graves are small, cubical blocks of copper- or iron-rich silica, very highly coloured, and intricately marked with surface electron channels. They contain the last mental output of a single dying ir-Grasnuavath. Using Homex Crystalscan Deep (Read) Ultrabeam decoders the emanations can be heard as fluctuating whistles. The contemporary military regime on the ir-Grasnuavath homeworld has outlawed all after-life paraphernalia and given permission for sale of the graves, of which on Tombworld there are an estimated billion. However, in obedience to the Community Law of Life Respect, sale is limited to one thousand items per year. Recordings are available, also translations.
Mind Grave 45000 gc
DubTexic recording (20 voices) with spoken translation 100 gc

PAN GALACTIC
STARTOUR DISPLAY TICKET

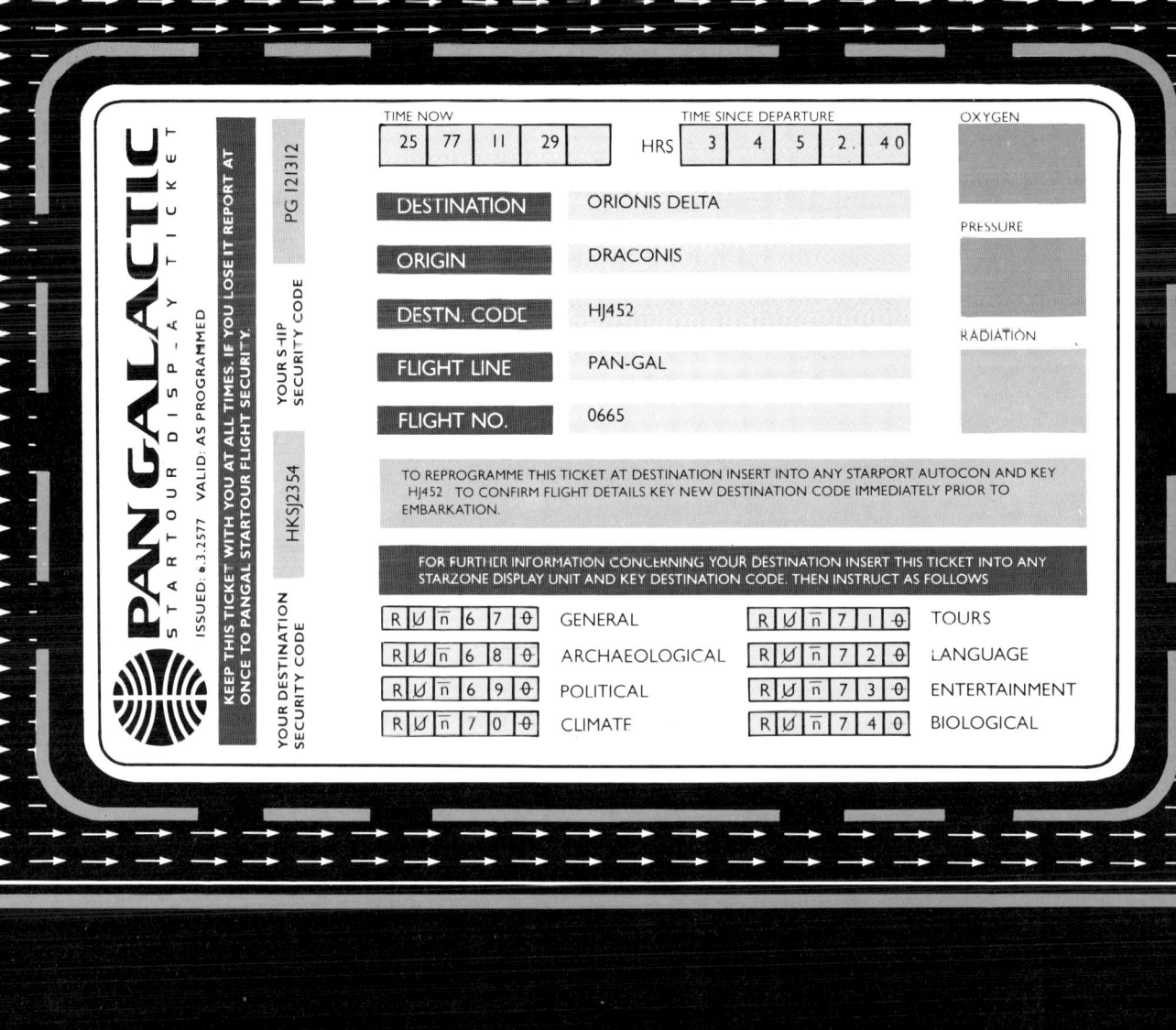

ISSUED: 6.3.2577 VALID: AS PROGRAMMED

KEEP THIS TICKET WITH YOU AT ALL TIMES. IF YOU LOSE IT REPORT AT ONCE TO PANGAL STARTOUR FLIGHT SECURITY.

YOUR SHIP SECURITY CODE: **PG 121312**

YOUR DESTINATION SECURITY CODE: **HKSJ2354**

TIME NOW					TIME SINCE DEPARTURE				
25	77	11	29	HRS	3	4	5	2	40

DESTINATION	ORIONIS DELTA
ORIGIN	DRACONIS
DESTN. CODE	HJ452
FLIGHT LINE	PAN-GAL
FLIGHT NO.	0665

OXYGEN

PRESSURE

RADIATION

TO REPROGRAMME THIS TICKET AT DESTINATION INSERT INTO ANY STARPORT AUTOCON AND KEY HJ452 TO CONFIRM FLIGHT DETAILS KEY NEW DESTINATION CODE IMMEDIATELY PRIOR TO EMBARKATION.

FOR FURTHER INFORMATION CONCERNING YOUR DESTINATION INSERT THIS TICKET INTO ANY STARZONE DISPLAY UNIT AND KEY DESTINATION CODE. THEN INSTRUCT AS FOLLOWS

R Ø n̄ 6 7 0	GENERAL		R Ø n̄ 7 1 0	TOURS
R Ø n̄ 6 8 0	ARCHAEOLOGICAL		R Ø n̄ 7 2 0	LANGUAGE
R Ø n̄ 6 9 0	POLITICAL		R Ø n̄ 7 3 0	ENTERTAINMENT
R Ø n̄ 7 0 0	CLIMATE		R Ø n̄ 7 4 0	BIOLOGICAL

TA · ORIONIS DELTA

```
ORIONIS DELTA SYSTEM
SOL-TYPE SUN
NINE PLANETS
ORIONIS DELTA III, OR BEHEMOTHS' WORLD,
IS EARTH-TYPE. THE 7TH PLANET A GAS
GIANT HAS MICRO-ORGANIC LIFE. NO
INTELLIGENT SPECIES. BEHEMOTHS' WORLD
HARBOURS ABUNDANT ANIMAL LIFE,
INCLUDING MASSIVE BEHEMOTHS THEMSELVES,
BUT ALSO A GREAT VARIETY OF MAMMALOID
LIFE WITH BETA-LEVEL POTENTIAL FOR
EVOLUTION TO SENTIENCE WITHIN 10
MILLION YEARS.
```

ORIONIS DELTA

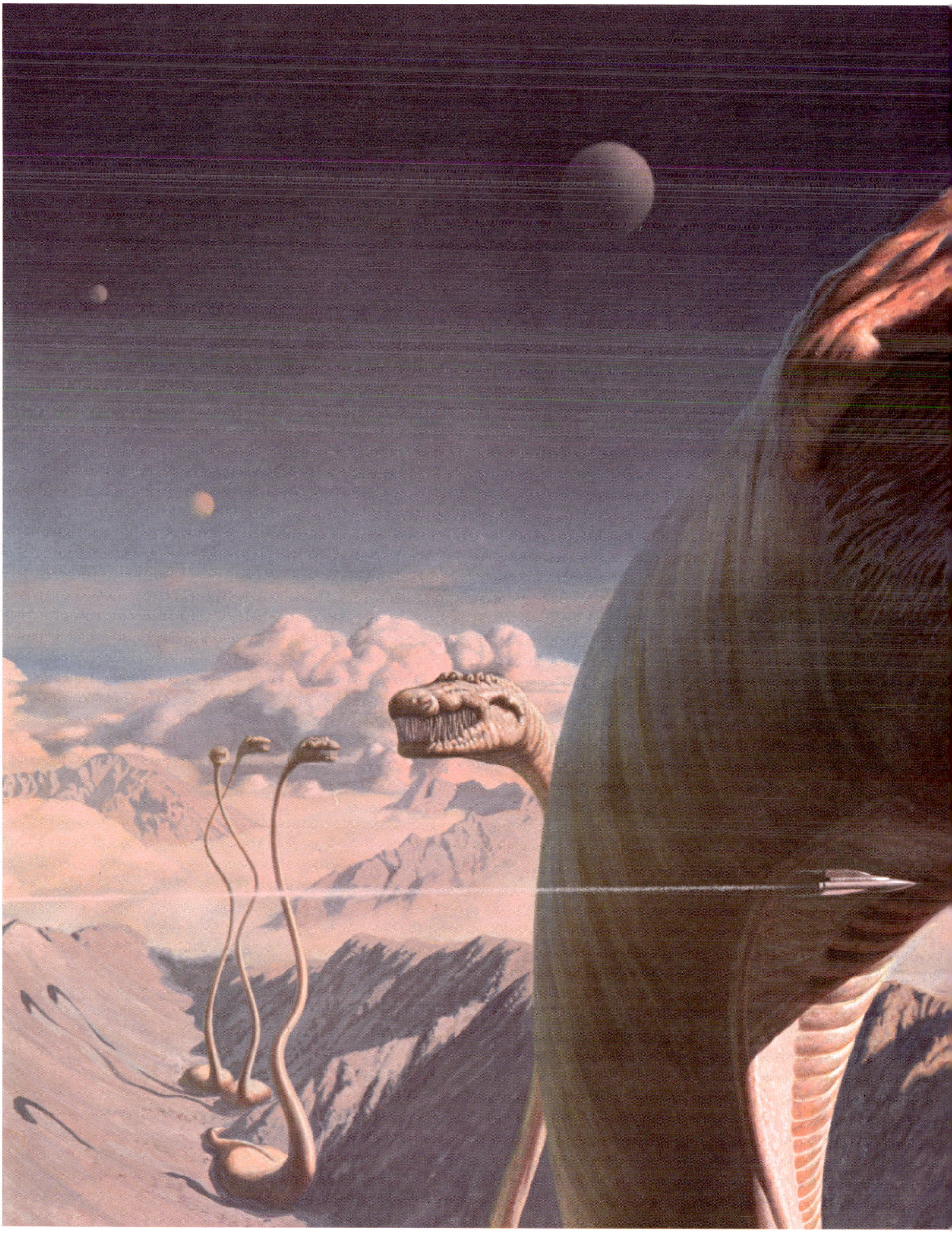

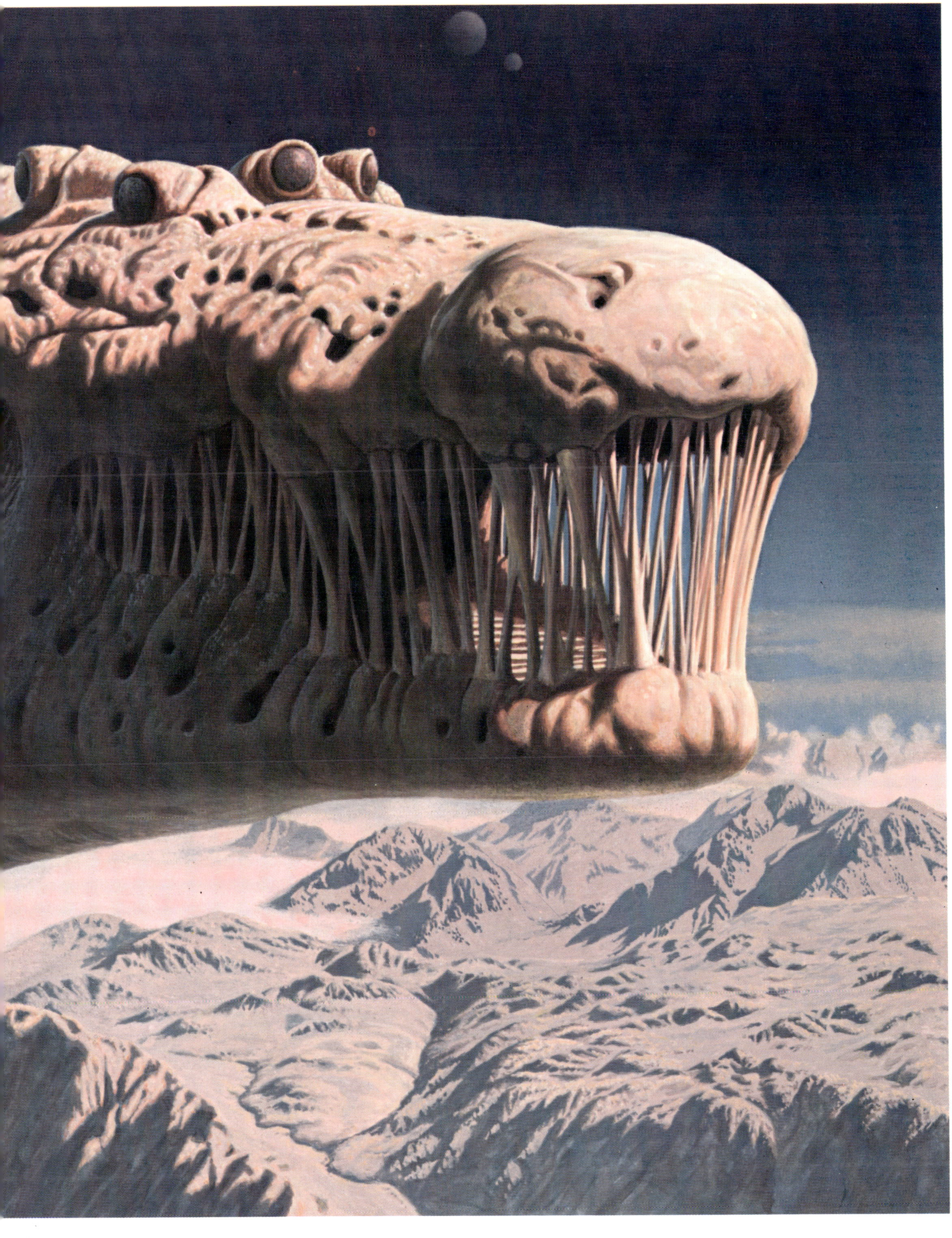

Personal diary Lelo. 6th December 2577: I've been neglecting my diary for too long. I keep forgetting. There's just so much to do! If I had my way I'd do an about-turn and go back to Tombworld. What a place that was! I don't think I could ever get too much of it. We hardly scratched the surface, we hardly saw one percent of what there is to see, and we were there for two weeks! Now we've come to see the last of the scheduled Wonders of the Galaxy, the Behemoths' World of Orionis Delta III. We've had a bit of a disaster too, and will miss our connecting flight to Hyperiona. I'll get to that in a moment. Behemoths' World is one of those places you just refuse to believe exist. It's quite astonishing, and the beasts, the Behemoths (as they are always called), are just incredible. There are only forty thousand on the whole planet! The world itself is slightly larger than Earth, but much less dense. I weigh only three-quarters of my normal weight here, and it gives you an incredible sense of confidence as you spring-foot along. It also helps the Behemoths. Forty thousand non-sentient creatures, and they hardly ever move. Their necks are hundreds of metres long, reaching right up to the higher atmosphere where they sieve air-borne 'plankton' – and incidentally, those plankton are sometimes human-sized, light-weight but voluminous. The heads are hysterical. They're immense. The neck muscles bulge and throb below and somehow manage to keep the skulls supported. We landed on one beast's head, and took a hike across one of its eye-ridges. We had to be roped to a stanchion driven into some horny, scaly skin where it wouldn't feel it. With our masks on you don't get the sense of atmospheric rarity, but you certainly feel the wind. And you get bombarded by organic material, blobby creatures, and insectiforms, and those struggling balloons, with their transparent arms and legs, that seem so humanoid. The Behemoth moans as it sucks them in, and air siphons from fossae all over its head. Its eyes don't seem to move at all, but its head sways in the wind. When you look down, its body (which is kilometres in length) looks tiny, almost silly. The neck is straight, with flotation bags inside, apparently. Its way of reproducing is bizarre. They don't have much pleasure, that's for sure.

We were only scheduled to stay here for a week, touring the world and studying the gigantic beasts, and attempting to

EXTRACT FROM: WONDERS OF THE GALACTIC ZOO, REV. ED. 2564

Behemoths (*Giganticus Orionis*) In our explorations of the galaxy we have found many strange life-forms, but none more bizarre than the Behemoths of Orionis Delta III – or Behemoths' World, as it is popularly known. These are by far the largest organic life-forms ever discovered, dwarfing the dinosaurs of ancient Earth just as the dinosaurs would dwarf an insect. The statistics of their size are staggering: a neck extending vertically to a recorded maximum of 1950 metres (twice the height of the tallest building on Earth!); a head the size of a cathedral; a body with a mass of untold thousands of tons (a precise figure has never been established). Their freakish evolution is one of the strangest stories of galactic zoology.

Archaeological excavations show that millions of years in the past the ancestors of the Behemoths, while huge enough, showed little evidence of the neck elongation which gives them such a startling appearance. In that primeval era the Behemoths were just one among a great variety of immense creatures (including predators which must have been the most fearsome animals ever to walk the soil of any planet). But the evolution of much smaller and more agile mammaloid forms spelled doom for the giants, just as happened on Earth and many other worlds. The mammaloids competed successfully for food, and the Behemoths' cousins were starved out of existence. The Behemoths' first advantage was that even then they did not feed on the ground; instead they survived, as now, by filtering from the air huge quantities of pseudo-plankton. These are abundant, jellyfish-like creatures, floating with the aid of helium sacs, which at that time swarmed in the lower atmosphere, feeding on micro-organisms.

The crucial factor triggering the Behemoths' development to their present form is believed to have been the evolution of flying mammaloids – in the first instance gliders, incapable of sustaining long flights, but eventually true fliers. As these became common the plankton, their numbers threatened as never before, ceased to be found in quantity near the ground. The only Behemoths which still had access to their food source were the largest, or those with the longest necks. The others slowly died out. (You must remember that all these changes took many thousands, even millions, of years.)

So it continued, the plankton retreating gradually to the highest level of the atmosphere at which they could live (the topmost stratum of micro-organisms) and the Behemoths developing their long necks through natural selection in pursuit.

How does the Behemoth's neck remain upright, duplicating a feat which human technology would have found impossible as little as 500 years ago? The answer is that the Behemoths' skeletons naturally contain (through processes we do not yet understand) reinforcing filaments of continuous pseudodiamond crystal (to use the non-technical term). It is a similar substance to the material which made possible the construction of the space elevators, and it gives their skeletons a tensile strength thousands of times that of ordinary bone. The neck also contains a series of helium sacs which act like a series of balloons moored to it and helping to pull it aloft.

Such an enormous mass presents many problems. The adult Behemoth is, of course, incapable of movement, and its neck cannot deviate more than 8 degrees from the vertical. Beyond those narrow limits it loses equilibrium, and the combined efforts of muscles and flotation sacs are insufficient to bring it upright again. One of the commonest causes of death among these naturally long-lived creatures is for the head to fall to the ground. Even if the neck does not rupture or the skull break the animal will quickly starve to death.

The creatures require an enormous intake of food to sustain them, despite the extreme slowness of their metabolism. The head has developed to great size in order to trap the maximum number of plankton, which are caught in innumerable air filters lining hundreds of air passages through the skull. These passages also serve to reduce the skull's wind resistance and thus improve the Behemoth's stability.

get into communication with them. This is more of a joke than anything, since the Behemoths, you are repeatedly told, are unintelligent. But they communicate their animal desires and fears on some super-auditory level, that's practically telepathy when you get down to it. Local superstition holds that the Behemoths are talking to themselves all the time, planning how they'll get rid of the intruders. Caroline experienced some wild dreams, imagining herself to be a Behemoth, and feeling the sensations of wind and rain on her neck, and the great longing (sorry) for reproduction. Perhaps that was the sort of contact that happens. Anyway, it only happened once, and then we had the disaster. We were touring a skeleton. On this world they take the bones of the beasts and convert them into tourist centres. It's an excellent idea since it negates the need to build human structures on an inhabited world. The skulls of the dead litter the planet, and take centuries to decay, apparently. Inside many skulls there are hotels, medical facilities, restaurants and theatres. Each building is inside either a socket, or one of the spaces where brain or other organs was lodged. The skull ridges, just bits of bone thrown up into a slender barrier inside to divide one bit of brain from another, are metres high, and several have been converted into monorails. So you can ride about inside this cavern, dreaming dreams of Behemoth pasts. Caroline, getting keen on the idea of doing some climbing, as we used to on Earth, starts to climb one of the wind caverns in the skeleton's backbone. She wanted to see inside the enclosed spaces that don't get built in, and run through the bone itself. Of course she fell. She didn't have ropes, and her so-called guides were two local lads who'd taken an obvious fancy to her and no doubt had plans to do their own bit of exploring once inside the cavity. I felt really angry, but she did look a sight. She only fell a little way, and most of that was an ungainly slide. But she broke her arm. I didn't realise she'd been so badly hurt, at first, but apparently her left upper arm had snapped clean through. With Quik-Knit she'll be okay in a couple of days, but it's held us up. **End entry.**

Reproduction is an obvious problem for an animal incapable of movement once it reaches maturity. The Behemoths solve it by a mechanism oddly reminiscent of that used by certain trees (e.g. the sycamore). Once a year the adult male produces huge quantities of sperm which it expels in floating clusters from an organ on its back, a process repeated at regular intervals over a period of 7-11 days. These clusters have enough buoyancy to carry them up to fifty kilometres on the wind. At the same time the female opens a sexual orifice on its back and waits for sperm – a single cell will do – to drift into it. It's a chancy process, not least because the floating sperm provide an extra food source for plankton, but enough reach their target to maintain the Behemoths' slow birth rate. The young are born alive about 42 weeks later; a single mother may produce several hundred. At birth they stand about four metres high and slightly resemble young giraffes; they are mobile quadrupeds at this stage. They are also cannibalistic – and indeed ravenously attack any potential food source. They grow very rapidly during the first hundred days, and birth is always timed to coincide with the plankton swarming season, when they are most abundant in the lower atmosphere. The few young Behemoths that survive lose mobility after about two years, although they take at least 20 years to reach adult mass, and 100 to grow to their maximum size.

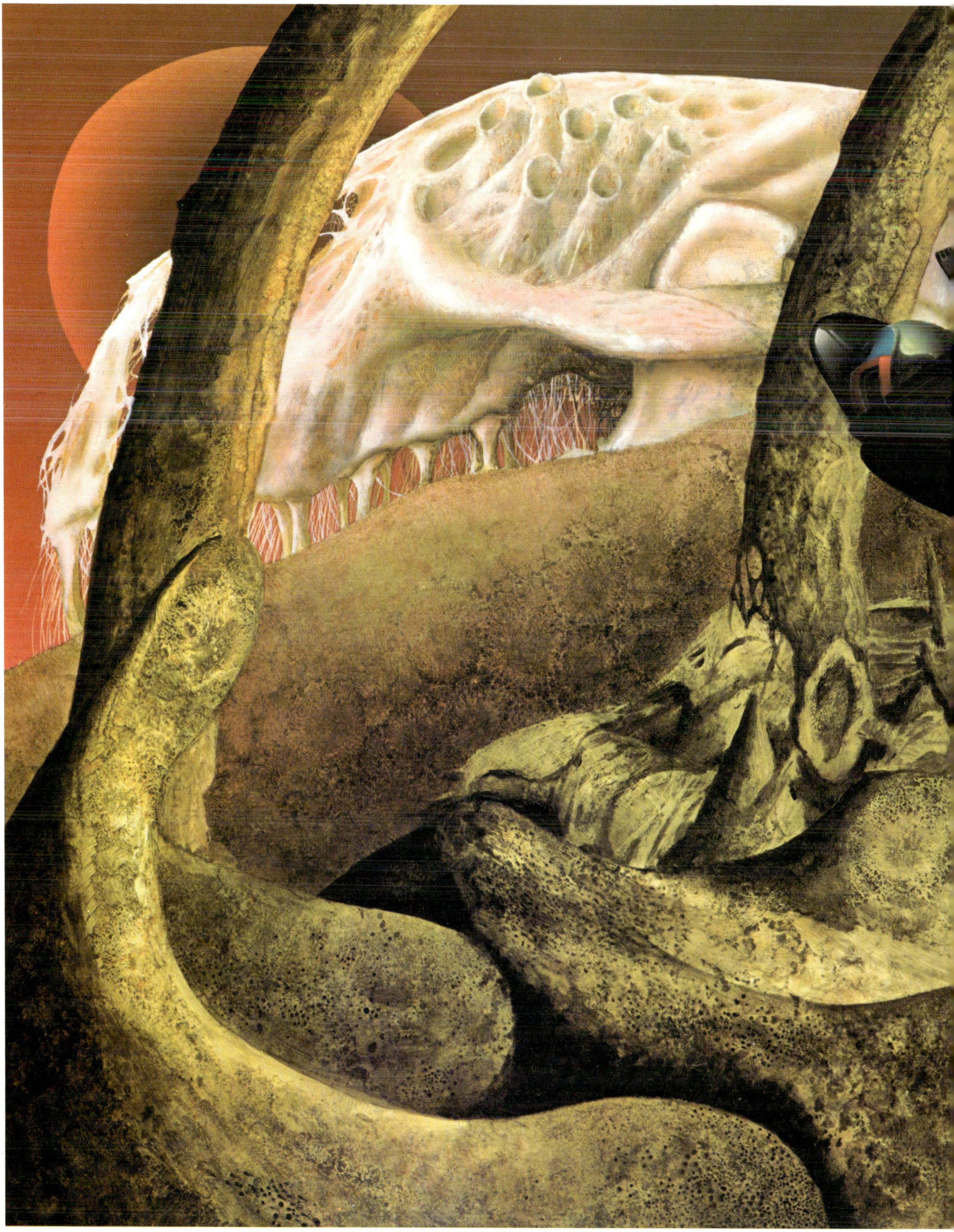

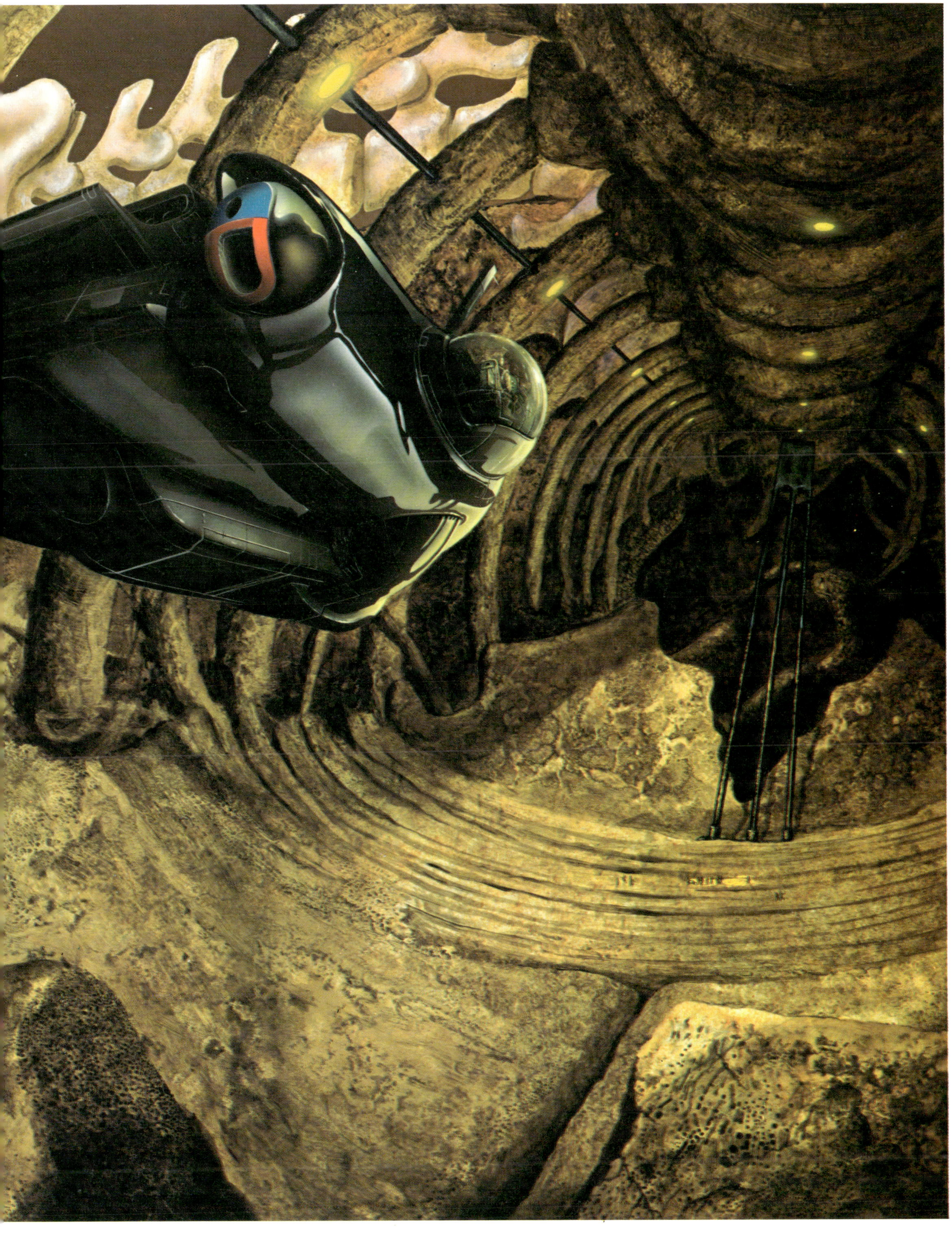

Personal diary Caroline. 7th December 2577: Mission accomplished! The feeling of relief is incredible, exhilarating. As of this moment my status as an agent is Permanent Inactive, which means effectively I'm retired (nobody can ever actually **leave** the service). So I'm free to return to normal life, with whatever changes result from this trip (quite a few, I hope). Leio will never know a thing. (If I ever show him this diary I'll have to do some editing.) It was all done very quickly and smoothly. We arrived here in Skull City VI on Behemoths' World and spent our first few days flying around, just marvelling at the absurd, incredible creatures. We even landed on the head of one. You have to be careful walking around in case you stray too near an air passage and get sucked in; it would be humiliating to end as a tiny crumb of a Behemoth's lunch. We chased 'plankton' some of which — tiny as they are compared to the Behemoths — looked sufficiently large and fearsome to me. Then, while exploring inside a skeleton — an amazing experience, like standing inside an organic cathedral — I faked a fall. An ambulance arrived almost too quickly and whisked me off to the hospital, where a surgeon from the service on Earth was waiting. Under anaesthetic he swiftly fractured my arm, removed the crystal, set the bone with Quik-Knit, treated my eyes with a chemical which painlessly dissolves the cameras, and that was that. A couple more days and I'll be out of hospital. Poor Leio's a little baffled as to how I managed to break my arm in such a trivial fall. I'd really like to tell him the whole story, but of course that isn't possible. (Even if I did, I expect he'd only think I'd been popping once too often.) The best news emerged from a visit this morning by a senior agent. She played back the recording I made in prison on Aurora. It was very unsettling listening to my own voice describing events of which I have no memory whatever. I've been trying since to summon up a mental picture of those happenings. Sometimes I think I've pinned down a faint recollection; but then I think I'm probably just reconstructing it from the playback. It's disorienting. It makes you wonder if other parts of your memory could be fake. You wake up one morning with a headache: is it really because of what you did last night, or is it because your entire previous existence has just been wiped out and replaced by a clever set of fake memories? There's no answer — it's one of those "How do I know

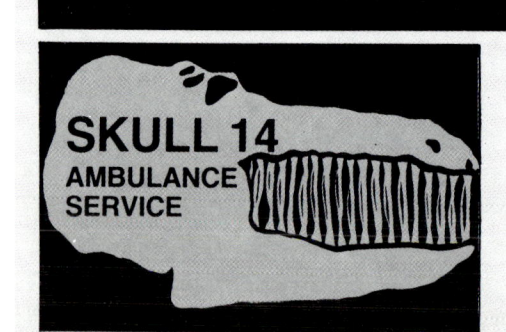

SKULL 14 AMBULANCE SERVICE

MEDCARE CENTRE

ORIONIS DELTA HEALTH SERVICE

G.M.O. 17792/BM/15

CALL OUT SHEET

AMBULANCE NO:	MEDCEN S-K6352
DRIVER:	ROBISEN E
DAY:	4* DECEMBER 2577 GST
TIME:	13.58
LOCATION OF ACCIDENT:	MERIDIANAL SPINAL FOSSA 2214 (0.5km STH SKULL ENTRY)
CASUALTIES:	ONE HUMAN FEMALE : HUMERAL FRACTURE
WHERE TAKEN:	CENTRE 14
TIME OF RETURN TO ON-CALL:	14.32
SIGNED:	*E. Robinson*

I exist?" sort of questions which are ultimately pointless. Anyway, it seems I improvised effectively on Aurora, and gathered important information. My hypersonic recordings show significant modifications to the DreadHulk's structure, and preliminary analysis suggest that our scientists should be able fairly readily to duplicate the Aurorans' work. The balance of power is maintained, and detente (one hopes) will continue with both sides knowing there is no advantage to be gained by force. It's sad that this kind of work is still needed, but until we're all united in a single co-operative I suppose it always will be. Maybe we could have trusted the Aurorans, but dare we take the chance? No. Whatever happens now, though, my part is over. All I need concentrate on is the remainder of the holiday. It's a pity we only have one more stop before returning home (and even that's going to be curtailed by this hospitalization), but I certainly intend to make the most of it. Hyperiona, entertainment world of the Galaxy . . . and about 10,000cr of spending money left . . . **End entry.**

NAME	SPECIES	MEDFILE NO	AGE	SEX
LURANSKI. C.	HOMO-SAPIENS	AxM317423ef	21	F

HOSPITAL NO	WARD/ENVIRONMENT
13	MOTHRA

NORMAL BASAL TEMP
B/F ELEMENT
ORGANIC STRUCTURE
EXO/ENDOSKEL
NORMAL PULSE
NORMAL B/F PRESSURE
SLEEP/WAKE CYCLE
OTHER NOTES

SIMPLE HUMERAL FRACTURE

DIETARY
HUMAN NORMAL

PHEROMONAL

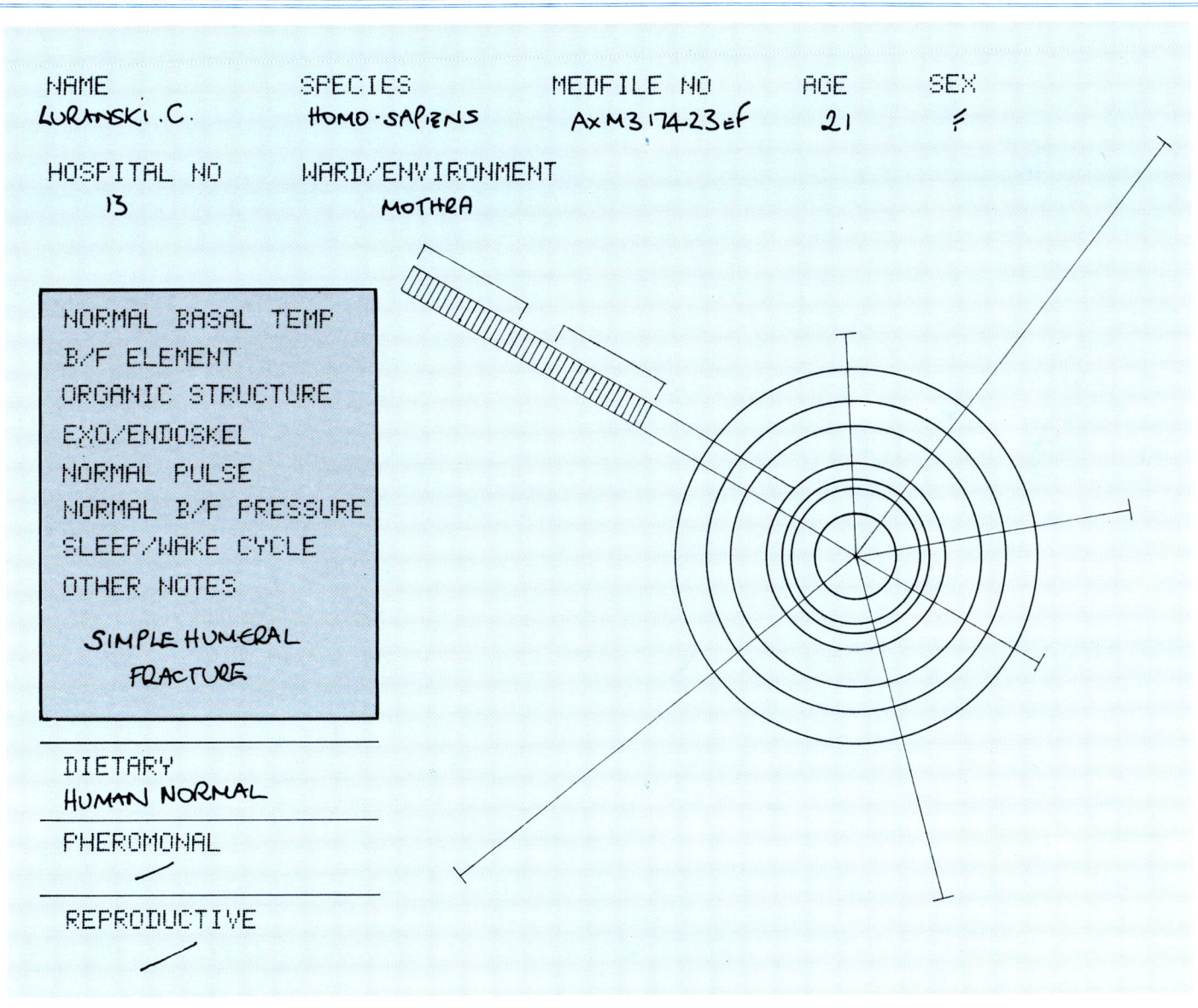

REPRODUCTIVE

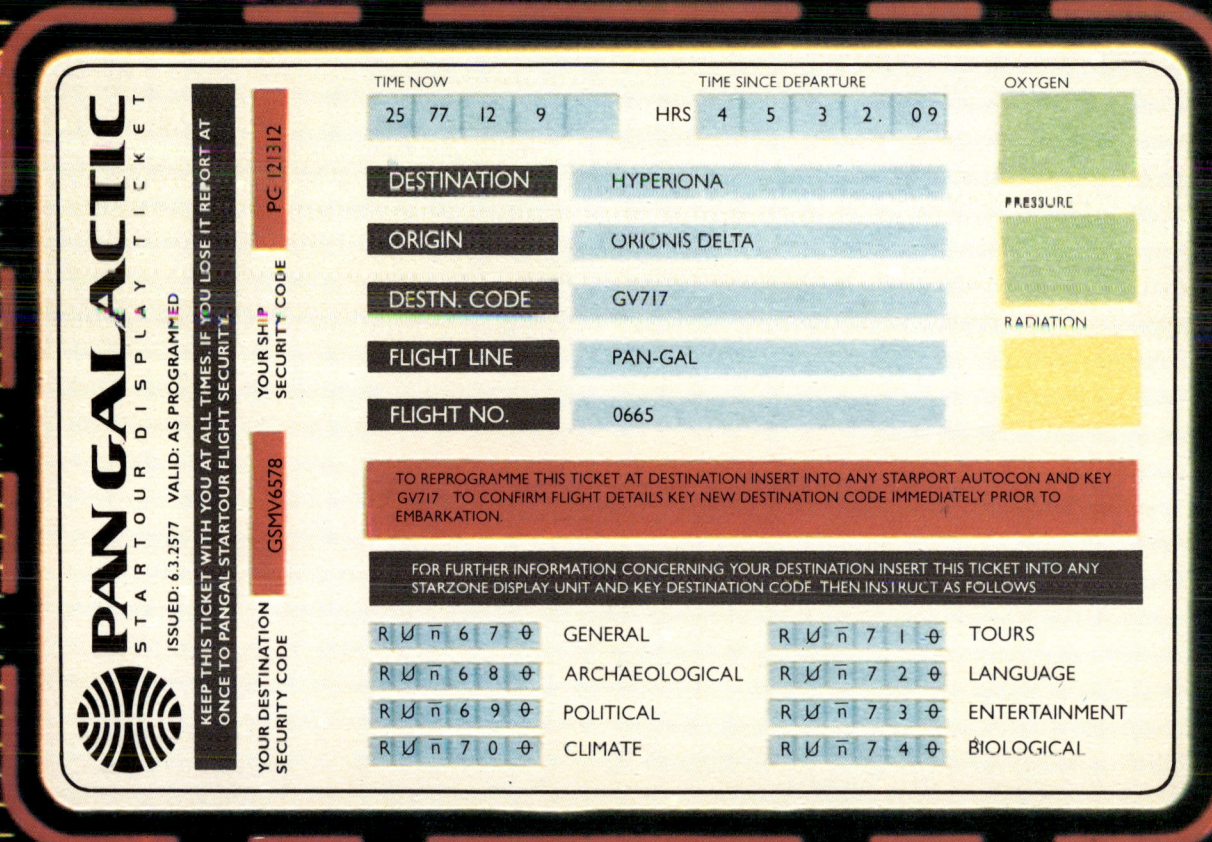

PAN GALACTIC
STARTOUR DISPLAY TICKET

ISSUED: 6.3.2577   VALID: AS PROGRAMMED

KEEP THIS TICKET WITH YOU AT ALL TIMES. IF YOU LOSE IT REPORT AT ONCE TO PANGAL STARTOUR FLIGHT SECURITY.

YOUR SHIP SECURITY CODE: GSMV6578

YOUR DESTINATION SECURITY CODE: PG 12/312

TIME NOW	TIME SINCE DEPARTURE
25 77 12 9	HRS 4 5 3 2 . 09

DESTINATION	HYPERIONA
ORIGIN	ORIONIS DELTA
DESTN. CODE	GV717
FLIGHT LINE	PAN-GAL
FLIGHT NO.	0665

OXYGEN
PRESSURE
RADIATION

TO REPROGRAMME THIS TICKET AT DESTINATION INSERT INTO ANY STARPORT AUTOCON AND KEY GV717 TO CONFIRM FLIGHT DETAILS KEY NEW DESTINATION CODE IMMEDIATELY PRIOR TO EMBARKATION.

FOR FURTHER INFORMATION CONCERNING YOUR DESTINATION INSERT THIS TICKET INTO ANY STARZONE DISPLAY UNIT AND KEY DESTINATION CODE. THEN INSTRUCT AS FOLLOWS

R U n 6 7 0	GENERAL	R U n 7 1 0	TOURS
R U n 6 8 0	ARCHAEOLOGICAL	R U n 7 2 0	LANGUAGE
R U n 6 9 0	POLITICAL	R U n 7 3 0	ENTERTAINMENT
R U n 7 0 0	CLIMATE	R U n 7 4 0	BIOLOGICAL

HYPERION · HYPERI

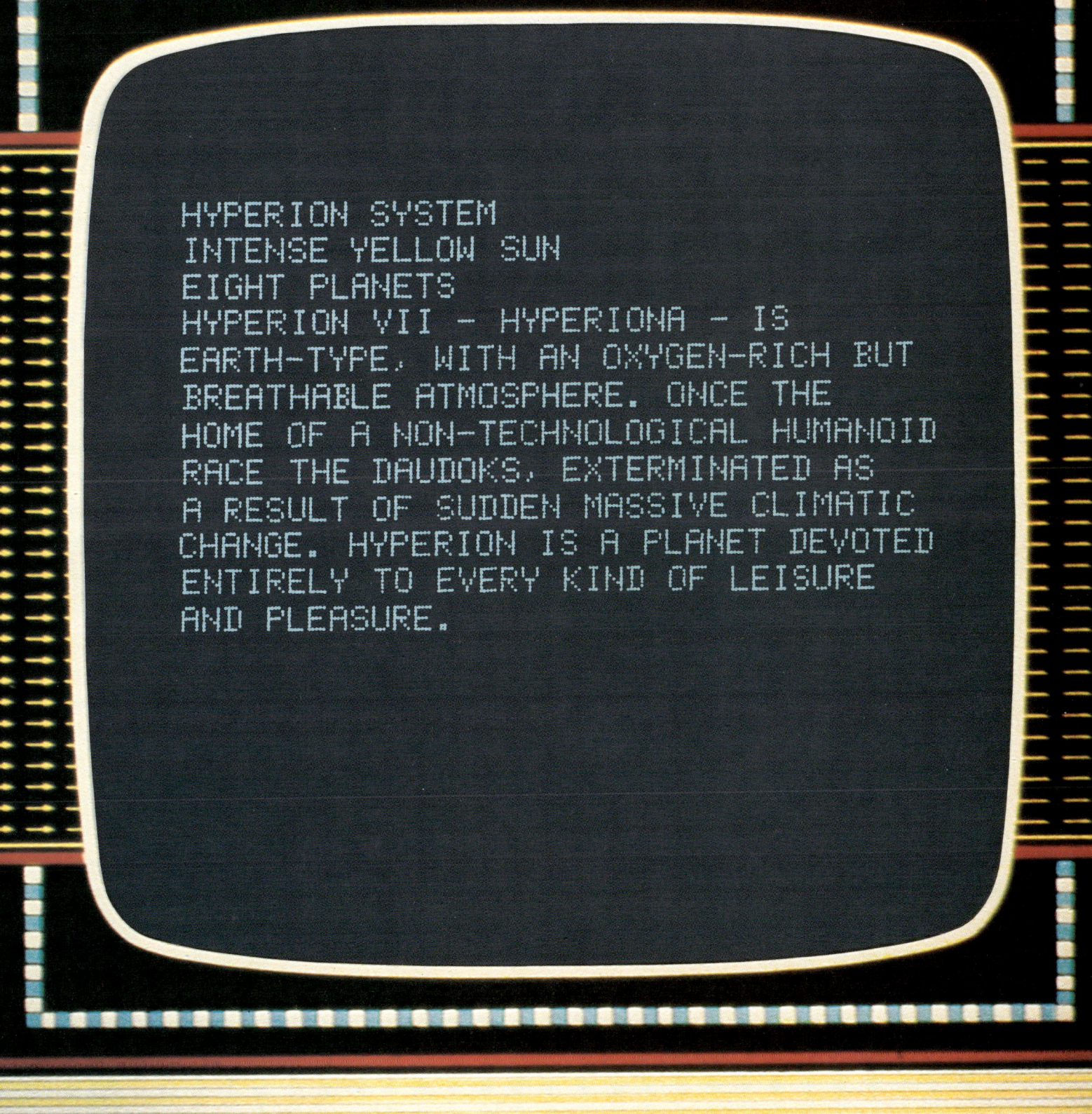

```
HYPERION SYSTEM
INTENSE YELLOW SUN
EIGHT PLANETS
HYPERION VII - HYPERIONA - IS
EARTH-TYPE, WITH AN OXYGEN-RICH BUT
BREATHABLE ATMOSPHERE. ONCE THE
HOME OF A NON-TECHNOLOGICAL HUMANOID
RACE THE DAUDOKS, EXTERMINATED AS
A RESULT OF SUDDEN MASSIVE CLIMATIC
CHANGE. HYPERION IS A PLANET DEVOTED
ENTIRELY TO EVERY KIND OF LEISURE
AND PLEASURE.
```

Personal diary Lelo. 19th December 2577: We're now six days behind schedule, but Pan-Galactic have been very good and re-arranged everything for us. And so here we are, ten days of total extravagance on the world that is called the Casino of the Galaxy .. and I can well believe it. I didn't realise that Caroline had such a liking for gambling, but she does, and she's spending and winning like crazy. Her arm is totally healed, and I've never seen her so happy, and so relaxed. When we're alone she's quite incredible, and I don't intend to go into any more detail. She took a trip to an erotidome, and instead of feeling jealous I actually thought it was a good idea. And I went myself. And that's something they really should permit on Earth! What an amazing place. It's costly, of course, but it's not seedy like you might expect it to be. It's like a huge food and drink orgy; everybody looks like they're enjoying themselves, even the girls and boys of the establishment. And once you're into the building, anything goes! And I mean anything. Most of the women are Jennies, that's from 'genetically modified' to be, perhaps, a metre tall, or three metres tall, or fat or thin, or with funny body parts that personally I didn't find very appealing. I spent most of my time with a normal-sized girl, having a normal – if excessive – relationship. Not all my time, mind you, but most of it. Hyperiona was once an inhabited world, so I believe, but the creatures that lived here never developed beyond a sort of alien Iron Age . . . clan wars, massacres, squabbling. And then a climatic change wiped them out. Now it's a solid city from North Pole to equator; millions of intelligent creatures live here, each species concentrated in its own areas. We're in Hyperiona City, which is the size of England, and is the only city that is totally mixed. There are forty human cities on Hyperiona, out of ten thousand. And every city, human or alien, is geared up for fun, gambling, sex and satiation. **End entry.**

GALACTOPLAZA 1 2

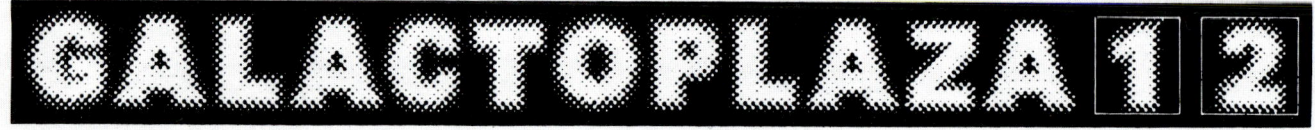

GALACTOPLAZA GROUP OF FILM COMPANIES IS PLEASED TO ANNOUNCE ITS
NEWWEEK PROGRAMME

GALACTOPLAZA 1

STARDAY FOR EIGHT FULL DAYS

STAR TREK
THE HOLOSHOW

They came from out of the past to save mankind. The screen's biggest, boldest most spectacular historical film this century!

Starring, DALE NAVABI as Captain Kirk, ELU ELTIRK as Spock, VIL SUDDABY as Bones and introducing RANDALA GRONG as 'Toops'.
Written by Ali Dead Frustar, based on 2-D recordings unearthed in the Washington Archives.
Directed by Kinadal Krish.

There have been remakes of remakes of remakes! But there's never been a remake like this remake!
HYPERION EVENING STAR

GALACTOPLAZA 2

STARDAY FOR EIGHT FULL DAYS

Lunis Bunala's

A Man and a Woman and a Thrumsk

They loved an alien, and it destroyed their humanity

Starring JONNI TRUFFEAU as John Truffeau
VERA VENUSA as 'The Maiden',
RIP LUMBOKA as Max Schanker and introducing DANNY GALACTIC as The Kid.

DIR. BY LUNIS BUNALA, PROD. BY QUIKFILMS CORPORATE.

Personal diary Caroline. 22nd December 2577: Hyperiona is certainly everything they say it is. In other circumstances I suppose I might find it all rather gross, rather too much of a neon extravaganza; as it is, I hardly knew where to start. I'm sure I've done enough over the past week either to reduce me to premature senility or to keep me young forever (depending on which theory you prefer). Leio's been having a good time too, but I think he's actually a little shocked at finding me so keen to try things: it doesn't fit his Platonic ideal image of me. We've spent a lot of time in linked Sensualoan, which was mind-blowing to say the least. I'd recommend anyone to find out what it's like to be Imuuka Delores . . . not to mention what it's like to be one of her consorts! No wonder this stuff is banned on Earth: it's so addictively enjoyable that the whole economy would grind to a halt. They say a lot of early users simply let themselves starve to death, and it's easy to see why. The Tactile Emporia have been fun, too . . . One of the interesting things is the huge variety of different species catered for. Each has its own specific areas of the planet, but everybody and everything comes together in Hyperiona City. I don't think I've seen so many aliens before in my entire life. There are areas of common interest — it seems that all intelligent species, irrespective of their other qualities, love to gamble; and Sensualoan is almost universal in appeal — but other pleasures seem species-specific. A couple of days ago I followed a sign promising me (if I were a Groon) the Spasm of seven lifetimes. Now the Groon, one might think, do not have a lot of fun. If they resemble anything it's a singularly morose species of oversized toad. But appearances can be deceptive. The Spasmic Chamber — as I was gloomily told by a Groon attendant in a tone of voice suggesting that his entire family had just died — is barred to other species, the reason being that the Spasm is an experience of such transcendent ecstasy that it's fatal to any species other than the Groon. (And to judge from the Groon I saw staggering out, it's fairly hard on them!) So far we've only dabbled at the casinos, but with only three full days left I intend to start trying them out in earnest. **End entry.**

SENSUALOAN

Have you ever wanted to feel the command of a battlecruiser engaged in interplanetary skirmish?

~ ~ ~

Have you ever wondered what it's like to be Imuuka Delores, making love to her transplanetary escorts?

~ ~ ~

What does it feel like to be an adult Ugranthik undergoing temporal transformation: body into energy, energy into time, time into void, and void into new body?

Now you can FIND OUT. Sensualoan, a branch of the Hyperion National Depository, can offer you a choice of more than a thousand such experiences, each approximately two hours long (Imuuka's recordings are considerably longer). Donated by four hundred of the galaxy's best known celebrities, politicians, beauties, studs and heroes, each experience is the *real* memory of a *real* event. Each sense is connected, and the experience will stay real for you.

A one day loan will cost you no more than 100 galactic credits. In that time you can dogfight with Auroran zip-craft, experience the love of an amorphous alien, undergo binary fission and be none the worse for it, see how it is to digest a rock . . .

Hundreds of such experiences at

SENSUALOAN
off Gemini MainWay, Level 15,
Serpens Heights.

RIGELLIAN LESSONS from expert in oral communication. Walk up or dial Hyp-5576BBM

Hyperion Erection and Demolition Experts. We are a team of three and prefer to operate together; ideal for Janusian tripods and human companies with more progressive attitudes.

INTERIOR DECORATOR: painting and stripping no problem for all you old-fash; Mick Angelo's can be accommodated; hold-vid available, and for those *real* primits full line of luxury leather and furs, black, blue, green and skin soft. Whatever your property we'll make sure it's snug.

THE OPHIUCHUS BALLET COMPANY

PRESENT

GRAVITY WELL

INDRA TUSCANA, EARTH'S MOST RENOWNED BALLERINA, DANCING WITH HYPERION'S OWN **WAYLAND GREEN** TO PROJUMIK'S GALACTIC-ALLY FAMOUS BALLET WITH FULL RANGE OF SPECIAL EFFECTS TO ACCOMPANY THIS TRAGIC TALE OF STAR-CROSSED LOVERS SUCKED TO THEIR DOOM IN A BLACK HOLE, ONLY TO BE REUNITED IN THE FABLED GOLDEN GALAXY THAT LIES BEYOND THE DEEPEST HOLES IN SPACE. WITH FULL DANCING SUPPORT (SEVEN DIFFERENT SPECIES) AND AUTO-MATED MUSIC BY STRIKACHORD (HYPERION) MUSICALS.

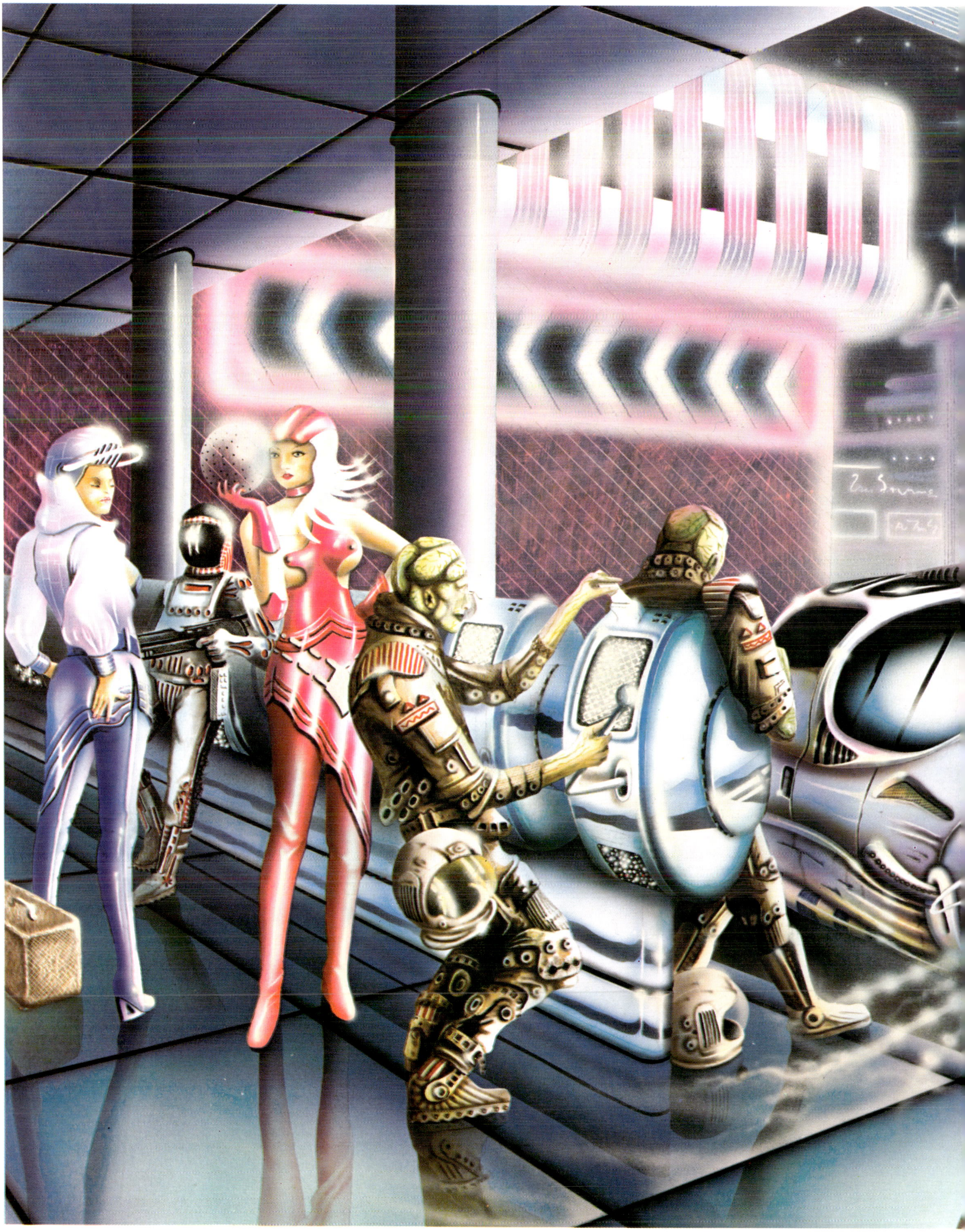

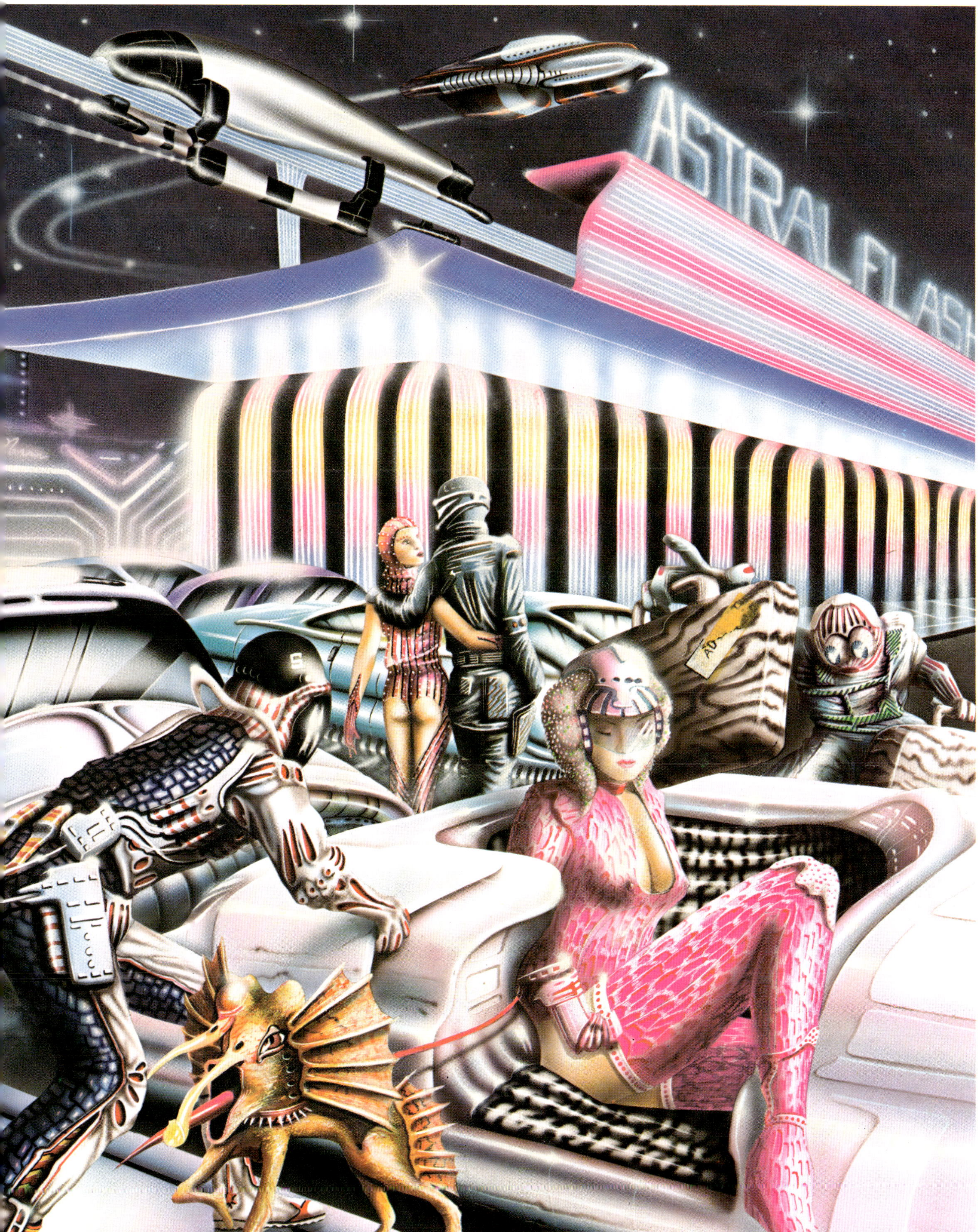
ASTRAL FLASH

THE *SEVEN STARS CASINO* IS PLEASED TO MAKE AVAILA
BAJIKASTA, USING THE *BAJIK'T* PACK

BAJIKASTA

SUIT: SKULLS CARD: MASTER
SUIT: RINGS CARD: SLAVE
VOID CARD: OMEGA
SUIT: SHIPS CARD: 7
SUIT: FLAMES CARD: SWORD
VOID CARD: ENTITY
SUIT: HEARTS CARD: CLOWN
SUIT: STARS CARD: QUEEN

Patrons are advised not to attempt participation unless they are well familiar with the complex and convoluted 'life rules' that are associated with play. The *bajik't*, who evolved the game, use marked stones; an adapted form of their ritual exchanges is becoming increasingly popular in the Galaxy; though much simplified, it is nevertheless a *dangerous* game, and only suitable for players with a strong mental disposition.

The *bajik't* pack consists of six suits, adapted from the *bajik't* symbols: ships, hearts, stars, rings, flames and skulls. There are *evolution cards* in each suit, numbered 1-11. There are five Master cards to each suit: Slave, Queen, Master, Clown and Sword. There are two Void cards, the Entity and the Omega. All the essential symbols derive from *bajik't* history, and the *bajik't* themselves call the essential game *alternatives*. Some human worlds limit the *evolution cards* to ten in each suit, which brings the pack closer to the familiar Earth pack. The playing area, decided by mutual consent, consists of 100 territories, arranged in a minimum of five concentric circles.

HOUSE PLAY MODIFICATIONS:

1. Allotment of role is made by dealing through the whole pack; thus two or more players may enter the life game with the same role.

**E A CONTINUOUS GAME OF
8 CARDS.**

The Omega and the Entity are allocated
arately, and each will thus play a double role.
The Omega 'makes play' when the Sword of
lls is shown.
The Entity 'makes play' when the Clown of any
 is shown.
Play drops to Hunt Level only when the six
ens are played.
Play drops to The Spiral when the six Masters
played.
The final killing may only be attempted when
 of Omega or Entity have declared their roles,
all six Swords are shown upon the middle ring
he play area.

THE SEVEN STARS CASINO
NOTICE TO PATRONS

The management of the Seven Stars Casino welcome you, and respectfully offer the following information which may help you enjoy your visit to the full.

Games available
The Seven Stars offers for your entertainment a full range of games of chance and skill. These include Trixstar (regular and involute versions), Stellar Red, Sirian Roulette (our special version of Shoot-the-Well, with variable collapsar program and two shots at a successful slingshot to double your chance of winning!), oldstyle poker and blackjack variants, tri-D chess and Go against programs to all levels, and Hyperiona's largest range of games machines.

House Limits
In line with Equity Commission recommendations a 1000g.c. limit operates in each game *except* Sirian Roulette, which has no limit. Minimum stake on all tables is 10g.c.

Refreshment
The house is pleased to present refreshment at all tables, with its compliments. In fulfilment of Commission regulations we are unable to provide hallucinogens or direct neural stimulants in the gaming halls, but relaxo-chambers are available for the use of patrons.

Children
For those too young to enjoy our main gaming halls we offer a full range of KidiGamble Fun-games, in the sub-basement Funroom. Alternatively, patrons may deposit under age children in the stasis chamber adjacent to the reception area.

Credit
The management are pleased to offer all patrons 24-hour credit up to individual limits. This period regretfully cannot be extended, and the management can accept no liability for the future welfare of patrons unable to meet this condition.

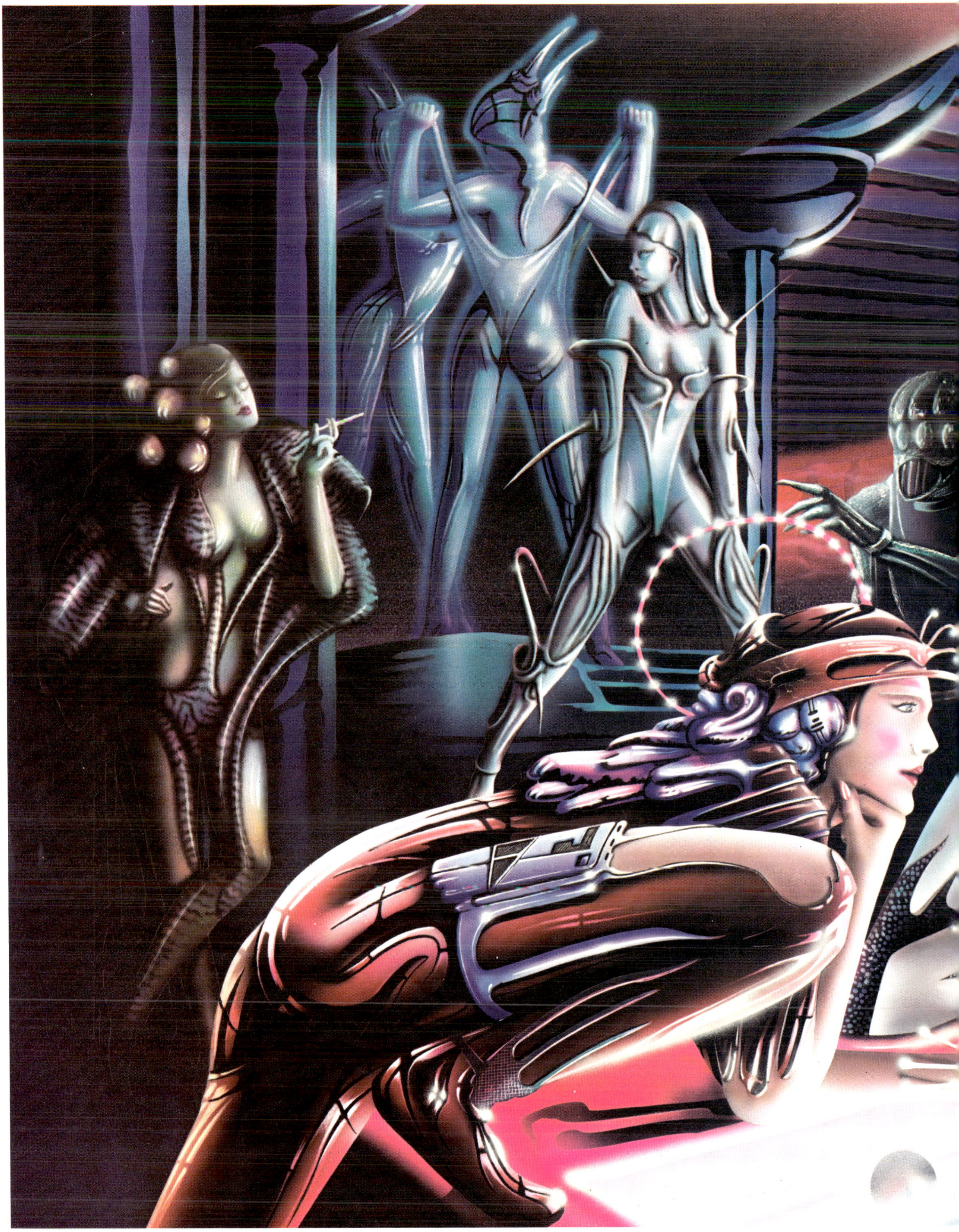

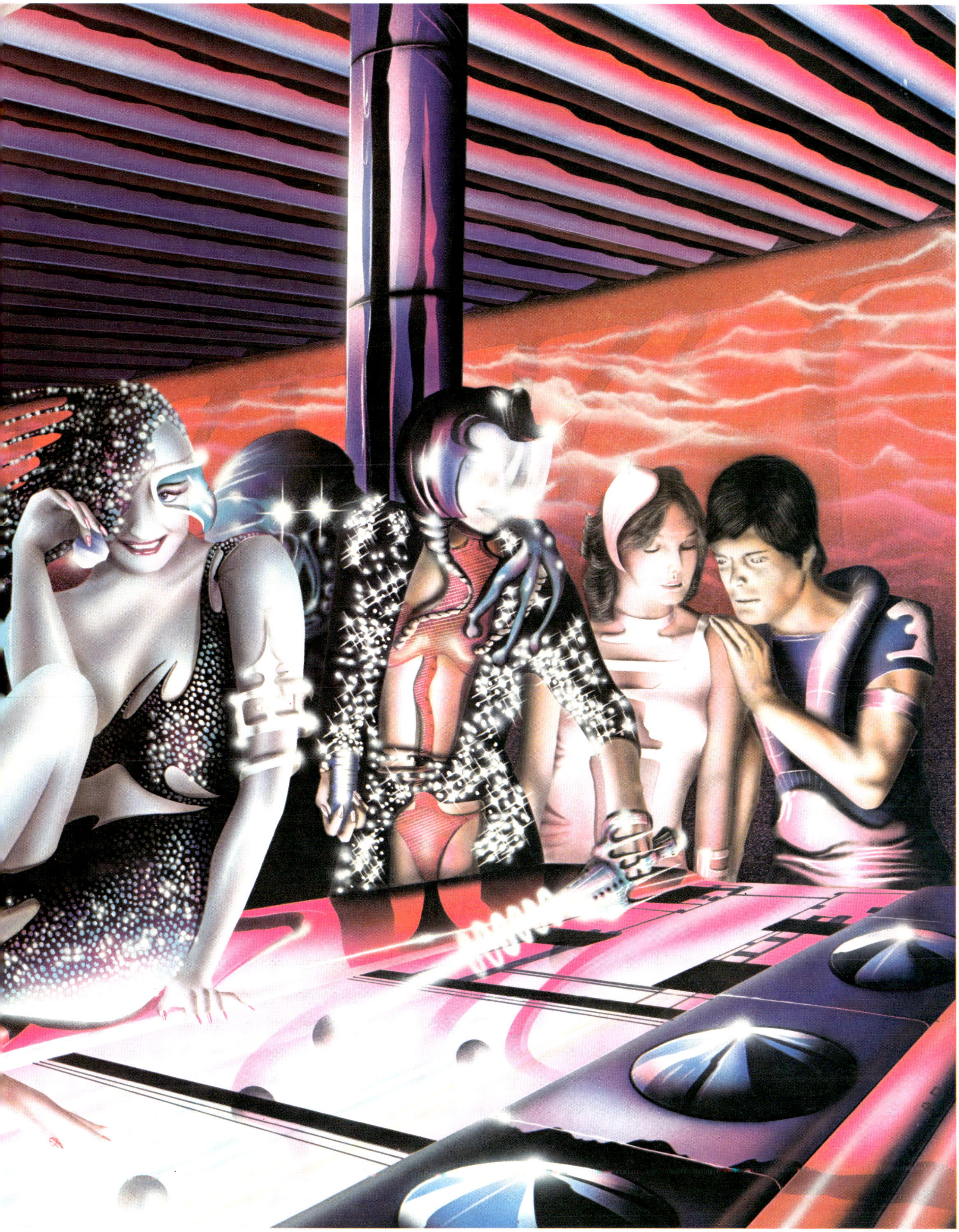

STAR CRAFTS

ALIEN FABRIC SPECIALISTS
19 GEMINI BVD.

2 Ig oz. Teralawy alimentary thread	1000 g.c.
12 ins sq. thisquasqua skin	064 g.c.

INTERGAL LIVE FABRIC REGISTRATION NO. Bha9300M Hyp

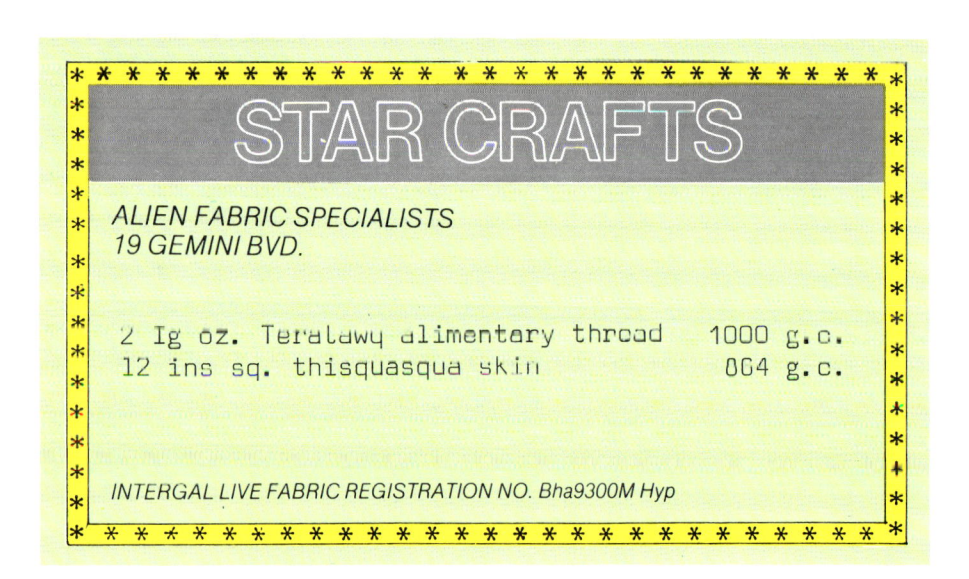

KAYS SPECIAL STORES

Specialists In The Old Fashioned
3 Sakanda Square

```
*/7   VEGAN ROUGH
      RIDER
*/4   RIGELLIAN
      TICKLERS
*/20  EPSILOX LUBE
      COLOURS
*/5   BETELESE
      GRAINLET
*/1   UH BOY
      MAXEXPANDER
      **AMT**
      000028
SUB   000120
TOT   000060
      000060
      000025
CSH   000293  +++
CHNG
```

Hyp275611

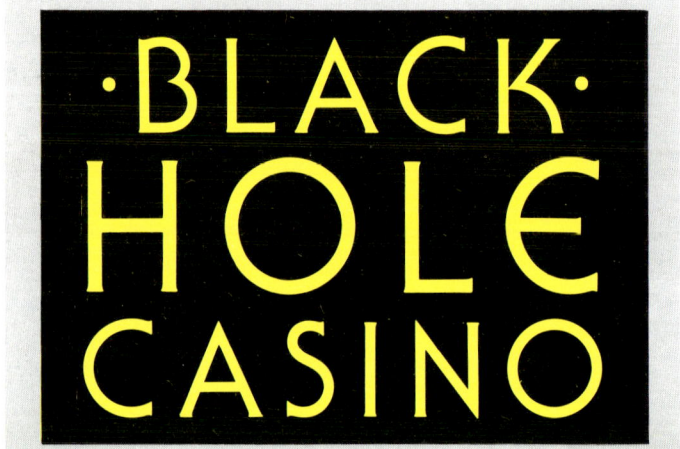

BLACK HOLE CASINO

Part of the Dream Dome Starset Strip Hyperion Central 5
343.22 (GST 12.23)

LEIO SCOTT	
GAME	TRIXSTAR
SCORE	⭐G 15 ⭐R 30 ⭐B 976
NET LOSS	901
NET GALACTIC CREDIT LOSS	2703 g.c.

The Black Hole Casino thanks you for your custom and gamesmanship and respectfully reminds you that you have until 343.23.midi (12.24.1200 GST) to effect credit transfer to Hyperio7769BHC12.

Love Touch Emporium

6 hrem 280
Dreamfloat 65
holovecs 100

445 G.c.

Thank you. Come again.
Cr67Blue10. Central Registry Love Tax charged at 15%

Hyperio Gulshan Tandoori Spices Restaurant

576 Block 7 (ground) Mainways South   vid Hyp-3336332

OPEN ALL DAY AND NIGHT

```
2x ----  82
1x ---- 101
2x ----  60
         243
   27%    66
1x ----  120
   73%    82
         511
```

Food Tax charged at 27%. Imported food taxed at 73%.

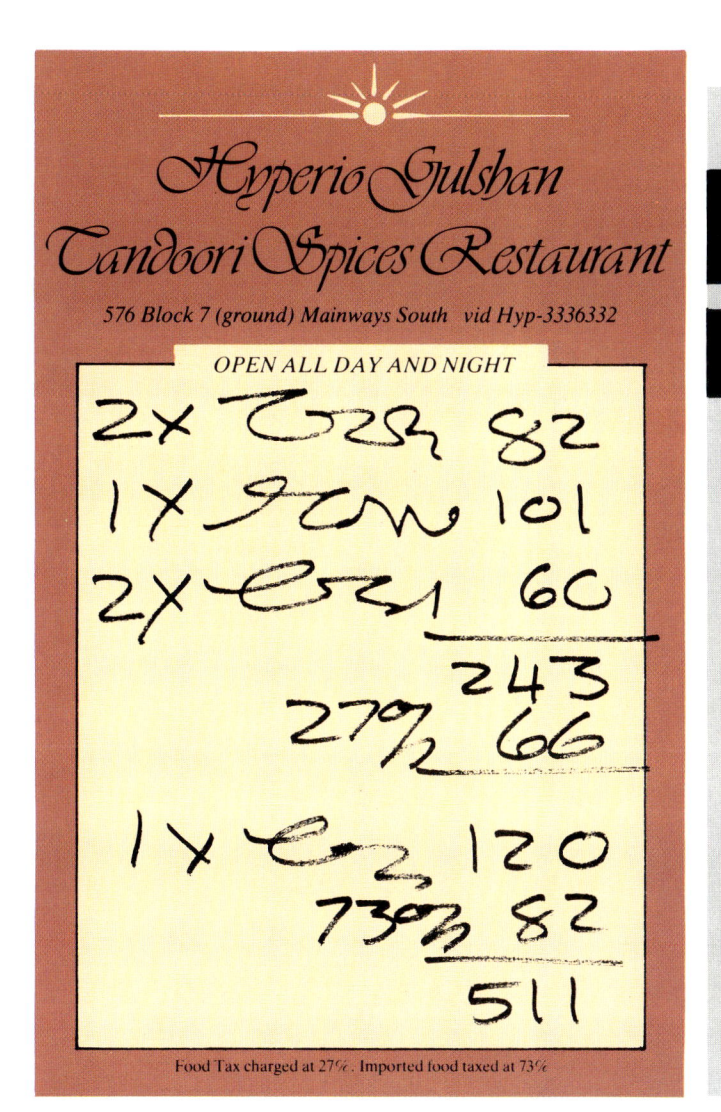

THORNIX HOLOMARKET

Mod17 Einstein Bvd.   Hyp. 45665M

	G	C
BILASER REPLACEMENT	0 0 0	3 8 8
THRUVIEW CLEANING FLUID	0 0 0	0 1 2
DEVELOPMENTS	0 0 0	0 3 2
HOLEROTICA 66PJ	0 0 0	0 7 2
HOLO CANON WIDE ANGLE	0 0 0	5 6 8
TOTAL	0 0 1	0 7 2

HyOps 667. Trade 14.

Customers Name: LEIO SCOTT
Credit code: N/A

For the best in UltraView and Dionix Optics.

TRANSWORLD MODELS INC.

356 mod.17 Columbus Highway   Ortygiaville Hyperion 56

model crafts from the whole Galaxy- imported and private enterprise items not available on Earth.

QNTY	ITEM		COST
1	Holotronic 4-D Galaxy kit plus Magellanic Clouds		700 g.c.
1	Eesiview Holoprojector for natural light.		568 g.c.
			* * * * * * * * * * * *
			1268 g.c.

tax is included in the price of all purchases

STARLINERS	ALIEN STRUCTURES	BASIC HOLOTRONICS	KLASTICS

Personal diary Lelo. 26th December, 2577: Suddenly it's all over, the whole holiday, all but the going home. It's hard to believe that six months have passed since we set off for Earthport; it seems like only last week. If I'm tired at the moment, it's only **because** of the night life on Hyperiona, not **with** the night life, which is a life I could lead for years. I didn't take to gambling so much as the sensuadomes, erotidomes, and the various non-gambling games. The best of these was the zero-gravity pool; you go into a huge room, in zero G, and there are twenty balls, and your opponent; you don't use a cue, you catch the cue-ball, getting penalised if you touch any of the others, then you toss the cue-ball at your target. Great fun. For exercise, though, the Night Run is something I wish we had back in London. This is a sort of city-wide chess-and-chase game where you can experience being hunted by any weapon — say a robot, or night eye — or warrior of your choice. You get allocated a role, and told a general game play. What makes it more fun is that there are actually two players in a room, watching you on a screen, and able to **force** moves upon you. It gets really tense, and yet I always survive; I guess I just have a natural talent for undercover work. While I've been playing at making myself fit, Caroline has spent days, quite literally, in the casinos, playing Stellar Red, a sort of complicated poker using four hundred different symbols, and Sirian Roulette, which I know of as Shoot-the-Well: you know, where you try and get a ball through a rotating black hole and into a specified target. She did well at first, but then her luck changed. She seemed to get let off a considerable debt she'd accumulated, which was fortunate, but I didn't like the fact that she vanished for thirty hours inside the Seven Stars Casino and kept laughing all the following day. **End entry.**

C·R·I·P·S

Confederation of Registered Interstellar Passe

CERTIFICATE OF SPACEWORTHINESS FOR TIME-SPACE- MATRIX-DISTO

Valid for 50 standard TSMD journeys in ships with fewer than 1000 such journeys logged at time of issue and with unconditional approval (Section Ci). Valid for 20 journeys in ships with 1000 or more logged TSMD journeys, or with conditional approval (Section Cii). All ships must report immediately for further inspection if Hull Integral Stability Ratio or Time Distortion Potential deviate on any single journey by more than 2% from figures recorded on this certificate. Failure to comply will lead to permanent withdrawal of certificate and may result in criminal proceedings.

DATE OF INSPECTION: 77/11/20. **INSPECTOR:** S.S. BILWAG

PART A

1	Name and registered no. of owner	INTERSUN HAULAGE GXT4142TM37
2	Class of ship	TROJAN II
3	Name and serial no.	AD ASTRA
4	Date of entering service (GST)	2498
5	Date and no. of previous certificate	2575.7.19
6	No. of TSMD journeys logged	1638
7	No. logged since previous inspection	47
8	*To be completed by commanding officer or authorized deputy* Report here any incidents since previous inspection, as required under Section III(vi)b of the TSMD Safety Regulations, 2435 (rev. 2561).	

2577/11/2   15.33 MILLISECOND TIME DISPLACEMENT RECORDED ON ROUTINE SIRIUS-EARTH TRANSIT

PART B Inspection rota (se

1	Hull type:	ZIRONTIX S
2	Charmed quark emission (meas	
3	Engine model:	ELDRED MAX
4	Time distortion potential (meas	

PART C (only one section t

i   This ship is awarded an uncondi
ii This ship is awarded a certificate modifications being made before

TSMD - STABILI

iii This ship is refused a further cert
iv This ship is refused a further ce (appeal against this ruling must inspection).

Signature of Inspector:

Personal diary Caroline. 27th December 2577: Well, Leio isn't too happy, but it was worth it. Eight thousand credits in a single evening — more than most people earn in a year. My gambling was under control at the Black Hole, where I'd spent two days (Leio came in from time to time, but mostly preferred other sorts of entertainment), only losing about three thousand (and that mainly on a single Trixstar shoot when I was sure I had a primary sequence). Then we both went to the Seven Stars to celebrate Christmas Day. That was when I got carried away. It's a much more classy place than the Black Hole, where I found all the Jennies touting for custom intrusive. We started playing Sirian Roulette — a local variant with two chances at a successful slingshot and no limit. I had a couple of good shots early on, and then started doubling up on my losses. Before Leio could do much about it I'd lost another 5000, which meant we owed about 3000 more than we had. This could have been difficult — Hyperiona casinos are not known for their generous and forgiving attitude towards debtors — but luckily I was able to make arrangements with the management to work off the debt. It only took a little over a day, and was quite easily done (if strenuous), and even instructive. Leio wants to know details, but I'm keeping them to myself. One unforeseen problem is the grounding of the liner we were to have travelled home on. We're almost penniless now, and can't afford to extend our stay until the ban is lifted. And as they are offering alternative transport Pan-Gal have no obligation to meet the cost of a delay. So we leave later today on an Intersun Haulage ship, the **Ad Astra**. We looked it over at the spaceport and frankly it looked a rustheap to me. It's an old freighter partly converted for passenger use, and its manning seems inadequate. I'd sooner stay than travel on it, but we have little choice. Leio says I worry too much, and that a little corrosion doesn't matter if the propulsion unit is sound. I wish I could share his confidence. **End entry.**

---

r Carriers

ON PASSENGER LINER

ched schedule for full analysis)

921	Integral Stability Ratio:	40:44
neridian point):	•000374-QJ	
Thrust (30 sec. at rest):	4716.22	
.5c under conditions of zero matrix turbulence):	1.4×10^{-7}	

mpleted)

rtificate for a further 20/50* journeys (*delete one).

rther 20 journeys conditional upon the following spection.

REFIT

ending completion of works listed in attached schedule and must be withdrawn forthwith from passenger service stered at local C.R.I.P.C. office within 14 days from date of

---

CHAOS AT SPACEPORT

as Pan-Gal withdraws liners from service in safety scare!

THOUSANDS OF PASSENGERS were stranded at Hyperiona Spaceport today as Pan-Galactic Spacelines temporarily withdrew from service their entire fleet of Titan class liners.

This shock action follows unconfirmed reports of structural weaknesses discovered in the Titronix Diamond Tuff-Shield hull of the Sirian Interworlds Titan liner *Canis Major*, which emerged everted from a routine TSMD flight last week, causing 9,427 fatalities – the worst ever space accident. Pan-Galactic said that the withdrawal was purely a precautionary measure. "There is every reason to suppose that any weaknesses in the hull of the *Canis Major* were a result of the accident rather than its cause," said a Pan-Gal spokesperson "but we are proud of our safety record and do not intend to take any chances." Preliminary tests already indicate that the hulls are structurally sound, and the liners are expected to return to service within 14 days.

Meanwhile, other spacelines using different models are hastily arranging extra flights to relieve congestion at the spaceport. Hyperiona is particularly badly hit by Pan-Gal's move, as 42% of all long-haul flights are made by their Titan liners. Intersun Haulage, the second largest carrier, has already announced plans for a temporary doubling of its number of flights. Pan-Gal confirm that all tickets are transferable to other carriers while their fleet remains out of service.

Competition Winners' luck runs out at casino

LEIO SCOTT AND Caroline Luranski – lucky winners of two places on the galactic trip of a lifetime – found their luck at an end last night when they paid a visit to the Seven Stars Casino in Hyperiona City. Leio and Caroline, whose dream trip has taken them to Aurora-Magellan, Tombworld, and many other exotic worlds, set out to celebrate their last night on Hyperiona before returning home to Earth. But before the evening was out they had lost every credit of their remaining spending money on the casino's tables.

"We just go carried away," said a rueful Leio afterwards. "It was the Sirian roulette that really finished us." "We're only glad it wasn't our own money," commented Caroline.

Worse was to follow for the couple when they learned of the cancellation of their Pan-Gal return flight to Earth (see main story). "We can't afford to stay any longer," said Caroline, "so we'll be trying to transfer to an Intersun Haulage liner tomorrow."

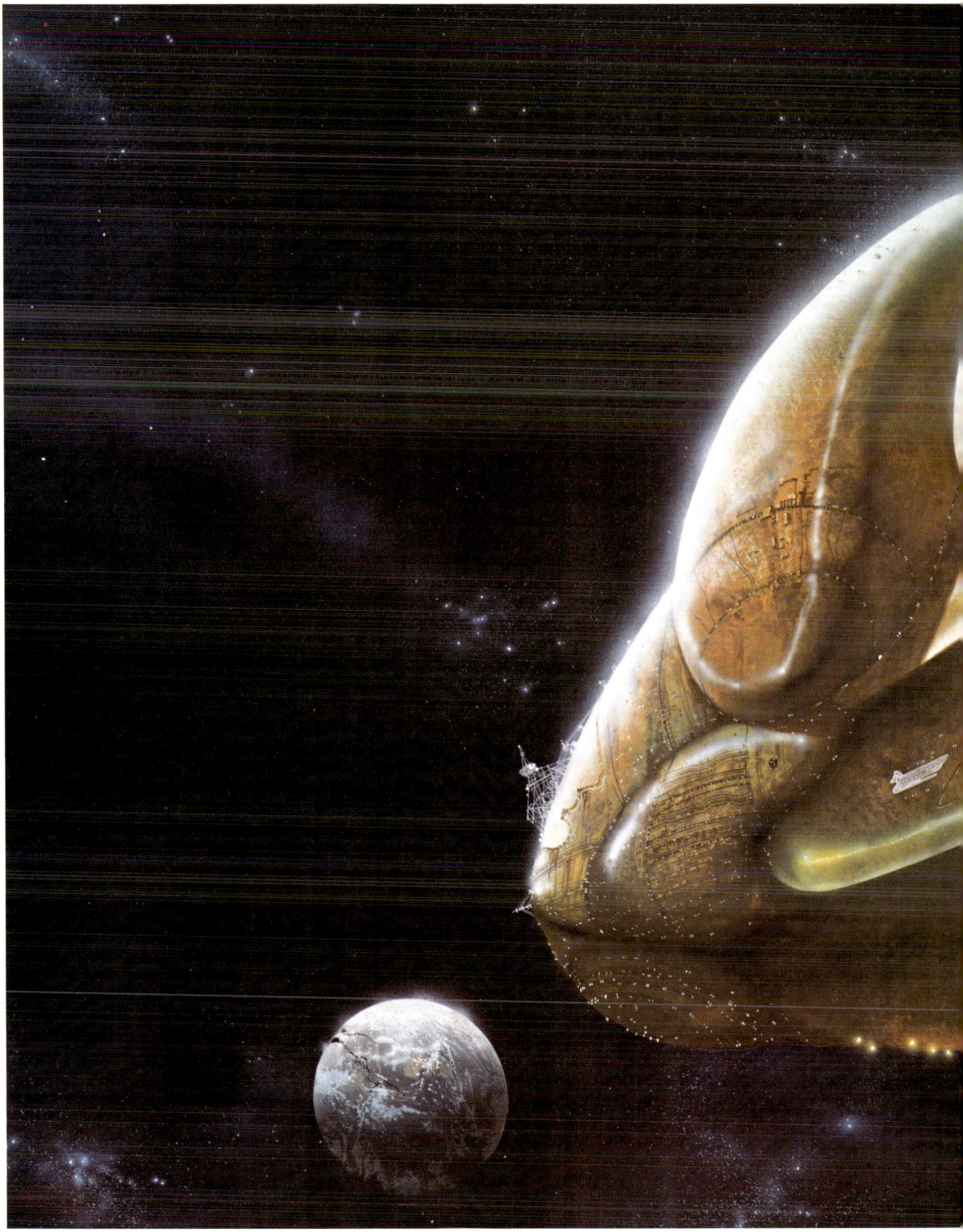

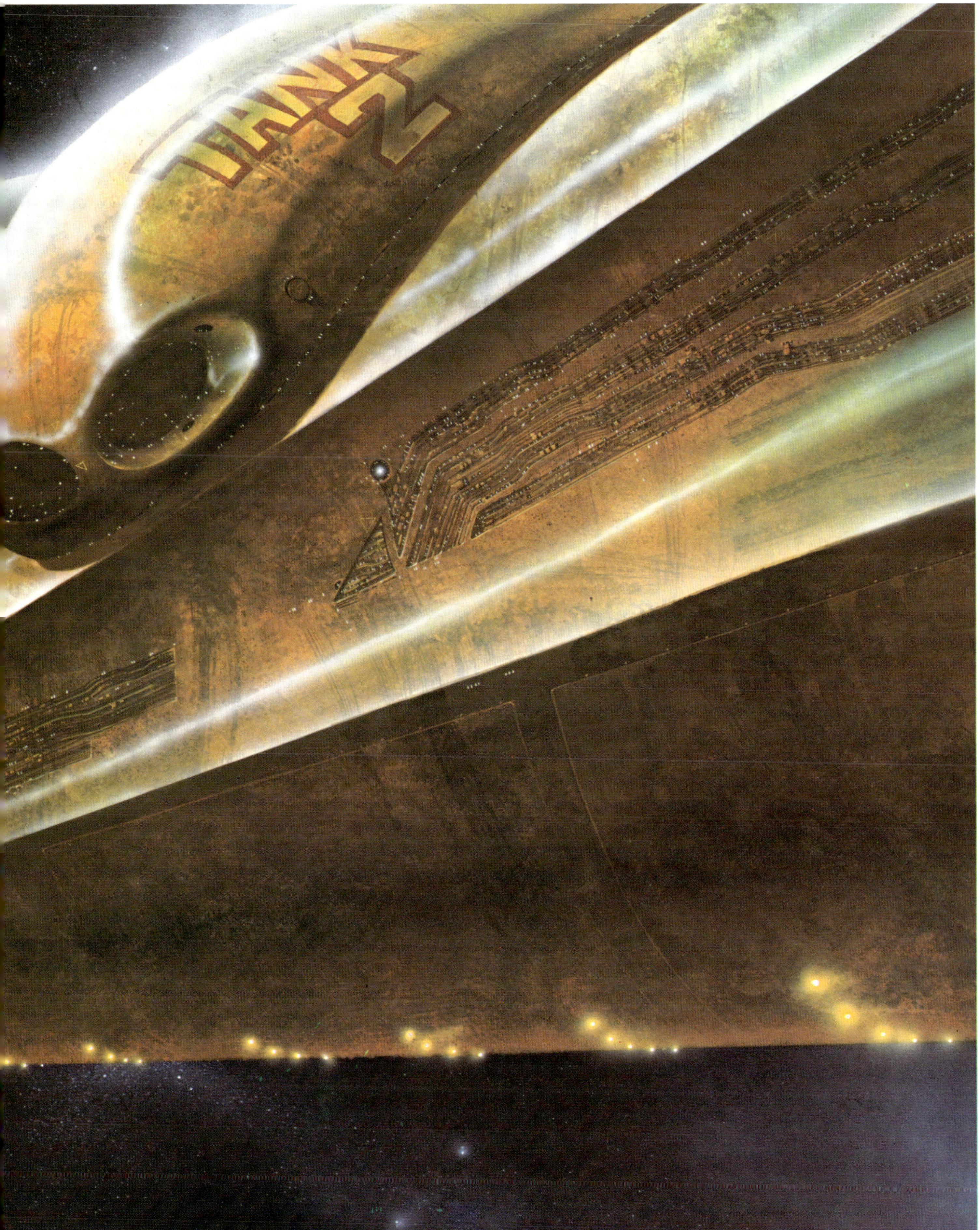

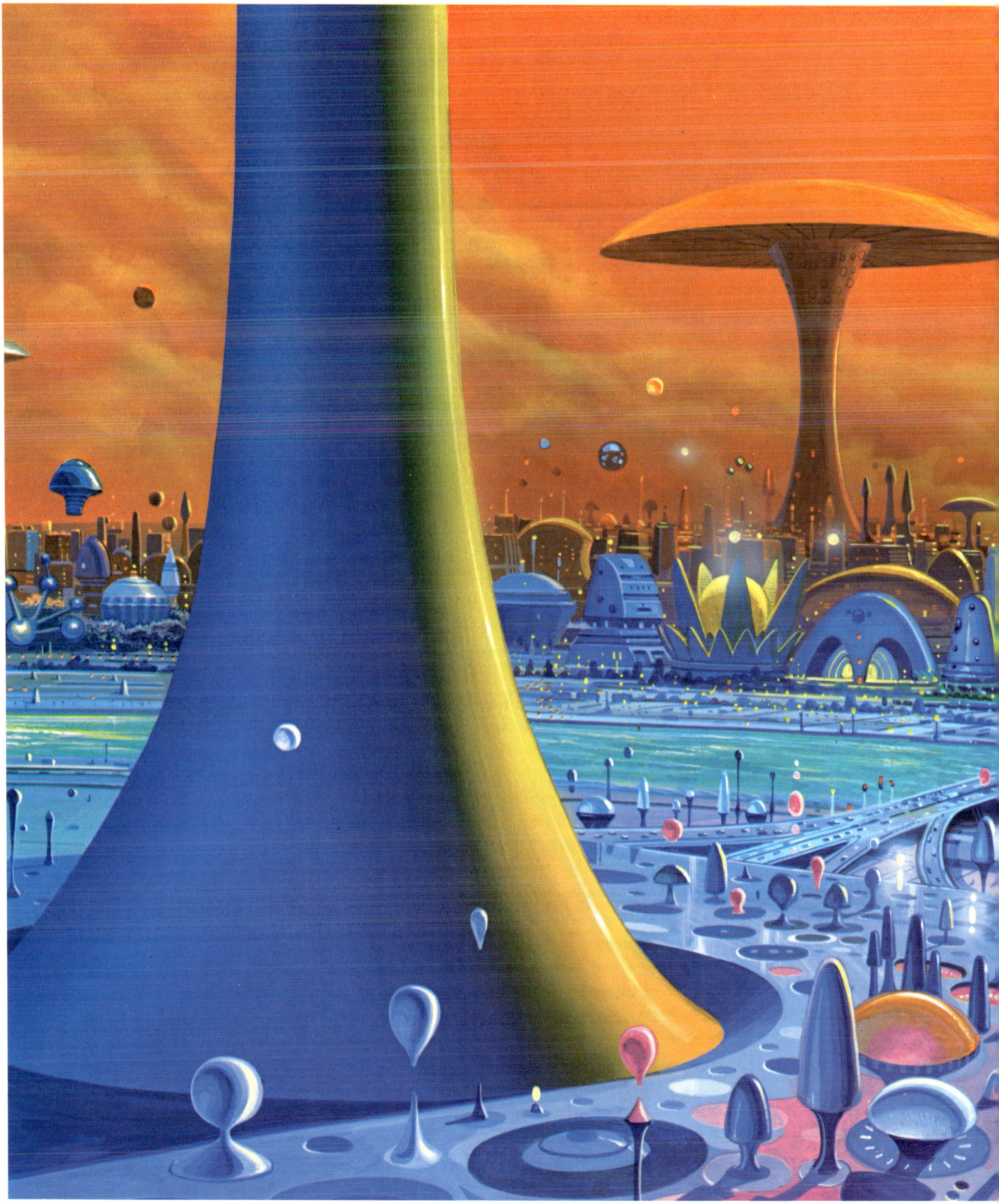

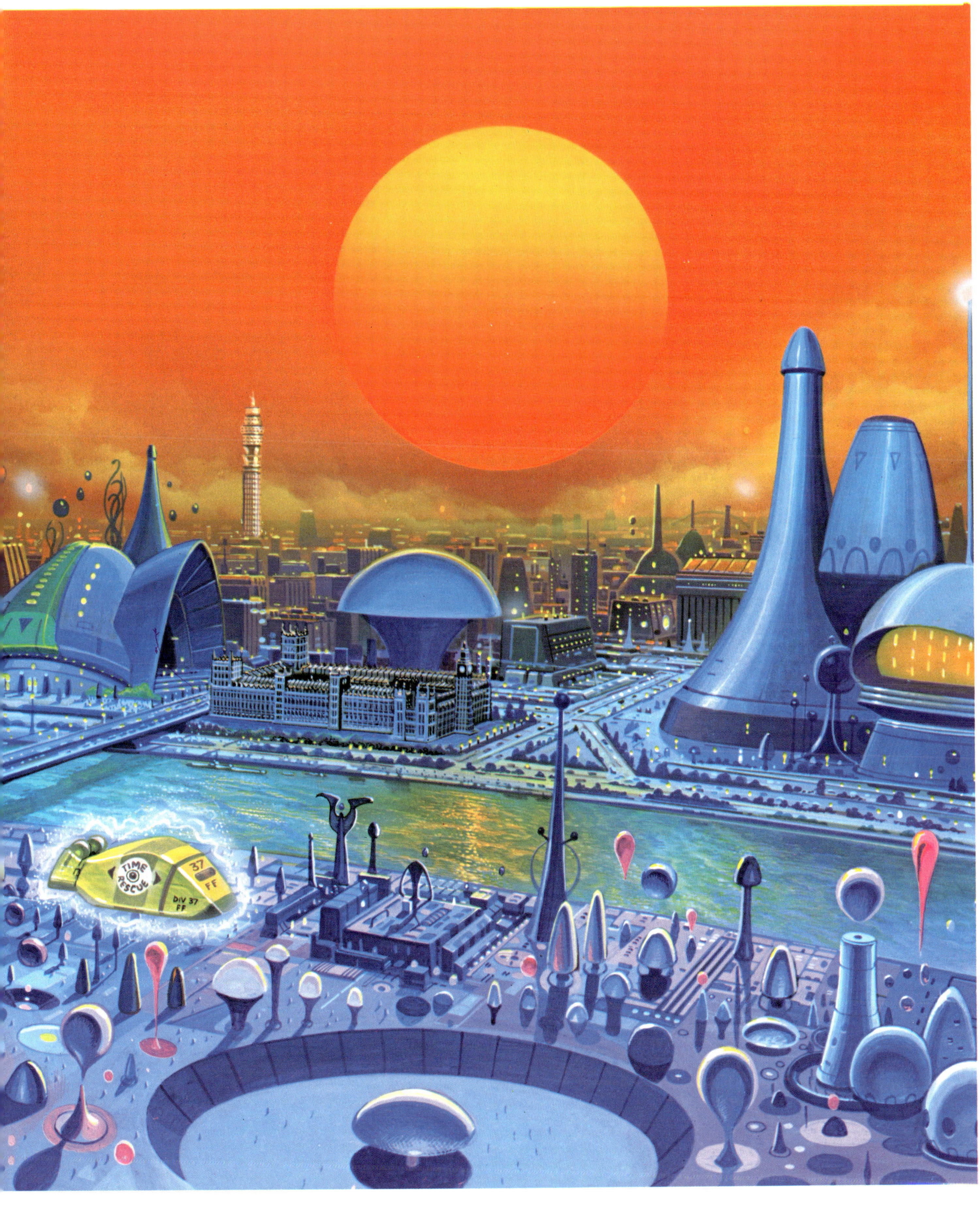
TIME RESCUE
37
FF
DIV 37
FF

Personal diary Lelo, 1st January 2578: As I record this, the towering shape of one of the most unusual vehicles I've ever encountered is just fading away; the last thing that vanishes is the name on its side: Time Rescue Inc. I have no idea whether the powers that be will even allow me to keep this diary entry, or even a memory of what has just occurred. What's happened is unbelievable, almost inconceivable. Everyone is still slightly stunned, shaking their heads and whispering as we file away to debarkation. My legs are like jelly. I haven't eaten a thing for a day, I've been so excited. We should have checked with Hyperiona Starport Control about that rust-bucket that brought us home; what an appallingly uncomfortable ship, and apparently it made the Earth run despite an unfavourable safety report. Result? It slipped its time-hold, and got displaced thousands of years into the future. Something to do with witch-space, the faster than light Universe, and the so-called TSMD-stress factor. When a ship is travelling so fast that it's outside space and time, its sub-atomic particles behave in a peculiar way; mass literally changes form to a particle that can only exist in witch-light. When more than 0.1 percent of the ship's mass changes permanently, it loses its ability to hold on to real time. We ended up in far-future Earth orbit. Several people shuttled down for a look before Time Rescue arrived, and I managed to see some of the pictures they brought back: great sinister-looking structures, strange activity, a pall of darkness; bits of London were still recognisable, but the river, they say, looked red. Then this damned great machine materialized and chased them back up to the ship, where it picked us all up, and brought us back to the present. We were told that only a mistake stopped us being picked up a second after we'd arrived in normal space, so we could all count ourselves lucky to have had even such a brief glimpse of our future world. The TR crew spoke strangely, and wore strange clothes; I have a feeling they came from future time themselves, but if the back-barrier theory is correct that's impossible. But now we're about to be processed through the Ring City, Terminal 15, and then down the elevator to Mount Kenya. Being so close to home again I can't wait to get back to Module 1328, to unpack, to see friends, and to get our film developed. This has been a terrific six months tour. **End diary.**

TIME RESCUE INC.
A SUBSIDIARY COMPANY OF OVERVIEW

fanEx: Over16722AL

REGISTERED OFFICES
Modules 1400-1420
Trudeau Building
Great State Central Park
NEWBISH 17 (Oldpipes)
ALASKA

TRANSTEMPORAL MEMO	at 2577.12.31 current time. (SSstandard)

Rescue of Passenger Ship after large TSMD failure and substantial Displacement of 257,723y, 6m, 12d, 3h, 3m, 17.64s.

SHIP NAME:	Ad Astra	COMPANY LINE:	Intersun Haulage (Quark-line)
CAPTAIN'S NAME:	Juno Kabazard	HUMAN OCCUPANTS:	208

Small group passengers brought to surface, close by Central London. No contact with indigenous population. Mild culture shock and programme Edison Mem Rack used.

TIME CRAFT:	Time CraftVisual exposure 10.54 min. Atomic exchange 0.00000007% mass, minimsed.

Est. cost of rescue 900 thou GC. Passengers disembarked at Earthport, Ring Terminus 15, PanGal elevator-way.

TR/TSIG FUTURESCAN 12.31. AT 13.04 STANDARD
TO ALL YEARMOTION VESSELS SUBSCANDER LONGHAUL. STELLAR VESSEL IDENT.
EARTH ORIGIN CIRCA 2570 DISPL. TIME FORWARD 257 TPLUS. TIGHTSCAN
OVEREARTH CONCENTER LONDON. HUMAN CARGO EST. 250. URGENT RESCUE CODE
GREEN 26 TIGHT CONTROL. MEMRACK ESSENT. WHO CAN GO?

Personal diary Caroline. 2nd January 2578: I hate to say I told you so, but I **knew** something would go wrong with the ship. We knew something was badly amiss as soon as we approached Earth orbit: no Ring City visible. The Captain announced a "slight" time displacement problem, but it was obviously more serious than that. A shuttle went down over London, following Time Rescue emergency procedures (though they allowed some passengers aboard, which is strictly contrary to regulations), and when they came back they were obviously in shock. I think Leio saw some pictures, but he wouldn't tell me what they showed. If so, he's lucky not to have had a memory erasure, Commandment 1-10 of Time Rescue being, "Thou shalt not bring back knowledge of the future". The rescue was efficiently managed. One odd thing about Time Rescue is that you don't have to wait for it: no sooner do you finish making your distress call than the Rescue vessel materializes (though on this occasion there was a slight delay through miscalculation). They make every effort to get people back to their own time with as little exposure as possible to the future: in bad cases, excess exposure has caused irreversible debilitating future shock. I was flattered to learn from the vessel's captain that they'd had special instructions that I was a Very Important Passenger. He also felt free to tell me that our displacement was over 250,000 years, one of the worst on record. It was a suitably dramatic conclusion to the holiday. And now it's over. We're back in our module: almost like moving into a new place after so long away. There has been a flurry of holonews interest, but that will soon die down. I've shown some of my holovids to the Boss, who seemed quite excited: there's a good chance they'll package them into a whole programme, in which case I should get my new post. There was a huge excess amount in my accumulated salary printout, which we've put down to computer windfall (though I know it's my payoff from the service). It will mean we'll still be able to do some interstellar travelling: both of us have developed a taste for it. I don't suppose the future holds anything as exciting as the last six months (and I hope not: it's a relief to get back to normal life), but it looks bright. I can just see us in 30 years' time, sitting in our new luxury penthouse module, pulling out our old holovids, and looking back nostalgically. **End diary.**

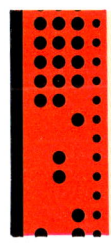

```
TR/TSIG TIMEDEEP 12.31. AT 13.50 STANDARD
RESPONDER RESPONDER YOUR TSIG 1304. DEEPTIMER VESSEL GORGON RPT.
GORGON IN TRANSIT SUBTIME 13000 ASCENDING. WILL BREAK TO FASTYEAR
THRUMAT. ETA SCAN SPACE 5 HOUR. HAVE CAPABILITY OF HUMAN STORAGE
TO 400. WILL BEACON DERELICT FOR HVA SALVAGE CRUISER.
```

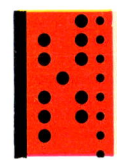

```
TR/TSIG 12.31. 1423. ROGER GORGON. ALL SUBSCANDER CEASE RESPONSE
STAND BY. GORGON, TIGHT SEAL INSTRUCTION PASSENGER FEMALE
LURANSKI RETURN ESSENTIAL CO OPERATIVE SECURITY.
```

---

hel4	**EARTHPORT TRANSIT CARD (DISEMBARKATION)**

NAME: CAROLINE LURANSKI

PASSPORT NO: Ea674921 - Ss LT4525399918

EARTHPORT

INCOMING FLIGHT NO:	LUGGAGE COLLECTION BAY:	POSTFLIGHT MEDICAL CHECK BAY NO:	TRANSIT BAY:
IS0372	A99	CA11	MK12

CUSTOMS DECLARATION (Please indicate colour): ✓ (green)

YOU ARE REMINDED THAT AN INCORRECT DECLARATION ON THIS TRANSIT CARD MAY RESULT IN CONFISCATION OF GOODS AND A FINE. PLEASE CHECK YOUR IMPORTS CAREFULLY AGAINST THE ALLOWANCE LISTS ON SCHEDULE EDIS 5

State Body Mass Of Livestock:	NONE	Is It Registered With Centace?	N/A
Have You Filled In Import Schedule 170 Gammad?	YES	State Excess	3Kg

SIGNED: Caroline Luranski   DATE: 2677-12-31

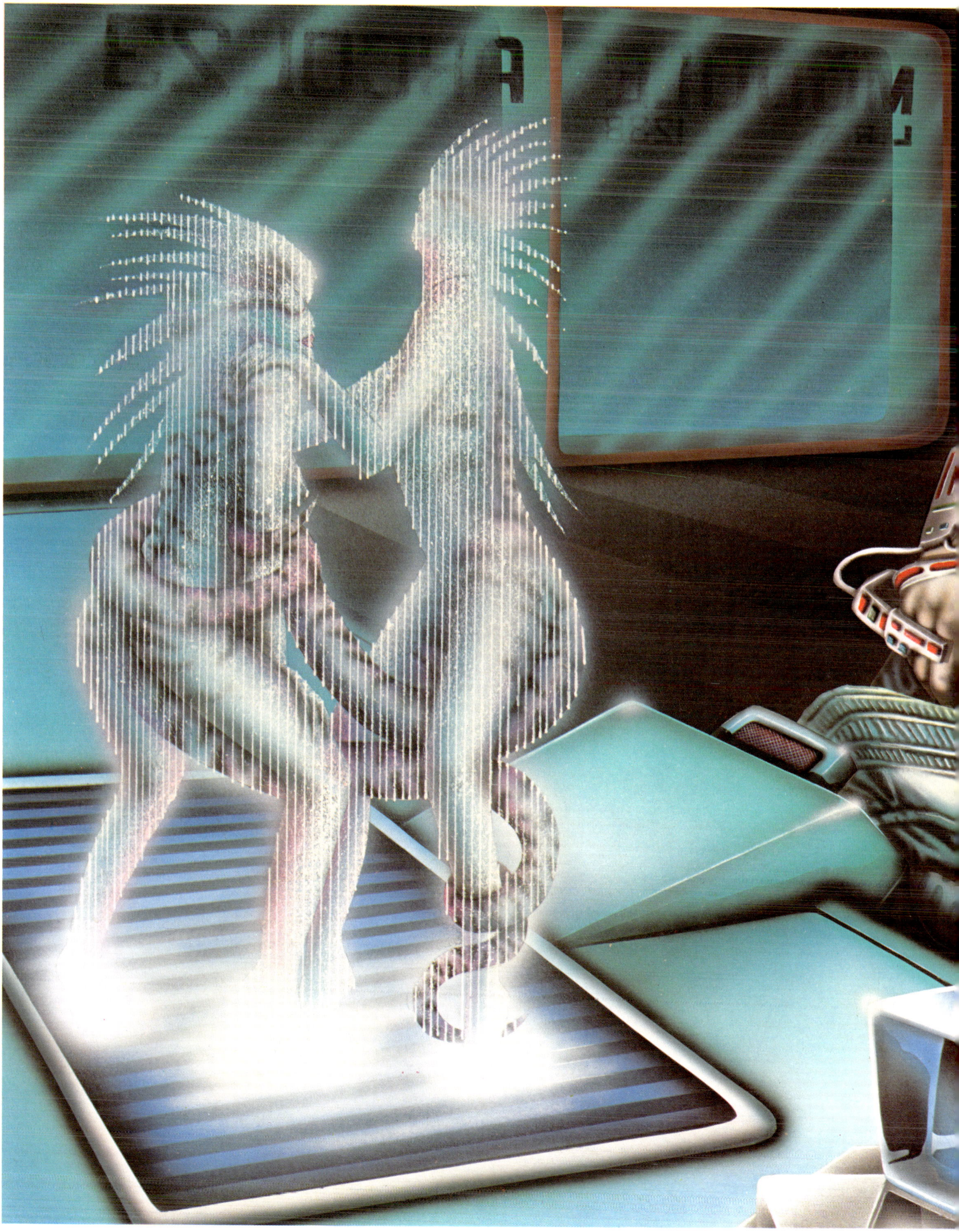

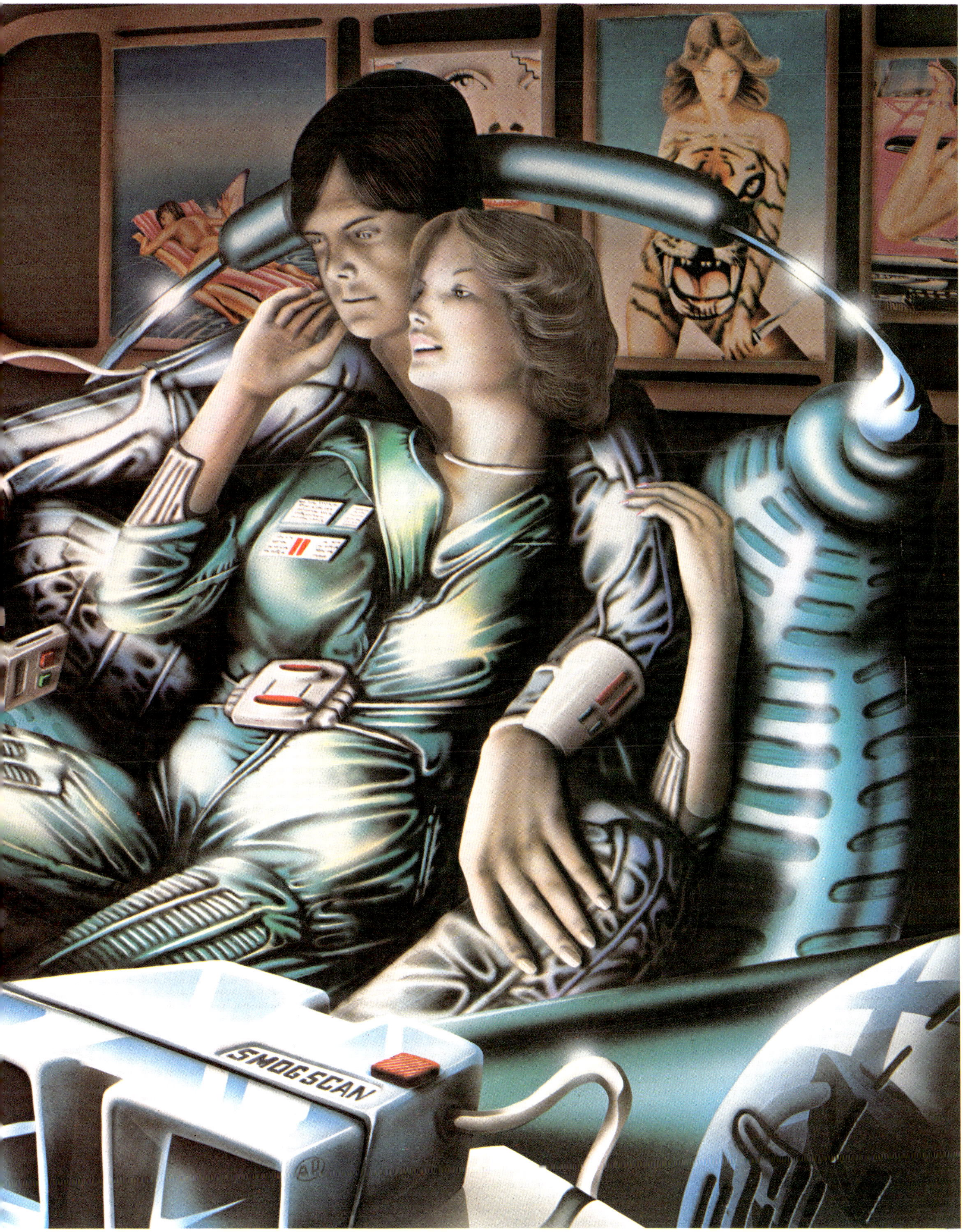
SMOGSCAN

ROBERT HOLDSTOCK is a young English writer with a growing reputation in the science fiction field. His novels include *Eye Among the Blind* (1976), *Earthwind* (1977), *Necromancer* (1978) and the forthcoming *Where Time Winds Blow* (1981). He acted as advisor on the popular and highly successful SF introduction *The Octopus encyclopaedia of SF*, recently edited "the most blatantly chauvinist SF anthology ever" (*Stars of Albion*, 1979) and is co-editor of the writer's magazine *Focus*.

MALCOLM EDWARDS was, until recently, the administrator of the Science Fiction Foundation in London; he is now a full-time writer and private book-dealer and editorial advisor to one of Britain's leading SF publishers. He was a contributing editor of *The Encyclopedia of Science Fiction*, has edited the critical magazines *Vector* and *Foundation*, and has published numerous reviews, as well as the popular *Spacecraft in Fact and Fiction*, co-written with Harry Harrison, and *Alien Landscapes*.

TONY ROBERTS was born in Worcestershire in 1950. He attended Wolverhampton Art College from 1967 to 1969, and Ravensbourne College of Art from 1969 to 1972. He works chiefly, though not exclusively, in science fiction. His work has appeared on numerous paperback covers and in SF art compilations. He is preoccupied with hardware and the visual impressiveness of modern technology — from Bertone-styled car-bodies to printed circuitry and robotics. He lives in Bromley, Kent, within sight of H.G.Wells birthplace.

TERRY OAKES was born in Merthyr Tydfil in 1945, where he still lives. He is a completely self-taught artist, and worked in a number of jobs while he learned the various tricks of his trade, developing his own inimitable style. He submitted folios of his work to publishers in London, and was encouraged and soon taken on by Young Artists. He works mainly as a cover artist.

JEFF RIDGE was born in St. Albans, in 1950, where he still lives. He specialised in Art whilst at Secondary School, and went straight into the printing industry, where he has worked as a Graphic Artist for the last eleven years. He is one of the most recent additions to the Young Artists agency, and has been doing cover and interior illustration, mostly in the science fiction field.

ANGUS McKIE was born in 1951, and educated at Jarrow Grammar School 1962-69, and Newcastle College of Art, where he studied Graphic Design, 1970-74. He spent a year working in an advertising agency and then submitted samples of science fiction drawings to Young Artists; he has been an illustrator ever since. He has been a fan of science fiction films since childhood, finding their appeal to be, like the paintings of John Martin and William Blake, their powerful imaginative visual feel.

BOB FOWKE was born in 1950, in Sussex. He passed through childhood, then trained for three years at the Somerset College of Art. He is a widely travelled man, and has lived in Paris for some time as well as in India. He has worked for many of the major British and American publishers.

ALAN DANIELS born 1947 in the wilderness beyond Watford Gap, he came to civilisation as soon as he was able. He studied sculpture under Leonard Schwartz of the Black Mountain School, then repaired to Sweden and other European countries to teach behavioural control and cybernetics. He returned to England to illustrate, and now works in a wide variety of commercial fields, from covers to advertising.

JIM BURNS was born in 1948 in Cardiff. He left school in 1966 to take up a career as a trainee pilot in the R.A.F. He left, after eighteen months, having soloed on 'Chipmunks' and 'Jet Provosts'. He then trained at Newport School of Art from 1968 to 1969 and at St. Martin's School of Art in London for the next three years. His diploma show was seen by John Spencer of Young Artists, and he was taken on immediately. He is well known for his jacket illustrations, and he recently collaborated with Harry Harrison on an illustrated novella, *Planet Story*.

ROBERT HOLDSTOCK

MALCOLM EDWARDS

COLIN HAY was born in 1947. He attended Edinburgh College of Art from 1965 to 1970. The main influences on his work are: military hardware, the architecture of the ancient world, the Gothic cathedrals, modern architecture, Turner, the Surrealists, Paul Klee, Paolozzi and Chris Foss.

LES EDWARDS was born in London, 1949, and was educated at the usual local schools, before training at Hornsey College of Art from 1968 to 1972. He moved straight into freelance illustration with the Young Artists Agency, painting covers, mostly for horror books, before branching into very many fields.

RICHARD SPARKS aged 23, is one of the brightest talents to emerge from St. Martin's School of Art in recent years. His imagination was early captured by the Pre-Raphaelites and the European Symbolists. He creates pictures that are rewarding to study for their subtle and significant detail, creating a marvellous empathy between words and art. He has recently been taken on by Artist Partners.

THEO PAGE F.R.S.A., F.S.I.A. is a master of his craft of technical drawing. He has worked on detailed technical illustrations and cutaways of Concorde, oil rigs, ocean liners and at the time of going to press he is on assignment abroad working for NATO. At other times he works from his own studio in Devon and is represented by Artist Partners in London.

ILLUSTRATIONS

EARTHPORT I
1 EARTHPORT/*JIM BURNS*
2 RING CITY/*TONY ROBERTS*
3 CUTAWAY OF JUPITER SHUTTLE/
THEO PAGE
INSET/*COLIN HAY*

STARPORT
1 STARPORT GANYMEDE/
TONY ROBERTS
2 CUTAWAY OF STARSHIP/
THEO PAGE
3 INSIDE GANYMEDE BASE/
TERRY OAKES

PLUTO
1 PLUTO/*COLIN PAGE*
2 THE DEAD WORLD SCROLL/
RICHARD SPARKS
3 STARSHIP ENTERS WITCHLIGHT/
ANGUS McKIE

ALTUXOR
1 RIFT VALLEY, VANDEZANDE'S WORLD/*TONY ROBERTS*
2 HUNDERAG ROCK/
RICHARD SPARKS

PLIAX
1 REFUGE/*JIM BURNS*
2 CHIKSTHA VARIETIES/
TERRY OAKES
3 THE SACRED WORLD/*BOB FOWKE*
4 CHIKSTHA CITY, PLIAX V/
ALAN DANIELS

STARGATE
1 SHIP PASSING THROUGH STARGATE/*TONY ROBERTS*

2 CRYSTAL PLANET/*LES EDWARDS*
3 PRISMOIDS/*RICHARD CLIFTON-DEY*
4 AURORA-MAGELLAN GUARDS WITH MURAL/*JIM BURNS*
5 AURORA-MAGELLAN CRUISER/
JEFF RIDGE

AURORA
1 DREADHULK/*LES EDWARDS*
2 SAFARIWORLD/*BOB FOWKE*
3 WEAPONS FOR SAFARIWORLD/
THEO PAGE
4 HUNTING PARTY/*BOB FOWKE*

DRACONIS B
1 TOMBWORLD/*LES EDWARDS*
2 HALL OF A THOUSAND RACES/
LES EDWARDS

ORIONIS DELTA
1 BEHEMOTHS' WORLD/
RICHARD CLIFTON-DEY
2 AMBULANCE INSIDE BEHEMOTH'S SKELETON/
JIM BURNS

HYPERIONA
1 HYPERIONA/*ALAN DANIELS*
2 INSIDE THE CASINO/
ALAN DANIELS
3 AD ASTRA APPROACHING EARTH/
TONY ROBERTS
4 LONDON 250,000 YEARS HENCE/
ANGUS McKIE
5 EPILOGUE: LOOKING BACK OVER THE HOLIDAY/*ALAN DANIELS*